Sea-gift
A Novel

by

Edwin W. Fuller

Sea-gift
A Novel
by Edwin W. Fuller

Copyright © 2024

All Rights reserved.

ISBN: 978-93-67148-86-0

Published by

DOUBLE 9 BOOKS

2/13-B, Ansari Road
Daryaganj, New Delhi – 110002
info@double9books.com
www.double9books.com
Tel. 011-40042856

This book is under public domain

ABOUT THE AUTHOR

Edwin W. Fuller was a 19th-century American author renowned for his maritime and nautical fiction. His works often reflect a deep fascination with the sea and the adventures associated with it. Fuller's writing is characterized by its vivid depiction of nautical life and its ability to transport readers to the heart of seafaring adventures. Fuller's background and experiences significantly influenced his literary output. He had a strong grasp of maritime terminology and the intricacies of life at sea, which is evident in his detailed and authentic portrayal of ship life and ocean exploration. His novels frequently feature themes of treasure hunting, exploration, and the personal and emotional journeys of characters navigating the challenges of the high seas. In Sea-gift: A Novel, Fuller combines historical setting with imaginative storytelling to create a compelling narrative filled with adventure and romance. His contributions to nautical fiction helped shape the genre, offering readers an engaging mix of historical detail and thrilling maritime escapades. Fuller's ability to blend historical accuracy with captivating storytelling ensures that his works remain a valued part of maritime literature.

CONTENTS

PREFACE... 7

CHAPTER I 8

CHAPTER II.. 12

CHAPTER III... 15

CHAPTER IV 18

CHAPTER V.. 28

CHAPTER VI 39

CHAPTER VII... 46

CHAPTER VIII.. 55

CHAPTER IX... 72

CHAPTER XII 79

CHAPTER XIII.. 88

CHAPTER XIV.. 93

CHAPTER XV 100

CHAPTER XVI.. 107

CHAPTER XVII 121

CHAPTER XVIII 137

CHAPTER XIX 143

CHAPTER XX 152

CHAPTER XXI.. 155

CHAPTER XXII... 165

CHAPTER XXIII 169

CHAPTER XXIV 175

CHAPTER XXV 180

CHAPTER XXVI 189

CHAPTER XXVII 193

CHAPTER XXVIII 198

CHAPTER XXIX 201

CHAPTER XXX 208

CHAPTER XXXI 216

CHAPTER XXXII 219

CHAPTER XXXIII 225

CHAPTER XXXIV 234

CHAPTER XXXV 241

CHAPTER XXXVI 249

CHAPTER XXXVII 256

CHAPTER XXXVIII 265

CHAPTER XXXIX 269

CHAPTER XL 271

CHAPTER XLI 274

CHAPTER XLII 280

CHAPTER XLIII 301

CHAPTER XLIV 310

CHAPTER XLV 313

CHAPTER XLVI 319

CHAPTER XLVII 324

PREFACE

Reader, my Book is before you!

If it has faults, you expect them; therefore excuse. If it has merit, you are surprised; therefore applaud.

E. W. F.

CHAPTER I

As the usages of society generally require an introduction between strangers before communications of any moment can transpire, I hasten now to introduce myself, that the readers hereof, as yet strangers, but whom I hope before long familiarly to call "gentle" and "dear," may acquire at least one element of interest in the narrative I propose to offer, namely, acquaintance with its subject—modesty forbids me to say hero.

I am, then, at your service, John— —; no, I cannot call my own name, it always sounds strange in my own mouth. I'll hand you my card in a moment; and while I am fingering nervously in my case for the best engraved one I reflect:

Why should you listen with the slightest attention to my history? How can I expect you to care any more for me and my affairs, than for anybody else and anybody else's affairs? What right have I to inflict upon you a recital of events, in no way connected with yourself, that three-fourths of you believe untrue, and that concerns parties you never saw and perhaps never will see? None, reader, none!

All the attention you give must be entirely gratuitous, except what I shall gain by tickling the selfish side of your nature; for I well know that you like or dislike a book in proportion as yourselves are flattered. This flattery, however, must not be the result of the author's effort, but your own. If the persons told of are beneath you in morals or intellect, then it is pleasant to reflect on your own superiority. Are they above you in these particulars? then you are pleased to associate with them, so to speak, and to assign to yourselves, in imagination, a similarity of conduct, under similar circumstances. The book must also possess an ingenuity of thought and expression that will make you conscious, to a flattering extent, of your own ingenuity in detecting it. Hence, often the most pleasant books to read are those that tell of simple things in such a way that you exclaim:

"I could have written that myself, if I had only thought of it."

To afford self-complacent comparisons to the conceited, to furnish evidences of their own ingenuity to the soi-disant original, and to give conscious improvement to the soberly studious, is a more difficult task than

I can undertake. I will simply tell my story, and leave the self-bees to suck what honey they please out of it.

Ah! I have at last found it. Here is my card:

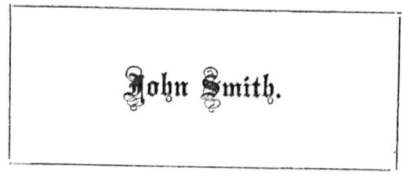

You smile; you know me? No, I beg pardon, I have never had the honor of your acquaintance. You may have known some of the Smiths, but not the members of our immediate family. John is an old family name with us. My father, grand and great grandfather, were all named John; in fact we could ascend the family tree six squares, without getting out of the Johns; and even the seventh, who was an H (H. T. Smith), was preceded by numerous Johns, only to be distinguished from each other by the middle initials. There was a John A. Smith, and a John B. Smith, and a John C. Smith; coming down so alphabetically that I used to think, when a child, that, as father and myself only had John for our names, a great many Smiths, whose names were lost, had already lived, and used up the balance of the alphabet for their middle initials.

Our family is a very large one, being represented in almost every nation on the globe; but its vast extent is a matter of pride, not reproach, with me. When I remember the long list of Warriors, Statesmen, Scholars, and the immense army of Usemen it has given to the world, I conceive that the world owes the name a debt of gratitude, and, being one of the creditors, I expect partial payment at least.

The name itself points to an artizan origin, but the sieve of centuries has filtered our blood clear of the last dust of the anvil, and it throbs in our veins with Heraclidean purity. Perhaps the majority of my connections were men of humble birth, but where the number is so immense, we can claim only those that are creditable. Consequently, the aforesaid tree, hanging up in our library, with dusty, tarnished frame, and an age-yellowed parchment, presented a very mottled appearance of groups of very little blocks, with very little "*Smiths*" written on them, and very large blocks, their names spelt in capitals, and with broad red lines connecting them to us. These last were Smiths who attained to something and were worth claiming. Away off in one corner, with a great quantity of zigzag lines to make it even connect at all, was the name of John Smith, with "Capt." prefixed, and the date 1609. Father used to take me on his knee, when I grew old enough to listen, and tell me long stories about my brave relative, who had fought with the Turks, slept on straw, (a fact which led me to believe that he was also a kinsman of Margaret Daw), dared the Indians, looked calmly at Powhatan's lifted club, and then flirted with his gentle protectress, Pocahontas. Her descendants, in Virginia, father told me, always claimed kin with our family, though the relationship was based entirely on this approximation to matrimony between our ancestors. I remember well that I did not wish to recognise, as relatives, the children of the mulatto her picture represented her to be; and I insisted that they be put down with the little blocks and little Smiths, until he informed me that many of them had become distinguished; and while it was quite a disgrace in society to have had a dark ancestor with kinky hair, it was quite an honor to have had a dark ancestor with straight hair. I have seen, in life, since then, that social distinction often turns upon less than the crook of a hair.

For our immediate family there were father and mother and I, after I came.

My father was wealthy, owning a very large plantation near Goldsboro, a fine residence in Wilmington, N. C., and some heavy renting real estate in New York.

Possessing the means for it, he was fond of display, and stood among the neighbors, in the country, as a proud, though popular man. They admired his pride because it was above their envy, while his uniform courtesy and kindness flattered all with whom he had intercourse. His carriage at elections was sure to be welcomed with cheers, as it drove on the grounds, though he could never be persuaded to dabble in the turbulent waters of politics. In town, some loved, some envied, but all respected him. His perfect integrity, his generosity, and his social qualities, secured for him, at all times, a large circle of friends, while there were some who, feeling socially equal, were surpassed by him in character, both in their own eyes and in public opinion; these, of course, regarded him with some disfavor.

But of mother no tongue spoke evil. Every one possesses a distinguishing idiosyncrasy; hers was goodness—all that was comprehended under St. Paul's "charity." There was no sounding brass or tinkling cymbal about her life; it was one of unselfish love, active benevolence, holy influence, and unassuming piety. I believe that the only command in the Bible she could not obey was, "Take up thy cross," for her angelic temperament made every duty a pleasure, and every sacrifice a source of happiness. Nor was she only theoretically good. She put her faith into constant practice. When her pew was vacant at church, the doctor was sure to be our visitor; the pupils in her Sabbath school class made an entire transfer of the affections they should have reserved for their own mothers to her; and our servants refrained from any insolence and disobedience out of the purest respect for her—a perfect anomaly in slavery. The meanest hut in town could boast her presence if there was sickness within its walls; and our dining-room servants brought a salver and napkin for charity delicacies as regularly as they laid the cloth. Yet her charity was not of that order which begins anywhere else but at home; everyone in our house felt that she had a deep interest in them. Her smile was almost constant, and when she did reprove there was a tone of regret about her words, as if they pained her more than they did the recipient.

She and father were very happy together, though they lacked congeniality. He was fond of display and gaiety, she fond of retirement and quiet; his heart chiefly on the world, her's all on heaven; he haughty though courteous, she gentle and kind; he formal, she good natured and easy in her every manner.

Father was a Polonius about dress, believing it should be "costly as thy purse can buy;" and he inundated mother's wardrobe with silks, brocade and velvets, and constantly replenished her *bijouterie* with jewels of rare value, till she was as much bewildered as Miss McFlimsey, from a cause just the reverse. I have often smiled to see her, just to please father, start to church in a magnificent train and exquisite bonnet, looking for all the world like a poor dove, dressed in peacock's plumage.

But I must not plunge into affairs too rapidly. Having given this short prologue before the curtain, I will now let it rise upon the first scene.

Ring the bell!

CHAPTER II

I was apparently expected, for, as I have been credibly informed, an extensive wardrobe had been prepared for me, and a whole drawer in the bureau appropriated for its storage. The said wardrobe consisted of several long sacerdotal robes, of the finest cambric; a dozen or more very unsacerdotal looking nether garments of linen and cambric, ruffled and trimmed with thread lace; a number of gowns of rich material; also a couple of flannel skirts, heavily embroidered, and seemingly intended only to tangle the feet; and quite a pile of unmentionables, with necessary fastenings.

There was also an elegant India muslin robe, trimmed with embroidery and fretted with lace, and a handsome lace cap, laid apart to themselves. These, as I afterwards learned, were intended for my baptismal suit.

I have thus particularized, because I am rather proud of having come into property so early.

One blustering night in the latter part of March I arrived, invaded the wardrobe, and appeared next morning on a pillow of state, ready to receive company. My appearance could not have been excessively prepossessing, as I formed no exception to the usual standard of æsthetic attainment exhibited by the little red monsters of my age. My hair was very thin and peach-fuzzy; eyes of uncertain hue, and apparently disgusted with the world and its sights, if we may judge from the persistency with which they kept the puffy, lashless lids closed; a dusty little forehead, that wrinkled so much when the eyes did open that one would suppose I had seen trouble, and "had losses" in the world from which I had so recently come; my mouth, purple and projecting with the upper lip, while the under lip was sucked in, after the most approved directions for pronouncing the Greek *phi*. The sleeves of my wrapper were rather too long (the usual fault in our first clothes, arising, perhaps, from the fact that while they are in process of construction there is no opportunity of trying them on us), and were rolled up around my tight-closed fists, which kept digging into my eyes with prize-fighting pertinacity.

The day following my advent being Sunday, and the place of my birth being in the country, many of the neighbors dropped in to see Mrs. Smith and the baby. All went through the same programme.

"How d'ye do, Mrs. Smith; I hope you came through well; but then this is your first. There's nothing like getting used to it. And where's the little dear?"

And without waiting for my mother's replies and thanks, they would turn to the nurse holding me in her lap on the pillow, and removing the wrapping from my face as carefully as if it were a bird, and would fly out, they would gaze at me mesmerically, cluck to me with a perseverance undamped by the want of effect, and finally turn away with the defiant assertion that I was the perfect image of both my parents; an assertion which would have been at least debatable, from the fact that my father was very dark in complexion and feature, and my mother very fair. Some even insisted on holding me, the spinster visitors being particularly desirous of this privilege; and getting me in their laps, they would examine the tightness of my clothing, and the temperature of my skin, with the well assumed criticism of experience. And if one found, on thrusting her hands beneath my clothes, that my feet were cold, most proudly and complacently she would unfold my garments, and expose my little splotched limbs to the fire. My feet and legs must have looked very pitiful indeed, sticking out of a wilderness of flannel like two slim beets, crossing each other with their little flat soles, as if I was born to be a tailor!

When the visitors were gone my father would come and gaze long and steadily into my face, then anxiously suggest that something must be the matter with me, because I was lying so still; and my mother would call for me to be brought to her, and after innumerable fixings, adjusting the cloth over my face this way, turning my head that way, hiding the point of one pin, pulling out another, straightening this and that fold of a garment— after all these nervousnesses, peculiar to young mothers, I would be found to be sleeping soundly; and then mother would regale herself with a long conversation between us, though it is more than probable she monopolized the talking.

But as my presence, so important to one household, had no effect whatever upon the old monarch of the glass and scythe, the days still managed to glide by, and with the crying spell at the morning bath, the troublesome feeding, father's fidgets and mother's anxiety, I arrived at the first era in baby life—*noticing*. What an important period! How many things were tried to attract my attention! Father whistled and clucked his mouth almost away; Aunt Hannah, my nurse, coming with my bottle, would tinkle on it with her thimble and sputter her lips to draw my blinking eyes towards her, and mother shook, successively and constantly, all her different bunches of keys over my face, in the vain endeavor to discover my favorite. Unconscious I, all the while lying on my back, vacantly staring to see the sounds. Mother now being able to sit up, it was her constant delight to have me in her lap, treating me as if I were a doll, and she a girl of ten; trying vainly to part and brush my scanty hair, making me sit up, while she kept my limber neck steady with one careful hand; and wearing my palms out teaching me to "patty cake." And such air castles as she would build for me! Telling me with as much emphasis as if I understood it all, and with each word, giving me a soft peck on the cheek with her forefinger.

"Never mind, tweetness! we'll do 'way from this old country house soon, and live in the town, and then, oh! the putty things Johnnie will have! A putty 'ittle tarriage and a g'eat big yocking horse, with a long mane and tail, and a 'ittle g'een wagon, and a 'ittle black dog, and ah! so many, many putties for a tweet 'ittle boy." Then chattering my chin in her ecstasy of love, till the titillation made me draw my face into a shape that might, by a very wide stretch of the imagination, be called a smile, she would scream for father to witness my display of intelligence. He, of course, would not believe it till I was chattered again; but instead of the laugh, the concussion of my gums would produce such plaintive wails that mother would apologise, with all the pleonasm of baby talk, and soothingly request me to "there, then, darling!"

My extreme youth prevented me from seeing the exact philosophy of "there then-ing" under pain, and I would continue my vocale till something more palatable to baby taste than baby talk would stop my mouth, and sleep's gentle wing would fan away my tears.

How long would a mother's patience watch my slumbers while she mused on the strange responsibility of her position! A soul given to her to form for good or evil; the potter's clay placed in her hands to make a vessel unto honor or dishonor! How fervent her prayer: "O, Father, guide me to guide him!"

What an impostor is the slumbering babe! His tiny hand, resting in dimpled fairness on your breast, seems to lift the veil of Futurity, and open to your view the brightest paths of flowery beauty, down which his feet shall patter with the innocence of childhood, run with the eager ambition of youth, stride with the honors of manhood, and totter with the feebleness of old age into the grave o'er which towers the marble tribute of a nation's love. Were the real curtain lifted, and Life's true pathway shown, how Earth's timid ones would shrink from its thorns and poisons, its bubble hopes and bitter cups. Thank God the Future is hidden, but the promise stands: "As thy days are, so shall thy strength be."

CHAPTER III

The year, growing old, began to feel ashamed of the jaunty green in which the spring and summer had decked him, and was laying aside his verdant garments, leaf by leaf, for the more dignified russet of autumn, when we—that is to say, father, mother and myself—prepared to return to our winter residence in Wilmington. I, of course, have no recollection of the journey, but have since been told that I stood it like a little soldier, though whether diminutive stature has anything to do with military fortitude I leave to nursery disputants to settle; as I believe their invariable encouragement to patience and endurance is the example of a fictitious officer of small size. The man has never been a child who has not been requested to take a dose of physic or bear a mustard plaster like a little captain, thereby inspiring himself with the greatest respect and admiration for the immense deglutitory capacity of that functionary, and the callosity of his epidermis.

The winter in turn passed away, and another spring and summer in the country, and we were returning again to town in the Fall, before I can begin to recollect things on my own account. What vague, undefined and grotesque memories they are! The carriage in which we travelled seems now to have been a chaos of shawls and baskets, from which father, mother and Aunt Hannah protruded helplessly, like pictures of fairies coming out of flowers. It was very cloudy, or at least everything now seems to have been gray when we started. The wheels commenced humming a drowsy tune, as they rolled through the sand, and soon hummed me to sleep; and when I awoke the carriage was going backward, and the sun had come out in the wrong place. Then we stopped at a well, near a house with a fat, wooden chimney, and an aspen tree in front, whose leaves seemed to be blinking all their eyes at me. A man in a broad-flapped hat came out with a gourd in his hand, and behind him a large yellow dog, that was tied to a piece of wood, and barked and jumped on each side of the string as if he wanted to shake it off. The well had a long pole, with a bucket at one end and a large stone at the other; and when Horace, our driver, went to it to draw some water for the horses, the stone seemed to fly up to the clouds. Then Horace filled the bucket and carried it to the horses, and I could hear them kissing it, as if they were so glad to see it; and, while I was listening at that, the man with the hat and dog handed in, at the carriage window, the great cool-looking gourd, with a long, crooked handle, down into which the water clicked, as if laughing, when father held it to me to drink.

After I had been bidden to "thank the kind gentleman, Johnnie," and done so, Horace strapped the bucket again under the carriage, got up to his seat, and the house and well moved back out of sight, just as the man sent the stone flying up again to the sky. All is a blank for a long time—till Horace drives over a snake, and they hold me up to the window to see it. My eyes can discover nothing but the shadow of the bucket swinging between the wheels; and ever afterwards a bucket, under one of the old fashioned carriages, is associated with a dead snake and a hot, sandy road. There is another sleepy blank, and I drowsily rouse up, as we drive into town, to find it dark, and the lights all in a hurry to go somewhere, chasing each other by the carriage window, till one bold blaze stops right in front of it, and father exclaims, "Here we are!"

We get out, shawls, chaos and all, and I am carried up some broad stone steps, into a large hall with bright lights, and on through to a strange room, where there are new faces among the servants, a little excrescence of a fireplace, filled with red coals, and a large table steaming with good smelling dishes. Everything, for an indefinite period after this, is confused and unsatisfactory, and I can eliminate nothing into distinct recollection but two series of events, which, from their frequent repetition, have become facts of memory, viz., rides in my little carriage, and, in educational phrase, corrections; more plainly, whippings.

What tortures I suffered in my carriage, children alone know. Enclosed on three sides by the leather curtains, I was confined in front by a strap, which was buckled across my breast, to keep me from falling out, and, thus cooped up like a criminal, I would sit, listening to the grinding, gritty sound of the wheels as they rolled over the flag stones, bumping my head against the framework, knocking my cap awry, and not knowing how to put it straight again, and suffering the misery of whining without being noticed—a source of much affliction, by the way, to many grown-up children—my nurse all the while walking behind, and pushing me along, engaged in too deep a conversation with other nurses to heed my murmuring!

One of my sorest trials was to pass the stores, and have some pert clerk stop my carriage and say:

"Hello! Auntie, whose child is that?"

"Col. Smith's, sir."

"Why," coming to me, and squatting down by the carriage, "I'll declare, he's a fine little fellow. How d'ye do, sir."

"Tell the gentleman how d'ye," persuades Aunt Hannah, who, like all nurses, is flattered by compliments to her protégé; but, before I can turn away in disgust, his tobacco-smelling moustache scratches my face. My greatest consolation, in all this persecution, was to meet little Lulie Mayland, my assigned sweetheart, though I was rather young for the blind god's arrow. Our nurses would lift us from our carriages and hold us up to kiss each other; and I would be in a perfect glee as she tried to put her little plump fingers into my eyes, and I felt her moist little mouth on my cheek. Putting me down in the foot of her carriage, we would be rolled home together, as happy and joyous as children only can be.

The other series of events to which I have alluded were, from their very frequency, fixed still more indelibly upon my mind; though the intense activity of certain cognitive faculties, during their occurrence, may have contributed somewhat to their retention. They were the immediate and inevitable consequence of any recusancy, on my part, in regard to the rules of the bath. I possessed the usual hydrophobic prejudice of extreme youth, and dreaded morning ablutions as Rome did the Gauls. Had I been old enough to have managed the bath myself I should not have cared, but to be washed like a dish, put into the tub, and spongeful after spongeful squeezed over me, was more than my good nature could submit to. Mother, finding her reasoning wasted, and her commands disregarded, would send for switches, and laying me across her lap, pour hot embers, as it seemed to me, on my naked legs. I did not stop to debate, which I might have done with propriety, whether the friction developed the latent heat of the rods, or whether they were actually set on fire and then applied; I simply recognized the fact, that unless the bath came the fire did, and I wisely chose the former. The embers' influence would last, on an average, about two days, when they would have to be again applied.

CHAPTER IV

I had been disturbing the centre of gravity of our globe for nine years, and had grown up into a mischievous, fun-making urchin—always out of the way when wanted, and in the way when not. I would have passed any committee on "boys," and probably taken the medal as the best specimen. I had fulfilled all the requisites of custom. I had torn out all my pockets with loads of marbles, knives, strings, stones, buttons, nails, &c. I had cut my hands and fingers, and fallen out of doors perhaps even more than was necessary. I could soil a ruffle with all the facility of contempt for such a feminine ornament. I could wear out shoes and tear a hat as quickly as the most reckless, and I had a real, first class aversion to "trying on" clothes in process of making; the rough edges of an unfinished jacket, rubbed into my neck by the fingers of the seamstress, not at all according with that placidity of temperament I had been advised to cultivate by the dogs-and-bears poetry, while the rapidity with which I could cover clean clothes with mud was, I fear, a matter of peculiar pride, as it was of certain punishment. My most perfect attribute of boyhood, however, was the devotion I bore my sweetheart, and the utter apathy and indifference with which I regarded all other girls.

Being such an one, I was highly gratified when mother said to me one day:

"Johnnie, we are going to give a dinner party next week, and as you will be without company, you may go over and invite Lulie Mayland."

"Oh! I'm so glad, I'm so glad," I sung out; "and I mean to go over right now, and tell her to come."

"No, no," said mother, smiling, and taking me by the jacket button, "we have not sent out our cards yet. Wait till Monday, then you may go."

I was disposed to whine at the delay, but she pinched my cheek as she got up from her chair, and said:

"No, you must do as I say, sir;" and left me, full of impatience for the advent of Monday. During the remainder of the week I exercised fully the child's faculty of being ubiquitous at home. The kitchen, however, received the largest share of my attention. I was around every table, dipping in every dish, and in the cook's way, to my fullest extent. If she turned around with a pan in her hand, it was sure to thump my head, and my anger thereat could only be appeased by letting me have a piece of dough to feel or a bowl to scrape. If eggs were to be beaten, I must try to froth them, till I was as full of foam as a half born Aphrodite; if flour was to be sifted, I was sure to get whitened; if spices were to be pounded I was certain to have my fingers mashed; and the burns I received, in trying to cook little dabs of cake, would have discouraged Mucius Scævola. Then my insatiate curiosity, and constant inquiries in regard to the numerous articles scattered around, would have worried out a less irascible nature than that of our cook; and by a final appeal to mother, and a command from headquarters, I would be forced to raise the siege, and retire from the field, with a jacket full of sugar and flour, sullenly licking my fingers in defiance.

Verily, children prove the old adage true: "Satan finds some mischief still for idle hands to do."

And yet how dear to us are their mischievous ways, and how blank and drear would childhood be without them! The sunshine of their presence is always brightest when flecked by little clouds of annoyance. And when your tenderest bud has been plucked by the Reaper, your heartstrings throb saddest o'er the toy that's broken, and your tears fall in torrents o'er the little torn garment, while the clothes neatly folded pass unnoticed by.

Early Monday morning I hurried over to tell Lulie. As I entered her gate I discovered her at play, near a large rose bush, but was surprised and troubled to see a strange boy with her. I had somehow, in my own mind at least, assumed a kind of proprietorship over her, and the presence of any one else, in whom she could take any interest whatever, was excessively annoying. I managed to creep up quite near, without being discovered, and stood for some time watching them, and feeling, in my jealousy, an almost irresistible desire to try a stone on the strange head. They were busy arranging a doll house, which consisted of rows of dirt piled up like fortifications, with lumps of moss for chairs and sofas, and an array of dolls that seemed to have been taken from the hospital, so much were they maimed in their legs and arms.

The strange boy and Lulie seemed very intimate, and bent their heads together, and talked in delighted and animated accents; he suggesting, and she listening and adopting his suggestions. And then he had on such new clothes, such a jaunty cap, such a blue jacket with bright buttons, and such boots with heels! In him I recognized a formidable rival, and concluded to retreat and give up all thoughts of the invitation. As I endeavored to slip away unobserved, I overturned a little tea set that was placed to one side, awaiting the completion of the house. At the noise they both turned around and saw me, and Lulie's face flushed a little as she exclaimed:

"There, now! see what you have done! turned over all my tea cups and broken I don't know how many!"

I offered, with all earnestness, the child's universal apology, "I didn't go to do it," but felt that it was not accepted, and that I, Lulie's acknowledged sweetheart, was not welcome. But boys are not oversensitive, and as I knew that to retire then would only make matters worse, I swallowed my confusion and joined in their play. Lulie did not introduce me to her companion, but I soon learned that his name was Frank, and that he was fast supplanting me in her favor. All my suggestions in regard to the disposition and arrangement of the furniture were at once overruled and disregarded for what he thought best.

All her questions and remarks were addressed to him, and they both seemed oblivious of my presence, save when they wished me to perform some office for them. Then Frank, as she called him, had such an insolent way of staring at me, and walking around with his hands stuck contemptuously into his trousers' pockets. And when we had completed the house, and were cleaning up, he raked away the earth with his boots, and made little ditches around the walls with his heels, and stamped the walks level; in short, made such a display of his morocco that I felt quite ashamed of my plain copper-tip shoes, and tried to hide them as much as possible by standing in the grass. After awhile it was proposed to get the doll's dinner ready, and then I thought of my errand. Without a moment's consideration for Frank's feeling, I broke out with: "Oh! Lulie, I forgot; you must come to our house to-morrow; we are going to have a dinner, and have got lots of good things cooked. There won't be any other girls there but you, and your pa and ma are coming, too. Won't you come?"

"I don't know," she replied, tying an apron on a very red-faced doll, with china feet, wooden legs, and her hair rubbed off the back of her head; "I don't want to go much, 'cause me and Frank are going to have a doll wedding to-morrow. Frank, let me tell you" — — breaking off suddenly, and putting the doll down with her face on the ground, and her wooden limbs very much exposed, she took Frank aside to whisper something to him. I inferred it was a proposal to invite me to their dinner, as he replied loud enough for me to hear:

"No, let's have it all by ourselves."

Lulie seemed to assent, and as I had become rather incensed at the whole proceedings, I turned off without another word, and went home. Children suffer as keenly, if not as long, in their little loves and jealousies as older people; and I was as unhappy during the remainder of the day as was Octavia while Anthony was in Egypt. Many were the castles I had built in the air, in all of which Lulie reigned as queen. My favorite dream was to imagine her and myself wrecked, and playing Robinson Crusoe on some desert island. I had loved to think how we would sit together by the beach and watch the frightened billows fleeing to the shore, or stroll through shadowy forests in search of fruits; and how I would defend her from the wolves and bears, and how tender and confiding she would be when she had no one but me to look to. And then, at night, how cosy and snug we would be in our cave, which would be always warmed and lighted by some means. And when the savages came how we would shut the great stone door, and be safe and secure. But I had now found in the sand, not the naked foot print Robinson saw, but a boot track, which conjured up more fears and suspicions than Defoe ever conceived; for it told of the presence of a cannibal for my heart.

The next day wore away and the guests began to arrive. Having nothing better to do, I stationed myself at the hall window to watch the carriages as they came up to our door, and their contents came out.

The first that arrived were the Cheyleighs, numbering Mr. Edward Cheyleigh and wife, a stylish old couple, who prided themselves on their family and position in society, and the two Misses Cheyleigh—ladies who had been in the market for some time, and as yet were unspoken. They were great sticklers for the usages of society, and dependent, in a great measure, on their social prestige and *en regle* manners for the attention they received. They were well aware of the fact, that while Mr. Cheyleigh had given balls and parties innumerable for their benefit, he had not yet given a wedding party, and to accomplish for him the privilege of giving one was and had been their constant aim, albeit its fervor was a little abated by its continued futility.

As they entered the hall, and found the hat and coat stands empty, Miss Ella, the younger, turned to her father, and with much petulance exclaimed:

"Now, pa, I hope you are satisfied; you would hurry us off, and now we are the very first. I declare it is really too bad."

"Yes, it is," chimes in Miss Gertrude, the elder, "and looks as if we were so dreadfully anxious to come."

"Well, my daughters," philosophises Mr. Cheyleigh, "somebody has to be the first, and we are fully ten minutes behind the time specified."

"Ten minutes!" exclaimed both young ladies, between the pronunciation of the "ten" and the "minutes," changing their faces from a frown to a smile, as mother, hearing their voices, appeared in the hall and welcomed them, taking the ladies off to the cloak room; while William, our servant, who had been leaning against the stair while their conversation was proceeding, recovered himself sufficiently to usher Mr. Cheyleigh into the parlor. Many others arrive and are passed in, until at length two young gentlemen approach, toss away their cigars, and stroll, as it were, up the steps, taking a long time to reach the door, and conversing in a low tone, which I could overhear.

"I wonder who is to be here to-day," said the first, frowning as if in pain, as he buttoned his glove with an effort; "dinners with old folks are devilish bores."

"I understand the two Misses Cheyleigh will be here, and that will be some relief," replied the other, pulling down his wristband, so as to show the white.

"Yes, quite a relief to you. From your devotion down at Bentric's last evening I should judge you were really in love with that long, languishing Gertrude."

"Hush, Cassell, I vow you shan't speak disrespectfully of her. I have a right to admire her, if she is a little oldish."

"Success to you, Berton! here goes for an hour's boredom with that little mincing, over vivacious Ella;" and he pulled the bell, muttering as he did so, "I say confound these small and select gatherings; a fellow is always put off with a fussy old maid, or a gassy old fogy, who'll talk you into an anatomy in five minutes."

"Any way," whispered the other, as William opened the door, "old Smith keeps good wine and feeds well."

They are followed in turn by others, till at last Dr. Mayland's carriage drives up, and, to my great surprise and delight, I recognise the curly little head of Lulie through the window. I was too much piqued by her conduct of the day before to run out and meet her, but sprang at her from behind the door, as she entered, in a conciliatory kind of way, and we both lost our stiffness in a hearty laugh. Without waiting for more arrivals I hurried her off to the nursery.

"I thought you were not coming," I began, as soon as we were fairly in, "but that you and that Frank somebody were to have a doll's party."

"Yes, but you see Frank and I fell out," she replied quickly, "and I think he is ever so mean."

"So do I," I responded warmly, "don't let's have anything more to do with him; we can always have more fun by ourselves, can't we?"

"Yes, we can; you are not mad because I said what I did yesterday, are you?"

"No, that I am not," I replied, delighted at the turn things had taken; "but come, Lulie, let me show you what father gave me on my birthday."

Sitting down together on the rug before the bright glowing fire, we took out of its box a little model of a house in separate pieces, and commenced to put it together. I sat and gazed at her, as she bent over the blocks, trying to make piece after piece fit; and she looked so beautiful, with one side of her face all red from the fire, and her clustering brown curls drooping so gracefully around it, that I could resist the inclination no longer, but leaned forward and kissed the glowing cheek.

"Oh stop!" she said, tossing her head without looking up; "you bother me so I can't build the house at all."

This was so much milder than I expected I tried another.

"Stop, I tell you," she exclaimed, feigning to strike me with one of the blocks; "see, you've tumbled all the top of the house off."

"I will stop," I said, looking at her very earnestly, "if you will give me a kiss of your own accord."

"Here, then," she said, raising her head; and throwing back her curls she put up her rosy lips, and I kissed her. People say children know nothing about love, but there was a thrill of pleasure and a smack of romance in that kiss before the nursery fire, that none which have ever since touched my lips have possessed.

We amused ourselves in various ways till the servant brought in our dinner, spread the nursery table, and, as I gave Lulie my high chair, piled up books in another for me, to bring me up to a comfortable level with our meal, then left us to enjoy it. We chewed out praises, and smacked out lavish encomiums on the skill of the cook, as we eagerly applied ourselves to her dainties; and when Lulie had sipped the last trembling particle of *blanc mange*, and added the *debris* of the last grape to the goodly pile on her fruit plate, we got down, instead of rising, from our chairs, and went from the nursery to the dining room. The ladies had withdrawn some time since, and the gentlemen had almost finished their wine. The two young men, who had characterized dinners with old folks as devilish bores, had excused themselves, and gone back to the parlors.

Finding nothing to interest us in the dry, stale jokes or political fanfarronade of the dining room party, we ran off to the parlors, and took our station on each side of the door, to watch all within. The ladies were grouped round the fires or examining the pictures, while Mr. Cassell and Miss Ella, Mr. Berton and Miss Gertrude, were promenading slowly the whole length of the rooms. We thought this was a great sign of love, and watched them with great interest. As they approached our end of the room we could hear very well, but when their backs were turned their words were gradually lost; so that our ideas of the tenor of their conversation were somewhat disconnected. Mr. Berton, who seemed interested in what he was saying, and Miss Gertrude equally so, approached first.

"Yes, indeed," he was saying, as they came into earshot, "we had a most charming time. The moonlight was as bright as day, and the Minnie scarcely rippled the water. The music, too, was better than usual, and we danced eight sets going down, besides the round dances. We missed you a great deal; everybody was inquiring for Miss Gertrude."

"Ella told me what a delightful excursion it was," replied Miss G., trying to pout bewitchingly, as if still vexed at her own absence. "I was so exceedingly unwell that ma would not hear to my going, and I had a real hard cry over it. When do we have another?"

"I am afraid not before another moon. We are talking, however, of getting up a picnic for the Sound next— —." They passed down the room, and out of hearing, as Cassell and Miss Ella came up, she all smiles, he all languor.

"You say they are from the western part of the State?" he inquired, with a drawl, as if he only pursued the subject because he was too lazy to find another.

"Yes," replied Miss Ella, with nervous vivacity, "from Charlotte, I think. They are quite an addition to our society, are they not?"

"Quite!" laconicised Cassell, as if he had done all for the subject that could be required of him.

"And then," she continued, "they are connected with the Cartoneaus of South Carolina, who, you know, are some of the first people in the State. Mr. Paning brought a letter of introduction to pa from Judge Francis Cartoneau.

He and ma called, of course, and were much pleased, though Mrs. Paning, ma thought, was a little stiff."

Lulie and I were immensely interested in this conversation, and eagerly listened for its further development.

Mr. Cassell paused awhile, as if to debate whether his system could stand a continuance of the conversation, then, with a resigned arch of his eyebrows to himself, asked:

"Do they intend to reside here?"

"Oh yes, they have bought Mr. Huxley's place, and are having it fitted up in magnificent style. When they move in I understand they intend giving a grand ball!"

Mr. Cassell paused again, then taking a flower from his lappel, bit it savagely, and asked:

"Have they any daughters?" as if it was the last question she might expect from him.

"No, they have only one child—a little boy—named Frank, after his uncle, Judge Cartoneau."

Cassell did not appear at all interested in the name of the little boy, but I was intensely so, and leaned in the door to hear more, but, unfortunately, they had passed down the room out of hearing, while Miss Gertrude and her beau came again into audience. They were still on the subject of the excursion, and Mr. Berton was verging towards the sentimental, while Miss Gertrude was encouraging him with all the art she could command.

"I'll vow I didn't, Miss Gerty; I sat apart almost the whole night, thinking of you."

"Why, Mr. Berton! Ella told me you were perfectly devoted to Miss Withers."

"Withers, indeed! she's perfectly horrid; but did you think enough of me to inquire what I did?"

"Of course, I——" Her remarks were broken off, as far as we were concerned, by the entrance of the gentlemen from the dining room. We tried to dodge, and get away, but two of them caught us, and holding us by the ears, asked our names—which question seems to be, with most people, a test of a child's intelligence. To answer it was a task I dreaded more than Hercules did the Augean stables. My name, short as it was, seemed to stretch into a length equal to the King of Siam's whenever I had to pronounce it; and I have often blessed the man who invented cards. There being no escape now, we drawled out, respectively, "John Smith" and "Lulie Mayland," and were released, one of our captors remarking as we scampered off:

"Smith, you and Mayland ought to raise them up for each other. They will make a fine match one of these days."

I fully forgave him for asking my name, and earnestly wished he might be a prophet.

Glad to get away, Lulie and I ran out into the back yard, and played till 'twas very dark, when one of the servants came to call us in. We found all the guests gone but Dr. and Mrs. Mayland, who were just entering their carriage. I bade Lulie a hasty good-bye, and turned back into the house, feeling a joyous flutter about the heart, as if a humming bird were enclosed in it and was struggling to escape. Mother met me in the hall, and said:

"John, it is so late you need not get your lesson to-night, but, as you are perhaps sleepy, you can go into the nursery, and I will come in and hear you say your prayers."

Though I was a good stout boy, mother could not get out of the old habit of seeing me to bed, and hearing me repeat my prayers aloud.

I entered the nursery, but instead of undressing, sat down by the fire, and began—

"Fancy unto fancy linking."

Again I was on the desert island, but the boot track had disappeared, and our snug grotto received the addition of a grate, a rug, and a house model. The savages came, and smacked their bloody lips through the bars of our cave, and yelled with eager desire to reach us, but I cared not. I was happy as long as those curls were drooping over the blocks, and I was stealing kisses from the rosy architect.

Mother came in, and broke my reverie. I got up, undressed, and kneeled down by her side. Laying my cheek on her knee, I commenced "Our father" with my tongue, while my mind was still in the grotto with Lulie. I had not repeated half, when a ferocious savage tore loose a bar, and was squeezing himself through the aperture, while I stood on the defensive, with one of the Corinthian columns of our little house for a weapon, ready to strike down the invaders. So vivid was the picture that even my tongue forgot its office, and with the broken prayer upon my lips I lay gazing into the glowing coals. Mother's hands touched my head as she said gently:

"My child, what are you thinking of? Remember, you are praying to the great God, who will not hear you unless you ask in earnest. If you were asking your father for something you wished very much would you not think of what you were saying?"

"Yes, ma'am," I replied, meekly, at length recalled from my vision.

"And do you not want God to take care of father and mother, and yourself, to-night?"

"Yes, ma'am."

"Then ask him as you ought." And with that soft hand upon my head all earthly visions vanished, and I repeated the oft-said prayer, with all of childhood's earnestness, and its simple, trusting faith.

I rose, got in the bed, received mother's good-night kiss, and, as I closed my eyes, Queen Mab's grey gnat coachman drove his atomic team across my nose, and Lulie, models, savages, Cassell, Miss Gertrude, and crestfallen Prank Paning, all danced before me, and danced me to sleep.

CHAPTER V

On the morning succeeding the day described in the last chapter, father startled me very much at the breakfast table, by asking:

"John, how would you like to commence school? you are getting too old to be playing all the time."

"Oh, ever so much!" I replied, eagerly, watching his face closely, to see if he was in earnest. "Ned Cheyleigh began last session, and I can read and spell as well as he can now, so it will be easy for me to keep up."

"Well, I saw Miss Hester Weck about it yesterday, and she said she would be very glad to take you, so you can get ready to start to-morrow morning."

I was too much excited to eat any more, but began teazing mother to begin right away on my school outfit.

"Mother, I want a satchel to carry my books in, and a basket for my luncheon; and, mother, please get me a string for my top, because all the boys play top, and I broke my string yesterday; and father, please sir, get me a knife to peel apples and to cut pencils with, and a piece of leather to make me a sling, and a— —"

"Hush, Johnnie," said mother, "be quiet, and I will be sure to have you ready. The school room is just around the corner, so you can come home for your lunch; and as your 'books' only consist of one 'Angell's First Book' you will hardly need a bag."

I gulped down a mouthful of food, then hastening from the table, I got my Reader and devoted the whole morning to picking out all the hard words and spelling them over. By dinner time I had mastered nearly all of them, and could read with considerable fluency the pathetic tale of retributive justice which befel the cruel James Killfly.

That evening when father came in he brought me a beautiful knife with a file blade in it. To possess a knife with a file blade had always been one of the unattained pinnacles of my ambition—this appurtenance, in my eyes, being the very *toga virilis* of cutlery; and as my property in this department had hitherto consisted of blunt pointed Barlows, and fatigued looking dog knives, with their edges purposely made dull, to be the undisputed owner of an exquisite pearl handled knife, with brightest blades, placed me at once upon the pinnacle, and I enjoyed the situation. I was never tired of opening and snapping the blades, and blowing my breath upon them, as the larger boys did, to test their metal. I trimmed my pencil quite away, because the cedar cut smoothly, and the chairs suffered as severely as Washington, Sr.'s, cherry tree did.

I rose next morning with the sun, and was busying everywhere in my preparations for school. Breakfast finished, with my book in my hand, and that adored knife in my pocket, I started with father for the school. I felt a little sinking about the heart as I kissed mother good-bye and descended the steps, and would, had I not been ashamed, have shrunk from the new life I was entering, and gone back to the old routine of play. As we turned our corner I looked back, and mother was still standing in the door, gazing thoughtfully after us. I could not then understand or appreciate her feelings, but I can now.

Miss Hester answered our tap at her door in person, and invited us in to a seat. I shrank closer to father as the curious eyes of the scholars were all turned towards me, and I found no kindly sympathy in the glances. Father took a seat and entered into conversation with Miss Hester, while I timidly surveyed the apartment where my ideas were to be taught to shoot.

Miss Hester Weck kept a small preparatory school for girls and boys, and ruled it with old maidish particularity. All the scholars had to sit up straight on three rows of benches, which were so arranged with reference to Miss Hester's seat that she could have a full view of all. None were allowed to speak or laugh, and as for rocking backwards and forwards, a motion believed by children to be conducive to study and essential to retention, the thing was unheard of in Miss Hester's school. Some, indeed, had tried it on first entering, but after one or two interviews with Miss Hester's rod they had learned to study in one position. On one side of the room was a row of pegs for the girls' hats and bonnets, and on the opposite side a similar row for the boys'. At one end of the room was the rostrum on which our monarch sat, and at the other was a long desk, covered with ink splotches, at which the scholars wrote. Having completed my survey of the room I turned my attention to the scholars, and scanned their faces closely, as I was to associate, more or less intimately, with all of them. They were all, with the exception of two or three, munching the corners of their books, and staring steadily at father and me. There were five occupants of the front bench, who, I thought, from their position, must be first grade scholars. The first was a tall, raw-boned girl, with sandy hair and freckled face, and light gray eyes, turned up at the corners, giving her a sinister and Chinese expression that assured me of victimization. Next to her was her brother, a small and sleepy second edition of herself, not at all revised or corrected. Then came a bright-eyed little fellow who was engaged in the pleasant diversion of making hideous faces at me. At his side was a fat, redheaded girl, who was the only one studying; and lastly, a stupid, tow-haired youth, whose straight flax hair looked as if it had been hung on his head to dry, and had dried stiff, and who was gazing at me as if I were vacancy.

The second bench held three girls and two boys, who resembled in many particulars those on the first bench. On number three I recognized, to my great joy, Ned Cheyleigh and Lulie Mayland, and to my annoyance Frank Paning. Before we had concluded our interchange of whispered salutations, father rose and said to Miss Hester:

"I will now leave him with you. He is a good boy and easy enough to manage, though a little inclined to mischief."

"Oh, I will take care of that," she said. "We will be first rate friends; won't we, Johnnie?"

Father left me, the door closed on him, and I was beginning to enter Life's shallowest waters alone.

"Come here, Johnnie," said Miss Hester, "let me see how much you know, so that I can put you in a class."

I rose, and with a great swelling knot in my throat, drew my book from my side pocket and carried it to her.

"How far have you been in this?" she said, as she carelessly fluttered over the leaves.

"I went clear through it, ma'am, under mother."

"Well, let me see how you spell; spell 'honest'?"

I had begun, at first, spelling by recollecting how the letters looked on the page, but mother had broken me from it and taught me to spell words by their sound. Accordingly I stammered out, while my eyes filled with tears and the knot in my throat almost choked me:

"O-n-n-e-s-t—Onnest."

At this Frank Paning led off with a laugh, followed by the whole school. A rap on Miss Hester's desk secured silence, and she proceeded.

"Don't be so frightened, child, try another word; spell 'Business.'"

Knowledge of everything, save the names of the letters, was gone, and I blindly blurted out:

"B-i-z-z-i-n-e-double ess!" I broke down completely and stood there trying to hide my crying, while the perverse tears would drop on the floor, and my nose, treacherous organ, required constant snuffling or the tell-tale use of my handkerchief.

Another titter was heard, but Miss Hester repressed it, and said in her kindest tone:

"Poor child, you are too much agitated to spell. I will put you, for the present, in a class with Lulie Mayland and Edward Cheyleigh. Go there, and let her show you where the lesson is."

As I started across the room a wad of chewed paper struck me in the face. I did not see who threw it, but Miss Hester did, and calling up Frank Paning gave him a sound whipping.

Sitting down with Ned and Lulie I felt more at my ease, and by the time recess was announced, felt like joining in the games. All was clatter and chatter as we poured from the door, and the scholars forgot I was a "newy" in the excitement of the play. The game of "goosey" was proposed and commenced. We separated to our bases, and at the call advanced. Scampering hither and thither, some tried to catch, some to be caught. I dodged, in good earnest, both boys and girls, and endeavored to reach the opposite base with a zeal that would have adorned a fanatic. But it was no use; the tall and freckled girl singled me out, and with a speed that would have disdained Atalanta's apples, pursued steadily, and with the utmost perseverance, after me. No matter how I twisted, turned and doubled, still she was behind me, nearer and nearer, never relaxing her speed, while with every backward glance I gave, her brown calico dress flew higher and higher, and her parrot-toed feet stepped over each other more and more swiftly.

Of course she overhauled me, and, catching me by the lower edge of my jacket, triumphantly dragged me backwards to the base, in the style known as "walking turkey." Throughout the whole game it was my fate to be caught by the girls, but I was not over timid on this score, and rather enjoyed it. At one o'clock I ran home for lunch, and gave father and mother a detailed account of my morning's experience, omitting the crying scene. I returned to the school room with a light heart, and, as children are not very formal, was soon acquainted with all the scholars. Frank met me first, and begged my pardon for his rudeness in the morning. He made himself so kind and attentive to me that my prejudices against him imperceptibly began to wear off, though I could not help observing that he was overbearing to those who were meaner dressed than himself, and whom he considered his inferiors.

As the days wore on I had time to form intimacies, and I found one friend in the school whom I could "grapple unto my soul with hooks of steel."

Between Edward Cheyleigh and myself there sprang up the most lasting friendship. He was the most noble hearted boy I ever knew. Manly and firm to the last degree, yet gentle and soft as a girl in his manners; full of life and gaiety, yet no amount of persuasion could make him yield his consent to what he thought was wrong. He was, in consequence, rather unpopular with the scholars, and I have often seen his face flush at a sneer about his being the favorite, after a refusal to join in some plan to worry Miss Hester. I used to admire his firmness and moral courage, and long to imitate his example, but I was too much afraid of the ridicule of the school, and I would often forfeit Ned's approval rather than face the jeers of so many.

As the session passed on I lost all my reserve, and, with the absence of embarrassment, came my love for fun. I was soon up to all the tricks of school, and an expert in their performance. I was perfect in the art of chewing and shooting paper, and William Tell took no more pride in his apple feat than did I in the accuracy with which I could plant a two inch pulp in a boy's forehead across the room, and never attract a glance from Miss Hester. I could gauge a pin to the exact desideratum of pain, as I inserted it just above my neighbor's point of contact with the bench. I could stand up and call out, "M' I g' out?" as loudly as the boldest, or assume, with perfect ease, the don't care expression and slinging gait, after a mortifying attempt at recitation. These accomplishments were only acquired after months of timidity and practice, but by degrees I became a ringleader in all the mischief, and many were the difficulties I became involved in. Frank Paning always joined us in our schemes, but somehow generally managed to escape the punishment that fell on the rest of us.

One day Miss Hester was later coming than usual. We had all assembled, and waited patiently for her some time, when Frank suddenly proposed that we bar her out, and make her give us holiday. His proposition was agreed to by several, of which I was the first; while all the girls, and two or three of the very small boys, went outside to wait for her. We commenced our operations with vigor, piling up chairs, tables, and Miss Hester's desk, against the door, in our haste turning the ink over the copy books and papers, and scattering the pens and rulers generally. As we concluded our arrangements, we observed Ned still inside, sitting quietly at his usual corner.

"Why, hallo, Ned!" said Frank, "I thought you were outside with the other girls. Why don't you go?"

"Because I don't wish to," Ned replied, quietly, rubbing out one figure on his slate with a wet forefinger and putting down another.

"But you won't tell on us, will you?" asks a timid one.

"I shall not tell on any one, as it is none of my business;" and Ned bent over his slate as if that was all he had to say.

"All right! here she comes 'round the corner," exclaimed two or three excited ones, peeping through a crevice in the window. "Wonder what the old lady will do?"

Sure enough Miss Hester was coming, walking with all the majesty of a teacher, and carrying demoralization to our garrison by her very presence. As she came up we could hear a chorus of shrill voices crying:

"Lor! Miss Hester, what do you think? the boys have locked us and you out, and say they won't let us in till you promise to give 'em holiday."

She did not reply, but we heard her come up the steps, and shake the door two or three times. Finding it barred, there was an ominous silence of a minute or two, then another more violent shake. The more timorous of our number now wished to open the door, and surrender unconditionally; but Frank and I, by dint of hard persuasion, and by representing to them that this course would not palliate their sin, induced them to hold out. She left the house, and went off, walking rapidly. The advocates of surrender now gained strength, but we argued and plead them into a little more obduracy. Before our council of war had ended Miss Hester returned with a carpenter, and we felt that the battle was hers. We got our books, took our seats, and watched, with anxious eyes, the door, as it creaked and strained with every blow. A moment more and it flew open, scattering our barricade in every direction, and Miss Hester marched in victorious. Having dismissed the carpenter, and put things to rights, she turned her attention to the perpetrators of the deed. We saw, from the miniature thunder cloud that had gathered between her brows, that there was no hope for mercy, so we prepared to meet our fate resignedly. Calling us all up in a row, she began at the top of the roll:

"Eliza Atly, were you inside or outside?"

Miss Eliza Atly, the freckled girl, with corner-drawn eyes, is delighted to testify that she was outside.

"Abram Barn, outside or inside?"

Abram Barn, the small, fat boy, with puffy cheeks and dry tow hair, bubbles out his answer as if it were liquid:

"Out chide, m'm!"

"Edward Cheyleigh?"

"Inside, ma'am."

"Edward! I am surprised at that. Did you bar the door against me?"

"No, madam."

"Do you know who did it?"

"Yes, ma'am, I do, but I cannot tell."

Miss Hester's face flushed, as she said, sternly:

"Those who conceal are as guilty as those who commit."

She proceeded down the roll, receiving confessions from some, and denials from others, till she came to Frank's name.

"Frank Paning," she said, with her darkest frown, "did you bar my door?"

"No, madam, I did not."

He had been nailing down the windows while we were barring the door.

"Did you see who did it?"

"I did not see any one do it. When I looked the door was all barred up tight."

Every one looked at him in amazement, but he replied by a smirk of conceit at his success.

"John Smith, did you help to keep me out?" thundered Miss Hester, her patience all gone.

"Yes, ma'am, I did."

"That will do; you can all take your seats."

My name completed the roll, and she laid aside the book, and took up the rod. After some remarks on the enormity of our offence, and the surprise she felt that some of her best scholars should have countenanced it, and that it was her unpleasant duty to punish all concerned, she proceeded to call up the offenders in order.

"Edward Cheyleigh, come here, sir. I regret very much the necessity of punishing you, as it is the first time, and I have never before even reproved you; but the offence is very grievous, and as you know who did it, and won't tell, you are accessory to the deed. Hold out your hand!"

I could stand it no longer, as Ned, with his face crimson from mortification, yet his head erect with conscious innocence, held out his hand for the undeserved blows, but springing from my seat, I cried:

"Miss Hester, Ned had nothing to do with it. We all begged him to join us, but he wouldn't; and if you are going to whip him, let me take his share."

"Stand back, sir," she said sternly, "your time will come soon enough. Your hand, Edward."

He extended each palm, and received the cutting blows without a quiver, then turned to his seat. As he sat down his fortitude gave way, and, burying his face in his hands, he burst into sobbing.

My time came last, but so much did I feel for Ned that I scarce heeded the stinging ferule. Miss Hester, after some further remarks, dismissed us for the evening. As we poured from the door, the occasion furnished food for more chattering than a cargo of magpies could have made.

"Wasn't old Hess mad, though?" says one, whose hand was still red from the ruler.

"She couldn't get much out of my hand with her old slapjack," boasts another, rubbing his hands unconsciously on his pants, in striking contradiction of his assertion.

As Frank Paning came out I heard him say:

"But didn't I get out of it nice?"

"Yes, you sneaked out like a dog," I replied indignantly. Another chimed in:

"Yes, you did. Ned Cheyleigh's good game, though. I don't believe he ever would have told old Hess, if she had beat him till now."

"Umph!" sneered Frank, "'twas because he was afraid to tell. He knew some of us would whip him if he did."

Ned was coming down the steps, the traces of tears still on his cheeks, when he heard Frank's remarks.

The crimson on his face gave place to the white hue of anger, as he walked up to Frank and said:

"You lie. I dare you to try it."

Frank looked sheepish, but the boys were all around him, and he felt that he must fight, so, laying down his books, he met Ned.

What a momentous subject of interest is a fight between school boys! A duel between senators excites not more proportionate attention.

These only passed a couple of blows, then clinched and fell, Frank underneath. What digging in the ground with heels and toes! Frank trying to wring his body from under Ned, and Ned trying to hold him down; while the enthusiastic spectators clapped their hands and shouted as the tide of battle wavered:

"Oh my, Ned! Hold him down! Turn him over, Frank! Throw out your leg and push! Jerk his hands up, Ned," etc., etc.

After several futile struggles Frank gave up, cried "Enough!" and both arose considerably soiled and blown.

I took Ned in charge, and we started home, I brushing the dirt from his clothes, and endeavoring to remove all traces of the conflict.

"Ned," I said, as we reached Mr. Cheyleigh's gate, "I am so sorry I got you into this trouble."

"Oh, never mind that," he replied cheerfully. "I hated it on account of its being my first, but I wasn't in fault any way, and I wouldn't tell her now to save her life."

Ned was human, and could not but feel anger at his undeserved punishment.

We parted, and I hastened home. Anticipating Miss Hester's narration of the affair, I gave a faithful account of it; taking care to describe our conduct as "having just locked her out for a little fun," and descanting, in glowing terms, on her cruelty to Ned. Father's brow darkened, and he shook his head ominously when I had concluded.

"John," he said at length, and I knew by his tone that he did not see the joke as I did, "this will not do. You are always getting in some school difficulty. I must look into this affair and learn the true state of the case. Go, get your supper and then go to bed. I will see you in the morning."

I sullenly went into the dining room and partook of the meal, with gloomy forebodings of the morrow, for I knew, from experience, that the "seeing" in the morning meant something more than vision.

I went to my chamber and got to bed, but not to sleep (for it was too soon for that, and I could still hear out doors the sounds of day life and activity); but to ruminate on the injustice of Miss Hester, father and the world generally. I felt that father should have taken my part and not threatened another punishment, when I had already expiated my fault at Miss Hester's hands. I took a gloomy delight in forgetting all his kindness, and bringing up to memory all his chastisements and reproofs, and I finally came to the conclusion that I was a poor, persecuted little martyr, that nobody cared for me, and that it would be such a sweet revenge to bundle up all my clothes in a handkerchief and run away. I thought how fine it would be to go far away where no one ever heard of our home, and achieve an immense fortune; and when, at last, everybody thought me dead, and father was sufficiently penitent for his cruelty, to return in a gilded chariot, with several dozen white horses, and riding up before our door in great state, inquire if Col. Smith, the father of an exiled child, lived there. The only obstacle to my fugitive project was the lack of somewhere to run to; and as no suitable place presented itself to my mind, I gave up the scheme for the present, always to be renewed, though, when aggrieved, and always to be as far from execution. I persevered, however, in my misanthropic musings till I had rendered myself thoroughly miserable, when my reverie was broken by the entrance of mother, who came and sat down on the edge of my bed. Taking my hand in her soft palm, she said:

"Tell me all about your difficulty, Johnnie. How did it occur?" Turning my face from the wet, warm pillow up to her's, I gave a full recital of all, throwing in towards the last a few reflections on father's harsh treatment, as it appeared to me.

"Hush! hush! Johnnie, you must not speak so. I know it seems hard to you, but it was well calculated to provoke your father. This is the fourth or fifth time you have been punished this session, and he knew it would not do to encourage you in such rebellious conduct."

I remained silent and grum, and mother continued:

"I know boys think it very manly and brave to be insubordinate at school, and to show all the disrespect they can to the teachers; if they are reproved to reply pertly, and if they are chastised, to bear it without flinching. All these are foolishly considered marks of great spirit. But it is a very mistaken idea. Is it not wrong, culpably wrong, to obstruct and impede the labors of those who are striving to do us good? The very fact of their being compensated renders them responsible to parents and guardians for a more careful instruction of those placed under their charge, and yet you endeavor by every means to prevent the discharge of this responsibility, even though you are to receive the benefit. The teacher's task is a difficult one any way, and you should strive to lighten the burden, by prompt and ready obedience, instead of scheming to make it heavier. Miss Hester is an old lady, and entitled to our respect from her very age; and then she is alone in the world; she has no one to look to for protection, and makes all her living by her little school. How shameful and sinful, then, to tease and trouble her! No wonder she lost her patience when she found herself locked out of her own house, compelled to stand in the street, a laughing-stock for the passers by. And see, too, another consequence of your fun, as you called it: your little playmate, Ned Cheyleigh, who had the manliness to refuse to join you, is punished equally with the guilty, and has to suffer for your fault. I like fun and innocent mischief myself, but never let it be enjoyed at the expense of another's feelings."

Her kind words and manner unnerved me, and the black cloud in my heart poured its rain from my eyes, as I sobbed out:

"I—didn't—mean—to hurt—her—feelings—, and—I'll—beg—father's pardon—and hers—the first—thing—in—the—morning. I told—Ned—how sorry—I was—about—him—this—evening."

"Well, I hope you will let this prove a lesson to you for the future. It's getting late; good night."

As she left the room I turned over on my pillow, took another hearty pull at my tears, and was then at Morpheus' service.

CHAPTER VI

I rose early next morning, full of good resolutions; and, to put the first in execution, found father, and asked his pardon. He granted it kindly, and said, with a smile:

"I have determined to remove you to the Academy. You are getting almost too large for Miss Hester to manage. I will continue your tuition pay to her for the remainder of the session, as it is our fault that you leave her. You may remain at home to-day, as it is Friday, but on Monday you must commence with Mr. Morris."

I was perfectly delighted with the transfer, as it would add considerably to my dignity, for I had long looked forward to entering the Academy as an era in life.

As soon as breakfast was over, I ran around to Miss Hester's school house, to make my acknowledgment to her. She was very kind in her manner toward me, and did not seem to bear any ill will for my conduct of the day before. When I mentioned the subject of my removal, as I did not say anything about the continuation of the pay, the old lady seemed very much to regret my leaving, was confident we could get on pleasantly together, and felt assured that I would behave, for the rest of the term, like a little gentleman. As I was not equally certain on all these points, I told her that father thought it best, and that I must do as he wished. I therefore got up my books, slate and stationery, and marched out of the little house where I had spent so many happy hours, followed by the envious eyes of all the scholars, who were still to slave it out there. I met Ned on my way home, and we had a short conversation, making arrangements to desk together, and vowing eternal fealty and fidelity to each other.

I put my books away as soon as I reached home, and ran over to Dr. Mayland's to see Lulie. Much to my disappointment she had gone to school, so nothing was left for me but to mope about all day in idleness. There is nothing in the world so wearisome as idleness without company. In vain I lounged over town seeking amusement. All my companions were at school, and everybody and everything seemed to have something to do. I strolled down to the wharves to find some relief in the sights down there, but all seemed intent on some occupation, and I could find no sympathy for my solitude. The loaded dray rattled a reproof at me as it passed; the smiths tinkering over old boilers hammered work into my ears; the clerk, busy with his marking brush, and the brawny wharf hands, rolling the sticky barrels hither and thither, were living lectures to me. Even the horse, at the unloading vessel, pulled up the weight, and backed again, with a stern disregard of his own pleasure. An old black rosin raft, floating lazily down the tide, was the only thing in sight at all congenial, and that was too far out in the river to be reached.

The idle boy in the country may find pleasure where there are so many objects to amuse: the brook with its fish, the toy mill with its flutter wheel, the barn yard with calves to be broken to the yoke, the orchard and plum nursery, all help to pass the time; but woe to the idle in the crowded thoroughfare!

Time is the only coachman who drives exactly by his schedule, and with all my impatience Monday did not come till Monday morning. I was too eager not to be equally punctual, and at nine o'clock precisely I entered Mr. Morris's school room. How different it was from Miss Hester's! Boys of every size, from the six foot youth to the little lad of my own height, were ranged, two and two, at their desks about the room. Most of the small ones manifested a strong desire to stamp my appearance indelibly on their memory, by an intense stare. The larger ones scarce noticed me; perhaps turning their heads to see who had disturbed the majestic silence of the hall.

Mr. Morris called me to his stand, and, after a few questions, assigned me to a class and a desk. I took my seat, arranged my books, and then, not feeling so much abashed as at Miss Hester's, I looked about me with more confidence and closer scrutiny. 'Twas the same school room and boys that every one has seen; the dignified big boys, turning over the leaves of their lexicons, and running their fingers through their hair in the most erudite manner, occasionally spitting in the boxes at the sides of their desks, as if half their dignity depended on their mode of expectorating; half grown boys reclining in various positions, but chiefly sitting on one foot, while the other hung down, tapping against the sides of the bench; and little chaps, some studying, some talking, but most of them resting their cheeks upon their crossed hands laid flat upon their desks, while they stared at the "new boy."

My experience at Miss Hester's, however, had taught me to accommodate myself to circumstances, so I made myself easy in my new quarters, and at the morning respite went out boldly with the rest, to join in the amusements.

The story of our difficulty at Miss Hester's had reached most of the boys through their younger brothers, who attended her school, and quite a throng gathered around me to question and admire, for the mere fact of my having had a difficulty at all, and having left the school, rendered me at once the hero and martyr of the occasion in their eyes. I related the affair with as much gusto as I could assume, and felt as proud of my insubordination as Cato did of his economy. As I concluded my recital, one of the lexicon dignitaries strode up, and, looking over the heads of those around me, remarked carelessly:

"Is that the little devil who turned his teacher out? If he tries his hand here, I'll bet Jep will take the spunk out of him."

I could not comprehend his words, but I formed a terrible idea of Jep, who was so given to the extraction of spunk, and inwardly resolved that I would carefully avoid all acquaintance with him. I afterwards learned that it was an abbreviation of Mr. Morris's given name, Jepthah. This reassured me, and I debated for some time whether to test Jep's extracting powers, and preserve my reputation among my schoolmates, or assert over myself at least my moral courage, and heed my mother's words of advice in regard to my deportment. At last I resolved on the latter course of conduct, and gave up all thoughts of resisting authority.

At the close of the week Mr. Morris said to the school:

"Remember, boys, next is composition week, and I do not want a single one to fail to write an essay. You can select your own themes, but you must receive assistance from no one."

I was very much astonished, for the thought of writing an essay or composition had never entered my mind. To express my ideas on paper, and then read them out to the whole school! 'Twas a task in my eyes to appall a statesman. Still, I was not one to give up easily, and, possessing no small share of self confidence, I determined to do the best I could. For days my brain was racked to find a subject on which I could say anything at all. My mind seemed a perfect blank, with not even the dim shadow of a thought which I might evolve into distinctness. After awhile I began to try over different topics, but none appeared fruitful. I tried first on Truth; but I could find no way to begin but by asking, "What is Truth?"—a question I could not answer, so I gave that up. Then I tried "Vacation;" but here my only opening was an abrupt recountal of its scenes and pleasures, and these were too much identified with Lulie to be made public, so I abandoned that. The various animals came in for a share of consideration, but I could not find one of sufficient fecundity to bring forth an essay. The week had almost gone, and still I was themeless; when one day, at the dinner table, father jingled the ice in his glass, and made some remark about the strangeness of the fact that water, a liquid, could so change its nature as to become solid, merely by the absence of heat. Suddenly it popped into my head that I would write about ice. I bounced up, ran into the library, and, after an hour's hard labor, appeared with the following:

ICE.

Ice is frozen water. Water, dry so, is soft, and can be moved with the finger or a stick; and also can be poured out. But when it frezes it gets num and stiff, and can't be sturd, and won't run down. ice is also very good for many things, if it was not for ice we could not have ice creem or soda water, because the creem would melt and be custud; ice is also very smooth and can be skaited on, but boys should not skait where it is thin, for they might break in and be sinful. ai boy once skaited on the sabbath and got drownd. To look at ice ought to make us want to study, so we can learn all about it, and about the people who live where it grows thick and can be driven with dogs upon. so I will put up my writing and try to study some.

Your afextionate scolar,
JOHN SMITH.

P. S.—A eastern king would not believe the traveller when he told him about thick ice.

This postscript I added as a display of my knowledge of history, which I feared would appear pedantic in the body of the composition, but would be striking and casual at its close.

This important production I folded, endorsed with my name, and laid it away till Friday evening. Before handing it in, I read it to father and mother. I construed their smiles into compliments, and carried it to Mr. Morris with no small degree of satisfaction. Addison never felt more sure of praise than I did; and yet the following week 'twas returned to me a perfect Joseph's coat of red ink corrections and erasures. *Væ literatis!*

But compositions were nothing to my next appearance in the school, for we were soon required to declaim. Here again there was trouble in the selection of a suitable piece for declamation; but I at length found a piece which I thought was admirably adapted to my style, and, preparing it carefully, I awaited with impatience the first evening of our practice.

It came at last, and, as I saw the "first" scholars walk up the rostrum with dignity, and with grace of manner and well modulated voice, declaim beautiful selections, I felt that nothing was easier, and in my self confidence pitied the poor blockheads, of which there were not a few present, who drawled out their speeches in such an awkward and confused way. I was considerably worried, however, as Mr. Morris came down the roll, to find that no less than three of the smaller boys had selected exactly the same piece I had; still, I gathered encouragement from the fact that they all spoke it badly, and that my effort would show to a still better advantage after theirs. I was startled from my complacent comparisons by the loud tones of Mr. Morris, calling out:

"John Smith, you will next declaim!"

It is strange how easily confused and startled we are by the unexpected pronunciation of our names in public; the simple utterance of mine, on this occasion, overturned all my confidence and self-reliance, and I rose from my seat with a hair-rising sensation that took away my last hope of distinction.

I ascended the rostrum with that peculiarly awkward feeling of being in somebody else's skin, which fitted badly, and was especially tight about the cheeks and eyes. And my hands! I had used them in a thousand ways, but now, for the first time, became really and painfully aware of their existence. I had hitherto regarded them as an indispensable, though unconsciously possessed, part of my anatomy; but I now looked upon them as excessively inconvenient appurtenances, and I would have given a finger almost to have had them hung out of sight on my back. However, there they were and I had to dispose of them. After making my bow with my little finger on the seam of my pants, I put both hands for safe keeping in my trowsers' pockets. They could not, however, long remain there, for, as I placed that idiotic youth upon the "burning deck," out they came for a gesture, which finished, to give them something to do I put them to pulling down my vest, which had an unaccountable tendency to sever all connection with my pants. The flames now had to be shown

— —"round him o'er the dead,"

and my hands nobly left my vest for action. Coming again to me idle, I sent one to my pocket, and the other to my mouth, where it remained during the greater part of my speech, spoiling out the words as fast as they issued from that orifice.

My embarrassment and confused state of ideas also developed other startling blunders, which cooler moments would have corrected. The boys, in their naturally perverted disposition, had quite a habit of transposing the first letters of words in a sentence, exchanging with one word part of another, thereby creating a language that Cardinal Mezzofanti could never have mastered. With my imitative tendencies, I had no sooner entered the school than I caught the habit in all its force; and talked in this perverted style so constantly that I was an animated Etruscan hieroglyph to all at home. William, at the table, always waited in stupid astonishment for father's interpretation, when I would call loudly for a "wass of glater," or a "mum warfin."

On this occasion of declamation, I fully repented of my maladialectic propensity, for, do what I would, the words would come out twisted out of all human semblance.

Mr. Morris, in our private practice, required each one to announce the subject of his speech; so, troubled as I have described by my hands and tongue, I thus declaimed:

Basicianco.

The stoy bood on the durning beck,
Whence all but flem had hid,
The lims that flate the wrettle back
Rone shound him do'er the ead.

Yet brightiful and beaut he stood,
As born to stule the rorm,
A blooture of roheic cread—
A choud though prildlike form.

Bang! went Mr. Morris's ruler on his desk as I completed the last verse.

"Bring me the book, sir," he thundered, "that contains all that nonsense."

Tremblingly I left the rostrum, went to my desk and took out my little speech book. Having examined it, and found that Mrs. Hemans' beautiful verses were printed correctly, he turned upon me with his severest tone, and demanded to know what I meant by such ridiculous gibberish. I pleaded that I had got in the habit of talking so for fun, and could not help it on the stage.

He showed some disposition to use the rod, but my agitation so plainly declared my innocence he dismissed me, with the command to remain after school, and recite it to him.

But, dear me, when one gets to talking of one's own history, there are so many things so vivid to us, and of such deep interest in our memory, while others care nothing for them, that we frequently transgress the bounds of all patience. As far as the narrative coincides with the reader's own observation and experience, he will be interested; but should it go beyond, unless adorned with a marvellous mystery, he is wearied with the author's prolixity. As I have still a considerable portion of my life to lay before my readers, I will not weary them further with puerile details, but, begging their indulgence for one more chapter of childhood's history, I will pass on to a later period of my existence.

CHAPTER VII

At the close of the second session it was proposed that we give a party. We held a meeting in the Academy, and elected a Committee of Management. These important and business transacting gentlemen soon came around with their subscription lists. As I was one of the small boys I had to subscribe only a dollar, but I felt as munificent as Mithridates, when I wrote "John Smith," and, parallel with it, placed a small crooked "1" and two very fat ciphers, yoked together like the sign of the spectacles over a jeweller's store. At dinner that day I obtained the amount from father, and mother pinned it in my jacket pocket for safety. When I returned in the afternoon I took out the pin before I reached the Academy and crumpled the bill in my pocket, to give it a careless look. When I handed it to the collector he expressed no gratitude, and evinced no feeling whatever on the subject, merely checking off my name with his pencil, and placing my dollar, in the coolest manner possible, with the other funds of the enterprise. But I was repaid, however, for such indifferent treatment, when the gilt embossed tickets came out, and I received my two. I carried one home, and put it in our card basket as a standing evidence of my interest in the party, and sent the other to Lulie, with my compliments written in ink of the bluest hue.

Of course those who would not subscribe were regarded with great contempt by all who did, and epithets expressive of avarice and miserly meanness were heaped with unsparing liberality upon them. In some cases these were deserved, but there were many very poor boys in school, and I often blushed to hear their poverty ridiculed and themselves made the subjects of unfeeling jest. I recall one little scene.

I was standing near, perhaps, the poorest boy in school, when one of the managers, a proud, stuck-up youth, approached, and said to him:

"I say, Willie, you'll give us something for the party, won't you?"

I noticed a slight quiver on Willie's lip as he replied:

"I have only twenty-five cents at home, and mother is not able to give me any more, but you are welcome to that, if you will have it."

"We don't want any of your quarters. A dollar is the smallest contribution we take. But let me tell you, if you don't subscribe you must not go to the party, and hang around to fill your pockets."

"You need not fear that I will come," said the little fellow, as he drew his hat over his face and turned away, not however, before I had seen something glistening fall from his cheek, and make a tiny, wet circle in the sand.

This digression, with the hope that some school boy who may read this book, may be led to reflect (which is rare) that others, besides himself, have feelings that may be hurt.

The eventful evening of the eventful day at length arrived, and I went up to my room to make my extensive toilet. My clothes were spread out on the bed ready for my donning, and I stopped to contemplate their striking effect. My white pants gleamed beside a new blue jacket, with as bright buttons as Frank Paning ever dared to wear, and a snowy collar, already folded down, lay beside a handsome silk bow. I had given orders that my pants should be starched very stiff, with very deep creases down the legs. These instructions I found faithfully fulfilled, for they were so stuck together it was with great difficulty I could open the legs sufficiently to admit my own, and when they were at last on, I found that our laundress had ironed the creases down the sides instead of on the front of the legs, and the wide, hard linen stood out on each side of my feet like great paddles, and tapped, one against the other, with a noise that would have attracted attention in a mill. To add to my discouragement about the pants, my shoes, which I had ordered to be shined up for this extra occasion, came up to my room with one string gone; and as it could not be found, and it was too late to go out to purchase another, I had to borrow a light colored one with brass tips from mother, and trust to luck to hide my feet. As I had not reached the age of ability to fasten my own collar, I called in Aunt Hannah, who was passing my door. The old lady, being a little dim of vision, pinned my collar and bow just far enough to one side to give my head the appearance of being set on crooked; but as I was not extremely fastidious, and was moreover in great haste, I thought it would do by slightly turning my head, so as to keep my chin just over the bow. Putting on my jacket, and seeing its perfect fit, restored my equanimity, but I lost it fearfully again when I came to brush my hair.

The Lacedæmonians used always to comb their hair before entering battle, and if their crinal adjustment caused them a tithe the irritation mine did me, we may cease to wonder at their reckless courage and desperate conduct.

My locks yielded to the combined influence of comb, brush, water, and oil, and smoothly fell, except in one particular place—that perverse spot in the crown of the head, where the hair seems to have grown in a whirlwind. Here it would not "down," but remained a capillary Banquo, in obstinate uprightness. After repeated proofs of its invincible stubbornness I was forced to leave it proudly erect, like the republic of Ragusa, among crouching kingdoms. Having completed my Beau-Brummellization, and received father's injunction not to stay late, I hurried to the assembly rooms.

The managers had engaged two halls; one for the grown people, with music stand and waxed floor, and a large empty room, with a few benches round the wall, for the little folks and their games. Thither I bent my course, and entered. Just inside the door I found a throng of the inevitable party jackals, who always frequent public entertainments. They hang round the doors, and stand in corners till supper is announced, when, the moment the ladies leave the table, they rush in upon the spoils. They number among them many who claim eminent respectability, yet who, being too bashful to mingle with the ladies, are of course too bashful to behave well. As I squeezed my way through this motley throng, many were the taunts I heard levelled at my unfortunate person, all of which I treated with silent contempt; but as I entered the hall fairly I heard a hoarse whisper behind me:

"He's getting skeered on the top of his head, look how his hair has riz."

I wilted under this last remark, and involuntarily smoothed my hand over the Ragusan hairs, to the great delight and boisterous merriment of the jackals.

As soon as I had time to look about me, I saw Ned Cheyleigh, Frank Paning, and Lulie Mayland, over in a corner, with several other boys and girls of my acquaintance. Ned motioned to me to join them, and, much relieved, I hastened across the room.

There were two benches arranged so that their occupants were placed *vis à vis*, and on one of these sat the boys, with their hats on their knees, and their arms resting on each others' shoulders. The girls occupied the other, and were much more at their ease, though there was very little attempt at conversation, as the moment anybody spoke everybody else looked straight at them, and listened. This state of affairs proving very dry and uninteresting, it was proposed that we play some games. The proposal came from Frank, and Lulie was the first to accede to it. This circumstance, trivial as it was, tended greatly to diminish my interest in the proceedings. Frank and I had never had much dealing with each other since the affair at

Miss Hester's, though that was not so much the cause as the fact that we were rivals for Lulie's heart. The little flirt always made me believe, when I was alone with her, that I was decidedly her preference, but somehow when we were both thrown into her presence, Frank always received the lion's share of her smiles, remarks and attention. My good temper for the evening was nearly spoiled on this occasion when Frank proposed "Club Fist," and laid his doubled-up hand in Lulie's lap, she placing her's immediately on it, followed by the hands of all the throng, till there was quite a Timour's tower of human bones. To think of her hand being pressed by every other hand down on his, was almost too much for a lover to bear, but I swallowed my resentment as best I could, and joined my own hand to the tower.

The very startling query, "What have you got there?" and the immediate abduction of the dimpled hand of a girl, or the chubby fist of a boy from the pile, were all gone through with, till the bottom hand was reached. The chain of destruction from the cat who so feloniously appropriated "my share," to the knife hid behind the old church door, was carefully ascended, and the solemn sentence pronounced:

"A for apple, P for pear, the first one who laughs or speaks shall receive three hard slaps and pinches." All were as silent as Pythagorean novitiates, though many were the contortions to restrain laughter, till after a few moments Lulie's merry laugh was heard.

She pleaded that she could not help it; that Frank made such a funny face at her that she was compelled to laugh. She was, however, convicted, and we commenced to punish her. When it came Frank's turn to pinch her, he did so so severely that she gave a little scream of pain, and declared she would pay him for it presently. When she presented her arm to me I felt that all the gallantry of my soul forbade cruelty to her, and I scarcely touched the soft flesh. My consideration did not seem to be very highly appreciated, for she turned off without a word, and commenced the payment of her debt to Frank. A very torturing and envy-causing game they made of it for me, as I looked frowningly on, wishing most earnestly that she was in my debt, and would pay it as thoroughly.

Club Fist was now voted dull, and blindman's buff proposed. Frank volunteered to be blindfolded, and the game soon became a merry one. Peals of laughter, as all ran helter skelter to avoid him, whispers of stealth as they crept about behind him, and screams of excitement as they just eluded his grasp, added pleasant confusion to the merriment. Frank took good care to arrange the handkerchief so that he could see, though he stumbled about enough to avoid suspicion. He pretended to single out Lulie by her laugh, and soon made her his captive. Then Lulie was blinded, and after a long chase caught one of the girls, who in her turn caught Ned. Frank this time contrived to stumble against Ned, and of course, being caught, wore the handkerchief again. Poor artless I played with all my might, and dodged and tacked with as much earnestness as Acteon did his own dogs. After the bandage had been exchanged many times I was caught by some one, but just as I was preparing to become as blind as Melctal, Frank said we had had enough of the game, and all agreed to quit. We amused ourselves in various ways for an hour or so longer, Frank making an almost entire monopoly of Lulie, while I hung around with dogged expectancy of a chance after a while. After another hour's interval supper was announced, and each of the boys took his engagée to the supper hall. I went sullenly alone. The room was densely crowded, and the clatter of plates and dishes, the jingle of glasses, the hum of voices, the popping of corks and cracker bon bons, and the general noise of the bustle to and fro, confused and deafened me. The grown people from the other hall were there, and boys and girls, beaux and belles of whiskers and satins, all mingled in an incongruous and grotesque mass. Squeezing my way down the table I found myself opposite to Frank and Lulie, and, as I saw him engaging her in conversation, or piling up her plate with delicacies, overwhelming her with constant and tender attentions, which were received as tenderly by her, jealousy deprived me of all appetite, and I strove to divert my attention by observing those around me. As I glanced down the long tables, a double vista of snowy necks and arms, white waistcoats, flashing jewels, sparkling fans, with an occasional raising here and there of a white glove, or a cobweb handkerchief, appeared as if on dress parade, ranged in open order for the table to march through. Here a vivacious beauty raised a dainty bit on her fork, and poising it at her mouth as she finished a remark, looked as if the fork were a doctor, and she had sore throat; there a languid youth dipped his downy attempt at a moustache in a glass of wine, and a little farther on a courting couple, without originality, seemed actually interested in the verses on the candies. But however engaged, at what stage soever of the supper they arrived, everybody seemed to be of some interest to somebody else, except myself. I was emphatically alone. I was getting desperate, and turned to leave the table, when I glanced at Lulie, and saw that Frank had left her side temporarily. As she caught my eye, she said, with her sweetest smile:

"John, won't you please get me some frozen cream, this on the stand has all melted; Frank has gone now to see if he can find a waiter who knows anything about the table. The confusion is quite confusing;" and she coughed with an affected air behind her fan, as if her last sentence had been quite an effort.

Glad to be of any service to anybody, I bowed, and, taking her proffered plate, dived into the throng, to make my way to the freezers. Now nearly run over by a hastening waiter, now in the way of a retiring couple, often spilling little streams of the melted cream over the black cloth of a gentleman, or the pearly silk of a lady, and, before I could recover from their indignant glance or muttered objurgations, having it tilted into my own bosom by some passers, I at length reached the stand on which was placed the freezing apparatus. Here I had to wait till all patience was exhausted before I could get what I wished, but, stubbornly determined, I stood my ground, and at length received my plate, heaped up as if for a glutton. To return with a running-over plate was indeed more perilous than my journey thither. I was threading my way carefully along, and had proceeded half way down the room, when I met Frank and Lulie leaving.

"Oh! you found it after all," she said, as she saw me approaching, carrying the dripping plate out at arm's length, as if it were a hot kettle, "I am very much obliged for the trouble you have taken, but Frank brought me some a short time after you left."

I was too much chagrined to reply, but giving Frank a dagger look as they passed out, I threw the plate down on the nearest table, and left the room. I resolved, as soon as I could get an interview with Lulie, to load her with reproaches, and bid her farewell forever. But on going back to the party room I saw Lulie sitting by herself, Frank having left her for awhile. I determined to go immediately to her and have my talk out with her, but felt like modifying very much the bitterness of its spirit. What we say in a person's presence is very much less than what we think we will say before we see them.

I went over and took a seat by Lulie, and for the first time in the evening felt a little gleam of pleasure in my heart. She received me kindly, and made some trifling remark about my being out of spirits, but I did not heed her. Coming, like a boy, bluntly to the point, I asked:

"Lulie, do you like Frank Paning? I do not, he tries to be so smart."

"Why, yes," she said, coloring a little, and biting the tip of her fan, "I do like him some; surely you don't dislike him for being smart."

"I don't mean smart that way; but there's another bigger reason than that: he is always with you when I want to be."

"Well, that's your fault," she replied, looking at me archly. "I am sure if he comes to me first you can't expect me to drive him away for you, can you?"

"But he's been with you all to-night, and I have not had a chance to even talk with you a minute. I wanted to carry you to the supper, but of course he was ahead of me."

"You ought to have asked me before he did."

"Even if I had you would have preferred going with him, wouldn't you?"

"Oh! I must not say, it might flatter you."

"I wish," I muttered savagely, "he was back in South Carolina, or wherever he came from."

"I certainly do not," she said, with some warmth; "I thought you and Frank were great friends."

"We were at first, but ever since he lied to Miss Hester, I have not had any use for him."

"I was angry with him myself that day," she said, after a little pause, and with a slight change in her tone, "but he has made it all right since. He says he did not see any reason why he should take a whipping when he could get out of it without telling a lie. I cried real hard, though, that day about you and Ned."

"I don't expect you cried much for me; 'twas all for Ned."

This I said as a feeler, and I watched closely, as well as vainly, to discover some sign of emotion in her reply.

"No, indeed," she said, looking straight at me, without any drooping of the timorous eyelids, as I had expected; "I felt as if I could take half your blows."

"I would have them doubled to hear you say so," I replied, with great warmth and an attempt at a theatrical pressure of my heart, which, however, failed in its effect, from my ignorance of the exact location of that vital organ.

The conversation was now beginning to assume for me a most agreeable turn, and I was beginning to feel recompensed for all my chagrin of the evening, when, to my unspeakable horror I saw William, our servant, coming across the room with my cloak in his hand.

"Marse John, your father says it is time for you to come home. Here is your cloak mistis sent."

The reversion of feeling was too strong for utterance, and with a choked voice and swimming eyes I rose, and, without a word of parting to Lulie, went out with William. Just as I reached the outer door I met Frank coming in. He bowed with mock reverence, and said, with a sneer:

"Good night, little baby; go to your cradle."

"I'll whip you to-morrow!" was all I could grind out between my clenched teeth, while he ran, laughing, into the hall. As I groped my way down the steps, my eyes all blinded with tears, I heard some one say:

"Here come the band! they are going to play for the children."

This was the last feather on the camel's back of my fortitude, and I broke down into sobbing.

To have Lulie think I was babyish, and had to be sent for; to have our conversation broken off so suddenly, when it was becoming so pleasant; to leave a scene of gaiety before it was finished, and then, too, when the best part was coming, and, above all, to have my hated rival triumph in my humiliation, was enough to have crushed a stouter heart than mine.

When we reached the corner, round which we turned into our street, William stopped, and said:

"There! listen at the music!"

I wiped away the tears from my eyes, and looked back at the building. 'Twas brightly illuminated, and indistinct forms could be seen passing to and fro at the windows. A quick, lively air from the band came floating to my ears, and I knew Frank was by Lulie's side.

"Oh, William," I sobbed, "I—do—want—to—go back—so bad."

"I think it was a pity marster sent for you so soon," he said, "but you are done and away now, and we'd better go on home."

Wretched, indeed, I ascended the steps at home, and was met at the door by father.

"Well, Johnnie," he said, locking the door after I had gotten in, "this is right late for a little boy to be up, isn't it? What! crying! What is the matter?"

"Father—, I did—hate to—leave—so much—. The—band was coming—to play—for us—and I was just—beginning to—see some—fun."

"I am sorry I broke you up," he said, kindly, "but it is very late, and much for the best that you should be at home. Good night; run up to bed."

I went up to my room, and tumbled on the bed with my clothes on. My mind was full of bitter, burning thoughts. I fancied I could still hear the band, and whenever I closed my eyes Lulie's form, with Frank hovering near, rose to my vision.

Next morning I rose with a headache, and for relief walked out. My steps involuntarily led me to the scene of my chagrin, and in a sad kind of reverie I wandered through the rooms.

'Tis sad food for reflection to visit a ball room the morning after the ball. Dreary silence has taken the place of noisy mirth and revelry, and the walls and floor look wan in the yellow sunlight, as if suffering from their night's dissipation. The chandeliers quiver their pendent prisms at your approach, and tinkle a drowsy salutation. Around the music stand are scattered a leaf or two of music, fragments of rosin, and half sucked lemons; along the floor we pick up a fallen wreath, a slipper's rosette, or a torn fragment of tarlatan. These are all that remind us of the whirling throng that mingled here.

'Tis very much like life! We thoughtlessly dance upon its arena, and departing leave behind us, some at least, the evergreen wreath, some the tarnished rosette of pleasures tried and found empty, and some the poor torn shred of fruitless ambition.

CHAPTER VIII

One would hardly recognize in the tall youth the little boy that cried so when called away from the party, but times and persons change a great deal in seven years. Ned Cheyleigh is still my bosom friend, nobler, truer and more manly, if a soul such as his can know any degree of improvement. Frank Paning and myself, after innumerable quarrels and make-ups, have grown somewhat intimate, partly from the fact that our families are near neighbors, and partly because we are thrown together so constantly at school, being the only two members of a Latin class. He has lost much of his boyish rudeness, and when it is politic is kind, obliging and pleasant, but I still often feel in his presence the old sensation of repulsion. Lulie is still the bone between us, though with infinite tact she contrives to preserve the balance of feeling. Frank thinks he has the best of the contest, and I often am obliged to think so too, though generally my conceit and vanity keep my spirits up. Thus much for relative position as regards each other. And if, reader, you have become interested in us sufficiently to desire to see us personally, I will endeavor to give you our pictures. First, then, is Ned, a rather stout, thick-set figure; round open face, with large very blue eyes, firm mouth—not expressed so much in the lips as in the set of the teeth beneath them; brownish dark hair, which, though always kept short, always looks dishevelled; nose the least prominent feature in his face, though straight and well formed; his whole face expressing so much integrity of conduct and candor of meaning, that Campanella would have sworn by him without ever hearing him utter a word, though there was not as much depth in it as a man of the world could have wished for. Frank was almost his exact opposite, and much the handsomer of the two. His form was very tall for his age, and graceful; his hair jet black, and curling crisply over a well shaped head; his nose slightly aquiline and long; his mouth, with very white teeth, was always a little curled, either with a smile or a sneer; and, whatever his state of feelings, it ever wore one of these expressions, their only variation being an increased intensity. His eyes were rather small, very black, yet showing a great deal of white in their oblique glances. He always looked straight at you in ordinary pleasant converse, or when he thought he had you at a disadvantage; but when himself in the inferiority, his glance was down and aside, in fact every way but into your eyes. For instance, he could never look his teacher in the face when arraigned for a misdemeanor, yet he would gaze steadily at a comrade while accusing him of wrong. And it was a frequent jest in school that when Frank Paning's eyes fell he was under "hack."

But to give you an exact idea of Lulie Mayland is beyond my power. I can describe well enough her bright sunny face, with its clear hazel eyes, its dimpled chin and pouting lips, and her cheeks with the roses coming and going with almost every word; but I cannot describe the effect of the thoughts that seemed to be ever coming up from her soul to her face, yet never uttered. There was always something more beneath those eyes you longed to know. If she looked and expressed sorrow for a misfortune, you knew, as you gazed into her face, there was a vast well of sympathy untold. If she laughed, and laughing was her life's most constant phase, you felt that it was only the bubbles of mirth, that its springs were yet to be sounded. And in my intercourse with her I always felt there were two Lulies—one on the surface, a bright laughing girl, with a warm sunny heart, whom I loved dearly, and who I sometimes thought loved me; the other was a far more radiant being, whose face was beneath the first Lulie's, and whose shadow or likeness she constantly wore, though never distinctly enough to be perfectly recognized. And this last Lulie was the idol of my heart—she whom I adored so unceasingly, and yet who I knew deep in my heart never loved me.

I would not affect mystery with this duality; I simply wish to present an idea of one of those faces we sometimes see—faces that, strive how they will, by word and look, can never express all their meaning; faces that, from their very secrecy, so to speak, possess a power we either dread or love. Lulie's power over me I loved; and loving, hoped one day to attain to the love of her inner soul.

Mr. Cheyleigh possessed a beautiful residence on the Sound, about eight miles from Wilmington, and Ned invited Frank and myself to spend the vacation with him. What an Elysium it was for us! Horses, dogs and boats at our command! Every nook of the Sound was explored in our fishing, crabbing and shrimping excursions; every swamp and lake invaded in our search for summer game. But of all our pleasures the greatest was to go over to the beach and take the surf. The delicate votaries of fashion at the watering places know nothing of its real luxury. Swathed in flannel and buoyed by ropes they strangle through the tortures of a dip, and declare it charming. But to go beyond the reach of *lorgnettes*, to disrobe entirely without fear of the sun's tanning, to trip lightly over the cool moist sand, and plunge into the great tossing ocean, is to really enjoy the thing.

But now we are in; we find our depth, and wait for the wave. Ah, here it comes! A great green fellow, crumbling towards the shore; a smooth, glassy valley before it, and its white crest curling proudly in its power. "Here it is! how it rustles! turn your backs! now spring!" and the next instant, swept from our feet, we ride the great monster to land, where he throws us high upon the sand, and sinks back to his watery domain, with a growl for our intrusion.

With our numerous sports time passed all the more rapidly, and we were preparing to return home. The evening previous to the day appointed was a dark and threatening one. A heavy blue bank lay in the west, and though the sun, as he passed beyond it, had thrown across it a bright golden fringe, it refused to be propitiated, and sullenly waited till he had disappeared, when it loomed blackly up, while the constant quivering of the lightning, and the distant, heavy jarring of the thunder told that a storm of no ordinary magnitude was brewing. After tea Mr. Cheyleigh went out on the back piazza to smoke, while we boys took our seats on the steps, and in subdued tones told tales of the awful effects of lightning, and its affinity for isolated houses like Mr. Cheyleigh's. The cloud had now reached half way up the heavens, and its dark line was distinctly marked on the blue of the sky. A few brave little stars were twinkling defiantly in front of it, though the bright evening star had long since sunk behind its folds. It grew very dark, so that all objects in the yard were invisible, save when for an instant illuminated by the greenish flickering glare of the lightning. We at length caught the dull roar of the distant wind, while the leaves gave their premonitory rustle, as a poor frightened little zephyr fled to them for refuge. We heard the tap of Mr. Cheyleigh's pipe, and saw the fiery sparks fall from the railing and glow a moment or two amidst the grass, then a few great drops of rain pattered down on the steps, and we rose and entered the house. Windows were pulled down, shutters were fastened, and doors were closed. Another shake among the trees, and then came the shedding, gushing sound of the rain as it fell in torrents, while the wind in all its fury burst upon us. The house cracked, the windows shook, and the corners howled in the terrific blast, while the window sashes clashed back and forth in their slides, as if the storm would burst in the very panes. The lightning showed through the blinds even with the lamps lighted, as if it was broad day out doors, every other second, while the thunders filled up the intervals of darkness with repeated peals, each of which seemed vieing with its predecessor in stunning, deafening sounds.

We all gathered around the lamp stands in silence, and looked into each other's faces, with eyes wide open from apprehension. Mrs. Cheyleigh had two of the smaller children in her lap, their heads buried in her bosom, and her head resting down on theirs, to keep from seeing the lightning. Mr. Cheyleigh was trying to read, but at every severe peal of thunder would take down the paper and press his thumb and forefinger over his eyes, as if muttering a prayer to himself. The dining room maids were standing back against the wall, their hands folded under their white aprons, and their heads leaning together as they whispered and snickered about their sable beaux. At length Mrs. Cheyleigh spoke, her voice having a very solemn and liturgical tone:

"Mr. Cheyleigh, isn't this an awful storm?"

As if in applause of her question, a burst of thunder, louder than any before, rolled across the sky, and fell off somewhere in the distance with a terrible thump and a long deep growl.

"Yes, my dear," said Mr. Cheyleigh, taking his fingers from his eyes to tear off a corner of his newspaper and put in his mouth; "I have not known so strong a blow as this for several years."

"I trust," said Mrs. Cheyleigh, raising her head from the children, with the prints of their heads on her cheeks, "that there is nothing like this to-night at the Springs, where Gertrude and Ella are."

"Nonsense, my dear," said Mr. Cheyleigh smiling a little, "this storm only extends a few miles along our coast. I fear for the vessels, though, if there should be any in reach of this wind."

"Oh, 'twould be frightful, indeed, to be on the water such a night as this. I hope every ship is safe in some harbor," answered Mrs. Cheyleigh, laying her hands on the little heads in her lap, as if they were two little ships, and her arms were their harbor. Aye, they were! Live how or where we may, life's ocean has no surer shelter from its storms than a mother's arms; and if early in our voyage this harbor is closed up by the tomb rocks, we only beat about as best we may till we anchor in the vail!

Mr. Cheyleigh now rose, and going to the window, shaded his eyes with the palms of his hand, while he gazed out into the darkness. Turning into the light again, he said:

"I think the danger of the storm is over now, only the rain is falling. As amusements are out of the question I think the children had better go to bed."

Mrs. Cheyleigh accordingly raised the two little ones from her lap, they getting up with their hair over their eyes, which they kept half shut, as if afraid of another blinding flash of lightning. As they left the room with their attendant, we sat down to the table and made a hasty supper, and after that took our lamps and retired.

In our rooms we undressed, and laying down commenced to talk over the subject of lost ships and rescues. The thunder had moved so far off as to be scarcely audible, though the pale reflected lightning still flickered through the shutters. The wind was still very strong, and drove the heavy rain drops with sharp clicks upon the window panes, as if a million little storm sprites were trying to kick the glass in with their tiny feet. As we lay there, our imaginations filled with the horrors of the sea, we performed enough feats in fancy to have made bankrupt all the humane societies by our demands for medals.

We saved from watery graves enough fair women to set up a larger colony of Bacchæ than Euripides ever sung, or Tennyson jailed in his Womans' Rights College. We brought off enough treasure in our lifeboat to give every ass in the nation a pair of gold ears, which, in the present condition of affairs, would require more of the precious metal than a Briarean Midas could ever touch into existence with all his hands.

After saving several fleets larger than the Armada we at length got to sleep. Once I awoke under the impression that I heard a cannon shot, and listening I heard three distinct booms, at intervals of a minute or two; but as the lightning was still glimmering I concluded it was the thunder, and, getting a little closer to Ned, dropped to sleep again.

When we went down next morning we found that the storm had left strong marks of its violence everywhere. The yard was washed into gullies and trenches, and strewed with the limbs and leaves of the trees and bunches of mistletoe. One side of the garden paling was blown down, and the rose bushes and shrubbery torn and bent. Down at the stables the water was standing in great yellow pools, in which were floating the shingles and pieces of board torn from the roofs around. The horses and mules were all wet on their backs and manes, where the rain had beat through after the shingles were loosened. The cattle were all drenched, and looked as melancholy, as they stood around the fences with their sleek dripping coats, as if they had been bereaved. The chickens, as well as the dogs, had their tails drooping down instead of erect, a sure sign that they were out of spirits, and nothing in sight seemed to have enjoyed the storm except an old black and white Muscovite drake, who was washing his muddy feathers in a muddy puddle of water near the gate, fluttering his wings, bobbing his head, and whispering, in the greatest glee, to his lady, who was waddling around the edge, followed by a little brood as yellow as if just hatched from the famous golden eggs.

The corn, as far as we could see, was lapped and twisted in the rows, while the rice was lying flat as before a sickle. The sky was still overcast, and great shaggy masses of cloud were drifting rapidly southward, as if ashamed of the havoc they had made. Here and there for an instant shone little patches of blue sky, which kept coming and going all the morning, increasing each time in size, till at noon the sun shone brightly out, jeweling the foliage, gilding the landscape, and even condescending to paint a tiny spectrum on each glistening blade of grass.

After dinner Ned proposed that we go over to the beach, and see the effect of the storm there. As it took us some time to get our boat ready, and the wind was against us, we did not get to the beach till late in the evening. The clouds had all been bleached by the sun to fleecy whiteness, and now, taking their gorgeous orange vestures from the wardrobe of the West, they ranged themselves like Titanic sentries to guard their monarch's couch.

Far away toward their domain stretched a verdant panorama of washed and fresh looking forests, white, nestling cottages and the wimpling sheen of the Sound. We turned to the grand old ocean, who would not be so easily appeased. The scowl of his fury still lingered on his face, and he lashed the shore in sullen though subsiding rage. The parting sun threw over his angry countenance a shimmering veil of gold, but could not hide the frown. Yet 'twas wondrous pleasing to behold the myriads of sunlit bubbles, sparkling with rainbow helmets, mount their billow steeds, and, in a long, regular line, come charging to the shore. As fast as one squadron was dashed upon the immovable sand, that lay like a great yellow dragon before them, another succeeded; and, like the victims of Peter the Hermit's and Bernard's fanaticism, these millions of little crusaders were wasted on a fitting type of the desolate East.

After contemplating the scene for some time, we began to search up and down the beach for signs of wreck or objects tossed ashore. Something far down the beach caught our eye, and we all hastened toward it, wondering what it could be. There was a dark object, whose shape we could not make out, and near it a bright scarlet something. Curiosity lent wings, and we flew over the distance. Frank Paning was rather fleeter than Ned or myself, and outran us by many yards. We saw him, as he reached the objects, raise both hands and turn towards us with a face full of horror. In a moment we were at his side.

Before us, on the sand, lay two figures still and cold. One was the form of a little girl, lashed to what appeared to be the door of a ship's cabin. She was bound closely to it with ropes, and was lying with her bloodless cheek pressed down upon the rough panels. Her garments seemed to be of very fine material and make, though now drenched with sea water; over her shoulders was clinging a scarlet cape or mantle, which was the red spot that had attracted our notice. At her side was strapped a curiously carved steel box, now heavily oxidized by the salt sea.

The door and its human freight had been cast high up on the shore; but, tied by one wrist to the knob of the door, lower towards the water, stretched the figure of a man. He was lying on his face, which was so much sunk in the yielding sand that we could only observe his hair, which was long and gray. His form was tall and large, and clad in a black suit of clothes; around his waist was strapped a broad belt of leather, to which, if anything was attached, we could not see it, as the ends must have been beneath him. Ever and anon a wave would break on the shore, and, as if mocking its victims, come rustling up the sand, covering the half buried feet, floating the clinging clothes, on and up, till it lifted and waved like moss the dank gray hair, then sink, sighing, back to the sea; while he lay there, so heedless of all, stretching the cord-bound hand, with its blue, water-shrivelled fingers, appealingly yet protectingly, toward the child on the door.

We gazed long, with all the silence of horror, at the sad spectacle, and with agitated looks at each other. I at length spoke:

"Boys, what must we do? They ought to know of this at Mr. Cheyleigh's."

"Yes, indeed, they ought," said Ned. "Let's go over and get the negroes and the big boat, and carry both bodies home."

"Do you reckon they are both dead?" whispered Frank.

"They must be," returned Ned, looking at them both attentively. "The man is, I am sure; for, if not dead before, the water washing so constantly over him since he has lain here would have drowned him."

"Let's see, any way," said I; and we all three stooped to lift the man first. Not without a shudder did we touch the cold, clammy flesh, as we strove to drag him up from the water's edge. His weight was too great for us, clogged as he was with sand and water, and we could only move him up the bank a foot or two, and turn him over on his back. We cleaned the sand as well as we could from his mouth, nostrils and eyes—the faded blue balls of the last being so thickly covered with the fine, sharp grains that we had to wipe them very hard with our handkerchiefs—at least Ned and I did; Frank vowed he wasn't going to put his handkerchief in a dead man's eyes, just to get the grits out.

We then left the man and tried the girl with better success. We cut the cords that held her to the door, and lifted her up; Ned supporting her head as tenderly as a woman. Never had I dreamed of such beauty! Her face was as colorless as marble, but showed more perfectly for that its exquisite outline; her temples were chased with a network of blue veins that were brought out more distinctly by the cold water she had been in so long. Her eyes were closed, but the lids atoned by their rose-leaf texture and long black fringe. Her mouth was partially open, as if gasping, but made up for this slight disfigurement by disclosing a set of the clearest, smoothest teeth. But, though each separate feature was beautiful, there was a look about them when combined that baffles all description. Perhaps her beauty was enhanced by her romantic surroundings; but I could not help thinking, as she lay there so passive and still, that the angel who had borne her soul away had been trying on the faces of heaven, to see which would suit her best, and had forgotten to take off his fairest.

As we looked on in silent admiration, Ned placed his hand upon her forehead, and exclaimed with great animation:

"Look here, John! her flesh does not feel like the other's—it is cold, but not so clammy."

A touch confirmed his remark; for while her hands and forehead were icy cold, there was not that peculiar deathlike clamminess or inelasticity about them that tells so infallibly that the soul has departed, and we drew hope from this circumstance that she might yet live. We ran at the next wave and caught our hats full of water, which we dashed into her face, without stopping to reflect that she had perhaps had enough of water for the present. We loosened her clothing as delicately as possible, and began chafing her hands and arms. Our anxiety to revive her made us almost drown her again with our hats of water, and in our eagerness we rubbed the tender flesh almost raw on her hands and arms.

In the midst of our efforts Ned, who was supporting her, exclaimed:

"Look! look! she drew her breath."

We gathered excitedly around and watched her closely, but her face was still marble—no sign of life in its pale outlines! After we had gazed a long while in the most intense suspense, a quick spasmodic gasp came through her parted lips, and a quiver played over her eyelids.

What a moment for our heroism! We felt that we were saving from the monster sea a fairer being than ever Palamon and Arcite tilted for. Beowulf, conquering the hideous Grendel, felt no more chivalric pride than did we, as our lovely waif lay with fitful breathings in our arms.

At length her respiration became more regular, and her eyes slowly unclosed. "Eyes" is a meagre word for the magnificent black orbs turned so timidly and wonderingly upon us; they probably served the commonplace purpose of vision, but the pleading eloquence of their look, and the emotions of fear and amazement which were almost audible in her gaze, declared their primary object to be expression.

Turning them restlessly from one to another of us, and failing to recognize any one, she closed them, as if in pain. Ned now ventured to speak, though we were almost afraid he would scare the soul away again that had been so hardly persuaded to return.

"Are you suffering now? Don't be alarmed, we are all friends."

Again she opened her eyes, looked wildly at him, then suddenly seemed to come to consciousness. With a frantic look of horror she cried out: "*Oh, padre! padre! oh donde està mi padre!*" and other frantic sentences, in a language unknown to us, and strove to rise to her feet. Ned and I assisted her, and she stood up on the sand. It was most unfortunate that she did so; for, as she gained her feet, her eyes fell on the corpse near the water, and, with a soul-piercing shriek, she sank to the earth, and all our efforts to revive her again were unavailing. As it had now grown quite dark we intended to hurry across the sound and tell Mr. Cheyleigh. Our sail boat being very small, it was thought best to leave one of us with the body, and to take the little girl in the boat over to the house. As it was not a pleasant solitude by any means, we drew pebbles to see who should remain, and it fell to my lot. Accordingly, Ned and Frank took up their fair burden, and promising me to make all the possible haste they could, went slowly up the banks to their boat. I saw them lay their charge down gently, hoist the sail and glide away in the darkness, and I was alone with the dead. The sun had long since gone down, and the red tinge of the sky was paling into the dusky gray of twilight. Far up and down the beach the dreary waste of waters grew drearier in the deepening shades, and the darkness fell so fast that when I looked up at the sky for a moment, and then turned to the sea, an hour seemed to have elapsed when measured by the increase of gloom. The sail of Ned's boat at last disappeared behind a point of land, and there was nothing for me to watch but the dead man's face and the moaning, tossing waters. It was now too dark to distinguish his features; there was only the ghastly white shape of his face, that, as I gazed so long upon it, seemed to make hideous grimaces at me—now sneering at my timidity, now opening its faded eyes to glare at me for having sent the little girl away; now shutting one eye and opening the other, sometimes reversing the face, putting the eyes in the chin and the mouth in the forehead; sometimes disappearing entirely, then suddenly coming back as white as ever. I would have fled up the beach, but I was afraid the corpse would spring up and run after me. And the whole scene was full of death! The stars seemed dead men's eyes, the sob of each wave was a dying groan, the white foam caps were dying faces, struggling for life, and a white gull, flying across the sky, was a cloth from the face of a corpse.

Suddenly a light came over the waters, and I looked up to find that the moon, at its full, was raising its great yellow disc from the waves. As if in kindly sympathy with me, the light came dancing over the burnished sea, but ceased its gambols at the shore, and threw its wan radiance over the dead face.

With the light I grew bolder, and rose and stood by the corpse, to see if it had moved. But it was lying as we had placed it, without a quiver in the face; and again I sat down upon the sand. Looking over the sound I saw Mr. Cheyleigh's boat coming, and the rapid flash of the dripping oars told that it was speeding well. Inexpressibly relieved, I went down to the landing and stood there, as unconcerned as if I had been pleasantly entertained on the beach. The rigging rattled as the sails came down, the keel grated on the sand, and Mr. Cheyleigh, Ned and Frank, and four stout negroes got out and went to the body. They wrapped it in blankets, laid it in the bottom of the boat, and with a stiff breeze and strong oars we soon glided under the shadow of Mr. Cheyleigh's boat house. Ned, Frank and I sprang out and ran ahead to see about the little girl.

Mrs. Cheyleigh was up in her chamber with her, and we could see only two or three excited negroes, who could tell nothing. We soon heard the negro men coming up the steps with their loaded, faltering tread, and we followed them into the back parlor, where, under Mr. Cheyleigh's direction, they deposited their burden, smoothed the blankets over him, and marched out, picking up their hats from the corners of the doors, where they had thrown them as they came into the "gretouse."

Mr. Cheyleigh then went up stairs to aid Mrs. Cheyleigh while we turned into the dining room, where they were just bringing in supper.

"I wonder what will be done with her if Mrs. Cheyleigh succeeds in bringing her to?" said Frank, as we took our seats near the open window.

This was something we had not thought of, and we were somewhat startled by the query; as we considered her ours by right of discovery, and her disposal, consequently, a matter of importance to each of us.

"I suppose," continued Frank, "she'll have to go to the Orphan Asylum."

I repudiated the idea with indignation.

"Never!" I said warmly; "if her friends do not come forward and claim her, I will get father to adopt her, as he has no other children beside me."

"Oh! perhaps you will," said Frank, with something of a sneer in his tone; "any way I claim an interest in her, and will have her for my sweetheart."

"You had better first learn whether she is alive or not," said Ned, reprovingly.

The waiting maid, Tildy, here interrupted us:

"Marse Ned, supper's ready; you reckon your mar's gwine to come down?"

"She don't want none, nohow," said Winny, another maid, coming into the room. "I jes come outen her room and she was a rubbing the little gal with brandy and mustard."

Tildy again put in, half to Winny and half to us:

"I wonder how come dey never stood de man on his head to let de water run outen his mouth?"

"Sheer! what you know 'bout it, gal?" rejoined Winny, giving her a push on the shoulder with the back of her hand. "I tell you what, doe Tildy, dey ain't no poor bokra; de little gal had on de finest underclose I ever see, mo' lace and stuff all round 'em; and when mistis was undressing her she taken off her neck er big gold chain with er locket hung to it. I taken it up and looked at it, and it's got a whole heap er sets in it, dat shines wors'n mistis's breastpin."

Mr. Cheyleigh here entered the room and said:

"Winny! your mistress wants a cup of hot tea and some toast carried up to her immediately. Come to the table, boys, Mrs. Cheyleigh will not be down to-night."

We sat down to the table, but could not eat for eager questions. Mr. C. informed us that, after much rubbing and many stimulants, the little girl had become conscious, and had been able to speak. She had addressed Mrs. C. at first in Spanish, but, on hearing her give some order to the servants, inquired if Mrs. C. spoke English, and learning that she did, used our language quite fluently. Mrs. C. had gotten her to bed and was trying to keep her from talking. She had, by a few questions, learned that the little girl was a Cuban; that her name was Carlotta Lola Rurlestone, and that she was lost from a ship the night before. She was constantly asking for her father, and Mrs. Cheyleigh had thought it best not to tell her of his death, but had evaded her queries as best she could. She was under the influence of an opiate now, and Mrs. C. wanted the house kept quiet.

After supper we had food enough for conversation till a late hour, when we retired only to dream of shipwrecks, and corpses, and half drowned girls.

At the breakfast table the following morning we were glad to meet Mrs. Cheyleigh, who was able to give us still more news about our little protégé. She told us she seemed much better, though feeble; that she recollected the scene now, and was weeping violently about her father's death; that her mother had been dead several years; that her father was a native of New Orleans, and that he and she had started to this country to spend the summer, as was their custom; that they had stormy weather for several days, and been driven somewhat from their course, and when the violent storm came on it was said that the ship was sinking; that her father had lashed her to a cabin door he had wrenched off, and, that he might not get separated from her, tied his wrist to its knob. He threw her into the water and tried to follow, but was jerked over by the weight of the door, and fell, striking his head violently against it. He seemed to be stunned, as he made no motion afterwards, but drifted about with the door, his face down in the water and his whole body sometimes out of sight. That the ship was soon blown off and out of sight, and that her agony was so great, as she saw her father drowning, and could not move to help him, that she had become insensible, and had known nothing more till she was in Mrs. Cheyleigh's room, though she remembered faintly seeing strange faces around her as in a dream.

"She is in constant distress about her father," continued Mrs. C., "but I hope that, with proper care and attention, she will recover. Mr. Cheyleigh has sent to town for Dr. Mayland, and also for the Coroner, who will hold his inquest as soon as possible."

Very soon after breakfast the Coroner arrived, and his jurymen began to drop in one by one.

We went out to the back piazza, where they were assembling, and walked among the crowd, listening to a confused jargon of questions in regard to the crops, wonderful tales of the ravages of the late storm, and surmises as to the drowned stranger, and the probable verdict that would be rendered.

The Coroner was a middle aged man, of great self-importance, who evidently thought an inquest a work of as great moment as a national negotiation. He took but little interest in the conversation of the others present, though he occasionally addressed some words to Mr. Cheyleigh, who was sitting near him. After considerable delay, and the assemblage of a large crowd of people, he pulled out his great fat silver watch, and said slowly:

"Well, I reckon we had as well begin. The morning is getting on smartly. Where is the body, Mr. Cheyleigh?"

Mr. Cheyleigh led the way, the Coroner and his jury following in single file till they reached the parlor. They crowded round the table to get a view of the corpse, all leaning forward, and holding their hats and hands behind them, as if they were tied there. The tall men looked on, while those small in stature moved round and round, vainly endeavoring to find a gap in the crowd to peep through.

The usual form of selecting and empanelling the jury was gone through with, and the Coroner commenced to examine the witnesses. Mr. Cheyleigh was first sworn.

"Mr. Cheyleigh," said the Coroner, walking his chair backward on the two hind legs a step or two, to gaze better at Mr. Cheyleigh through a pair of very broad rimmed silver specs, "will you please to state all you know about the finding of this body."

Mr. Cheyleigh came forward very gravely, and proceeded to relate his knowledge of the affair with a declamatory style, and with such long words that I did not know whether he meant to confuse the Coroner by using language above his two-syllable comprehension, or was acting under the common impulse of human nature to display proficiency in any department which has not been attained by those listening.

"The first information," he began, with a salutatory wave of his hand, "which I received of the discovery of the bodies was imparted to me by my son and his friend. Immediately on receipt of this intelligence I took the large boat, and with some of my negroes we rapidly made the transit of the Sound. Their report of the melancholy catastrophe was unhappily confirmed, for in close proximity to the water's edge lay this body. Edward and Frank brought the little girl over with them when they came for me, and Mrs. Cheyleigh has succeeded in resuscitating her. The man had apparently been inanimate for a period of some length, as his flesh had undergone considerable contraction from contact with the water—at least was contracted around the bones and features; the body proper was very much distended. He had been tied by one hand to the door of a ship's cabin, though the boys had cut the cord. I placed the body in the boat, and brought it where you now see it."

The Coroner moved his head up and down, slowly at first, then faster and in shorter spaces, till it came to rest, like a spring pendulum, as who should say:

"Just as I expected; all just as I expected;" and then, with a look of legal sagacity that would have adorned an Ellenborough, asked:

"Did you bring the door over with you?"

"I deemed that altogether unnecessary, but I took from the man's waist a pouch containing some money and one or two checks for large amounts on New York houses. I also found a very fine watch and chain; the upper lid of the watch bears a bouquet of diamonds and the initials H. V. R. Here is the watch and pouch."

He passed them to the Coroner, who examined every part as minutely as if he were identifying stolen property, and having satisfied himself that the articles did not belong to him, passed them on to the others, who each examined them in the same critical way.

"What, then, Mr. Cheyleigh," resumed the Coroner, after they had all finished their tedious examination of the articles, and returned them to Mr. C., "do you think was the cause of his death?"

"Strangulation, sir, from the influx of water into the larynx, and the consequent exclusion of air."

"Exactly—exactly, Mr. Cheyleigh; that will do, sir. Did you say your son found the bodies?"

"He and two of his friends."

"We can examine him, then?"

"Certainly, sir."

Ned was a little confused as he came forward, and kept passing his hand nervously over his tumbled hair. The Coroner assumed a mild, patronizing air, and said:

"Well, my son, what can you tell us of this affair?" Ned swallowed once or twice, and began:

"After the storm, John Smith, Frank Paning and myself thought we would go over to the banks and take a view of the ocean. When we got over the sky was fair, but the— —"

"Never mind about the sky, my son," interrupts the Coroner, "just tell what you know about the dead man."

"Well," resumed Ned, with a long breath, and another swallow, "John Smith saw them first, and we all ran to them and tried to move the man, but found him rather heavy, we then cut the cords, and lifted up the little girl— —"

"Stop! stop! don't tell about the girl, let us hear about the man."

"I don't know anything particular about him, except that he was dead."

"How was he lying when you found him?"

"His feet were in the water and his face was in the sand. One arm was doubled under him so, and the other—the one tied to the door knob—was stretched out so."

Ned here attempted to assume a descriptive attitude.

"Did the knot appear to have been tied by himself or somebody else?"

"It was a slip knot, and could have been fastened by himself."

"Did he lie as if the water had washed him up, or somebody had placed him there?"

"I think he was thrown up by the waves, sir."

"You didn't see any tracks or boat marks about?"

"No, sir."

"That will do. I don't think it is worth while to examine anymore witnesses. Gentlemen, you can make up your verdict."

We accordingly left the room, while twelve good citizens endeavored most earnestly to ascertain what they already knew—the manner of the dead man's death.

When we got out we found Horace waiting for Frank and myself with the carriage and horses.

We packed up our valises, made Ned promise to come to see us, left a kiss for our little foundling, and were soon rolling towards home.

Father and mother were as much interested in my news as I could have desired, and as I dwelt upon the beauty of the little girl and her lonely condition, I saw by the tear in mother's eye, and the serious shade on father's face, that I had made an impression. After recounting all in as vivid terms as I could command, I begged father to adopt her, offering as arguments many facts which he perhaps knew as well as I: that he was able to do it; that she would not be a great expense; that she would be company for mother when I was away; that I wanted a sister just like her, and would love and care for her tenderly, and wound up by declaring I would rather starve than have her sent to the Orphan Asylum.

"Well, well, don't be so impatient, my son," said father, relapsing into a smile, "even if I were inclined to adopt your suggestion there are many preliminaries to be arranged. I must see Cheyleigh, as she is now under his charge, and I must write to her friends in Cuba, where you say she came from. Then, perhaps, she may not be willing to come and live with us. You will have to restrain your eagerness till your mother and I consult about what is best to be done."

I was obliged to rest content with this. I went down town in the afternoon and recited to every acquaintance I met our wonderful adventure. The sun was nearly down when I was interrupted in the midst of my narrative by a servant, who came to tell me that there was a lady at home who wished to see me. I wound up my story and hurried home, wondering who it could be. To my utter surprise and pleasure I found Lulie Mayland in the sitting room, looking prettier and brighter than ever. She smiled delightfully when I pressed her hand and said, with a little blush:

"It's strange, isn't it, for a lady to call on a gentleman? but you must excuse me now. Pa has just returned from the Sound and has been telling me about the little girl you found. My curiosity was so excited I determined to come to see you and learn all about it, as you would not call and tell me. Promise me you won't think strange of it."

"Oh, Lulie, the bare idea of such formality between old friends!" I said, taking a seat near her.

"Well, we will not deem it a breach of form for the sake of old times."

"What a pity it is," said I, half musing, "that people grow older and colder in their natures. We were so happy as children. Do you remember the day in the nursery, long ago?"

"Yes, I believe I do; but tell me about your Sound adventure now, I am all impatience to hear that."

I detailed minutely every circumstance connected with the affair, and dwelt particularly upon the little girl's superb beauty, hoping thereby to raise a spark of envy in Lulie's heart, for I was piqued at her only believing to remember about the nursery scene. As I pictured to her the wavy black hair, the gazelle like eyes and chiselled features of Carlotta, I thought I detected a glance towards the opposite mirrors, where her own tumbled curls and merry blue eyes were reflected. When I had concluded she sat for some time in thought, then softly said:

"No father—no mother—no home!"

I knew then that envy found no room in a heart so full of pity and love.

"What is to be done with her?" she said, at length.

"I don't know; I am trying to get father to adopt her, and I think he is half inclined to do so."

"Oh, that would be splendid," she said, brightening at the thought; "I could see her so often, and we would be such dear friends. Do beg Col. Smith to bring her here."

"You may rest assured I will do my utmost, if it is only to get you over here sometimes, as you now have to make formal explanations for a single visit."

"Indeed, I expect you have other motives for your petition. Somebody's heart, perhaps, aids somebody's lips in begging."

"Never!" I said, with great emphasis; "she is truly lovely, but there is only one heart in the world I care to — —"

"I am very much obliged to you, Johnnie, for your narration," she said, rising to go, "it has interested me very much."

"The obligation is mine," I said, with a profound bow, "for your kind attention. 'Twas really a pleasure to talk with such a listener."

I escorted her home, and sat with her some time on the stoop, and felt more than ever that I was completely her slave. She seemed to have thrown around me an inflexible chain, one which I could not bend to get nearer her heart, and one which I could not break to get away. Every word of her conversation was so chosen that, while it kept alive my hopes, it did not satisfy them, and yet she skilfully permitted no word of love making to pass between us; all was carried on by innuendo; and, when I bade her good evening, I felt convinced that she did not love me, but dreaded to wound me by the disclosure.

CHAPTER IX

"John, I saw Cheyleigh in town to-day, and we have arranged all the matters about bringing up your sister, as I suppose you will call her, to live with us. Your mother and yourself must go down for her in the carriage the day after to-morrow." Thus spoke father, as he pushed his chair back from the tea table, about a week after my return from the Sound.

I deemed it dignified only to say, "Yes, sir."

"My dear," he continued, addressing mother, and taking a cigar from his case, "you have some clothing getting ready for her, have you not? As she didn't bring her baggage on the door I presume her wardrobe is scanty, so much so that she can exclaim, with the fallen Cardinal:

'My robe,
    And my integrity to Heaven, is all
    I dare now call mine own.'"

"Oh, Col. Smith," said mother, reproachfully, "do not jest at her misfortunes."

"Not jesting, my dear, not jesting; but, since poor Wolsey's time, I suppose she is the only one who could boast any integrity, when limited to a single robe. However, we have not proved her yet—Wolsey may still be alone."

"That is worse than jesting," returned mother, with a smile the good Samaritan might have worn, "you are blotting her with suspicion before you have ever seen her."

"We will assume, then, for your good hearted sake," said father, blowing out the words on each side of the cigar he was lighting, "that she is an angel, and let her prove her wings."

"I am sure that she will," said mother, as she rang her table bell for the servants to clear off the tea things.

The next day was one of preparation, and the room intended for Carlotta was fixed up like a fairy bower. The morning after, mother and I were whirling rapidly toward the Sound in our open carriage, the top thrown back to catch the fresh breeze. What a pleasure was such a drive on such a morning, with such horses, through such scenery, on such an errand!

Neither of us spoke, but leaned upon the side cushions of the carriage, listening to the rapid trample of the horses' feet and the singing of the wheels over the level roads as we flashed along; now through slim, quiet woods, where the sunshine drove away the shade from half the ground; now through thick luxuriant trees, grouping themselves with dense foliage-curtains around dark unrippled pools, where Artemis could have bathed with perfect modesty, and from which, now, a lonely heron, startled by our wheels, slowly rose with his blue noiseless wings; now through a swampy hollow, where the laurel poured from its white cups exquisite perfume, and now through the solemn forests, where the patriarch oaks waved their gray moss-hair, and the towering pines stretched their broad arms benignly over all, as if to invoke a blessing from the blue heavens above.

At last Mervue, as Mr. Cheyleigh's place was called, with its long avenue of oaks, came in view, and in a few moments our horses, lathered with foam, were prancing with unspent fire at the door. Mrs. Cheyleigh, Ned and two of the children, with Carlotta, met us at the steps. Mrs. Cheyleigh had told her of our coming, and her great speaking eyes were turned inquiringly upon us. Mother did not wait for introduction or salutation, but rushed forward and clasped her in her arms. Carlotta seemed in an instant to sound the depths of mother's tender love, and her first touch was an electric flow of sympathy. Throwing her arms around mother's neck she burst into convulsive sobbing. It touched every one present. Mrs. Cheyleigh wept; Ned turned into the house with his handkerchief to his face, while I, trying to hide my emotion, was ruthlessly plucking and snapping the tendrils of a jasmine that was clambering over the sides of the porch—little Sue Cheyleigh, in the artless curiosity of childhood, walking around to look at my eyes, in order to discover whether I was crying or not. The first paroxysm of grief over, mother gently released Carlotta, and Mrs. Cheyleigh, with that half hoarse tone which always succeeds tears, invited us in. Carlotta grasped mother tightly by the hand and we followed Mrs. Cheyleigh into the house. Having now an opportunity to observe her closely, I found that Carlotta was not such a little girl as I had supposed—being, in fact, nearly as old and as large as Lulie. Mother, Mrs. C. and the children taking seats in the large, cool sitting room, Ned and myself went out to the stables to see about the horses. When I returned to the sitting room I found mother and Carlotta alone— Mrs. Cheyleigh having excused herself for a short time to attend to domestic affairs. Mother was sitting near an open window, gently stroking Carlotta's head, which lay confidingly in her lap. They were talking, and, not wishing to interrupt, I took my seat quietly near them.

"And you are willing to come with us and be our child?" mother said, bending over her.

"If you all are willing to take me," said Carlotta, "I will try to deserve your love."

"We love you already, my darling child, and will love you more and more each day."

"I believe you, and trust you, ma'am; but oh! my father, my dear, dead father! how I wish that I were with you in the ground!" and the poor child broke down into sobbing.

"Hush, dear," said mother, gently; "do not speak so; God has seen fit to spare you——"

"I know He has, but I wish He had not; 'twould be far sweeter than life to lie by father's side, though it is cold. But oh!" she continued, raising up her head to look in mother's face, and taking her hand, "I am so ungrateful to you; you are so good to offer me a home, and yet I shrink from going where I have no right to go, except the right of your kindness."

"That shall be the surest right of all," said mother, kissing her forehead; "but you must not feel dependent. We do not take you because we pity you, but because we want just such a daughter to live with and love us."

"Then, will you promise me, ma'am, if you ever tire of me, that you will send me away? You can do it without unkindness, because papa had a great deal of money, and you can pay some one to take care of me. Will you promise me?"

"Yes, dear, I will promise you to send you away whenever we get tired of you. But, in the meantime, I do not want you to feel humble in our home, as if you were a charity child. Col. Smith has examined your father's papers, and finds that you are possessed of considerable wealth. He has written to your father's agent, who was named in the papers, and to the American Consul at Havana. He will probably go to Cuba himself next month, to see about the appointment of a guardian and the settlement of your estate. Have you no relatives at all there?"

"I have a cousin, who lives on the other side of the island, but I have not seen him since I was a very little child. Mother was an orphan, like myself, and came from Spain to Cuba with an old uncle, who died after she was married to papa. We had many acquaintances, but no relatives anywhere in the island except the cousin I have spoken of. I have heard papa speak of having relatives in New Orleans, but I do not know their names."

"Well, you are composed now; try to remain so. Do not give up to those sad feelings when you feel them coming on."

"I do struggle hard, Mrs. Smith, to keep from crying; but whenever I commence thinking about the evening of the storm—and I cannot help thinking about it—I remember how happy papa and I were sitting together in our state room, and, though the wind had been high for a day or two, we felt so secure, for the steamer was thought to be the strongest one on the line. I remember so well his holding me by the hand, and saying:

"'I think the wind is lulling, Lottie, bird; we will be safe to-morrow.' And then came that terrible cry that the ship was sinking; and we ran together out on the deck, only to find the crew in a panic, and the storm wilder than ever. Papa dragged me back to the cabin, tore off the door, tied me to it, and—— Oh! I cannot, cannot think of it without crying. Do not blame me, I cannot help it." And her eyes filled again, and her lip quivered with suppressed feeling.

"Dear child, you know I do not blame you; only try by every means to keep your mind from reverting to the painful scene. I will not offer consolation now, for I well know how deceitful it sounds to the bereaved to hear those who are not, quoting scripture passages to recommend resignation and submission. The beautiful sacred words are meant as a sympathy, not as a teaching. When your lips are lifted farther from this cup of gall we will go together to the Fount of Life and drink its sweet waters."

Mrs. Cheyleigh now returned to the room, and the conversation, ceasing between mother and Carlotta, became general. So many and varied were the topics to be discussed that the morning passed rapidly away; dinner came on, and the afternoon siesta, in hammocks swung in the verandas, where the sea breeze came cool and refreshing, was enjoyed, when the sinking sun reminded us that it was time to order the carriage.

When Carlotta came to tell Mrs. C. good-bye, and thank her for her kindness, she had nearly lost control of herself again, but, with an effort, she kept her tears back and entered the carriage. The shadows which had been hiding from the sun all day around the roots of the trees were now stretching out at great length, and spreading into all kinds of fantastic shapes, though they still kept the trees between them and the glaring eye they dreaded so much. The scenery through which we passed was all drowsiness, instead of the vivacity of the morning. The sun had gone down and the twilight was fading when we stopped at our door. Father and Lulie Mayland were standing on the stoop, waiting for us. Father took Carlotta in his arms out of the carriage and pressed her to him tenderly, while I was helping mother out. Lulie was then presented to her, and, after a kiss and embrace, they went up the steps hand-in-hand, as fast friends as if they had known and loved each other from their birth. We went into the dining room, where early summer tea was already laid. Carlotta did not wish anything, and mother withdrew in a short time with her. After the silence that succeeded, for a few seconds, their retirement, father said (and I knew by the twinkle in his eye he was enjoying the thorns on which I sat):

"Lulie," sighting at her with one eye through his iced tea, "I am afraid you will have a powerful rival in Carlotta. You must secure all your beaux with double chains or she will steal them away. I think one is proving recreant already, if I may judge from the glances of admiration he lavished upon her just now at the table."

My face was crimson, and the consciousness that it was so made the hue only deeper. To be teased about the girl I loved, before her face, by father, too, was the very climax of embarrassment to me. I glanced at Lulie, and found her not in the least disconcerted.

"Oh, John is so fickle," she replied, laughing, "that I can never count on him for more than a day or two. If he deserts me, however, I shall not be desolate, as I have several others under my thumb, you know."

Embarrassment is very much increased by being contrasted with coolness and ease, and mine received a tenfold impulse from Lulie's light way of treating the matter.

"Really," continued father, "you are quite a belle; but I am surprised that John should have withdrawn so easily from the contest. I thought you had more perseverance, my son. Surely, you did not encourage him, Lulie?"

"Yes, indeed I did, but he was not to be caught, and I have given him up as a hopeless case."

I vainly endeavored to swallow my confusion with large gulps of tea; the tea somehow slipped by and left the confusion sticking in my throat, but I managed to jerk out the words:

"If you ever gave any encouragement I did not know it."

"Ha! ha! ha!" laughed father. "Very good, my son, very good. But suppose she were to offer encouragement now, would you come back? Try him once more, Lulie. I would enjoy the courtship very much."

"I am willing," she said, demurely; but I thought I detected a smile towards father, as if they were in conspiracy.

"Now, John," continued father, "she says she is ready, and will return a favorable answer. How will you commence? Don't blurt out 'I love you!' as that would be unexpected and sudden; come to it gradually, and the slower you are in getting to the point the surer will your answer be 'Yes.'"

I could stand it no longer, but rose from the table and walked from the room, not, however, before hearing Lulie say:

"I don't quite agree with you, Col. Smith. I can't bear a slow courting fellow. If he loves much it won't take him long to tell it. There! you have run John off. I like him ever so much, only he is very timid."

I went out and sat on the stoop in no pleasant frame of mind. I was provoked with father for teasing me; I was provoked with myself for being teased, and I was provoked with Lulie for not being teased.

"She cannot love me or she would not treat the matter so lightly," I soliloquized, grinding white circles on the brown stone with my boot heel. "She thinks me timid, too; I'll prove my boldness the first opportunity I get."

Father and Lulie now came out and sat down, but no further allusion was made to the dining room topic. We spoke of our intended trip to the plantation near Goldsboro', and Lulie agreed, if her pa was willing, to go up and spend the remainder of the summer with us, as it would be very pleasant for her to be with Carlotta. After talking for some time of the pleasures of the country, Lulie rose to go, and I, of course, accompanied her.

So far from proving my boldness I walked by her side in awkward silence till she spoke.

"Why did you let your father tease you so to-night, Johnnie?"

"He didn't tease me," I returned, with Munchausen mendacity. "I didn't care a straw for what he said, only I did not choose to be spoken of so before a lady."

"I'll wager Frank Paning would not have been disconcerted," she said. "He has more self-possession than any one I ever saw."

"I don't care what in the thunder Frank Paning has; I don't want to be like him," I said, savagely.

"I did not intend to offend you, sir; I am obliged to you for your escort thus far, but, since you are so incensed, will need your services no farther," she said, very quietly, taking her hand from my arm.

"I beg a thousand pardons, Lulie; I was rude and hasty, but so many constant allusions to Paning irritate me beyond measure. He must be very dear to you from the repeated mention of his name."

"Oh, no, that does not follow at all. I think very well of him, as he is attentive and kind; but here we are at our gate; won't you come in?"

"Thanks! not to-night. Let me ask pardon again, Lulie, for my very harsh words on the way."

"Do not mention it; 'tis forgotten with me. Good night!"

My feelings, as I walked homeward, were very much mingled. There was always pleasure and pain in being with Lulie. Young as she was she already possessed consummate skill in swaying the feelings—now by some bewitching word or look raising your hopes, then dashing them to earth by some sarcasm, or worse, an allusion to some other favorite. She had reduced her game to a science, and always pitted special rivals against each other. Frank was sure to be my thorn. A single remark, evincing a preference for him, was enough to disturb my equanimity for an evening. So, in my thoughts this evening there was pain, yet a sweet pleasure, too, in the reflection that, in our retired country seat up in Wayne, I would have her all to myself; that I could see her every day, and talk as long and freely as I chose, with all the adjuncts and concomitants of love—woods, birds, brooks, bowers, meadows and moonshine.

Just as I reached our gate I met Frank Paning himself, hurrying up street to his home.

"Hello, John!" he said, lightly, as we stopped, "where have you been? Over to the Doc's, I suppose. I am getting jealous. Lulie must be looked to."

"There is no danger," I replied; "you are certainly the idol there."

"Oh, you tell me that to blind me, but I know a thing or two. By the way, how is our little foundling. I heard to-day that your folks had brought her here to raise up as a wife for you. I suppose you wish to train her up to suit you, so she will not have to learn your ways after marriage."

"You heard a most infamous falsehood, then, and you can tell your informant I said so," I replied, the blood rushing to my face.

"Well, don't get mad about it; I was only joking. I want to call on her; when will she receive company?"

"Not in a year or two," I said, emphatically. "She is going up the country next week, and will not return till the fall, when she will commence school, and be closely occupied with her studies."

"I see it is plain you fear rivals. I will not trouble you."

Before I could reply he was gone.

CHAPTER XII

The morning is misty and damp, as father, mother, Carlotta, Lulie and I stand under the great shed at the dépôt, waiting for the car doors to be unlocked. It is very early, and nobody seems stirring except those immediately connected with the train about to start. There are a dozen or more people standing in groups, waiting on the same event as ourselves. They all yawn a great deal, rub their eyes, wish they were back in bed, and wonder how long before the brakesman comes to open the car doors. The train itself lies on the track like a great headless serpent (for the engine has not yet been put on), whose red and yellow sides are full of latticed eyes. At last the brakesman, in a blue coat, striped shirt and glazed cap, comes along, whistling the last popular ballad, unlocks the door with a rattle, and shouts "Walk in, ladies and gentlemen."

We crowd in and select our seats on the side from the sun, if it should come out. Father turns over the seat in front, that it may face the other one, lays his shawl in the corner, hangs up the basket containing our lunch, sits down, pulls off his glove with his teeth, thrusts his hand under his duster, draws out and looks at his watch, shuts it with a snap, and says indistinctly, through the fingers of his glove:

"It will be fifteen minutes before we start."

People continue to arrive and crowd in, singly and in parties. The individuals consist of a very fat old gentleman, with a broad hat soiled around the band, a duster too short by six inches for his long black coat, and a large red bandanna handkerchief, worn altogether in his hand; a fancy dressed young gentleman, who looks in the door a moment and concludes to finish his cigar upon the platform, with one foot lifted to the railing, where he can tap the heel of his boot with a leg-headed cane; a rather rough man with a very large moustache, who passes through the coach very often and slams the door very hard, gets between two seats to lean half way out of the window to tell some one, who is named Bill, "Hello!" and to ask "when will you be up?" lets down the window with a bang, and lolls across the seat with one foot hanging in the aisle; a middle aged maiden lady, dressed, of course, in black bombazine, with a green veil, a large basket with a scolloped top, a canary of yellow and black dignity in a white and green cage, furnished with seed, sand, and inconvenient water cups; an old lady under the care of the conductor, walking very slow, with a horn handled stick, a large flowered bandbox and a white cloth bag; she wears a dark fly bonnet, which she takes off when she sits down and displays a white cap, ruffled around her face, which is very much wrinkled, and has white, thin hairs about the chin; she shows a disposition to breathe hard, and to look around vacantly from the side seat at the end of the cars, where the conductor has placed her, and to talk to no one in particular with a voice like a cat-bird's with a bad cold.

The parties who enter are generally composed of tall, resigned looking gentlemen, burdened with innumerable boxes and bundles, patient and pale wives, in gray travelling dresses and lead colored veils, which they hold in one corner of their mouths, to show only one fourth of the face: sleepy looking, large boys, with badly fitting clothes, who stumble along the aisle behind their parents, as if they were still dreaming; smaller boys and girls following, holding each other by the hand, each in the fallacious belief that they are taking care of the other; and mulatto nurses, carrying in their arms very white headed babies, naturally lachrymose and nasally aqueous.

Having seen all these and many more come in, I raise the window. Everything is dripping with fog, and the moisture is trickling in little crooked streams down the sides of the coaches. The express wagon comes rattling down, and I can hear them unloading, with an occasional ejaculation bordering on the profane. Then I hear the bell of the engine as it comes out of the yard, and stews and hisses, backing down the track, nearer and nearer till it touches—then, with a loud clack-up of the coaches, everybody is jerked forward, the train glides back a foot or two, and it is coupled on. All is comparatively still now, and there is nothing to remind us of the immense power to which we are attached, except the odor of the smoke, which is rolling in black masses along the roof of the shed, and the faint singing of the steam.

I take my head in and find everybody either dozing or staring stupidly out of the window. Father is reclining in his seat, mother is resting her cheek upon her hand, with closed eyes, and Carlotta and Lulie, finding it too damp to raise the window, have looked through the glass till their breath has dimmed it, and wiping it with their hands, have left the print of their fingers in circles on the pane.

William now brings father the checks for the baggage, the whistle sounds, the bell rings, a few loud coughs from the great monster that draws us, and we glide from under the roof, creep under the bridge, jog along the suburbs, rattle into full speed, and roar out of sight of the town; the last sign of which is a little negro, standing in the door of a hut on the embankment above, waving his rag of a hat, as if to wish us good speed. Trees fly by, fences like long serpents wriggle past, and the whole country becomes a passing panorama!

The sun rises, and, dispelling the fog, shines out bright and sultry. People, aroused by the stir, begin to talk. Children become thirsty. The lady opposite, with two little girls and a baby, tells the nurse to hand her the basket, and opening it to get out the silver mug, sends the nurse after water. The nurse totters down the coach, rocks backward and forward while drawing the water, and totters back, steadying herself by the arms of the seats, and spilling a little water at every step. The little camels gulp it down as if the cars were Sahara!

The conductor staggers in and calls for tickets. Old gentlemen untie many-stringed pocket-books, old ladies open their reticules, and young gentlemen point to their hat bands. He passes out, and the whistle sounds. The brakes-man rushes to the wheel and gives a turn, then holds his cap on with one hand, and swings off by the railing to look ahead. Another whistle, another turn, and we grind into a small station, where we stop for a minute or two; then on and on we fly, faster for the short delay. The morning wears away, and we get out our luncheon. Broiled chicken and cold tongue! how they are associated with travelling! Their very odor is suggestive of the rattle of the train! We had scarce finished eating when the whistle sounded for Goldsboro'. We got off and found Aleck, one of the farm hands, waiting for us with the spring wagon, as Horace, he said, had not yet got up with the carriage. We all clambered up, and were soon rolling over a level, though dusty, road to our country place.

As the rattling wagon was not a very pleasant place for conversation, I had leisure to observe Carlotta, and to mark the effects of diversion on her beautiful face. Many traces of sadness were gone, and there was even brightness in her eyes. Such eyes I have never seen. There was a *velvet* expression about them, for to the soft rich effect of that fabric alone can I compare those orbs and their setting; and I thought, as I gazed at them, that the soul must be a rare one indeed that possessed such windows. She seemed trying to shake off reflections on her own misfortunes, and for others' sake, if not her own, to be cheerful. She sat next to mother, to whom she was already fondly attached, and whose tender heart fully reciprocated her love. Lulie was all gaiety, and father was undignified enough to be droll; some of his remarks even drawing a smile from Carlotta, though only such a smile a soul in serge can wear; a smile that seems begun in forgetfulness, and finished with repentance for its levity.

The afternoon was far advanced when we drove up the long avenue of trees that led to the house.

The place had been built by my great grandfather, and the house and all the premises were on the old style.

The great-house, as it was termed by the negroes, was a large two-story one, with narrow green blinds, a large wing extending back, and piazzas running almost all the way round. The chimneys were very broad, and were built half up with rock, then finished off with brick. The front porch had an arched roof over it, and was furnished with two stiff benches on each side. There was a magnificent grove in front, in one corner of which was a large pond or lake, on which a flock of geese were swimming. To the left of the house stood a large capacious kitchen, painted red, and behind and around the house were ranged the dairy, smoke house, &c., all of the same ruddy hue. Back of the yard were the long rows of negro cabins, with their martin poles, and little gardens in front of them, and a few hundred yards off, in a small growth of trees, stood the house for the overseer, Mr. Bemby. As we drove up to the yard gate a large bull-dog, chained in his kennel, commenced barking furiously, and this brought yelping around the house half a dozen curs and hounds belonging to the negroes. These were followed in turn by a troop of little negroes, who ran to the gate, shouting in great glee:

"Yon's marster and mistis."

Then ensued a scuffle for the honor of opening the gate, and a shrill chorus of "How dye's" as we entered the yard. Mrs. Bemby came down the steps to meet us, and took us into the cool, large front room, where she aided mother and the girls to take off their bonnets and hats, then conducted them to their chambers. She soon returned to father and myself, with waiter and goblets of ice water.

"Col. Smith," she said, as she placed the water on the table, "Mrs. Smith said you've got her keys; and, Mister John, your room is ready whenever you wish to go up."

"Thank you, Mrs. Bemby," I replied, as father arose and went to mother's chamber, "I will wait here awhile, as it is the coolest place I have seen to-day." "I must go see about supper," she said, taking up the key basket and holding it against herself while she searched for a key; "don't, the niggers will get every thing wrong. I 'spected to move over to-day to our house, but Mr. Bemby, he was so busy a plowing, I couldn't get all the things away; so, if you find any of Ben's things in your room, let 'em stay till in the morning. It ingenerly takes me a fortnit to get straight when I come from home to the great'us, or from the great'us to home."

I surveyed her and the room while she was speaking, and found her impress on every article. The room was always used as a sitting room, and had so many doors and windows that it was a perfect breeze generator. The chairs were ranged two and two under every window, as if to let the wind cool them. Father's lounge was drawn in the middle of the room, with its bright chintz covering tucked in so tightly that it seemed to say to me, "Come and lie down, I will not let you sink in and be hot, but will bear you up, that you may get the breeze." The floor was so clean and shining that I longed to get down and sleep with my face on the cool boards. Even the old fashioned piano, with its yellow keys and little straight legs, had such a tight, scant cover, that it seemed to have taken off its trousers for the summer. The broad fireplace was clayed as white as snow, and stuffed full of feathery fennel, and on the high, quaintly carved mantel, were plaster images, sheep with very red eyes, a studious boy with a slate, and his nose knocked off, and very erect Napoleon Bonaparte, with very large legs, one of which had grown to a stump, in a way that would have held him faster than St. Helena. Between these mementoes of itinerant Italians were ranged double rows of red and green apples, with Hardee precision. There were several old portraits in the room, and these had the gauze looped up around them, as if to give them air. A tall old clock, with a dignified face, and a lazy second-hand, that waited every time for the clock to tick before it would jump, stood in its corner—the long pendulum passing to and fro by the little glass door near the bottom, as if it didn't care if I did see it, and would as lief stop as not. And then its drowsy tick! Argus would have closed all his eyes if he could have heard it for five minutes! A large yellow and white cat, with both ears cropped, lay asleep in Mrs. Bemby's work basket, which sat near the door, and a frisky gray kitten on the hearth was catching at the flies in the fennel. And I thought, as I looked around, if Mrs. Bemby could impart such a cool, clean look to every thing by her short residence in the house, what must her little home be up on the hill, under those great shady poplars.

Mrs. B. having found her key, came to her work basket, shook the cat out of it (the cat coming down slowly on her fore feet, and bringing her hind feet down a second or two afterwards, as if half inclined to let them stay up in the air), and gathering up her work, left the room. I rose and went up stairs, where I found everything equally antique, and as clean and cool. I ordered up my trunk, and having made my toilet I went down, feeling very much refreshed. The girls soon appeared, and we spent the remainder of the afternoon exploring the old house. In the old parlor, in the library—with long high shelves of books—up in the old dusty garrets, down in the basement, everywhere that there was anything to show, I carried Carlotta and Lulie, listening to Lulie's bright laugh and admiring Carlotta's brightening beauty. From the house we walked out into the grove, down to the orchard, and, with our hats full of apples and peaches, at last took our seats on the green mossy rocks at the spring. As Lulie and Carlotta took their seats together, and seemed so absorbed in each other, I found that the first little cloud in this country trip was beginning to gather; that cloud was—and I blushed for shame at the thought—Carlotta's presence. I knew that she and Lulie would be inseparable, when I wanted Lulie all to myself. I felt that I must give up all hopes of private chats; that I would have no opportunity to tell my love; that all my courtship must be carried on by looks, and that, I knew, would be unsatisfactory, as Lulie never returned my tender glances; yet I could not help admiring Carlotta, and loving to be with her. She was so exquisitely beautiful that I could sit and watch her for hours and never weary; but she was too sad and serious yet to be congenial, and I felt that she was a bar to my intercourse with Lulie, and could scarcely refrain from wishing we had never found her. All the better part of my nature would rise up indignantly at the unkindness of such thoughts, but still I would have them. Youth, in love, is excusable for many follies.

While the girls were talking in a low tone together I was leaning on my elbow, flipping the parings of the peaches into the water, and indulging a somewhat bitter train of reflection over my disappointment, when the tea bell rang. We hastened to the house, and met father at the door, who said:

"Come in to tea. Mrs. Bemby has not had time to prepare supper at her house, so I have invited her and Mr. Bemby, and Ben, their son, to eat with us to-night. Ben is rather a queer case, but you mustn't laugh when you meet him, as it would hurt Mrs. Bemby's feelings very much."

We went down stairs to the dining room, where we were introduced to Mr. B. and son. Mr. Bemby was a large dark man, with a kind, pleasant face, but rough and sun-burnt in his appearance. He seemed very much at his ease, as he knew father and mother so well, and greeted us cordially, remarking to me, as he shook my hand:

"You've growed a'most outen my knowledge, Mr. Smith, but I hain't seen you sence you was a mighty little chap."

As soon as I looked at Ben I knew I had found a rare case, and I felt that he would contribute no small amount to my enjoyment. He was very tall and stout, being nearly six feet high, though he was apparently not done growing. He had a clear gray eye, full of intelligence, but that always looked as if it was laughing to itself; his nose was prominent between his eyes, but flattened at the end by an unskilful operation for hair-lip, when he was a child; his upper lip, from the same cause, had a deep scar in it, and was tucked in his under lip, as if he was sucking something from a spoon. When he laughed he showed only his under teeth, which were well set, but stained yellow from the use of tobacco; his laugh itself was a very singular one for a young person, though I have sometimes heard very old and sedate people laugh so. When he was amused his face assumed a broad grin two or three seconds before a sound was heard, and then from deep within came a series of short or long grunts, according to the intensity of his feelings; if he was very much amused the grunts were lengthened almost to groans—one beginning as the other left off; if he was only laughing slightly they were short enough to be a kind of chuckle. The best illustration of his laugh I can find is a thunder cloud—first the lightning on his face, after awhile the thunder rumbling up from within. Very often his face, in ordinary converse, would, like sheet lightning, flash out a laugh, while no sound at all would be heard.

Mother was suffering with headache from the day's fatigue and sent in her excuse, and the request that Mrs. Bemby would take the head of the table, and make the tea and coffee. Mrs. B—— accordingly took her seat, and while she is arranging the cups, let me introduce her more thoroughly by a brief description. A very stout old lady, with thin gray hairs, tucked into a small knot by a large horn comb, small blue eyes, with the under lid much nearer the pupil than the upper, giving her always a very pleasant but surprised look; a fat face, with scarcely a wrinkle, a loose under lip, and a tongue that threatened with every word to come out, so that all her words seemed to have been fattening before she spoke them. Her form was very large, so that she looked like a tierce of good nature. Her whole appearance was of that kind, that if you had seen her at the door of a house, as you were travelling, you would have stopped for refreshment, knowing that everything would be clean, and in that agreeable profusion that one always enjoys after a journey.

Mrs. Bemby was free and unembarrassed in her manner; Mr. Bemby unconcerned; but Ben evidently felt awkward, and was depending upon observation of the conduct of others for his table deportment.

"Colonel Smith," said Mrs. B—— to father, after grace had been said, "will you take some tea or coffee?"

"I'll take a cup of each," said he. "I am a little peculiar about that, and generally ice my tea while I drink my coffee."

"If I had a' known that I could a' had some friz for you, sir."

"No matter, Mrs. Bemby. I can soon cool it here."

"Miss Lulie, which will you have?"

"I will thank you for a glass of milk."

"Well, Miss Carlotta?"

"A cup of tea, if you please."

"Mr. John, tea or coffee?"

"Coffee, I believe, madam."

"Old man, you'll have coffee, I know," she said, putting the sugar in Mr. B—— 's cup.

Poor Ben had been watching carefully, but could not possibly decide what was *au fait* under the circumstances, so that when his turn came he resolved, as the safest course, to follow father's example, and, in response to his mother's inquiry, replied that he would take some of both, and "sorter cool the tea while he was getting down the coffee."

Mrs. Bemby's eyes certainly looked natural in their surprise at his answer. Lulie, whose face had been red with restrained laughter since she had seen him, now broke into an irresistible titter, to which Ben replied by a grin, without a sound.

"Ben," said his mother, still looking at him through her specs, "you must be a fool; give him some buttermilk, Harriet."

There was silence for some time, and then father said:

"Ben, do you ever catch any fish, now?"

"Yes, sir; I ketched a cat 'tother day, big as a bucket."

"Caught a cat, eh," said father, setting aside his coffee, and drawing the tea to him. "You must have baited with a mouse."

"Nor, sir, I baited with a worrum. Cats bites at worrums fine."

Lulie could restrain her curiosity no longer, but asked, with all earnestness, if it was a real cat, with tail, claws and all.

Ben gave a great many long grunts as he said, "Sho', its got a tail, but tain't got no claws, 'cause its a fish."

"Oh!" said Lulie, with her hand to her mouth, and a glance at me.

I ventured to ask if there were many squirrels on the plantation.

Ben bit a large semicircle out of a biscuit, and said through the crumbs:

"The trees is just a breakin' with 'em. I went to a mulberry this mornin', and th'was sixty odd on one limb!"

"Why, Ben," said father, looking up, "that couldn't have been so."

"Well, they mightn't a' been; but three hundred and over ran outen the tree when I shot."

Ben is not the only one I have met whose stories grew bigger as they repeated them.

Mrs. Bemby now interrupted him.

"Ben, you talked mighty nigh enough. Let somebody else have a mouth."

Ben, thus rebuked, was silent, and father and Mr. B— — talked about the farm, while Carlotta and Lulie occasionally whispered, and I ate in silence.

After the meal the Bembys left for their house, Ben having promised to take me hunting and fishing in all the best places; and we went out to the front porch to talk over our plans for pleasure. Father went to the library to read, mother was resting in her room, nobody in the porch but Carlotta, Lulie and I; and again I felt that Carlotta was in the way.

CHAPTER XIII

The sky was just reddening when I came down next morning and commenced to get my gun and accoutrements, to try my hand at hunting. Father called me as I was about to leave the house, and told me to come to the back door. There I found a negro boy, thirteen or fourteen years of age, in his shirt sleeves, a clean white shirt, and copperas checked pants, held up by suspenders of the same cloth, fastened on them by little sticks; one hand resting up against the house, and one bare foot scratching the top of the other.

"John," said father, as I came out in the porch, gun in hand, "this is Reuben, one of Hannah's children. You may take him for your valet. He knows all the best hunting and fishing places around here. When you go to Goldsboro' you can get him some more suitable livery."

"Thank you, sir; he will suit me exactly. How do you like it, Reuben?"

Reuben could only snicker and rub his hand on the weather boarding, as an acknowledgment of his favor.

"I am about to start hunting now; can you carry me to a place where I can kill some squirrels?"

"Yes, sir; ef I c'n git Unker Jack's Trip, and go over 'gin the big spring field, you kin find a sight on 'em."

"Well, run and get Trip, and come on."

He ran down to the quarters, and soon came back with a little blue-spotted, curl-tailed dog, which he declared could "find 'em eben ef dey wan't dere!"

After getting over fences, jumping ditches, tramping through dewy grass, and breaking through wet corn till my feet were drenched and my clothes saturated, we at last struck the woods. What splendid woods they were for hunting. Dignified, patriarchal oaks, matronly cedars, young dandy hickories, love-sick maiden-pines, that sighed in the breeze, and families of saplings! Reuben here thought we would find the game, and told Trip to "look about." The little canine obeyed, and was soon out of sight.

We moved cautiously about, listening; nor did we have to wait very long before Reuben recognized his short, quick bark, and, with the ejaculation, "dat's him," ran rapidly towards the place. I followed as fast as the nature of the undergrowth would permit, and we soon found Trip sitting on his tail, under a large oak, whose thick leaves concealed all but the lowest branches. I looked long and vainly towards the top; nothing could I see but the deep green leaves. Reuben, however, got off some distance from the tree, and, walking backwards, and looking with hand-shaded eyes, soon cried out, "Yon he is; cum year, marse John; you c'n see 'im." I ran eagerly to him, and gazed intently to where he pointed, and by his continued indications of the exact limb and fork, I was at last persuaded that I did see a small gray knot near the body of the tree. I levelled my gun and fired; all was still for awhile, and then the shot came pattering back on the trees a little way off. Another shot, and the gray knot ran out to the end of the limb.

"Dat's him; I know'd it was," shouted Reuben, while I was so much excited I could hardly load. Before I could get the shot down the squirrel sprang from the tree to another, the slender twigs bending under him, and the wet leaves showering down the dew. But Reuben and Trip were watching, and soon found him in a fairer place. I now aim more carefully, and fire; he falls several feet, then catches and recovers himself; another barrel, and he turns under limb, holding on by his feet. Before I can load again he slowly releases, foot by foot, his hold upon the limb, and comes tumbling headlong down, striking the ground with a heavy sound. Reuben and Trip are in great glee over it, while I look on with assumed indifference, for it is my first squirrel, though I had played great destruction among the rice birds near town.

I was just putting the caps on my gun when I was startled by the report of another gun close at hand. I soon heard the thumping of the ramrod, and a little while after the bushes parted, and the long figure of Ben Bemby emerged, his gray eyes gleaming under a broad wool hat without any band, and his scarred lip drawn into a smile. A large bunch of squirrels hung in his hand, and a long single-barrel gun rested on his shoulder.

"Mornin'. What luck?" he said, resting his gun on the ground, and throwing back his hat to wipe the perspiration from his forehead with his forefinger.

"One fine fellow," I said, holding my trophy up.

Ben chuckled a little, and said:

"Four shots to one; that's sorter bad. I got seven outer nine. That ere little pop-stick of yourn won't reach these trees."

I did not fancy any slur on the shooting qualities of my gun, which was a very handsome Wesley Richards, a present from father the winter before, and I offered to prove that it would shoot as far as his.

"Jumerlacky! Why, I can fetch a squrl when he is outer sight with this old gun."

"How do you aim at him?" I inquired, smiling at his earnestness.

"I just git me a hicker nut hull, with the print where a squrl's been a cuttin', and rub it in the shot, and when I fire, don't keer which way I takes sight, the shot goes right arter the squrl what cut the nut, and all I got to do is to look roun' and see what tree he's a gwine to fall from."

I expressed a great desire to see his gun perform, and asked if he had killed any that morning without seeing them.

"Not 'zactly," he replied, changing his squirrels from one hand to the other; "but one run up such a high tree he got t'other side of a cloud."

"How did you get at him?"

"Jus' shot wher he went thew; when he drapped he was right smarten wet, an' it rained purtty peart thew the shot holes in the cloud."

"Which one of those was it?" I asked, pointing to the bunch in his hand.

"This here biggest un," he said, holding him up by the tail.

"Why, he doesn't seem to be wet now?"

"Nor; he dried, like, comin' thew the air."

I was uncertain whether he was a little flighty or was trying to quiz me, thinking I was city-green, and a look into his laughing grey eye rather confirming this last supposition, I was about to change the conversation, when Trip's bark a little way off in the woods called our attention to him. We found the squirrel in the very top of a tree that did almost seem in the clouds.

"Lemme see you knock him out wi' your little double-bar'l toot-a-poo."

With the steadiest aim I could command, I gave him both barrels, one after the other, with no result whatever, my piece being a short bird gun, and the tree top an immense distance from the ground.

Ben said, "Now, let the old gal speak," and sighting the old brown barrel a second, he fired. The squirrel made a frantic leap into the air, and fell right into Trip's mouth. Reuben was in a dance of excitement, but felt that he must take my gun's part.

"Marse John's gun's new; 'taint got used to shootin' yet."

"What d'you know 'bout guns, you little devil's ink ball?" said Ben, turning to Reuben; "why d'nt you open your mouth when Satan was a paintin' you, and git some black on your teeth. Well, Mr. Smith, less knock along todes home; its mos' your breakfus time."

"Won't you go and take breakfast with me?"

"Nor, siree. Th' old man said I was fool 'nough last night to last a seas'n; but I'll come in short to see them ladies agin, for sho' they're fine 'uns."

"You must be sure to come. You think they are pretty, do you?"

"Well, I do exactly that thing. I've got a gal nigh here I thought was some on purtty, but she ain't a pint cup to these here."

"Which do you think is the best looking?"

"That's 'bout as hard to tell as buyin' knives. That ere curly head un is five mules and a bunch er bells, and ef 'twant for t'other would beat the world; but that black-eyed un, wh'sh! She c'n jus' look at you, and make you set still forever. Why, you c'n run er fishin' pole in her eyes up to the hand'l and never tech bott'm."

"Polyphemus would be a mole to her, if her eyes were as deep as that," I replied, laughing at his extravagance.

"I never heerd of Polly Whatchoucallem, but ef she looked like this ere wun, I'd trade Viney Dodge for her, and giv 'em boot."

"I expect Miss Viney will soon have cause for jealousy?"

"Nor, siree. Miss Kerlotter, I think the old lady sed her name was, is a darned sight too fine for me. You can't sew silk truck on to homespun; and Viney suits my cloth the bes', for she's three treddle sarge, and a thread to spare."

There was a fork here in the path, and we separated. I reached home just as the family were sitting down to breakfast. I exhibited my game, and was complimented for my skill.

After breakfast I went to the library, while the girls busied themselves aiding mother in her domestic arrangements. Before leaving the table they made me promise to take them fishing in the evening, or rather Lulie did, for Carlotta expressed her preference for remaining at home with mother, and I saw in her face that her intuitive tact had taught her that I preferred to be alone with Lulie. She was tenderly devoted to mother, and would often leave gay, frolicsome Lulie to sit by her, and talk on "grown up" subjects, as Lulie would call them. With father she was reserved, though respectful and grateful, and studied to please him in every way. Toward me she was gentle and kind, but shy, as if she was afraid of being teased about me.

I cannot describe my feelings for her. There was a thrill every time I met those great black eyes that I had never felt before, but I could not call it love, for Lulie engrossed all there was of that in my nature.

There was a magnetism about her that affected me strongly, and made me feel that, were we at all intimate, she would possess an unbounded influence over me, and that its exercise would constitute my supreme happiness.

The tender pity and brotherly love I had expected to feel were all gone, for she did not need them; the vast resources of her own deep soul, and the sympathy and love of mother, seemed to be enough for her. In all my thoughts I could only long for her friendship, and I felt that if I could awaken in her an interest in me as a friend, so that I could go to her ear and tell my troubles or joys, I would be the happier. In the common converse of our family circle I always looked to her first after my remarks, and her smile was a far greater reward to me than Lulie's, perhaps because it meant more. And if I had done wrong I would rather ten times Lulie should know it than Carlotta; yet, with all these feelings, resembling so much indices of love, there was no spark of it in my heart. Her very beauty seemed to fix a great gulf between us, and down in my soul I felt that she would never love me, except as a member of the same family. With these thoughts came the image of Lulie—bright, laughing Lulie—whose heart I could get so near to, if I could not call it mine; who was something human, like myself, and whom I loved so tenderly without the slightest shade of awe. And I longed for the time when I could tell her of it.

CHAPTER XIV

The afternoon was still and sultry, as I gazed out of my window, leaning on the sill, and waiting for Reuben to bring my fishing poles and bait.

From the corn fields in the distance a trembling haze was continually rising, and I could hear the occasional song of the negroes, as they moved behind their plows slowly up and down the long green rows. In the yard all was still; the chickens, with palpitating throats, were lying under the bushes, flirting the cool dark earth up into their feathers; and the ducks were gathered around the cool trough at the well, bubbling the water with their bills, and shaking their wings as if they wished to dive in it, if the trough were just wide enough; the bull-dog, at the door of his kennel, was lying on his side, with his head stretched out on the earth, from which he would raise it constantly to snap at the flies biting his flanks. A solitary peacock, with his tail all pulled out for the feathers, was sitting on the fence, with his blue neck and coroneted head reverted, as if gazing at the absence of his plumage. Down at the quarters I could catch the changing hum of the spinning wheel, making echo to the nasal minor strains of a negro woman at the wash tub. Everything was calculated to inspire reverie, and I leaned there, thinking of the cool shady bank of the creek, and of Lulie and myself sitting there alone; and musing on the pleasure of the evening, and wondering if anything would occur to mar it, I drew my eyes from the scenes in the yard, and gazed down the side of the house, noticing every little dent in the planking and the dark rain marks under the nails; and dropping bits of paper at a lazy red wasp that was crawling slowly up the weather-boarding. Reuben, passing under my window with the poles and a gourd full of worms, broke my reverie, and taking my hat and gloves I went down stairs, where Lulie was already awaiting me, looking sweeter than ever in a pink gingham sun-bonnet. Holding an umbrella carefully over her, Reuben leading the way with the poles, I went down the avenue through a long lane, down a wooded hill, and stopped at "de bes' fishin' hole on de creek," as Reuben called it. 'Twas a steep grassy bank under a large sycamore, at a sudden curve in the stream, where the water, running down heedlessly, struck the bank, and hurried off with many a curling dimple of confusion for its carelessness. After Reuben had undone and baited our lines, I dismissed him, and we both took our seats, pole in hand.

The thick branches overhead made an impervious shade, except where they opened here and there to let a little ray of sunlight dance upon the water. The lines, serpent-like, curled down from the poles, and the painted float circled up and down the eddy, but with no other motion but what the water gave. Presently Lulie's stood still, then bobbed under and up, while the water rings retreated from it as if afraid; again it goes down, and Lulie—like all lady fishers—gave the pole such a jerk that the line and its hooked victim were lodged in the branches above. All my efforts to disengage it were unavailing till, at last, I broke off the line, and threw pieces of stick at the little fish till I battered it down, its mouth torn out by the hook, and its shining scales all beaten off. Lulie took her little victim in her hand very tenderly, and almost shed tears over it. She declared she would never come fishing again; that it was mean and cruel to catch the poor little creatures out of the water when they were so happy.

"And, John," she continued, "I am so sorry I broke your hook and line, when you had fixed it up so nicely for me; I know you are really mad with me about it."

I did not notice her remark about the hook and line, but said (winding the broken line around the pole, and laying it behind us on the grass):

"Your compassion and pity for the little fish are so sweet, Lulie, that I wish I could be transformed into one, like another Indur."

The old roguish twinkle came back to her eyes as she said:

"You can have my compassion now if you will be caught like this fish."

"You know how quickly I would be, Lulie, but all your lines are occupied."

"No, indeed, John, you are the one in fault; but, then, you are completely fastened by a hook baited with a pair of dark Cuban eyes."

"Of course, Lulie, you refer to Carlotta; you are entirely mistaken; she is only a sister, and a very reserved and distant sister at that. I admire her beauty, but cannot love her."

"Well, you look at her as if you did, any way, and I feel every time that we three are together, that you are wishing I had not come up here to spoil your pleasure, and be in the way."

"Lulie!" I said softly, as I sat down by her on the cool green moss, and as I said it a hot flush came over my face, for I felt there was no retreat after such a tone, and that I must now tell her what I had been hinting at by action and word through my life from a child. She, too, well knew what I meant, for she dropped her eyes from mine, and laying down the little fish, commenced to pick from her finger, with great earnestness and effort, a bright scale that adhered to it.

"Let me get it off," I said, taking her hand and flipping off the scale, but still keeping the hand in mine; "Lulie, I am holding the hand of the only girl in the world that I love. It is no jest now, but solemn earnest truth. Darling, your own heart tells you how I have idolized you from a child, and my heart tells me how I adore you now. Sometimes I have felt that you did not care for me, and my despair has been worse than eternal death; at other times I've thought, perhaps, you did return my love, and the happiness would have been supreme but for the dread uncertainty. But oh! Lulie, I can endure it no longer; tell me, dearest, if you——"

She drew her hand suddenly from mine, and placing both hands over her eyes, she burst into convulsive sobbing. I put my arm around her, and tried to take her hands from her eyes. She turned towards me, putting both arms around my neck, laid her face, streaming with tears, on my shoulder, and cried as if her little heart would break. I sat still, supporting her, and not knowing what to do or say. Gradually her hands relaxed their clasp, and she raised her head from my shoulder, and, wiping her eyes with her handkerchief, which she tremblingly drew forth, said, with a tear-hoarse voice and a great sob:

"Oh!—John!"

"Lulie, darling," I said, gazing at her tenderly, "have I distressed you so much, and is it painful to you to know that I love you?"

"Yes, yes, dear John, the deepest pain, because—because I cannot love you in return."

"Not love me! Oh, Lulie! After all the years of fondest fidelity!"

"John, I do love you as the dearest friend I have on earth; as the one of all others in whom I can confide most implicitly; and because I love and esteem you so dearly your avowal of love causes me such intense pain. I could tell another I did not love him without remorse, but I know your noble heart is so truly in earnest, and its love is so sincere, that it almost kills me to turn it away and to offer only in return that bitterest of all words—friendship. But, John, by all the magnanimity of your generous nature, I beseech you not to hate me now, but hold me still as the same little Lulie of the nursery, when our hearts knew love as only childhood's friendship."

I sat as if in a dream, and only murmured:

"Hate you, Lulie! Never! never!"

After a long pause, I at length said:

I trust, as you believe in my honor, you will not think I am influenced by any hope of thus supplanting him in your favor. I bow to your decision of this evening as final, nor would I cause you to revoke it, if I could, by maligning him."

"John, I believe you; and I thank you more than I can tell for your intended kindness, but 'tis better that we speak no further on this subject. It might beget unpleasant feelings, and I would not feel, nor have you feel, one shade of anger, for the world. My heart is sad enough when I think what a change one hour has wrought. No more the same John and Lulie we have ever been; no more the same playful attentions you have always paid me, nor the same thoughtless encouragement I have given. Respectful courtesy now our only intercourse. Oh, how little did I think, when I lightly returned your looks and smiles of love, to what it all would lead!"

"Lulie, darling, I cannot feel anger toward you, whatever you do; but, even if you hate me for it, I must tell you of Frank Paning. He is utterly destitute of principle. He does not love you, and if he did would only love you as his slave. He is tyrannical and overbearing, yet sycophantic in his nature, imposing on the weak and cringing to the strong. He is free and forward in the presence of ladies, and impure and slanderous in his remarks about them behind their backs. I have known him to leave a company of ladies, and then, for the mere applause of a vulgar throng, make witticisms on their appearance and manners that would have caused a blush in Cyprus. He does not bear a proper respect for you, for I have heard him publicly boast of your love, and make remarks that I have been forced to resent."

"John, do not revile him any more. You perhaps mean well, but 'tis an utter waste of breath. For years I have loved and trusted him; and if an angel were to stand upon the rippling water there and warn me, I would not believe Frank false. When I gave him my heart I gave him my life, and, though you and all the world turn against him, I will cling to him and trust him, and when he spurns me I will die."

"May God protect you, Lulie, my own love, from all wrong," and I kissed gently and respectfully her dear, soft cheek, henceforth to be for other lips. She did not reproach me, but sat gazing at the dancing sunlight on the water. I rose and took up the pole that we had left set in the bank. A fish had hung itself upon the hook, and, utterly exhausted by its unheeded efforts to disengage itself, came up from the water limp and motionless. Putting it on our string, and tying up our tackle, I assisted Lulie over the rail fence, and we ascended the hill and walked up the lane in silence.

Reader! did you ever love earnestly and devotedly? Did you ever, after months, perhaps years, of doubt and hesitation, at last make up your mind

I assented, but asked what he wanted with another horse when he already had several he did not use.

"But this is something extra, my son, and I did not buy him for myself, but for a friend of mine. You will find his name on the bill of shipment."

I looked at it again, and saw that the Bay line had received, in good order, but subject to a score of risks, one horse, to be sent to John Smith, Jr., at Goldsboro', N. C. I thanked him with all the gratitude I could command under the conflict of feelings, and we all went out to the front porch, and sat there till the twilight darkened into night. Carlotta, with Lulie, took her seat on the steps, and I could hear her rich voice even laughing heartily at times as they talked together in low tones. I was glad that she was resuming her cheerfulness, and felt that I ought to join them, and not be so silent and moody in my own home. But I somehow wanted to be near mother to-night, and let her hand caress my head, because I was in trouble.

CHAPTER XV

The sun shining into my eyes next morning awoke me, and turning over I heard the rattle and rub of the brush as Reuben polished away on my boots, just outside the door.

"Reuben," I yawned, "has Horace fed the horses?" Reuben came into the room, with one boot casing his arm up to the elbow, like an ill-shaped boxing glove, and the brush still flying up and down the shining instep.

"I d'no, sir, spec he has doe, st—too!" and he stopped to spit on the end of the brush, as if he wished to spit the hairs away, "he allays de fust one up on de plantash'n."

"Well, as soon as you get through with the boots, tell him to hitch the gray horses to the spring wagon directly after breakfast; I am going to town; and tell him to put in my saddle and bridle, as I want to ride my horse back."

"Which un, Marse John?" said Reuben, as he set the boots by my bedside, "how's one horse gwine to pull de wagin back here agin?"

"Dry up, and go tell Horace what I said. It is a new horse I am going after, and you have got to attend to him for me, and you can ride him to water every day."

"Golly, dat's 'lishus; won't dese quarter niggers stand back," and he ran down stairs, cutting an audible shuffle every third step.

I was just tying on my cravat when Reuben returned, with a lengthened visage and a woful tale.

"Unken Horris was a waterin' de horses, and when I tole him, he said marster dun tole him, and dat was nough; and just cause I tole him to hurry up, he tuk and cut me mos' in two with de carridge whip."

"I expect you were impudent to him; but he ought not to have struck you when I sent you. I will see him about it after breakfast."

This silenced but did not satisfy Reuben, who, like all negroes, was anxious enough to see swift punishment fall on one who had offended against himself, though he would have been full of sympathy for one who suffered for any offence, however grievous, against a white person.

As we drove into Goldsboro', an hour afterwards, the whistle sounded, and the morning train came into sight, nodding up the track; the engine steamed by like a great hog rooting its way along; then the baggage car, its door open, and the baggage master leaning out; then the coaches, and, as they all came to a stop, amid the shouts of a dozen white aproned waiters, who were vowing that every passenger had plenty of time to eat the most delicious breakfast ever prepared, Frank and Ned, guns in hand, came down the car steps. I welcomed them warmly, being delighted to see Ned, and determined that I would crush every feeling of repugnance to Frank, and receive him with the hospitality of a Southern home. As we walked up to our wagon, where our grays were prancing and snorting at the train, Reuben came around from the hotel stables, whither I had sent him for my new horse, leading him by the halter. I almost forgot to breathe in my rapt admiration. He was the most perfect specimen of horse flesh I had ever seen. His color was the deepest chestnut or claret, and his hair looked as if it was just wound from the cocoon, and his large prominent eye had a soft intelligent expression that was almost human. His limbs were as delicate as a gazelle's, yet had that peculiar turn of the rounded muscles that told of desert born ancestors. There was nothing of the charger about him—no thunder-clothed neck, nor trumpet-like nostril; all was dainty symmetry, but the symmetry of a form that could not know fatigue.

I could not tell whether he would drive or not, but I felt that it would almost be a sin to clog such superb motion with harness. I ordered Reuben to put the saddle and bridle on him, and turned to Ned and Frank, and asked their opinion of him.

"I'll vow he's a beauty, John," said Frank, as we put the valises in the wagon; "let me ride him home for you, and find out his bad points, if he has any."

I could not refuse, and with much chagrin and disappointment saw Frank gallop fleetly on ahead of the wagon, as we rattled on towards home. Ned and I had much to talk about, and almost before we were aware of it, were driving down the avenue.

Frank had waited for us to come up, and now cantered along by the side of the wagon, descanting the praises of my steed in unmeasured terms.

When we entered the house, and Ned and Frank were met by the family, I was really sorry for Lulie, so great was her embarrassment. She could not bear to torture me by greeting Frank with the cordiality their relations demanded, and she could not bear to hurt his feelings by treating him coldly without a cause. Frank noticed her confusion, and asked, in his free and easy way, "Why, Lulie, what is the matter with you. Have you become so rustic already as to be frightened out of your wits by the presence of gentlemen?"

"Don't let him tease you, Lulie," said mother, coming to her aid; "Frank has mistaken the roses which our fresh air has given her for blushes at his presence."

"Not at all, Mrs. Smith; I am too much of a *connoisseur* in ladies' faces to mistake confusion for health. I will leave it to Miss Rurleston if Lulie wasn't ashamed to meet us."

But Carlotta, with her face all bright with animation, was deeply engaged in questioning Ned about Mr. and Mrs. Cheyleigh, and expressing her gratitude for their kindness, and did not hear his remark.

"Well, boys," interrupted mother, "I suppose you are both dusty and warm, and wish to go to your rooms. John, show them up; and remember one thing, you came up here to enjoy yourselves; do so to the fullest extent. Everything on the premises that will serve your amusement is at your service; the house and furniture are old, so you need not fear to be as boisterous as you please. When you come down from your rooms your breakfast will be ready, or I will send it up, if you prefer it."

"You are very kind," said both, "we will soon be down."

I had persuaded mother to fix the large room for us all three, so that we could enjoy ourselves more together than if formally separated.

As soon as we got into our room, and Frank had thrown off his duster and coat, he broke forth in his praises of Carlotta.

"I'll vow she is superb; my life! what an eye she has! I had no idea, when I wrapped her up in our jackets on the beach, and she looked so cold and pitiful, that she was such a beauty. Ned, she seemed to tackle to you strongly. I could not make her hear me."

"She was only asking me about home. You know she staid there several days before she came up to Col. Smith's."

"She's devilish grave, though," said Frank, pouring the basin full of water.

"Remember, Frank, what she has so recently passed through," said I; "she is really bright when she can forget her bereavement; then, too, she is contrasted here with Lulie, who is all life and gaiety."

"Ah!" said Frank, wiping the words out of his mouth with the towel, "Lulie is the star after all. If she just had Carlotta's beauty she would break all your hearts. I wonder what she meant, though, by being so confoundedly sour towards me. I believe I'll try a little game with Carlotta, any way, and see what grit she is made of, if for nothing more than to *pique* Lulie."

"Frank, you forget Carlotta is my sister, now," I said, gravely enough to let him see that I was in earnest, yet not enough so to offend him, as he was my guest.

"*Pardons, mille pardons, monsieur,*" he replied, folding a clean collar, and nodding to me gaily.

"Frank," said Ned, dusting his hat, "you are terribly conceited. How do you know that your attentions to Miss Rurleston will *pique* Lulie?"

"Oh, that's my biz, you know," returned Frank, shutting one eye at him; "but I am afraid we are keeping Mrs. Smith's breakfast waiting; let's go down."

As we reached the basement stairs Lulie called me out to the porch, while Ned and Frank went down. She was very much agitated as she said:

"John, I must go home to-morrow."

"Go home, Lulie!"

"Yes; it will be a perfect torture to remain here with you and Frank. He does not know of anything having passed between us, and will be constantly rallying me about a confusion I cannot conceal, when I think that you are watching me and suffering with every smile I give him. Oh, John, I am very unhappy about it all."

"And poor I am the cause of all. But, Lulie, you must not go. What will they all think of your leaving so suddenly, when you came up to spend the summer? I am afraid they will think there is something unpleasant between you and Carlotta or myself. Lulie, if you will only stay, I will promise not to be miserable, however loving you are to Frank, and I will endeavor to arrange all our plans so that you will not be placed in a single embarrassing situation."

"Your motives are all kind, John, but I alone know how I will suffer by remaining here. I must return, and I have called you now to ask that you aid me to take my departure without any unpleasantness. I will make it all right with Carlotta, and I want you to assure Mrs. Smith that neither she nor any of the family have given me the slightest cause for leaving. If it will make your explanation easier, you can even hint at something between Frank and myself. Colonel Smith, you know, leaves day after to-morrow for Havana, and, as he has to go through Wilmington, I can go down with him."

"So much the more reason for your not going. Father's absence will make it lonely here, and we cannot spare you."

"Do not, dear John, persuade me any longer. I am positively determined. Now, won't you please help me to get off without so much surprise and resistance on the part of others," and she twisted one little finger into the button-hole of my coat, and looked up at me with such earnest entreaty in her eyes, that I readily promised to give her all the aid in my power.

By way of fulfilling this promise, I sought an interview with mother, and, after a little confidence in regard to Frank and myself, and by hard persuasion, made her promise not to express more than conventional surprise and regret at the announcement of Lulie's intention. I had a short talk with father to the same effect, while Lulie was alone with Carlotta, down under the arbor; so that at the dinner table, when Lulie proposed to accompany father to Wilmington, there was no great outcry against it.

All expressed regret. Ned vowed it was a shame for her to leave just as they reached here, and Frank simply smiled, but a smile so like a sneer I could not tell whether he was pleased or otherwise with the announcement.

After dinner we separated for our afternoon siesta, Frank, Ned and I going up to our cool, large room, where, drawing our beds between the windows, with a soft breeze playing over us, we enjoyed that prince of luxuries, an afternoon nap. When we awoke, bathed, dressed, and went down stairs, we found the sun quite low down the sky, and Ben Bemby out in the front porch, with Carlotta and Lulie, who were both laughing at his quaint remarks. I introduced my companions, Ned shaking him warmly by the hand, Frank saying carelessly, with a stare, "How are you?" and then, as they all proposed to go to the orchard for fruit, I excused myself for a ride. Once upon Phlegon, my beautiful courser, flying along through grass-bordered wood paths, now reining up on some hill to get a view of the sunset, now pausing at a gurgling branch, down in some valley, to see him lower his tapering neck and dip his spreading nostrils in the bubbling waters, then on again, with freshened speed and tighter rein, I almost forgot that Lulie did not love me.

That night, after the lamps were lit in the parlor, father came in and declared we must lay aside all dignity and have a real romp. As he agreed to join us we assented, and for hours the house sounded like bedlam. Carlotta, at mother's request, participated, and her beauty was as much enhanced by the animation of the excitement as is a diamond when it is brought to the light.

What a delightful thing is a romp in the country, when you can make just as much noise as you please, and no one will care; when there is no nervous old lady over the way, to send over and beg that you be more quiet, as she has the headache; no simple minded policemen, to knock at the door and inquire if there is a fire; no next door neighbor to present you as a nuisance!

We fully enjoyed the rural privilege, and the old clock in the corner had rung out its warning many times unheeded, when our games were broken up, as far as the ladies were concerned, by the entrance of a bat, for there are few things they are more genuinely afraid of than a little leather-wing. Like the eyes of a well executed portrait, the bat seems to follow you wherever you crouch in the room, and dips with regular precision and nicety of distance at your head, however low you bow it. Verily, the woman who can stand the flutter of its dusky wings is a heroine, beside whom Daemeneta is insignificant! A broom and pair of tongs soon secured its expulsion, and allowed Carlotta and Lulie to return to the room. Taking up the lamp, and looking at the clock in the sitting room, we found it late, and, bidding each other "good night," we went to our rooms.

"John," said Frank, pushing off one boot with the toe of his other, "Miss Rurleston is your sister now, I know, but you must excuse me for saying she is superb. I'll sw — — vow her eyes set me crazy. Lulie ain't a whiff to her. By the way," he continued, getting up in his stocking feet and shirt sleeves to stand before the mirror, while he took off his collar and tie, "I wonder what put the little goose into the notion of going home?"

"Frank," said Ned, from the bed, where he had thrown himself, half undressed, to cool off, "if you do claim Lulie as your sweetheart, you shan't speak of her so disrespectfully. She is an old friend of mine, and I will defend her from any such epithets."

"Well, parson," returned Frank, sitting down on the other bed, "I will call her the madam, or her highness, if you desire, but I do think it is confounded shabby in her to leave us now. I'll make up for it with the black eyes, though. Excuse me again, 'brother' John."

I felt that I could not trust myself to reply, and there was a silence for a few minutes, during which Ned yawned, and slided off the bed to his knees to say his prayers.

"Oh, John, I forgot to tell you," said Frank, "that long, tow-headed booby, who was here this evening, said he had a fine place for fishing tomorrow, and we promised to go with him, if it did not conflict with any of your plans."

"Not at all," said I, "but I must go down and tell mother, that she may have breakfast early."

"No; she already knows about it, and promised to have us up at sunrise."

"Of course, I am in for anything you all say."

"Let's go to sleep," said Ned, as he got up from his prayers, and fell over on the bed. We let!

CHAPTER XVI

We were yet at the table when Reuben came in to announce that Mr. Bemby's son had come. We went out to the porch, where he was sitting, his elbow on the railing, his chin on his elbow, his white wool hat, without a band, hanging down like the eaves of a barn over his wheat straw hair, his red fuzzy wrists, sticking about three inches out of his coarse flax coat sleeves, and his broad copper riveted shoes gaping so wide about his bony ankles that they seemed to have frightened his speckled pants half way up his legs; his poles, lashed together with old leather shoe strings, stood against the railing, and his bait-gourd sat on the bench at his side. He greeted us with a "good mornin' to you," and a smile, without any sound whatever. We all shook hands with him, Frank barely tipping his fingers, then went back into the house to get our hats and tackle. Reuben came out with our dinner in a large basket and we were about to start, when Frank ran back up stairs, and soon joined us, holding his coat over something against his side. As soon as we got into the lane he took out a large black bottle of whisky and a bundle of cigars. I said nothing, but I could see that Ned was disturbed that Frank should attempt to do the "fast" with us, for neither of us were yet sophisticated enough to smoke or drink. Ben, however, smiled, and prolonged his laugh as he shook the bottle and watched the bead.

"That's fine as cat hair," he said, returning the bottle to Frank. "Licker's purtty much like er hole in the groun'; keeps you warm in winter and cool in summer; but less pearten er little; we got er right smart ways to walk now, an' it'll be hot enough presn'ly to curl er turckle's shell."

We accordingly walked on rapidly, Ned and I together, and Frank and Ben. Frank, however, had too much of the haughty about him for Ben, who soon fell back and gave us the benefit of his ever-going tongue.

"How far is the place where you expect to fish, Mr. Bemby?" inquired Ned.

"None er your misters for me; jus' call me Ben," said he, shifting his poles from one shoulder to another. "I'm er gwine to take you up to old Nancy Mucket's hole."

"Nancy who?" I asked. "What in the world do they call it by such a name, for?"

"'Cause old Nancy Mucket got drownded there. I have heerd daddy tell 'bout it er thous'n times. Old Nance was er mon'sus fisher, an' old Dave Mucket tole her whatever she done not to tech his ash pole. Nance she tuck it right down an' went to the creek. She never come back by night, an' next day they drug the creek, and pulled her up from the bottom, where she was hung under er root. She had the very ash pole in her grip, and when the corrunner sot on her, ole Dave he come up and shuck his head mighty solemn like, and talks: 'Nance, I tole you so; whenever wimmin gits to doin' men's doos they gits into trouble. God made 'em she folks fus, and they'll have to stay she till the worl busts.' Daddy mighty offen tells mo'er 'bout it when she wants to go roun' by herself or drive to town."

"Is it a good place to fish?" asked Frank.

"Tain't bad," said Ben, laconically, at the same time throwing his legs, one after the other, over a low rail fence, and saying, "Here's the place!"

We followed him over the fence, and through some tangled vines, and stopped at the water's edge; the bank covered with short, thick grass, the shade perfectly dense, the yellow waters of the creek curdled with clear rings and ripples from a noisy branch, that bubbled limpidly from the coolest of springs over the whitest of pebbles.

Just where the clear and muddy water mingled, Ben affirmed the fish would bite best. We undid our poles and baited our hooks. Ben and Frank had a little unpleasantness, arising from Frank's claiming a place for his pole to the detriment of Ben's position. His manner and words were so insulting that Ben was about to strike him, when Ned and I interfered, and prevented blows.

We found, as Ben had said, it was a capital place to fish, for we were kept busily employed in attending to our poles. Ben, however, easily beat us all. He some way had a knack of fixing his bait and spitting on his hook, so that his line would scarcely touch the water before a fish would seize it.

The morning waned, however, and the sun had laid the shadows of the poles directly under them, when we all agreed that it was time for lunch.

We carried our basket up to the spring, which bubbled out of a large rock, and where Nature had spread us a table with a green velvet cloth. Ham sandwiches, with just enough mustard, broiled and devilled fowl, cold tongue, with the parsley between the slices, together with heaps of covered fruit pies, and mother's especial boast, biscuit glacé, in the whitest of paper, to say nothing of a barrow full of peaches and melons which Reuben rolled down from the house, and placed to cool in a pond dammed up for the occasion; all were presented to appetites sharpened by the sport of the morning. Reversing the order of Aladdin's feast, our viands disappeared with as wonderful celerity as his appeared. After we had fairly choked the branch with a mound of water-melon rinds and peach parings, we took our seats farther up on the grass, and left Reuben to clear up the table. Frank now drew forth his bottle of brandy and proposed that each one of us should tell a short story, entirely his own, and that he who could tell the most improbable, should have the bottle to himself. Ben stretched himself out on the grass, with his arm under his head, and said, drowsily, as he tore off with his teeth a large quid of tobacco from a twist he drew from his pocket:

"Blaze away wi' yer lies. I'm a biled mullen stalk ef I can't win at that game."

Ned firmly declared he did not want any of the brandy, but said he would tell his story with the rest, merely to help out the fun. By request I was excused, that I might act as judge, and Frank, rapping on the bottle with his knife, asked Ned to begin. Ned reclined on one elbow, and said:

NED'S STORY

"I will tell you what happened in the western part of the State, for Frank's benefit. Our family were summering at a small town near the mountains some years ago, when a circus passed through that section, stopping for a day at our town. Every wall of every house that presented surface enough had for weeks been spread over with the marvellous high colored illustrations of what were to be seen under that mighty, mystic canvas. They were the same pictures, or I should rather say works of art, combining the airy lightness and licensed fancy of Correggio with the Dutch fidelity of Rembrandt, which you have, perhaps, all seen at different times pasted, with weather-proof adherence, to any visible portion of public places. There were troops of monkeys, done in the blackest of colors, swinging from the greenest of trees, across the widest and bluest of rivers, by tails of impossible length and elasticity. There were ibexes leaping into bottomless abysses, thereby defeating the design of the artist, who would have them to alight upon their horns. There was the traditional polar bear, defending her cubs and leisurely lunching on a sandwich of two seals and a sailor. The actual bear in the circus, I have found by long experience, invariably dies at the previous stopping place, bequeathing, tenderly, its skin to the public of to-morrow, thereby undergoing a constancy of death and a multitude of bequests that would startle the profundity of a probate judge. There were pleasant side groups of men lassoing the giraffe and zebra, tripping the rhinoceros, and tearing off tigers from the very hams of elephants, on whose backs were huddled not quite a full regiment of soldiers in all stages of the manual of arms. But the chef *d'œuvre* was the centre-piece, as large as life, representing the clown, dressed in the American flag, with stars left out, with a hat reaching too infinite a point with its peak to be measured by any rule in conic sections, and cheeks too flamingly hectic for medical aid, handing, with the utmost gravity, a dish of boiled eggs to a sedate and diminutive mule, seated on its haunches, with its fore feet up on a barrel as its table—the only position, by the way, in which I think a mule could be safely approached with anything so far from its usual bill of fare as eggs."

"Dog gone yo circus picturs!" interrupted Ben, raising up on one elbow to spit a stream of tobacco juice several yards behind us, "I c'n see them might' nigh every year stuck 'gin the warehouse over in town; go on wi yo yarn."

"Well," continued Ned, kindly taking no affront at Ben's abrupt interruption, "I will hasten on. I merely wished to show how public expectation was worked up to a high pitch. After awhile the day came, and with it the circus—wagon after wagon, with tent poles and furniture; then the cages with the animals, all closed except the little lattice at the top, through which could now and then be heard the scream of a monkey or the cough of a lion, and then the gorgeous, gilded band chariot, with its music. Negroes, and boys, of which I was one, were almost crazy with excitement; we danced and shouted along the sidewalk in a promiscuous throng, ever keeping up with the long train of plumed horses drawing after them the gilded dragon, with its backful of brazen melody. But our glee was hushed into a very silence of admiration as we saw coming far behind the band chariot, with solemn grandeur, the great elephant, its broad ears waving like dusky fans, and its proboscis twisting, like a great serpent cut in two, slowly from side to side as he came on, looming like a gigantic tower, through the dust. As he approached and passed us, his small eyes twinkling so knowingly on the crowd, his keeper on a dappled horse, pacing along so fearlessly by his ponderous foreleg, and his dog trotting carelessly under his curling trunk, the open mouths of the crowd must have relieved him to a considerable extent of the dust he seemed to deprecate so much by his fanning ears.

"Well, to hurry on without so much detail, the canvas was pitched, the keeper carried the elephant to the river to cool out, and then brought him up, and tied him to one of the posts of the market house, which was near the pavilion, till the afternoon performance should commence. At the hour he went round, decked in his Oriental costume, and undid the fastening, and spoke in some unknown tongue to his mammoth charge. The elephant started, made a step forward and stopped, with a shrill cry of pain. The keeper looked up surprised, then uttering a few genuine American oaths, ordered him to move. Again the elephant made a great effort, and again stood still, with a prolonged scream. The keeper, now furious, approached, and drove his short training spike into him again and again. With each stab the poor creature would shriek and strain to the uttermost its cumbrous limbs, but all in vain, it could not move from where it stood. There was something so new in this apparent obstinacy that the keeper commenced to examine his position. He found one of the market house posts nearly pulled from its place, and the elephant's tail, stretched to its last tenacity, sticking out straight as a poker towards the post, though not touching it by several inches, and having no visible connection whatever with it. Again he urged the animal forward, and again the elephant did his best to move. Just before his tail pulled out by the roots the post gave way, and tumbling over, hung dangling at the elephant's heels. The keeper took the post in his hands, and, looking closely, found that a little spider had spun a web from the elephant's tail to the post, and that this invisible thread had held him stronger than a chain of steel. Such a crowd had now gathered that the keeper found the elephant was drawing more people than the circus proper (or improper), and ordered him to move, that he might carry him under the canvas. The elephant obeying, moved forward, but the motion of his body set the post to swinging like a pendulum, which, increasing in its oscillation, at last commenced to thump him in the side harder than he fancied was comfortable. The thumps became more violent as he increased his speed, till, at last becoming frenzied with the blows, and the shouts, and hootings of the crowd, he broke away from the keeper, and ran hither and thither in the streets as fast as his unwieldy body could move, knocking over signs and boxes, breaking racks, frightening horses, and occasionally jostling over a clumsy man or two. At last he plunged through the great wide door of the court house, scraping his back against the brick arch as he did so. The post here fortunately got across the door and checked him. He pulled frantically, but the little web would not break; he then bent himself around as far as an elephant might, and tried to tear it off with his proboscis. The web, however, was so fine that it cut into even his tough trunk, and burying itself under the skin, held his proboscis fast to his tail. In his efforts now to disengage himself he fell, and lay helpless on the ground, and at last had to be rolled with an immense handspike over and over, like a very large hoop, till he got to the tent, or canvas, under which he was rolled, and perhaps unfastened.

"The prominent gentlemen of the town obtained part of the web, and forwarded it, with proper credentials, to several scientific societies for analysis. They each gave a different opinion in regard to the cause of its wonderful tenacity, but the people about the town always believed, and with very good reason, too, that the spider which spun it had been feeding on the beef brought to that market; and thus accounting for it, they ceased to wonder at the toughness of the web."

"Ned, that's a jolly good yarn," said Frank, tossing the serpentine paring of a peach over his shoulder, and puffing out one jaw with a large section of the luscious fruit.

"Less hear the lord juke tell his'n," said Ben, nodding towards Frank, and pushing himself up backwards by his hands to a large tree, against which he leaned, and folded his arms around one doubled-up knee; "should'n be suppris'n ef he can tell a buster, he's in such good practice."

"Well," replied I, "we will leave all discussion of the merits of each one's story to the umpire, and proceed. Frank, it is your time next."

FRANK'S STORY

"I hardly know what to tell," he said, taking aim at Ben's foot with the peach stone he had been sucking. "Ned has fairly taken the wind out of my sails. Let me see; I believe I'll tell you what happened to me once when I was very small. I was out one day in the mountains bird-nesting—a wicked employment, by the way, which perhaps accounts for my mishap—and found a very large hawk's nest. It was in the very top of a ragged old pine, that grew upon the edge of the most frightful precipice in the country. It was a sheer descent of five or six hundred feet, looking almost perpendicular, though in some places it bulged out with rugged rocks, and in others retreated into caves. All down the face of the cliff were little scrubby bushes, which grew straight out for an inch or two, then suddenly turned up in their course, as if determined to see beyond the great rocky wall that towered so far above them. The old pine had endured the agony of fear for centuries, for though its gnarled trunk leaned far over the abyss, the limbs had all turned toward the firm earth, and stretched their hard, knotty hands appealingly to the surrounding forest. Rain after rain had washed away the soil and left the roots exposed, till half the foundation stood over the precipice and added its weight to the leaning trunk. It was not without much hesitation and debate with myself that I prepared to ascend. I reasoned, however, that if it had stood that long through wind and storm it would not take such a still, calm day to fall; and then, even if its foundation was precarious, my weight would be so infinitely small, compared with its own, that it would never make a perceptible addition. The temptation, too, was a great one, for I had seen the hawk, one of the largest kind, fly away as I approached, and then the climbing was very easy, for a ladder-like vine wound its leafy folds clear up to the top, like a great green serpent seeking the eggs. I took off my jacket and commenced to ascend. With well rubbed pants and an irritating quantity of pine bark next to my skin I reached the first limb, where I rested;

then went on to the top, like going up stairs. At last I reached the nest, and there—rich reward for my trouble—lay four brown splotched eggs. Before I proceeded to take them out and tie them in my handkerchief I took a glance at my position. One look satisfied me, and made me faint and dizzy. From my standpoint the tree seemed to stretch out horizontally over the chasm which yawned hungrily below, and, looking at it as I did, through the branches of the tree, it seemed far deeper and more awful than it really was. Far down at the bottom, where the trees and shrubs shrank to the level of a green plush-looking surface, two or three cows were grazing, and they appeared just the size of the toy cows in my Noah's ark. As I had to descend to the level of the valley on my way home, I could not resist the boyish temptation to throw my hat out into the air and let it float down; I accordingly balanced it nicely and let it go. It sank steadily for a little while, then began to rock from side to side, and finally relapsed into the regular spiral descent, twisting down and down till my eyes could not follow the tiny speck. While gazing down to discover it, if possible, I was startled by a sharp crack near the foot of the tree; another and another followed, and I looked in terror at the roots, to find that the ground was rising slowly upward in a slanting direction from me. The tree was giving way, and gradually sinking more and more swiftly over that hell of destruction. I heard the tearing up of the roots and the sh—sh of the foliage through the air, and I knew no more.

"When I awoke I was swinging delightfully, as if in a hammock. Thick leaves were all around me, and when I parted them and looked out my position was plain. I had caught in the net work of vines in the top of the tree, and was now hanging by one strand of rope-like vine to the tree, which was dangling, top downwards, about fifty feet above me. I found, to my great comfort, that I was in a comparatively safe bed, well padded with abundant leaves, and held by strong cords which branched from the vine rope. This was so twined about the trunk of the inverted tree that it could not become detached; so that my only real danger was that the immense tree itself, hanging above me by a few roots that had not given way, might at any moment break from its slight support and plunge, with me beneath it, into the vast depths below. The very hopelessness of my position made me perfectly reckless and indifferent; and finding that the motion of my descent had given me a considerable swing, I endeavored to augment it by the constant change of my position, leaning first on one side, then on the other. I succeeded so well that I was soon sweeping through an arc of an hundred feet, with a rush through the air at every swoop that made my cheeks tingle. With every swing I increased my speed, and there is no telling to what extent I might have carried the wild excitement of the moment, had I not been checked by coming in violent contact with the face of the precipice. The blow almost stunned me, but it fortunately stopped my swing, and, with a gradually decreasing oscillation, I lay still in my nest of leaves. When I awoke 'twas late in the afternoon, and I found that I was extremely hungry. I ate two of the hawk eggs and felt relieved. I put the other two away, resolved not to touch them till I was absolutely compelled.

Having nothing better to do, I amused myself by swinging again, though I took good care not to swing far enough to strike the side of the cliff. The sun at last went down, and darkness crept over the dismal woods. Far up above, the stars began to twinkle brightly in the sky, and far down below, the dark void grew intensely black. With a trembling dread of the dark grim night, and yet with a strange sense of security—a feeling of safety from all other dangers—I tried to go to sleep. With a faithful remembrance of the old lady's instructions I said my prayers as well as the distraught condition of my mind would allow.

All through the long dreary night I was dozing off, only to dream that I was falling from my nest, and to awake with a cold shudder of horror.

After dreary hours of these terrors I hailed with delight the faint beams of approaching day. Brighter and brighter grew the sky, till, with a sudden flood of gold, the sun rose upon the world. What a bright, warm feeling of hope morning brings to the weary watcher! I knew that friends would soon be on the search, and I lay in constant expectation of their shouts. Nor had I long to wait; for soon the woods were ringing with their loud halloos, as they called and listened for my voice. At length I saw a party far below pick up my hat, and from their anxious grouping around it, and busy search among the rocks immediately afterwards, I knew they thought I had fallen over the precipice and was lying, a mangled corpse, somewhere near. I called and called in vain; they moved slowly hither and thither, and finally passed out of sight, carrying my hat with them.

My heart sank within me, and, burying my face in the leaves of my pillow, I sobbed and moaned most piteously. Suddenly, in the very acme of my anguish, I heard my name called aloud, and, looking up through my tears, saw half a score of friendly, anxious faces looking down from the edge of the cliff. Half ashamed of my weakness, yet still crying for joy, I shouted, and begged them for Heaven's sake to help me out of my terrible predicament. They had no ropes with them, and it was a long way to town where they could be procured, so I could see there was an animated discussion among them in reference to the best ways and means to relief. I heard one say, in an angry tone, 'I tell you it's a sho' thing. The wind hain't never turned it, and I'll bet my own life agin your pus, and that's empty, that it'll hold him for ever. Look at them ribs, man! Sheer! let her drap. I'll be 'sponsible for his life.'

The next instant an enormous blue cotton umbrella dropped down beside me, and a rough voice shouted, 'Put your foot in the crook of the handle; hold her up stiff; she'll let you down square.'

Whether the femininity of the umbrella inspired confidence, or the desperate state of my feelings urged me on, I cannot say, but getting on the edge of my nest, putting my foot in the strong oak curved handle for a stirrup, and grasping the staff firmly, I slipped from the vines, and floated slowly down, the old umbrella popping and straining as if it was going to fly to pieces. But with the exception of rubbing the edges on the rocks, and straightening out the ribs by the pressure of the atmosphere, I landed safely at the foot of the precipice, where I found the old man sobbing over my hat as if I was dead. He no sooner found that I was really unhurt than he put up his handkerchief, and cut a before long switch, with which he thrashed me soundly right the assembled throng of friends. I thought then, and still think, it was a singular way of thanking Providence for my safe delivery. This is about all I have to tell, except that the old gent had a gold handle put on the old cotton umbrella.

'Go ahead, now, what's-your-name; let us hear what you can do in the shape of a yarn.'

Frank drew the fruit basket to him, searched through it for the largest peach, and, hastily peeling it, threw himself back on the grass to listen to Ben."

Ben very deliberately rose, and tossed away his quid of tobacco, took some water to cleanse his mouth, and walked to a bush near by, from which he cut a large branch with an old horn-handle knife, out of which he blew almost a pipeful of tobacco crumbs before opening the blade. Taking his seat again, he commenced to trim up his switch and to tell his STORY

BEN'S STORY

"Your two friends, John, has both on 'em told good yarns, but they went mighty fur from home to get 'em. I'm a gwine to tell you what happened right up yonder at the house. Some time along the fust of last year mo'er took her up a house pig, to raise offen the slops and peelins. It growed and fattened a power, and was soon 'bout the likeliest hog on the plantation, only it got so cussed tame twould'n never git outer nobody's way, and was a continuwell being stepped on, and drug outer the house by the leg. Arter the little fool had been grown awhile, she come up one day with eleven pigs, as lively as you ever see, and pime blank like her, a squealin' and runnin' everywhere they hadn't orter. I heard a riddle wonst 'bout a pig under a gate makin' a noise, but he ain't a lighten-bug's lamp to a pig when he's hungry. The older they got the wuss they squealed, till dad said as how he could'n stand it no longer, the sow and pigs had to be moved; so me and him bilt a pen 'bout two hundred yards from the house, and driv 'em down to it. There was a free nigger, with a yard full of children, livin' 'bout as fur from the pen as we did; and the fust night after we'd put 'em up, long todes bed time, I heer a pig squeal like dyin', but I thought perhaps he'd got cut out of his suck, and I never thought on 'em agin till next morning, when I went down to feed 'em; two of the pigs was bloody behind, and, when I looked close, thare tails was gone. I knowed 'twas the niggers, for a fried pig's tail is the best thing a nigger knows how to eat. I tole the ole man 'bout it soon's I got back, and he said how we'd wait till the next mornin'. When we went to the pen agin thare was two more tails gone, and two more bloody pigs. Daddy sot on a rail sometime a studin, then he said, sudden-like:

'Bengermin, go to the house, and fetch me a shingle an my powder horn, an the big gimblet.'

I ran off, a wond'rin' what in the crashen the ole man was gwine to do with a gimblet and a shingle. Soon as I come back he tole me to get in the pen, and ketch one of the pigs with his tail on. When I histed one up, he tuk him and tied his tail out straight on the shingle, so it twould'n bend. He tuk the gimblet, and started in the tip end of the pig's tail, and bored it clear out. The bloody shavins come a bilin' up round the grooves of the gimblet, and the pig squealed till the air 'peared to be full of hopper grasses, tryin' to kick in my years. When daddy pulled the gimblet out, the tail looked like a holler skin quill, and would hold 'bout a double load of powder. Daddy poured it chock full, then put a fo-penny nail, with a gun cap on the eend of it, down 'mongst the powder, so that it'd go off if any thing totch it, and then tied it all up with horse hair. When I put him back in the pen that pig didn't have nary a curl to his tail; it stuck out as straight and stiff as if it was a handel to tote him by. We fixed two more in the same way, and then went home. Next morning, when we went down, we found one pig dead, with his hams ready baked, and his back bone drove through his forehead six inches. His tail itself was split open like a shot fire-cracker, and bent backerds like a shelled pea hull. The other two tails had just shot straight without bustin', but the kick of the powder had lifted up their hind legs so high they could'n git 'em down agin, and they was walkin' round the pen on thare forefeet samer'n a circus man. When we came to zamine the pen we found three niggers' fingers blowed off, and sticking to a rail, and little kinks of wooly hair were layin' round as thick as if it had snowed black. Daddy and me then went up to the nigger's house, where we found a good size boy and girl with their hands tied up, and thare heads burnt slick on top. When we asked 'em 'bout it, the boy said the girl was a nussin the baby, and went down to the pen to keep the baby quiet, and he just went along for company like. He said they got to the pen, and was a peepin' through the rails, when one of the pigs come to scratch hisself, and soon's he begin to rub he busted all to pieces. They were mighty badly skeered, and, to keep 'em so, daddy tole 'em them was some thunder-tailed hogs he got from the South. We never had another hog troubled in the least, and when hog-killing time came daddy found it mighty hard to get the hands to help him. That's the end of my yarn."

And Ben got up and walked to the spring, where a large curved handled gourd hung on a stick cut for the purpose, and, disdaining Reuben's offer of a glass, took the gourd, and dipping up half the spring, drank till the long crooked handle curled over his hat, and bent back like an officer's plume in a windy parade. When he had resumed his seat on the grass all three called for my judgment, and, with an assumption of great solemnity and dignity, I proceeded to render it.

"The object, gentlemen, of a wonderful story, or yarn, as it is vulgarly called, is not only to excite wonder, but also to evoke a pleasant surprise by discovering relations between dissimilar or contrary things, which we did not think of as possibly existing. If these dissimilars or contraries are too far apart for the mind to recognize any possible relation, then the narration becomes unpleasantly absurd, and we shrink from contemplating it. If, however, apparently improbable relations are brought out in a way that renders them possible, we are surprised and pleased with the discovery. Hence, the most exaggerated narrations are not always the most entertaining, and we derive most pleasure from hearing or reading those stories where improbabilities are unexpectedly brought within the range of possibility, or if beyond it, the fact is ingeniously concealed by possible concomitants. Thus, Munchausen's descent from the moon by a rope of cut straw is not half so pleasant a story as the firing his gun by sparks drawn from his eye with his fists. So, were you to tell an audience that you saw a mole move a mountain no one would be pleased or surprised, as the mind would have no effort to pronounce it entirely false; but if you should say you saw a fly trained to play a tune by buzzing his wings from the top to the bottom of a wine glass, the minds of your hearers would be pleasantly occupied for a while in eliminating the true from the false, and your story would be applauded.

Ned, to-day, in his story, erred by placing his relations too far apart. A spider and an elephant! There is no exercise of ingenuity in detecting the falsity of the statement, and the story, from its very improbability, is almost out of the range of competition for the prize. Frank has so mixed his that I scarcely know how to render an opinion in regard to it. The impossible parts are utterly so, and the possible are so easily probable we are not surprised. To Ben, then, I award the prize, as having produced the most entertaining story, exciting pleasant surprise in each development, and discovering possibilities in the most unthought of relations."

"Oh! blow your philosophic nonsense, John," said Frank, handing Ben the bottle of brandy; "you got it out of a book, and I'm the devil's apprentice if I didn't earn the brandy fairly."

Ben proffered us the bottle, but Ned and I declined. Frank, however, took it, and, with more swagger than swallow, turned it up to his mouth. Ben poured himself out a glassful, and the bottle was set aside for a smoke. Frank drew forth his cigars, Ben his pipe. Strange to say, I dreaded more to appear squeamish before Ben, whom I looked upon as an inferior, than I did either of the others, and with a blush for my weakness took a cigar. Ned declined again, for which Frank called him Parson Conscience, and we proceeded to light. Oh, dire beginning of troubles! I first bit off the end of my cigar, and could not get the end out of my mouth. I sputtered and spit, and twisted my face into more hideous contortions than Medusa ever wore, but I could not eject that little crumbling fragment of tobacco. Now under my tongue, now in the roof of my mouth, and now going down like a pill. I finally had to take it out disgracefully with my fingers. Getting over that, I lit the cigar—a hard black cigar—and commenced to smoke. With the exception of the pain I experienced from crossing my eyes to look at the end of my cigar, I got on very well for several puffs, then I found that I could not expel all the smoke from my mouth, a little would remain and get up my nose or go down into my lungs. I expectorated, too, very constantly, so that my throat became so insufferably dry, I swallowed just once to relieve it, and oh! the bitter, burning taste that went groping down to my stomach! Clear my throat as I would I could not get it up; more and more bitter it became with each succeeding puff. And now a singular sensation came on; a cloud of swan's down, or carded tow steeped in this same nauseating bitterness, seemed slowly ascending up into my brain, and piling up in sickening oppression just behind my eyeballs, so that I felt a constant desire to close them and roll them inward to see this feathery pain. I felt no interest in the conversation and was absent in all my replies to questions addressed to me, but I tried to look careless and at ease. I even took off my hat and leaned back against a tree, as if in a high state of enjoyment, and tried to flip off the ashes from my cigar with the air of an old smoker. Not understanding this sleight-of-hand practice, my third finger passed so slowly under the burning end that it came out the other side loaded with ashes, and ornamented with a large white blister.

"Smith, how do you like your weed?" said Frank, blowing out a cloud of smoke, holding his cigar daintily between his fore and middle fingers.

"Very much 'ndeed," I said faintly; "'tis very fragrant."

The tow or down now pressed so hard and bitterly upon my eyeballs that it confused my vision. Frank, Ned and Ben were continually changing places, and their conversation seemed to belong to a different period of my life. Objects were still enough when I gazed steadily at them, but when I winked and then looked, they would seem to be in different places. I tried closing my eyes for relief, but the great downy mass of nausea crowding my brain was almost visible, and I was glad to open them again. Still the bitter, burning taste in my mouth kept going down into my stomach, yet lingering with its sickening flavor on my palate. A cold perspiration stood on my forehead and hands, and I felt that I was looking deadly pale. I made an attempt at a yawn to conceal my faint voice, and said:

"I believe I will take a nap. Wake me if the fish bite."

I got up and tried to walk to a little hillock a few steps off; but at every step the ground seemed to rise in a steep hill or sink into a fearful declivity before my feet, and I staggered like a drunken man.

"Hello, Smith; has the cigar got you? I thought you had better pluck."

I was too faint to answer, but fell down, with my head hid by a tree, and with many death-like heavings sank into a drowsy unconsciousness. When I awoke it was late in the afternoon, and all was still around me. Staggering to my feet I heard the distant hum of voices, and taking a deep draught of the cool spring water to slake my feverish thirst, I walked unsteadily down to the creek, where I found my companions fishing with fine success. My vision was not sufficiently restored to admit of my angling, so I sat on the fence and yawningly watched the others till it was time to go home. With well filled baskets Ben, Frank and Ned walked along merrily, while I stalked on miserably, with a throbbing in my temples and an awkward consciousness of being ashamed of everybody, and especially of myself.

At supper I drank a little tea, and, pleading a headache, hurried up to my room. As soon as the servants had been served, mother came up stairs to look after me. She found me with some fever and symptoms of violent cold. A kiss when she came into the room told her I had been smoking, and she smiled as she passed her hand gently over my head, and said:

"John, you have been smoking to-day, and, from your restless, impatient look, you expect a long lecture, but I will wait before I say what I have to say on the subject. I want you to get to sleep now. It is so warm I will open the window, and take out the lamp to prevent the insects coming in, and I hope you will become composed."

She left the room, and I began that hardest of all tasks—trying to go to sleep. An intensely hot night! just light enough out doors to make a checked square of the window; not a leaf quivering; not a sound without but the incessant quavers of the katydids; down stairs the noise and mirth of merry converse!

Tossing from side to side of the bed; now shaking up my pillow, then reversing my position, and lying with my head at the foot board; then stretching directly across the bed, with my hands hanging down over the sides; in all positions I vainly sought a cool place. The very sheets, except that they were wrinkled, seemed to have just come from under the iron; and even the mahogany of the foot board, when I laid my cheek against it, felt tepidly disagreeable. At last, after trying every conceivable position on the bed, I fell asleep with my feet pressed against the cool wall, and while watching a firefly that had gotten into the room, and was flashing his tiny lamp hither and thither as he flitted along the ceiling, trying to escape. My slumber was uneasy and fitful, and I was dreaming of strange oppressions and sensations, and continually waking, to hear the laughter and mirth down stairs.

Perhaps conscience added a thorn to my pillow; but I could remember no definite sin I had committed. The cigar was surely not wrong, for father, and a great many others who were good, smoked. I could not then analyze my moral nature and detect the wrong, but years have since shown me 'twas in the lack of moral courage, in the yielding to what I was ashamed of, simply because I was ashamed to refuse.

Very young men deem the cigar an important adjunct to manhood, and when they smoke to look manly, the oath and glass are not far off. A good rule in forming this almost national habit is to light your first cigar before father or mother without a blush, and the harm resulting will be solely physical.

CHAPTER XVII

Father and Lulie have been gone an hour; father on his way to Havana, Lulie returning to Wilmington. Frank and Ned have gone with them over to town. I am lying on a lounge in the hall, and mother and Carlotta are sitting near me, arranging flowers for the parlor vases. Lulie got off without much trouble with the assistance of mother's tact; Ned expressing great surprise, while Frank was almost rude in his solicitations to her to remain. Dear little darling, how tenderly she bade me farewell, whispering as she pressed my hand, "Don't be hurt at my leaving, John, 'tis for your sake as much as mine!"

My eyes are closed, and mother and Carlotta think I am asleep, but through a scarcely lifted lid I am watching Carlotta, feasting my eyes on her beautiful face and form. She is sitting just inside the hall door, with a lap full of flowers, and though I cannot see her face, I gaze on an arm and hand that Phidias might dream of, but never carve.

Her muslin sleeve was turned up to her shoulder, to be out of the way, and the flesh, soft and snowy, swelled out from the richly worked undersleeve, and almost imperceptibly tapered to the elbow, with here and there a tiny thread of blue, winding its way under the transparent skin. At the elbow two dimples showed where the liquid flesh eddied round the curve, and a slope of perfect grace carried it to the wrist; here no knots disfigured, no roughness marred it, but, smooth and delicate, the wrist became a fitting bridge between such a hand and arm. Her hair, caught back by a crimson velvet band, fell in a dark shower over her shoulders; not the wiry ringlets, nor the hard straight locks that all are familiar with, but in soft undulating waves it fell, as if fairies were trembling the silken strands. Her profile was exquisite, and the beautiful proportion of each feature, and the delicate tints that overspread them, formed altogether a picture that has rarely been surpassed for loveliness. The peculiar witchery of the face, as I gazed upon it, was enhanced by an occasional frown and arch of the pencilled brow, as she endeavored to draw a refractory thread through the stems of the flowers.

Mother, at last speaking, broke the spell that bound me.

"Carlotta, darling, Col. Smith told you of the letter he received from your father's agent in Havana, did he not?"

"He told me of it, and also showed me the letter. Papa always thought his agent very trusty, and I suppose Col. Smith will find everything arranged properly."

After another pause, mother asked again:

"Who is this cousin who claims the estate?"

"He is mother's half nephew. He was always a great favorite with papa, and staid almost half his time with us, though his home was on the other side of the island. Papa used to promise him, when I was a very little girl, that I should be his wife, but he was so much older than I, I could never love him."

Though my fealty to Lulie was unchanged, I could not help thinking what a splendid thing it would be to have the promise of such a love as hers.

"But," continued mother, shaking the dew from a flower as she placed it with the others, "would you not marry him when you are grown, to get back so much wealth and riches. Remember, he has your father's will, making him the sole heir in case of your death, and he has also the affidavit of the captain of the vessel in which you sailed, that yourself and father were both lost, and could not possibly have been saved."

"I would despise him," she said, scornfully, snapping a stem as she spoke, "if he tried to get anything wrongfully. But Col. Smith has all papa's papers with him, and Cousin Herrara is too noble, I know, to do anything mean or sordid!"

She brushed the rose leaves from her lap, and placed the bouquet she had arranged in the basket of a Parian marble porter on the mantel; then coming back to mother, she kneeled down by her side, and laying her cheek sideways on mother's knee, with that peculiar winning way of her's, said softly:

"I hope Col. Smith will be able to save me something to repay you all for your goodness to me, for I cannot stay under your roof as a charity outcast, and it would kill me to leave you now, I have learned to love you so."

"My dear child," said mother, laying her hand on her soft, dark hair, "the very idea of compensating us for the greatest pleasure of our lives! Colonel Smith has gone to Havana solely on your account. Thank heaven we have as much as we want, and you may feel that you have a daughter's place in our household, and will never, never be a burden. Who knows," she added, playfully patting her head and glancing toward my couch, "but what you may be a daughter, indeed, to us one of these days."

"Oh, Mrs. Smith," said Carlotta so earnestly, that I opened my eyes in time to see the scarlet tinge of her cheeks, "you do not know how you hurt me when you say that. 'Twould make me hate the very thought of your son, whom I now esteem so much, to think that I was taken into your family to please him; that I was being raised to suit his fancy; that my character was being moulded after his model of a woman; that it was being constantly said of me, as I have heard it said: 'Mrs. Smith is training her up for her son.' Will I not shrink from his very presence when I feel that he looks upon me as his to love or not, just as he likes?"

"My dear child," said mother, looking surprised, "my words were almost without meaning. Forgive me, and I will endeavor to prevent any allusion, in this house at least, that may wound your feelings."

I here turned over, and moving my arms about showed signs of waking. This put an end to the conversation. Mother coming to the couch found me with considerable fever, and becoming alarmed sent Reuben off after the doctor. In truth I did feel a little badly, though I had been so interested in the conversation that I had not thought of my feelings. My eyeballs were hot and red, and felt as if they were full of sand; my breath burnt my nostrils as it came out, and my tongue was dry and coated. An hour of feverish restlessness elapsed before we heard the doctor's horse plodding up the avenue in a slow jog-trot, the fastest speed known to the medical fraternity. The doctor himself was equally deliberate in tying him to the rack, crossing the stirrups over the back of the saddle with the utmost care, and finally marching up the steps as if he was a pall-bearer at a funeral. He laid his hat on the seat in the porch, put his gloves in the crown, and laid his riding switch across them, as if it was to guard them. He at length advanced into the house and met mother.

"How d'ye do, madam; a very warm day, madam," he said, shaking her hand with one of his, and rubbing the bald place on his head with the other, as if all the heat of the day had centred there.

"It is very sultry indeed, sir," replied mother, as he released her hand. "Reuben, hand a glass of water, or perhaps, sir, you would prefer wine?"

"Much obliged, madam, but water will do. Best for this weather, madam."

While the water was being brought he sat down near the door and waited patiently, without deigning to notice me, as if anything connected with his profession was farthest from his thoughts.

"Who is sick, madam?" he inquired, when he had replaced the empty goblet on Reuben's waiter.

"My son, sir," said mother, conducting him to my lounge. "I don't know that he is sick much, but he is feverish, and fever always frightens me."

"And very properly, madam, for it is a sure sign that something is wrong in the system. Should always be taken in hand at once."

He felt my pulse a long time, slipping his fingers up and down my wrist, as if he were playing the violin; then felt my forehead, touching it as he would a loaf of bread, to see if it were warm, and bade me put out my tongue. He put on his specs and bent over it, as if he were looking for a splinter, requesting mother to stand just a little out of the light, madam, and rubbing it with the end of his little finger, took off his spectacles triumphantly, and turning to mother said:

"There is no danger, madam; very slight fever; only a trifling disorder of the system. A good sized blue pill is all that I would recommend at present. If you have any blue mass in the house I will make it for you before I leave."

The box of *pil hydrarg* was accordingly brought, and a cup of flour, from which he soon produced a pellet the size of a robin's egg, which I was to swallow. There might be almost said to be only two medicines known to the physicians of eastern Carolina, so constantly are they required in their practice, and they are as certain to administer mercury or quinine as Dr. Sangrado, of Valladolid, was to let blood or give warm water. I certainly did not bless their mercurial predilections that morning, and saw the old doctor ride off with an earnest wish that he had a pill, as large as the conventional brick, to roll around his hat on his head.

He had hardly gotten out of sight when mother came to the couch with the pill in the hollow of one hand and a glass of water in the other.

"Here, son, try to swallow this. The doctor thinks it best that you should take it."

I sat upon the side of the bed, asked for a bucket, in case of accidents, and took the pill in my hand. I found it soft, and sticky as putty, but with reckless desperation I laid it far back on my tongue, and took a great gulp of water. With a toss of my head I made a tremendous swallow, but a wad of air, many times larger than my mouth, got before the water and barred its progress down. Most of it got into my windpipe; the pill, with the flour coating washed off, and its nauseous taste revealed, rolled down against my front teeth and stuck there. Shades of Epicurus! how I heaved! Tearing it away from my teeth with my fingers I dashed it down, and vowed that no doctor's authority could ever compel me to the attempt again.

Whether the very taste of the pill had a good effect or not, that evening I was much better, and next morning felt perfectly well.

As it was the Sabbath, I was anxious to go to church with mother, Frank and Ned, but mother feared for me to take the sultry ride, and so I was to stay at home. To my surprise Carlotta asked leave to stay at home also, though she removed the flattering unction I had laid to my heart, that she staid to be with me, by telling mother she wished to spend the morning in her room. After breakfast the carriage came round, and mother, Ned and Frank, left for the church, which was a little country appointment, about four miles distant.

As soon as they were gone Carlotta went to her room, and, taking a book, I went out doors and lay down on the grass, beneath a large cedar at one end of the house.

There are four kinds of days in the year, coming one in each season, on which I feel an unaccountable, though not unpleasant melancholy. Days when I want to get far away to myself, and muse in undisturbed loneliness. Days when Memory, not Fancy, holds her court, and scenes and faces long forgotten spring up from her dusty sepulchres, and throng her shrine and ask for tears. Days that make a prison of the Present, a worthless bauble of the Future, and lift only to our heart's embrace the golden Past, gone from life forever! Brighter than it ever really was, its pains forgotten, only its joys remembered! Like a dead friend, it is dearer now than ever, and we weep because we cannot turn life's current back.

One of these days comes in winter, when, after a cloudy morning and noon, the sun sets cold and clear; when the wind with a hollow moan sweeps over the bare fields; when the long lines of wild ducks, clearly defined against the red sky, wind their way up the bends of the river, along whose banks the naked trees stretch their arms like the masts and yards of weird ships; when the blue birds, with their plaintive notes, huddle in the clumps of withered leaves on the oaks in the grove, and the very cows, plodding homeward, low mournfully, as if in response to Nature's dreariness.

Another day is in Autumn, when Nature, wrapping herself in a hazy robe, seems to lift her hand and say, "Hush, do not break my slumber," as she dozes into dreaminess. The sun himself half closes his glaring eye, and looks upon the world with a drowsy smile, and the purple sky droops upon the horizon as if Atlas were weary of his load. When the zephyrs are asleep, and the leaves on the trees are wan for want of exercise; when the crowing of the cock sounds like a yawn, and the little fly-catcher, perched, as is its custom, on a dead and leafless limb, breathes its one little song as if it was its last sigh. Such a day as Buchanan Read describes in his "Closing Scene;" the most exquisite verses ever penned by an American:

"All sights seemed mellowed and all sounds subdued,
The hills seemed farther, and the streams sang low,
As in a dream the distant woodman hewed
His winter log, with many a muffled blow.

"On slumbrous wings the vulture held his flight,
The dove scarce heard its sighing mate's complaint;
And like a star, slow drowning in the light,
The village church vane seemed to pale and faint.

"Alone from out the stubble piped the quail,
And croaked the crow through all the dreary gloom;
Alone the pheasant, drumming in the vale,
Made echo to the distant cottage loom."

Another day for reverie is such a day as this—a summer Sabbath in the country. Sabbath is stamped on the entire premises. The negroes, bedecked in all the finery of ribbons and beads, have just trooped in long droves through the gate and gone to preaching. Down at the quarters there is one old negro sitting at the door of her cabin, with her head bowed down to her knees as she ties around it her broad yellow kerchief. Her slight motion as she does this, and the faint monotonous wail of an infant left in her care, are all the evidences of life in the long row of tenements.

The horses and mules all walk solemnly about in the clover lot, and the sheep graze under the trees in the orchard, without a bleat to disturb the serene quiet of the morning. Tiger, the great bull-dog, is lying stretched out at the door of his kennel, watching with his small bleared eyes a hen and brood that are scratching fearlessly almost in his jaws. A mocking bird, down at the old graveyard, is alone forgetful of the day, and, perched upon the very topmost bough of the willow, is burdening the air with the joyous trills of his melody.

Overhead the great blue ocean of the sky is dotted here and there with fantastic white clouds, melting into various shapes as they grandly sail across its depths.

Propping my head with my hand, I lay and gazed up at the sky and around at the beauty of the day, and gave myself up to musing. Of course my mind turned to Lulie, and the terrible blight she had given my hopes, and, as the romance of my youthful mind intensified a thousand fold the nature of my disappointment, and my feelings were already made tender by the influences of the day, my heart could only find relief in tears, and turning my face over in the long cool grass I wept till I fell asleep. I had lain thus perhaps an hour, when a little bird, hopping in the branches overhead, rained down a shower of cedar balls upon me, and I raised up to find Carlotta standing by me. She started as I looked up, and said, without any embarrassment:

"I came out to the porch a few moments since, and saw you lying so still I was afraid you might be sick. Is there anything I can do for you?"

"No, thanks for your kindness, I do not need anything at all," I replied, raising myself from the grass; "but sit down here with me, I want to talk with you."

She hesitated a moment, then sat down near me.

"Day before yesterday, when you and mother were talking together in the hall, you thought me asleep," I said, after a pause of some seconds—a pause that is always awkward when you are expected to say something, and do not know what to say—"but I was not, and am now glad that I heard every word you both said."

Her face burned for a second, then became paler than before, as she exclaimed:

"Oh! why did you not speak, and stop my unkind and hasty words. Glad, did you say? how could you be glad to know that I had purposely shunned your presence, and shrunk from your most casual approach?"

"I was glad, because I had found the key to your conduct, and then knew why you had acted so coldly towards me, and refused so persistently the friendship I longed to offer. I was glad, because I knew then that the distance between us was not caused by enmity, but your sensitive nature."

Looking at me pleadingly with her eloquent eyes, and with a tremor in her soft voice, she said:

"Will you not appreciate my feelings, then, and forgive me?"

"I do appreciate your feelings," I said, with warmth, "and, appreciating them, have nothing to forgive. I have been pained that you seemed to mistrust me; that the love and devotion my brother's heart would fain have offered, was put aside, and that you wrapped yourself in such a robe of icy reserve; but I understand it all now, and you may trust me to use all my efforts to prevent the recurrence of any occasion that would cause you mortification or regret."

"Thank you, my kind brother, for your consideration of my feelings," she returned, warmly; "but let me add a word before we leave the subject: My annoyance has not been caused by the fact that your name, *as yours*, was coupled with mine, but that the very kindness of your family in taking me under their roof, is made, in the estimation of others, an obligation that places me at your disposal;" and the pride of her high-born soul burned in her glorious eyes, as she spoke.

"Well, we understand each other now," I said, soothingly, "and let us make this agreement—that whenever we are unobserved we will be trustful and confiding, as brother and sister should be, but when occasion demands we will be reserved and distant, without offence."

"I agree most cordially," she said, "and will henceforth place an implicit confidence in you as my truest friend."

She motioned as if to go, but it was so pleasant—something so new—to converse with her, to watch the play of her beautiful features, to catch the light of her great dark eyes, as she looked into my face as if to see my words, that I strove to detain her.

"Do not leave me yet, Carlotta. My heart is very sad today. Will you let me unburden it to you? It seems silly, I know, but I do so long to have some one to confide in; some one I can trust as I can you."

"You may trust me, John," she said, hesitating as she called my name for the first time.

After a pause, I said, biting a blade of grass with my lips—

"I had been weeping, Carlotta, when you came to me—weeping because the beautiful day made me sad."

"You sad? you weeping? you, who are so full of life and gaiety!" she said, looking at me with surprise; then adding, in a tone of deep sadness, as she thought of herself, "alas! what cause can *you* have for tears, in such a happy home, surrounded by those you hold most dear."

"What better cause for tears than disappointed love? Carlotta, I have loved Lulie since I could remember, and if ever one life can be bound in another mine has been in her's, and yet she does not love me. From her own lips I have learned this bitter truth. I could bear up had I one gleam of hope; but all is dark, and far worse than the extinction of hope is the knowledge that she loves another. Oh, heaven! how it grinds me to the earth to feel that he, who is most unworthy, should receive her smiles; that a love I would give my life for is wasted on one who regards it as the trifle of a day."

I paused and looked gloomily up at the bright blue sky, where a fleecy Delos floated.

"I, too, think her love is wasted on Frank Paning," said Carlotta, as I looked again at her face. "He may admire her beauty, and no doubt feels flattered by her preference, but he does not love her as she thinks he does. It will be a sad day with her when she learns the truth."

"Yes," I replied, savagely; "she will then know what I feel."

"Do not speak harshly of her, John, for while she loves Frank Paning, yet I believe she esteems you more."

"But how can you speak for her feelings?" I asked, with a faint touch of a sneer in my tone.

"Because she has told me all," she replied coolly.

"A perjured little——"

"Hush!" she exclaimed, looking at me reprovingly. "Do not judge her too hastily. She only told me part; I inferred the rest. Her heart seemed as if it would break the night after you went fishing together, and, when I sought to know the cause of her grief, she would only say she had made you unhappy. Hers is a fond, true heart, and I only wish it were given away more worthily."

"But what do you know of Paning's sentiments?" I asked with some surprise. "Perhaps he may be very devoted to her."

"I have very good reasons for knowing," she said, with a peculiar smile; "but yonder are some of the negroes returning from church. I must go in and have dinner arranged before the carriage returns."

She went into the house and left me wondering what she could mean. Can she love him, too, I thought, and is it because she herself has his heart that she knows Lulie has it not?

I began to grow desperate with the thought of my rival's second conquest, when the sound of the carriage diverted my attention, and mother, Frank and Ned came into the house.

"Oh, you needn't have dinner for us," said Frank to Carlotta, as he drew a glass of ice-water for himself, and drank it. "We have already dined sumptuously."

Mother nodded her head as Carlotta looked at her inquiringly. "Yes, my dear, we've had dinner. Mrs. Bemby invited us to her table, and of course we could not refuse."

"How did you like the sermon, Ned, and what kind of people were there?" I asked. "Tell me all about it."

"The sermon was very good in its way," said Ned, "and the people somewhat amusing; but you must get Frank to give you full details. I could not do the subject justice."

I could do nothing else but ask Frank for the narration, though I was not particularly anxious to hear his voice.

"Well," replied Frank, nothing loth to do the talking, "long before we got to the church we began to pass crowds of people who were walking thither; the men dressed in long sack coats of homespun, with immensely loose pants and dusty shoes, most of them carrying in their arms bare-legged, white-headed babies, who were employed in looking backwards over their fathers' shoulders, and mostly gnawing very large fat biscuits; the women were arrayed in bright flowered calico robes, which they kicked up behind at every step. They all had stick tooth brushes in their mouths, and long-tailed fly bonnets, which they carried in their hands. Then we passed others who, a little better off, were riding in red painted wagons, drawn by rope-harnessed mules, which trotted along so briskly, under the kindly influences of overgrown boys and hickory sticks, that the folks in the body were jolted from side to side of their split bottomed chairs. Then we overtook the cumbrous carriages of the well-to-do farmers, with heavy-headed, clumsy-footed horses, the low boots full of fodder, and large trunks full of dinner, strapped on behind. As many of these and other vehicles as we passed, yet when we got to the church we found the grove full of horses, buggies, carriages and wagons, and so many people out doors that I began to fear the preacher would have no congregation.

"At the foot of every tree in sight was a group of men engaged in the solemn occupation of whittling twigs and spitting. When we got to the door of the church, which was a large barn-looking structure, we found it full, and with difficulty got seats near the door. Such a mixture of people I never saw before. Here a silk by the side of cotton check, a broadcloth coat touching a copperas striped one, and a silk hat resting in the window with one of wheat straw, bound with green ribbon. As I could see very little but the backs of the people's heads, I cannot tell much about the congregation, except that the men for the most part had very long and very dry hair, which they wore bushy, while the women had theirs plaited in two strings and crossed like wicker-basket handles. The girls wore straw hats trimmed with ribbons, whose colors were of the rainbow that we may imagine would appear on a cloudy day. The elderly ladies wore bonnets that looked as if Noah's wife had made them for pastime while she was in the ark, and had fitted them on the goat's head for the want of a better block. The preacher himself was queer looking, and had a monotonous drawling tone." (Here Frank got up in the floor to imitate his style.) "Ah! my brethren and sistern-er, where are we to-day? 'Ere we are in the narrer road.'"

"Tut, tut, Frank," said mother, quickly, "that will never do. Jest about the people if you want to, but remember the sanctity of the pulpit."

"But it does not matter, Mrs. Smith, if we have a little fun at their expense; they don't belong to our church, and he wasn't preaching to us."

"It makes no difference," said mother, rising to go down to the dining room; "he was preaching the Gospel of Christ, and, however defective his sermon, we should not ridicule it."

"I'll show some other time," said Frank, as mother left the room. "But where was I? Oh, the preacher. Well, when the sermon was finished we all went out, and Mrs. Ben or Bem something soon found us, and insisted that we should eat with her.

"All over the grove the white cloths were being spread like gigantic snow flakes, and almost as numerous. Scores of negroes and ladies were unpacking great boxes, containing biscuit, rolls, cakes, ham, fowls, pickles, apples and peaches, and everybody was asking everybody else to dine with them. There was a good sized crowd at Mrs. Bemby's table when we went up. They were not introduced, but they all made us room, and bowed confusedly. Mrs. Smith knew and spoke to several of them while we took our part out in staring.

"Mrs. Bemby begged us to help ourselves, and every one acted on her kind suggestion with quite a zest. Country belles, pulling off their cotton gloves, alternated the bites at chicken and bread so rapidly and successfully that they were soon sucking the bones like candy, while the beaux cut symmetrical squares out of corn bread sandwiches, and played the flute on long ears of roasted corn, with unctuous smiles and impeded attempts at conversation with chewed words. Mr. and Mrs. B—— did not eat anything, but served the table, with cordial entreaties to all to spare not; Mrs. B—— distributing the bread and sweetmeats with a lavish hand, and Mr. B—— cutting the meats—his mode of dealing with a ham being very unique as well as effective. Standing it up on one end, and holding the hock in one hand, he sawed the knife across it like an Italian playing the fiddle, producing far more satisfactory results, however, than all the army of diminutive violinists Italy has sent forth. That great gawk of a Ben, instead of helping was perched on a wagon, idly kicking the wheels with his feet as he munched on an apple, and gravely winking at Ned and myself, in acknowledgment of acquaintance. Altogether the dinner was excellent, and, after our ride to the church, and our boredom in it, was particularly relished. There, I have talked enough; get Ned to tell you the balance."

"There is no more to tell," said Ned, as mother called to us from the basement to come down and eat watermelons. "I can corroborate all that Frank has told, except his account of the sermon. That was very good, and much to the point, though it was plain and without ornament."

I went down with the rest, but was afraid, for my fever's sake, to indulge in melons. If you would know whether it was any temptation to me or not, imagine a sultry afternoon, a cool breezy basement, four or five large melons, just from the ice house, like a row of victims with a knife in each pink frozen heart!

I felt tired of hearing them talk and seeing them eat, so I took my hat and strolled down to Mr. Bemby's to find Ben, and enjoy a talk with him. He was nowhere in sight, and I tapped at the door. At Mrs. Bemby's "Come in!" I opened the door, and instead of Ben found three strange ladies, who were discussing with profound interest the events of the day.

"Come in, honey; you look mighty feeble yet; how do you feel to-day?" said Mrs. Bemby, kindly, as she met me. "This is Col. Smith's son, Mrs. Bailey and Miss Viney Dodge; Col. Smith's son! Mrs. Dodge," she shouted in the ear of the oldest and most withered of the three ladies, who was armed with an orchestra looking instrument in the shape of an immense ear trumpet. Mrs. Bemby had to put her mouth right down to the opening, and shout my name out twice before she and I became acquainted. I shook hands with the old and bowed to the young lady, who gave me a curtesy in return that shoved her chair back almost out of range of her reseating figure. Her figure was very stumpy; her complexion very sallow; her hair very sandy, and her skin very freckled. Her hands were covered with half fingered blue gloves, and were employed, one in lying in her lap, the fingers folded and the thumb stiffly erect, as a sentinel over their repose; the other in holding, in as compressed a ball as possible, a dingy cotton handkerchief, which she constantly used, after a premonitory snuffle, by rubbing her nose very hard upwards, as if she wished to elevate its depressed point.

Mrs. B— — informed me that Ben would be in shortly, and I took the chair she offered and looked at the visitors; they looked at each other, and then there was a silence of some seconds.

"You beedn sorter poorly, haidn't you?" said Mrs. Dodge, adjusting her trumpet and leaning towards me.

"Yes, ma'am!" I shouted, making my reply more affirmative by a number of up and down motions of my head.

"Umphum! Haidn't had the summer complaint, is you? You look a little thidn."

I transversed the motion of my head very rapidly, and signed the negative many times.

"A leetle lodomy, drapped in ellum bark tea's mighty good for it;" and the old lady, satisfied with her catechism, turned her trumpet and her interrogative features toward the others.

Mrs. Bemby remarked having seen mother and the others at church that morning. Mrs. Bailey then took up the thread of the discourse where I had broken it off by entering.

"As I was a saying, sister Bemby," she resumed, "it does me a sight of good to listen to Brother Weekly's preaching. He is so searchin' to the sinners and comfortin' to the saints. His sermins are well pinted, too, and not writ, neither. I jist know in my soul, d'liver me from a writ sermin."

"Umph?" said Mrs. Dodge, in a prolonged note of inquiry, levelling her dread instrument on the speaker. Mrs. Bailey very kindly screamed the words into her ear.

"Ah, yes, I knowed 'twas good this mordn-ing, tho' I couldn't hear, for I sorter felt it. Brother Weekly is always powerful in his lastly, and whedn I see old Udncle Jacob Sawney slap Sister Brewer in the back, and old Miss Parkidns twiss her cheer roudn to the wall, and git my Viney here to untie her specks, so she could rub her eyes, I knowed he was a having great freedobm; and thedn he got a leetle louder, and I thought I heerd him say: 'He'll meet us at the gate, Hisself;' and somethidng told me in my heart he meadnt the Lord, and I wadnted to go just thedn, for 'pears to me I'd be more welcome like ef He told me to come in."

"Yes," resumed Mrs. Bailey, without noticing her interruption; "and did you notice, Sister Bemby, how he brought it out about the tares and the wheat. Seems to me, if I was a sinner I couldn't bear the thought of being sifted out and throwed away like a no 'count cockle grain."

"That was uncommon clear, Sister Bailey," returned Mrs. Bemby, "about putting in the sickle and reaping all together, then sortin' out the good and bad."

"That it was, Sister Bemby," agreed Mrs. Bailey, making a spade out of her tooth brush, and spading up half an ounce of snuff into her mouth.

There was another pause, and I looked uneasily out of the window, to see if I could discover anything of Ben, while Miss Viney rubbed her nose up again, and shot invisible marbles with the idle thumb in her lap.

Deaf old Mrs. Dodge again spoke:

"It's a mighty cobmfort, Sister Bemby, to have odne's chilldn a growin' up right. There's my Viney, she's been a perfesser nigh upodn five year, and haidn't backslid yit. Why dodn't you talk to Ben, Sister Bemby? He's a clever 'nough boy, but he's so mischeevous. Sedce I lost my hearidn I look 'round some in church, and no longer'n this mordning I see Ben holding up a streaked lizzard by the tail, fixing to put him on old Miss Judy Yates, who's the feardest of 'em in the world. Brother Bemby seed him jist in time to stop him."

"I know it, Sister Dodge," shouted Mrs. Bemby in the trumpet's mouth, "and I have talked to him a heap of times, but Ben says he ain't a going to die soon, and that he'll be a preacher yet, and he makes me laugh so I have to let him alone."

"Is you a lover of the Lord, sir?" Mrs. Dodge inquired, pointedly addressing me.

"I am afraid not as I ought to be," I said, confusedly, shaking my head.

"Well, you ought to love Him with all your heart whedn you think what He's dodne fur you."

I bowed an acknowledgment of the truth of her remark, and told Mrs. Bemby I would go out and look for Ben.

Not finding him anywhere I turned homeward, thinking on the glorious Gospel of the Son of God—a Gospel that, with the same words, can comfort sister Bailey's simple heart, and bind up one bruised beneath a velvet robe—a Gospel for all the world! deep enough to baffle the sage—simple enough to save a child. God alone can be its Author!

Go to the rustic church, with its rude unpainted seats, its plain deal pulpit, with a pitcher of water and a cloth covered Bible on the unvarnished slab. Sit with the simple, illiterate congregation, and listen to the unpolished man in the pulpit as, with an effort, he slowly reads his text: "For God so loved the world that He gave His only begotten Son, that whosoever believeth in Him should not perish but have eternal life."

Hear the story of the Cross told without rhetoric, and mark the faces around you, how they glow with faith and shine with tears.

Then let us stand on the broad stone steps beneath the clanging chimes and gilded spire. See the white-gloved drivers curb the prancing steeds— the liveried footmen hold the blazoned door, while silken trains sweep down the carriage step and rustle up the aisle. Let us go in and stand in the purpled gloom of the soft stained light. The golden legend over the chancel is illegible in the darkness, and only the bright figures on the windows up in the vaulted roof show that the glorious sunlight is over the earth. The tufted aisles make no echo to the footsteps, and the only sound is the occasional closing of a pew door by the silent ushers. The cushioned seats are filled, the gas jets around the preacher's stand are lit, and all is so hushed we almost expect the sermon to be whispered, when, with a trembling sob, as if its very pipes were sinful, the organ's wail of penitence is heard. Moaning and groaning at the very bottom of its voice, it grows louder and higher, till its weird minor strains peal through the church, as if its windy heart will burst, and still higher and higher it screams and shrieks, in its agony of remorse, then, with a galop down the scale, it breaks out into a lively polka of forgiveness, and is as happy as an organ can be, till its jig-and-break-down *repertoire* is exhausted, when it stands on one leg of a note and waits for the singing. A low, soft trill, like a mocking bird's song at night, breaks forth from we know not where, and its quivering melody fills the vast edifice; but ere we have discovered its source or meaning it is joined by another sound—a high zooning tone—like a bee far up in the air. This follows the first through all its wonderful manœuvres, and a faint conception begins to dawn on us that perhaps a song is intended. This idea is entertained for a few seconds, when it is forever put to flight by the sudden, sonorous bellowing of a bull over its slaughtered kindred, and while its terrible tones are thundering from the floor to the roof, we find that it, too, is following the others, and adding its powerful roar to their melody. But surprises are not over yet, for just as the three get fairly under way, they are quickly joined by a bronchial cat, unusually hoarse, that also takes after the others, though on a lower key and in strange fuzzy tones. This zoological *vocale* is persevered in by the four till, at last, they approximate a tune. We have some light thrown on the subject from the remark of a gentleman with an eye-glass to a lady with diamonds sitting just in front of us:

"Trilla's soprano is better to-day in *Te Deum* than 'twas last evening in *Trovatore*, but Catta's contralto is horrid." "Taurini's bass is magnificent, though, isn't it?" the young fop adds in a whisper, as, with a long orchestral flourish, the organ ceases to play and the services commence. Worshipping God by proxy! Because Taurini has a richer, better voice, and can say "We praise Thee, oh! God" in a deeper tone than we, we pay him to say it in our most holy place, careless whether an oath were last on his lips, or an early bar-room his only preparation for the Sabbath. But all is so different from the little wooden church, that we almost feel that they are serving another God with a different religion. We feel out of place and disappointed, and are about to leave, when the preacher ascends the pulpit and announces his text:

"For God so loved the world that He gave His only begotten Son, that whosoever believeth in Him should not perish but have eternal life."

We are at home now; the same verse that has brought tears from the simple minded, carries conviction to the heart of the rich and the wise. Though the service in its appointments may be fanciful—though the sermon be burdened with rhetorical roses, or ridiculous in rustic exposition, or flagrant misconstruction—Christ's words stand forth with the same grandeur of simplicity and force as they did when the trembling, conscience-convicted Sanhedrimite sought Him in the darkness, and received the light of God.

CHAPTER XVIII

The first of October found us all again in Wilmington. Father returned from Havana the latter part of September, having completed all the necessary arrangements in reference to Carlotta's property. He found the agent reliable, and having proved the death and identity of Mr. Rurleston, he administered on the estate, and qualified as guardian for Carlotta under the Spanish law.

Ned and I began the winter in hard study, as our last session in a preparatory school. Frank, however, declared his intention of going to Chapel Hill, the seat of the University of North Carolina, in January, and joining the Freshman Class, half advanced, getting the advantage of a year's start by the half session.

Sure enough, in January he left for the Hill, and we soon received letters from him telling of the wonderful charms of college life, and of the rapid progress he was making in his studies.

The spring passed and Frank came home a Sophomore. Ned and I felt quite tame before him, though his foppish ways and overbearing air only added to the dislike I entertained for him.

Lulie, poor thing, was as proud of him as if he had been her son, and whenever we met was continually quoting what Frank said, and telling what Frank did. In the kindness of her dear little heart she ever tried to consider my feelings, and it was the inadvertence of these remarks in my presence that made them doubly painful.

Between Carlotta and myself there had sprung up a strong, confidential friendship. She was so beautiful in person and character, so pure, so trusting, that had it not have been for our daily intimacy, I could have loved her even to the effacing of Lulie's image. As it was, she was only my best friend, and Lulie my hopeless idol.

A trip to Smithville closed our vacation, and we began to get ready for college. All the arrangements were made, and the day before our departure came round. Ned, who, of course, was to be my chum, had come into town with his baggage, and was to stay all night with me, to be ready for the early morning train. That night, after tea, he ran over to Dr. Mayland's to tell Lulie good-bye, and Carlotta and I took our seat on the stoop. Neither of us spoke for some time, for I felt really sad now that the time had come for parting.

"You will write to me while I am gone, Carlotta?" I said, at length. "I will enjoy a letter from you more than from any one else I know."

"Yes," she said, smiling. "I will write if you will promise to reply faithfully, and not to make fun of my letters."

"That would be impossible, even if I were not too anxious to hear from home and from you. I will miss your bright face and sunny smiles sadly while I am away," I continued, looking up at the stars slowly coming out, "for no matter where I am, or whom I am with, I never feel so well satisfied and happy as when I am with you."

"It is I, indeed, who will miss you," she said, with the least possible sigh, "for you have been so kind and attentive, so considerate of all my wishes, yet so unobtrusive in your attentions, that I can never get another to fill your place."

"You will not forget me, then?" I said, drawing a little nearer to her.

"Never!"

She looked so beautiful in the soft twilight, as she gazed at me earnestly and said this "Never!" that I did more than I intended—I took her hand and pressed it in mine, though I tried to do it in a brotherly way. But there was a thrill in her touch, nevertheless. I could see her face flush, even in the twilight, as she drew her hand once or twice, as if she would take it away.

"Carlotta," I said, still holding her hand, "I have told you how I once loved Lulie——"

"And there she is now," she said, quickly withdrawing her hand, then putting it back in mine, as if it was nothing to be ashamed of.

Sure enough, Lulie, Frank and Ned crossed over from Dr. Mayland's and approached our stoop.

"John, I have come over to say good-bye, as you would not come to see me," said Lulie, seating herself at Carlotta's feet.

"'Twas because I thought you would, of course, be engaged for to-night, not because I did not want to," I replied, in a tone divided between a sneer and a smile.

"You know I am always glad to see you, John," she said, rising again to her feet; "but we have not long to stay, Frank, and had better go now, as he is so ungracious, even on the eve of parting."

"Pardon me, Lulie," I said, her words recalling me to a sense of propriety. "Do not let us part in bad humor."

"Certainly not," she replied; "but," changing the subject, "do you not dread the ordeal of initiation? Frank says, though, he will not let the fellows, as he calls them, trouble you much."

"We are obliged to Frank for his kind intentions, but hope to be able to take care of ourselves," I replied, my ungracious feelings returning reinforced.

"I've a great notion to let you fellows alone, and let our class have its own way with you," said Frank, tapping the railing with a little gold headed switch he called a cane.

I had it on my tongue to tell him that I wished he would, but I restrained myself, and only said that I hoped we could stand it.

Lulie gave me her hand most cordially, and bade us both farewell, and she and Frank walked away—she looking up at him and talking to him as if her life was his, and he walking on as if only a toy hung upon his arm.

Father returned from down town, and, requesting my presence in the library, I left Ned with Carlotta and went in the house. Father was seated at his *escritoire* and motioned me to a chair near him. "As you leave very early in the morning," he said, through his teeth, holding between them one end of a tape he was tying around a bundle of papers he had assorted, "I thought we had best arrange our money matters to-night."

He took a roll of bank bills from a drawer, and, counting out a goodly heap, pushed it towards me, saying, "That will be enough for all your expenses till late in the session. Whenever you find you need more, write and I will remit. I do not want you to be extravagant, my son, neither do I want you to be a niggard; I will, however, trust to your own good sense to regulate your expenditure."

I folded the money up, and, putting it in my purse, was about to leave, when he closed the desk, and, jingling the keys into his pockets, said:

"Sit down a moment, John, I want to say a few words to you in reference to your conduct while you are away. I am sure your mother has instructed you thoroughly in your Christian duty, and, therefore, I do not fear that I shall ever be mortified by a letter confessing debauch and dissipation. I trust that your early training, with your own sense of propriety, will deter you from anything so ruinous; but I have a word or two of advice in regard to your deportment towards your fellow students and to your instructors. I have been at college myself and know something of what I say. You will, of course, be teased, or 'devilled,' as they term it, unmercifully. Every conceivable effort will be made to mortify you, and to present you in most ridiculous attitudes, and every one in the class above you will try his wits at your expense. You will be made the victim of many a practical joke, and will suffer frequent inconvenience from the temporary abstraction of your books or the derangement of your furniture. Bear every thing with quiet dignity, do not attempt to reply to anything that is said, and, if possible, keep from showing in the slightest way that you are teased. If their efforts are without success they will soon desist, and you will be unmolested. It is a most contemptible and barbarous practice, this striving to wound and crush the feelings of another, simply because he is a stranger, as if that fact alone did not entitle him to more consideration. I hope, John, that when you join this privileged class of persecutors you will never indulge in anything so unfeeling.

"To recommend care in the selection of your associates is a piece of advice as important as it is trite. Associates will be forced upon you by the location of your room, by your class and your boarding house. Look well to a student's moral and social status before you take him as a companion. Do not feel flattered into any concessions of your principles by an intimacy with a member of a higher class. While a Fresh, you would feel quite honored by an invitation to the room of a Senior, and you would find it very hard to refuse a drink with him, lest you should appear squeamish in his eyes. But remember that advancement is only a question of time and study, and possess independence enough to refuse all solicitations to evil, however flattering to your vanity they be. Ned, I am glad to learn, will room with you, and he and your books will be society enough for you, if you study as *you* now think, and *I* hope you will.

"In regard to your deportment towards your tutors I have a word to say, and then I have done my rather tedious exhortation. Be polite and dignified in their presence, be attentive in the lecture room, but not ostentatiously so, making a pretence of continually gazing at the professor, being the first to answer fly questions, or selecting a seat very near his desk, as there is nothing more displeasing to him than the endeavor of a student to make up for lack of merit by sycophantic fawning. While it is well to establish a personal acquaintance and good understanding with all those under whose instruction you are placed, yet do not make a display of intimacy with them, as the reputation of a 'boot-lick' is easily earned, and is exceedingly odious. The most disagreeable temptation to which you will be exposed is to join rebellion against college authority. You will be continually solicited to aid in schemes to break the laws of the institution, to annoy the professors, and to deface and misplace college property. Every conceivable plan for the defeat of the very objects of the institution will be set on foot, and you will be scoffed at and ridiculed if you refuse to join. Will you have the moral courage to refuse in the face of a jeering class? I hope so, my son. You will find it easy after the first time or two, and you will be respected all the more for your firmness. Write to your mother and myself often, and write freely. Tell us of your trials and difficulties, and express all your feelings without hesitation. But, lest my much advice may seem to evince a doubt of your strength of character, I will cease. Let's go to Carlotta and Ned."

He lowered the gas, and as we walked out of the library laid his arm on my shoulder in a tender way, that I have never forgotten—for a caress was a novelty from him.

That night, as Ned and I were about to go up to our rooms, I kissed mother good night, and said to her:

"Have you no parting advice for me, mother? I believe everybody has had some kind of valedictory for me."

She drew me to her and said, smiling, as she parted my hair with one hand:

"I have nothing special to say, John, even though you are going away from me for the first time. I have endeavored from your infancy to instruct you in your duty to your fellow man, as well as to God. It now only remains with you to perform that duty. The one great thing I have always striven to impress upon your mind is to act from principle. Whatever you propose to do, consider carefully whether it be in itself right—not whether the time or occasion renders it so. I have placed your Bible in your trunk; read it without fail once every day, and, as you have always done, seek counsel of Heaven; and if my poor prayers will avail anything, you will ever be fortified with grace and courage from on high."

In my room, as I undressed, I could not help looking around at the familiar articles of furniture, in order to remember exactly how the room looked after I was gone. Everything had a farewell for me.

The very bureau seemed to sigh as I took my toilet articles from its slab; and the chairs, with their worn rounds and knife-notched backs, seemed to creak an humble good-bye; the rug that I had scorched so often making squibs; the pitcher, whose lip I had broken by jerking it against a table, when a cat with a fit, on whose head I was pouring water, suddenly revived and sprang up under my hand; the book-case, through whose glass doors peeped the familiar faces of Swiss Family Robinson, Sandford and Merton, Tom Brown at Rugby, and the portentous covers of Latin Grammar, Greek Reader, Cæsar, Virgil and Sallust; the closet, with my gun and sporting furniture, and the bed, with its flowered coverlid, all looked as if they would be sad after I was gone, and as I went to sleep I felt prematurely homesick.

CHAPTER XIX

Father awoke us by coming into our room with the lamp and telling us that Horace was waiting with the carriage. We were up and dressed by the time William had carried down our trunks. We went down to the dining room, where the gas was burning with the sleepy glare it always has in the morning, as if it had just waked from a sound nap. I felt no appetite, but gulped down an egg, a bit of steak and some coffee, as if it were medicine. Horace sent in word that we had best hurry, as he had heard the engine blow for backing down some time ago. I slipped on my linen duster, pulled on one glove, told the servants good-bye with half a dollar each, pressed father's hand, received mother's fond embrace and fervent "God bless you, my child," and touched Carlotta's lips with a thrill the hurry could not damp, and Ned and I were rattling over the pavement to the depot. As soon as my eyes recovered from the glare of the gaslight I found that day had dawned and objects were plainly visible. The dwelling houses were all closed, except where an extra smart housemaid here and there had opened the shutters, and was sweeping off the steps. Nobody was astir in the streets yet except one or two butchers' carts, rattling on to the market house with their loads of beef. We rolled on down through the business part of the city, where sleepy porters, in their shirt sleeves, were taking down shutters and sprinkling and sweeping out the stores; on past the newspaper offices, where they were still working by gaslight, and where little newsboys were coming out with bundles of damp papers; on down Market street, past drowsy drays, with lazy negro drivers slapping the fat, sluggish horses with the ends of the reins; on, till we whirled round the corner at the river, where the chilly morning breeze was rippling the water and clicking the wavelets against the sides of the vessels and rafts that lay on the gray river, without other signs of life than a sailor leaning over the railing, dipping up water with his bucket and rope, or a negro cooking his breakfast at the door of his raft's cabin. The rigging, wet with mist, stretched like immense spider webs from yard to yard, and the jack, left out all night, drooped straight down the mast. How familiar is every log and piece of timber in the wharf! Every barrel and hogshead is an acquaintance, and every spot we pass the scene of some boyish frolic. Everybody that sees us bows and says good-bye, and we almost feel sure that the town will pass resolutions of regret at our departure.

We reach the train just in time, and find Frank already on board, with seats reserved for us. He is pleasant towards me, and seems to bear no ill feeling for my rudeness. Being a good talker, he enlivened the tedium of travel with accounts of college life, and gave us many valuable points in regard to our demeanor, instructing us how to "dodge devilling," and offering his assistance with as much conceit as kindness.

When we reached Raleigh, there was a delay of some minutes, and the train was soon crowded in the aisles with those getting out and those coming in. As we sat watching them Frank suddenly exclaimed, "Yonder's Carrover and Brazon, as I am a sinner!" and I saw two young men lounging up the aisle from the rear door. One of them filled my idea of what a senior ought to be. His beaver was tipped just a little on one side of a head covered with a profusion of rich brown curls, his face handsome, though pale, and ornamented with a dainty moustache and goatee; his form tall and graceful, and his dress very elegant but not foppish. He also carried a gold headed cane, larger and heavier than Frank's. His companion impressed me very disagreeably. He was short and thick of stature, with a bold, red face, staring pale blue eyes and a carrotty frizz of hair. He was dressed in very flashy style, and his linen was frowzy and rumpled. He greeted Frank with boisterous cordiality, and took the seat immediately behind us. The tall and elegant young man, I thought, greeted Frank very coolly, as if there was not much intimacy between them. He took a seat some distance off, and taking the *British Quarterly Review* from his travelling bag, was soon buried in its pages.

Brazon, as soon as there was a pause in Frank's conversation, leaned over and asked us politely how far up the road we were going.

"Only to Durham's station," I replied, feeling complimented by his notice.

"Then you are going to Chapel Hill?"

"Yes," I said, turning in my seat, so as to look at him; "you have been at college there, have you not?"

"Oh, yes," he replied, his pale eyes twinkling maliciously. "May I ask what class you intend to join?"

"The Fresh, I suppose, unless the professors——" but before I could finish the sentence he shouted in a loud tone: "Hello! Frank! here are a couple of Fresh, regular green ones, too. That's right," he said, addressing us, and patting me on the shoulder, "sit together on the same bench, like good little boys. Did mamma and papa tie you together, for fear you'd get lost? That's clever, my children, do as your pairients tell you and the devil will give you candy some day."

I was so taken by surprise at the sudden change in his tone from the polite to the jeering, that I sat with a burning face under his ridicule, while the car was shaking with the laughter of the passengers at our discomfiture, and never thought of resenting it. Frank, however, who had gone to the other end of the car to get some water, returned and saw the position of affairs. He caught Brazon by the arm, exclaiming:

"What the devil are you doing, Brazon? These gentlemen are particular friends of mine. You must have forgotten yourself."

"No I didn't, either. How could I know they were your friends when you said nothing about them? But since they are, I beg pardon. Introduce me and we will shake hands round and be friends."

It was with some hesitation I took his proffered hand; but I felt that it were best to make no enemies on my first entrance into college.

We all talked pleasantly together during the few minutes it took the train to reach Durham's, and, getting off there, found a number of hacks waiting to convey us to the Hill. There were many others going there, so we hastened to secure the best hack, and were soon jogging over that worst of roads. Carrover secured a seat in another vehicle, but gave it up to a lady and child, and took a place with us.

We stopped only once to cool out the horses, under some large trees by a well, when Carrover opened his travelling case, and taking out a silver flask offered it first to Ned and myself. We both declined, but I found that, in this my first temptation, it was difficult to refuse, so afraid was I of seeming boyish. The other three all complimented its contents by a plentiful inhibition, as the driver checked up his horses' heads and we resumed our journey.

When we reined up at the hotel we found the steps thronged with the Sophs, waiting for the hacks to bring in their victims. As soon as we got out we were surrounded by a score of them, all leering in our faces and yelling "Fresh! Fresh!" as if they had the article to sell.

With most impudent effrontery they gathered around us, each vieing with the others in casting ridicule upon us; nor were witty sallies alone the extent of their teasing; many of the coarsest personalities were indulged in. No one seemed to enjoy it much, and only an absurd sense of what was due a foolish college custom urged them on.

"Look what a big trunk," said one, striking my solitary piece of baggage with his cane hard enough to nearly blister the leather; "I'll bet he has homespun cake in there. Fresh, let me sleep with you," he continued, taking my arm, with every appearance of friendship, "but no, you are too dirty," releasing me with a gesture of disgust.

"Hoopee! what a foot!" said another, stooping down to take an exaggerated measurement of my foot. "Fresh, how do you get your boots on without a crane to lift your feet?"

"Well, Fresh," said a pert little fellow to Ned, "what is the price of tallow where you live? It ought to be very cheap if that is a sample in your face." As Ned was really very sallow this remark called forth a general laugh, during which we walked up the steps into the office, the crowd opening before and closing behind us in a continuous yell of ridicule and shame, heaped on us in every conceivable way.

Frank's friends all seemed glad to see him, but, even amid the storm of persecution that surrounded us, I could not help noticing that they all wore flash clothes, and had inflamed eyes and a profane swagger. Frank told us that it was out of his power to shield us from devilment in such a crowd, but that he would get us rooms for the night and we would be safe in them. He went in to see the proprietor and we were left standing in the midst of a deriding throng. 1 never felt so much like a culprit in my life. Nowhere could I look and find a single glance of sympathy. On every side were hoots, hisses and vulgar witticisms; and the attempt to utter a word was only the signal for such a roar as would drown every syllable. While standing thus, a tall, languid youth, with drooping side whiskers and a pair of gold eye-glasses, pushed his way through the crowd and asked, "What Fresh are these you have here? Introduce me." Some one shouted: "That is Mr. Danvers, Fresh; speak to him."

"How do you do, gentlemen? I am most happy to see you with us," said Danvers, offering his hand in the most cordial manner. Eager to touch somebody's hand that would sympathize, I extended mine gladly, but ere I touched his he drew it back with the sneer, "Oh, no, Fresh, you must wash yours first; you've been travelling, you know."

"Shame! shame! Danvers. A Junior devilling Fresh!" exclaimed several voices.

"I confess," said Danvers, turning off, laughing; "but it was such a good thing. They are greener than verdure itself, and will swallow anything you offer!"

Frank now came to us and said he had secured rooms, and that we could go up now if we wished. Of course we wished to do so, and once in, and the door locked, we gave vent to our feelings in no measured terms, both feeling assured that neither Huguenots nor Waldenses ever felt the bitterness of persecution as we did, and both wishing at heart that we were again at home.

We had scarcely bathed and gotten rid of the dust of travel when the gong sounded for supper. We went down and found the tables occupied entirely by the students, as there was little or no travel to such a retired village, from the outside world. A bevy of Sophomores rose on our appearance and escorted us to the table, and, drawing back our chairs, held them for us. Bewildered by their strange attentions, we attempted to seat ourselves, but, of course, found the chairs *non sub nobis*. I recovered myself, but Ned plumped heavily down upon the floor, to the boisterous merriment of the whole room.

At last seated, and served by the regular attendants, we attempted to eat, but every mouthful was declared enormous by those watching us, every action said to be ill mannered, and our whole demeanor so criticised that our appetites departed and we felt no desire for food. If we had, there would have been little opportunity for its gratification. If I chanced to turn my head, a teaspoonful of salt went into my tea. If I asked the waiter for a biscuit, my tormentor across the table would pour a dozen into my plate. Silver forks and napkin rings were dropped into my pockets, and the proprietor called to identify his property. When we rose we were escorted from the room by the same guard of honor, even to the door of our room, where they left us for the night.

Ned and I sat down on the side of our beds and looked out of the windows at the red evening sky, fast paling into twilight, and we felt dreary and lonely indeed. Frank was off with some of his friends, and we were afraid to venture out lest a renewal of purgatorial tortures should assail us. After awhile we could hear the noisy throng down stairs going away in twos and threes for their evening stroll, and, discovering from the window that they had all departed, I proposed to Ned that, as it was fast growing dark, we slip down stairs and take a stroll, as it was too sultry to remain in our room. As we came out into the hotel porch a lazy Senior, who was sitting with his feet on the railing, quietly smoking, with the enviable tranquillity of might, said to us—

"Ah, Fresh," as we went down the steps, "don't let the Sophs find you before you get back. Whenever you see a party of more than two approaching, cross over, for only the Sophs go in numbers."

We thanked him, and walked up the street to the very road by which we had come in. We turned into this, and walked on till we came to a small eminence overlooking a little landscape, and on this knoll we sat down to gaze on the scene and to condole with each other in our troubles.

The woods and plains below were bathed in the glorious light of the full orbed moon, which had risen, like a goddess of serenity, from the horizon. White night clouds floated lightly across her face, shaking off flakes of fleece into the blue sea around them.

"Ned," I said at length, "I look on the moon now as an old friend. It is the only familiar thing I can see, and I feel a positive affection for it."

"So do I," he replied, "and it seems doubly dear when I remember that, while it is beaming so placidly on us, it is also looking down upon the dear ones at home, and that, while we are so far apart, yet we can both gaze up at the same object, and imagine it a great mirror, in which each of us can see the others."

"Ah! 'home, sweet home!' I never knew the depth of meaning in the words before. I wonder what they all are doing there now. Would you not give a great deal just to drop in among them for a minute or two?"

"I would, indeed; but yonder come some of our tormentors. I think we had better turn back and meet them."

A half dozen or more students were approaching, laughing and talking loudly; and, judging from their tones and appearance that they were Sophs, we thought the best we could do would be to pass them, if possible, on the shaded side of the road, and, by an unconcerned air, to go by unnoticed. We had not got opposite before they detected us, and, with a shout of "Fresh! Fresh!" surrounded us. Every form of insult capable of conveyance by language was heaped upon us, yet so rapid and constant the stream that no one in particular could be selected on whom to resent it.

They turned back with us and impeded our progress by every conceivable means, thrusting their faces in front of ours, so that to advance would be to touch theirs; standing in front of us, so that we were compelled to go around them, and yelling with all their vociferous might into our ears the traditional Fresh song or chant, whose diabolical burden is the harsh and brutish bellowing (with a leader and a chorus) of these syllables: "Toot, toot, toot-tat-toot. Ba-a-a-h!" We had returned nearly to the hotel in this undignified manner, the throng of persecutors gathering strength as we entered the streets, till we were completely surrounded—those in front walking backwards, and stopping every now and then suddenly, that we might be jostled against by those who were thronging behind, all bellowing the pandemoniacal chorus, without words and still less tune. Sedate professors looked gravely at the noisy procession, as it successively passed their gates, and made a pretence of trying to recognize the offenders in the moonlight; young ladies came to their doors and laughed, as we marched by like culprits; and even negroes stopped in the streets to gaze and snicker at our predicament. I was choking with rage and indignation, but did not well know how to help myself. Ned, usually so quiet, was, I could see, terribly roused, and his prudence was fast yielding to his wrath. As we approached the hotel he could contain himself no longer, but, stopping short and taking advantage of the momentary lull, said:

"A foolish custom gives you the right to tease and worry me inside of college bounds, and I am willing to bear my part there, but I deny that right in the public streets, and shall treat all further molestation as an insult. Let me pass, sir!"

This last remark was addressed to a coarse, burly fellow, who was standing immediately in front of Ned, with his eyes open very wide, as if in wonder. As Ned ceased speaking he thrust his great red face right into Ned's with a derisive laugh. The next instant the blood was gushing from his nose, as Ned struck him with all his might in the face. This was the signal for a general *melee*. I had hardly time to spring forward and ward off a blow from Ned's head when a cane fell heavily on my own, making the whole place dance around with me, and increasing my sphere of stellar observation wonderfully. I made out to grapple with the nearest adversary, while Ned went down under twice his weight. The fencing saved me from a similar fate, and I had almost succeeded in turning my antagonist under, when the cry of "Faculty! Faculty!" was raised, and, as if by magic, every student fled, leaving Ned and me to claim the honors of the field, if the couple of tall gentlemen in dark clothes that were now seen approaching were disposed to accord us any.

"Ned, are you hurt much?" I inquired anxiously, assisting him to rise.

"No; are you?" he replied.

"No, only a little thump on the head; but yonder are some of the Faculty coming, and, if we do not wish to be involved in a long trial, we'd better run."

"I am surprised at you, John. Run! what for? I should act precisely the same way under the same circumstances again."

The two figures we had seen had come up to us by this time, and proved to be only a couple of students, members of the Senior class, and one of whom I recognized as Mr. Carrover, my travelling acquaintance.

"What's the row?" he said, looking at us inquiringly, as we were brushing the dust from our clothes. "Oh, I see, Sophs devilling you and you resisted; right, too. They have no privileges beyond the campus. Come, go back with us, we will see that you are not molested further to-night."

We were about to proceed to the hotel, when Carrover's companion spoke, for the first time, with a soft, rich voice:

"Charlie, you forget me. I shall have to introduce myself. DeVare is my name——"

"DeVare, I beg your pardon," said Carrover, hastily, "let me introduce you to Mr. Cheyleigh, of Wilmington, and Mr. Smith, of the same place."

"I am very happy to know you both," he said pleasantly, offering his hand, "any assistance Charlie or myself can give you in dodging the Sophs will be cheerfully rendered."

We thanked him, and brushing the dust of conflict from our clothes with our handkerchiefs, walked back with them to the hotel. The porch steps were thronged with students talking about our difficulty.

"The scamps showed fight, did they," said one, as we approached; "that's too high for Fresh—they must be taken down."

"Yes," echoed another, "a good smoke will bring 'em 'round ."

"How came they to fight? Was anybody hurt?" asked another.

"Why, we were just devilling them a little," said the first speaker, when one of 'em asked Burly to let him pass, as if he were the Sultan, and, because Burly didn't make his obeisance, put a smasher on his nose. Ellerton tapped one a little with his cane, and I was choking the one that hit Burly, but the mutton-headed Faculty broke us up."

We had reached the steps by this time, and passed through the crowd without molestation. Carrover turned when he got in the porch and said, addressing the students:

"It was mean enough to devil Fresh in the streets, without a dozen of you trying to beat two. If anything further is attempted to-night DeVare and myself will remain with them and help them to defend themselves."

"Whoo-ee," shouted a half dozen voices, "that won't do, Carrover; too plain a bid. Drum for your club more secretly."

We only noticed that this sally rather confused Carrover, when, thinking it prudent to withdraw, we slipped off to our room unnoticed, and locked and bolted the door. We lit our lamps and examined the results of our struggle. A little knot on my head, and a torn collar on Ned's part, completed our list of casualties. Summing up the events of the day, we came to the conclusion that college life was not such a very fine thing after all, and that John Howard Payne was extremely sensible when he wrote

"There's no place like home."

CHAPTER XX

Our second day was spent in the ordeal of examination, in the selection and arrangement of our room, and engaging board at the most eligible place. Our room, at the suggestion of Mr. Carrover, was chosen in the South Building, and after innumerable expenditures, and Ned's taste for arrangement, it really looked comfortable and home like. We passed the different departments of study without any serious difficulty, and the bell for evening prayers found us ready for the session's work.

We took a little stroll after tea, and were fortunate in meeting no one. Returning to our room and lighting up, we got our books and commenced to prepare, with all the interest of novelty, our lessons for the morrow. We had not been thus engaged more than half an hour when there arose in a distant part of the campus the most diabolical din conceivable: a fiendish combination of all the disagreeable noises produceable. Tin horns, tin pan drums, bells, whistles, paper trumpets, and the *vox humana* in its loudest, harshest notes, all roared forth their terrible discord on the still night air.

We leaned out of our window and listened to this caravan of horrid sounds approaching, till it entered the South Building. Even then we did not suspect its destination, and not till we heard the procession tramping noisily up the stairs leading to our room did the truth flash upon us that we were the intended victims. It was too late to fasten the door. In a moment the room was full of our tormentors, each one trying to drown the other's clamor by extra exertion on his own part. They formed a circle around us and beat, and blew, and shouted till we were deafened and stupefied with the noise.

Suddenly it ceased—everything was ominously still, and with sober face every one commenced active preparation for the more serious business of the evening. The door was closed and locked, the bed was stripped and the sheets hung up at the windows, with their edges stuffed in the cracks. Each then drew forth from his pocket an enormous pipe, and putting tobacco in it, began to smoke. Not the ordinary puffs of a pleasure whiff, but lighting about half a pipe full they would put more tobacco in on the fire, and instead of drawing, blow with all their might, ejecting from the bowl of the pipe a stream as large, and almost as solid as a man's wrist. As soon as I divined their object I got up and lay down across the bed, taking the pillow in my hand, that I might lay my face in it if it became very bad.

The great volumes of smoke, rolling up to the ceiling, now began to spread into a thickening vapor that filled the room, growing denser and denser every second, and I found myself constantly coughing. Another minute and the moving forms of the smokers could scarcely be seen, while the lamp standing on the mantel was only a dim halo in the white fog. The smokers now had to relieve each other, placing a guard at the door to prevent our exit. Thicker and thicker grew the cloud, till the lungs, wearied with incessant coughing, almost refused to inhale the bitter, sickening air. My eyes streaming with water closed themselves in spite of me, and my eyeballs were crossed with the nausea. I pressed my face down into the pillow for relief, but even that seemed a bag of tobacco, that was driving its dust into my throat. Every particle of air had its concomitant particle of smoke, and with every wretched gasp I gulped down a wad of poison.

A ton of weight seemed pressing on my chest, and my eyeballs almost started from my head in my intense efforts to feed my famished lungs, and to prevent the suffocation I was enduring. A few more gasps and a death-like sickness seized me; the smoke closed around my head like the band of the Inquisition, and pressed all consciousness and sensation out. With a blinding rush of darkness over my brain I fainted.

The first thing I knew as a fact of consciousness was a vague perception of the odor of camphor and brandy; then I knew that my hands were being violently chafed, and that something cold and wet lay on my forehead. My temples ached with a dull, unrelievable pain, and a deadly nausea seemed to pervade the very atmosphere. I opened my eyes and found that I was in a strange room, on a strange bed, around which were grouped half a dozen forms with anxious, fear-whitened faces. Some were holding bottles, some basins of water, and all intently watching my face for signs of returning consciousness. I swallowed a little of the brandy they held to my lips, and as it burnt its way through my system I found strength to speak. Sitting upon the side of the bed, with the support of two of those attending, I asked, in an idiotic way:

"What—are—you all doing here? Where—am—I?"

Their courage and effrontery revived as I revived, and their propensity for devilling returned as I returned to consciousness. There was a pause after I had spoken, and then a deep voice answered, in solemn tones:

"You are in hell! As soon as you can walk we will go down to the sulphur lake. Pyrophylax, see that the chains are candescent and send in a bowl of melted lead; he looks thirsty."

The utter confusion of ideas consequent upon my loss of consciousness, and the miserable feelings I was enduring, rendered this assertion not at all improbable to me, and I would not have been very much surprised to have seen the brazen gate flung open, and the aimless chasers of the giddy flag the great Guelph saw in his Inferno, racing around the arid sand. At this point, however, some one said that I had had enough for one time, and offered to show me the way back to my room. Supported by his arm I staggered along the hall to my own room, which had been deserted and opened, to allow the smoke to clear out. The door was open, the windows raised, and the breeze, like a kind housewife, had swept the smoke away, but its disgusting smell still clung to the curtains and the walls.

Poor Ned was lying on the bed in a profound sleep. His corpse-like paleness, however, showed how much he had suffered, and the bucket near the bed side bore testimony to his sickness. It would have been cruel to have aroused him, so I lay gently down beside him and slept till morning.

A sick headache next day, and an intense smell of tobacco clinging to everything tangible, alone told us of the night's scene, and it slipped back, with the ever passing pains and pleasures of life, into memory's great reservoir.

CHAPTER XXI

At last we were fairly inducted into college life, and commenced a regular routine of daily duties. Our room was pleasantly situated, and all our neighbors agreeable. As new victims continued to arrive we were forsaken by the Sophs, much to our delight, and were permitted to enjoy a good meal at the table unmolested.

Ned and I had formed as yet no circle of acquaintance. We were together nearly all the time, and having made up our minds, according to the invariable rule, to study harder than anybody ever did, we did not care much for the society of others. We both studied hard, and our progress in the various branches of instruction was, we thought, satisfactory. There was this difference between us, however—Ned studied uniformly, while I studied by impulse. The result was that while many of my daily lessons exceeded Ned's in preparation and recitation, yet his average was far greater than mine. Ned studied to learn *all* his lesson—to know every part of it; while I often picked over those points on which I thought I should most likely be examined. He studied to master the subject—to become acquainted with a language or to understand a problem; I studied to make a good recitation. He stored up for the future; I looked no farther ahead than the next morning's lecture.

I remember well, when we got to reading Homer, Ned would worry a whole morning over an idiom; and passages that I found no difficulty at all in rendering would afford him an hour's work with lexicon and grammar. I had a shorter way of doing things. I would take my Anthon's Edition— great friend of the student!—and, with the aid of its voluminous references, and the notes in Kühner, I would easily cram all that it was probable the professor would touch upon. Simple, easy parts, that I was sure he would not notice, had to take care of themselves. When we went in to recite, all the portions I had prepared so carefully were given to others to render or construe, while I would be taken up on some part I had thought too simple for my attention, and would be found woefully ignorant. So, about twice a month I would make a brilliant recitation, the balance of the time failures.

I suffered, too, from that great cheat of life, the self-promise to "turn over a new leaf." Regularly every Monday morning, in accordance with the previous week's resolve, I would start afresh, and, after tremendous application and intense mental effort, would go to the section room and pass the hour without being noticed. Leaving it without having had an opportunity to manifest my diligence, I would feel a little less careful about Tuesday's preparation. After another day of silence I would merely glance at Wednesday's lessons; and Thursday, with just a peep between the pages, I would be called to recite, and fail signally. The mortification would then evoke the firm resolve to "turn over a new leaf," but, inasmuch as the next day was Friday, I would conclude to wait till Monday. So Friday would go without study, and the next week would come and join the retreating line of its predecessors, and nothing would be accomplished but a slowly increasing indifference to failure, and a growing inability to reform. And in all my life since then there has still predominated that fault, turning over new leaves, and letting the very first breeze of difficulty flutter them lightly back again!

Is there anybody like me, or do my readers all paste their leaves down as they turn them over? If you do not you will never get farther in the book of reform than the preface!

But, whether we worked or idled, the days ever passed on Ned and I were taking our stroll one evening in the early part of the fall. We had just turned our faces back towards the college when a gentleman and lady on horseback approached. Before I could withdraw my eyes from an impolite stare, they had passed and were sweeping on far ahead.

From that moment study was at an end for me. Soul and body was wrapped in admiration of this beautiful vision, that had flitted by like a dream. Yet I had not seen her face; only the glorious wealth of golden hair, mingling and tossing with the long blue plume in her cap; only the superb form, gracefully swaying to the motion of her prancing steed; only the flutter of a rich white skirt beneath the blue velvet robe, and my heart was gone.

"Great Heavens!" I exclaimed, grasping Ned's arm, "what a beauty! Who is she, Ned?"

"How should I know?" he replied, coolly. "I suppose it is DeVare's sweetheart, as this is the second time I have seen him out riding with her."

"DeVare! then I may yet know her and be happy. Won't it be glorious, old fellow?" and I slapped Ned's shoulder exultingly.

"Just half crazy, that's all you are as yet, John."

"But see, Ned, they are returning. My throbbing heart, be still, that I may gaze!"

As she again flashed by the wondrous beauty of her face and form made my jesting extravagance to Ned seem almost reasonable. I could think or talk of nothing else till we reached our room, and as soon as the lamps were lit, and I thought DeVare was in his room, I went to it. I found only Carrover there, but he said DeVare would be in presently, and told me to wait.

Carrover and DeVare roomed together, and, as their rooms were on the same floor, and very near ours, we had become very intimate with them. Our intimacy was strengthened and made more pleasant by Ned and me becoming members of their club, so that they became our fastest friends, and we had even reached the point of calling them Charlie and Ramie. While I liked them both, yet Raymond DeVare was my favorite. Carrover was courteous and kind, but there was always a slight touch of frigidity about him—a formality I could never quite penetrate—and as constantly as I was thrown in his company I could never feel at perfect ease; I always felt younger, more unsophisticated and more capable of making blunders when he was looking at me than at any other time. He was so quiet and possessed in his air of *savoir faire* that I always feared he was thinking that all I did was out of time or place, and was pitying my ignorance. This feeling was not strong enough to constrain me in his presence, or suppress my flow of spirits, but when with him I was always conscious of a slight hesitation in word and action. With DeVare it was different. He was even more refined and gentle than Carrover, but he thought too much of others to think he knew more, and while he was the most brilliant man in his class, yet his nature's vocabulary had no such word as conceit in it. He always made me feel that I knew as much as he did, and, whenever we conversed, afforded me the pleasure of believing that I was very entertaining. He never ridiculed anybody, and I felt that I could eat peas with my knife, under his eye, and he never would remind me that it was customary to use a fork. He had that instinctive and yet cultivated delicacy that cared for another's feelings as if they were his own. Yet, when anything was wrong, he always condemned it with firmness, yet without bitterness. His moral character was spotless.

But I am digressing again. I was waiting, then, for him to come to his room. I lolled down on the bed while Carrover continued to study.

In a few moments we heard DeVare's step, and he came into the room.

"Well," I said, rising up on one elbow, "I have been waiting for you a long time. Now, tell who was that superb woman you were riding with this afternoon, and where does she live? My heart is hers eternally. I'll vow, Ramie, I never saw as much beauty done up in one bundle before."

DeVare frowned his brows at me and motioned his head towards Carrover, but as I thought he meant I would disturb him, I lowered my voice and went on:

"Please tell me about her, Ramie. I know you love her. You couldn't be with her and not love her. Promise me you'll take me to see her and I'll hush, and let Charlie get his lesson."

I looked at Charlie as I spoke and found him still intent on his page, but smiling peculiarly, as if there was something ridiculous in Blackstone.

"By the way, Charlie," said DeVare, as if my question was forgotten, "what do you think of the case for the Moot Court to-morrow evening?"

"I had not given it much thought," said Carrover, going to the bookcase for a volume; "what was the statement of facts?"

"Oh, bother the Moot Court," I said, getting off the bed, I'm on another kind of court now. Tell me about the girl, DeVare, and I'll leave you and Carrover to your old, dry discussions."

"Jack, you are persistent," said DeVare, with a laugh in the corner of each eye, as if he foresaw my confusion, "the lady I was riding with this afternoon was Miss Lillian Carrover, Charlie's sister."

I felt a hot tingle run up my cheeks, then run down again, and I glanced hurriedly at Carrover. He was still standing at the bookcase with his back toward me, and seemed as if he had not heard our conversation. I first thought of asking his pardon, but on second thought I changed the subject, and, after making one or two common-place remarks, left the room, resolving in the future not to be so free with my tongue.

The next day Ramie assured me that Carrover had not thought anything of it, and told me that if I still desired her acquaintance he would take much pleasure in introducing me. I informed him that no other thought or hope had been entertained by me since I had seen her, and besought him to make his convenience as early as possible.

We fixed on the morrow's night as the time of our visit, and the pages of my books were all blank to my preoccupied thoughts for the next twenty-four hours.

Virgil wrote about Lillian instead of Amaryllis, and stolid Socrates seemed to advise the cultivation of love for an angel in blue velvet. An equation of the fourth degree on the blackboard resolved itself into a horse, with a leg for each degree; and the only thing in the Algebra of any interest to me was the concrete example about the saddle and bridle being changed by mountings of different value. I was constantly with DeVare when not in lecture, and gathered from him, in reference to my sudden flame, that she was Carrover's only sister; that she was a North Carolinian by birth, but had been adopted by a rich uncle in New York; that she had been a Fifth Avenue belle since her fifteenth year; that she had returned in the last spring from an extended European tour; that she had made a conquest of all the hearts from Saratoga to the White Sulphur during the past summer; and, while staying at the last named springs, had met with Miss Minnie, our Professor's daughter, an old playmate and friend. Reviving the old intimacy, she had agreed to come to North Carolina with her, and spend part of the winter at the University.

On the morrow's afternoon DeVare showed me a delicately perfumed billet-doux, in most exquisite chirography, stating that Miss Carrover would be most happy to see Mr. DeVare and his friend from half past nine to ten and half. As the parlors of the favorite young ladies at the University were crowded every night, the plan had been adopted of engaging the hours, so that a young lady could specify the hour at which she would receive a visit from a gentleman, and he was not at liberty to stay longer unless he was specially invited, and no others had come in. Where there were so many students to so few ladies this served to avoid confusion, and gave the many who wished to call something like a chance to be heard, each for himself.

That evening, immediately after tea, I commenced getting ready, and after completely exhausting my wardrobe and patience, felt but poorly prepared to be introduced to a young lady who had actually been to Europe, and reigned as one of the queens of our metropolitan society.

As we neared the door I wondered that DeVare could be so cool and composed, while my heart was fluttering so that my limbs caught the tremor, and, in spite of the warm, pleasant night, persisted in having the ague. I saw that the curtain was down as we knocked at the door, but there was the reflection of light within, and the murmur of several voices. I had been thinking all the time of what to say first. I felt that I could get on very well after the conversation started, but how to fill up with appropriate remarks that dismal silence just after the introduction, was more than my inexperience could compass. I had made up some absurd compliment about the beautiful northern flower blooming still sweetly in southern soil, but the rat-tat of the knocker dissipated every collected thought, and left my mind blanker than before.

A servant answered our knock; we hung our hats on the stand. I arranged my cravat and smoothed on my glove for the thirty-seventh time, and the next thing I knew I was in a throng of faces, from which rose up one with a wavy mass of tawny hair, drooping sleepy eyes, and red lips, that parted over smooth white teeth. I thought I heard DeVare's voice, as in a dream: "Miss Carrover, allow me to introduce my friend, Mr. Smith," and I bowed till the part in my hair alone was visible.

There was another lady in the room, Miss Minnie, the daughter of the Professor, and I took the only seat in sight, which was near her. Notwithstanding our engagement, the parlor was full of gentlemen, and, to my horror, many of them were Sophs. There was quite a crowd of these around Miss Minnie, who was a vivacious little personage, full of mischief and wit, and dispensing her smiles and bon mots around with generous impartiality. As the conversation had begun before I entered I could not very well join in, and as no one addressed any remark to me, I sat bolt upright in my chair, with one arm thrown, with an attempt at ease, over the back, while the other fumbled at my watch chain.

DeVare had found a seat near Miss Carrover, and was soon absorbed in conversation with her—supposing, of course, that after an introduction I would have nothing to do but proceed to enjoyment. A procedure not always of consummate ease!

As I was sitting very near the circle around Miss Minnie, I soon found that I was not only the object of their mischievous glances but also of their wit. Their tones were just loud enough for me to hear, and after each sally all would join in a laugh, which Miss Minnie often led. From this they began to address themselves to me, calling me Fresh, asking what I had come for, and if I was not ashamed to use the parlor mirror to dress by. (I had been unconsciously adjusting my cravat in the mirror over the mantel.)

As I was not certain whether the Sophs' prerogative extended to a private parlor or not, I was afraid to say anything, but sat still, while my embarrassment drove the blood almost through my cheeks, and beaded my forehead with great drops of perspiration.

Miss Minnie then inquired if I would sit still or take a seat nearer the fire—the point of her remark lying in fact that it was quite a warm night, and there was not a spark in the fireplace.

I tried to say "No, thank you," but not recognizing my own voice, cut it off with "No——," which itself was so meekly stammered it had no decided negative character; but it had the effect of raising all the voices of the Sophs, who cried out:

"Oh, how impolite, Fresh, to say no to a lady! Where did you learn your manners? How extremely vulgar!"

I was just on the point of rushing from the room when DeVare's attention was attracted at this outcry, and he took in the position of affairs at a glance. His face was aglow with scorn and indignation as he rose from Miss Carrover's side and strode to our part of the room.

"Gentlemen," he said—looking with withering contempt on the circle around Miss Minnie, "though the term is a misnomer—I have introduced Mr. Smith here: an insult to him is an insult to me. The presence of ladies is no place for a quarrel, but I characterize your conduct as ungentlemanly, and will be ready to hear from any of you at any time. You know my name and the number of my room. Miss Minnie, pardon me, but I am surprised that you should have allowed or encouraged such conduct in your house."

"Really, Mr. DeVare, you are not in earnest?" said Miss Minnie, with imperturbable good humor. "Why, I thought even the ladies had a right to tease the Fresh."

"That is just as you please to think, Miss Minnie," he replied, with one of his bows; "the gentlemen have heard my opinion of *their* conduct."

"Lil, you and I will leave the parlor if the gentlemen wish to fight," said Miss Minnie, making a pretence of rising to leave the room.

Miss Carrover looked at her with a shake of her head, and with her soft rich voice said: "Minnie!" Then, turning to DeVare—

"Come here, Mr. DeVare, Minnie is only jesting. Mr. Smith," addressing me, "have you seen these stereoscopic views of the University? My brother had them taken last spring. Take a seat here on the sofa and look them over with me, and see if you can recognize them all."

Her manner was so composed and gracious that we were all reseated and everything quiet before we knew it. I had felt so miserably wretched while DeVare and Miss Minnie were speaking that I felt eternally grateful to Miss Carrover for relieving me, even though she treated me as if I were very young, in doing it.

In a moment or two all save DeVare and myself rose to leave—Brazon, who was the ringleader in Miss Minnie's persecuting circle, scowling malignantly at DeVare as he bowed himself out.

As soon as they had gone Miss Minnie came to where I was sitting, and, with winning frankness, offered her hand, saying:

"It was very naughty in me, Mr. Smith, to tease you. I beg pardon, and promise not to do so any more."

I caught her hand convulsively, and assured her of my entire forgiveness, and implored her not to give herself any trouble on my account, and much more to the same incoherent effect.

She drew her hand gently from mine, and calling DeVare, said—

"Mr. DeVare, let's take those seats by the window; I have a fuss to make up with you, too."

DeVare, of course, complied, and I was left alone on the sofa with Miss Carrover. We still had the box of pictures in our hands, but as soon as DeVare left she closed the box and said:

"Let's put these tiresome old pictures up, and talk some. Tell me all about the way the Sophs treated you when you first came."

To be near such superb beauty was almost too much for my poor sentimental heart; and then to have her wish to hear me talk, and even prescribe the subject, as if my words would be full of so much interest! I was stupid for awhile with surprise, and sat for nearly half a minute gazing abstractedly and impolitely in her face. Indeed, 'twas well worth gazing on.

Her hair was not done up regularly, but caught in great loose folds around her head, so as to best set off her face, and was rolled back from her clear white forehead in a great golden wave—yet its color was not altogether golden; it had a tinge of red that made it glow with a tawny light. Her skin was perfectly smooth and clear, and of wax-like whiteness, tinged with a bright peach pink on her cheeks. But her chief charms were her eyes and mouth. Her eyes were hazel or dark gray, I could never tell which, shaded with very long lashes and deep upper lids, that gave them a dreamy, languid expression, that always impresses us as most beautiful, we know not why. Her mouth was small, and very much arched at the corners; her lips bright red, and her teeth perfectly white; the upper lip protruded slightly, as if she was ever a little surprised, and this, combined with a constant slight arch of the eyebrows, imparted an air of interest in all you said, notwithstanding the languor of her general expression. Her beauty was Dudu's, and Byron well knew its fascinating power.

As soon as I recovered from my brief contemplation of her face I made an attempt to give her my experience as a Fresh, and what with the pleasure of talking at all to her, and her interest in my subject, and continued ejaculations of pity, I began to wish the fellows had done me much worse than they had, it was so delightful to have her listen to the recital of my woes. When I told her of my fainting under the smoking, she smiled such a lazy little smile, and said, "I did not know gentlemen indulged in such feminine weaknesses."

"But the air was so noxious, Miss Carrover, no one could have borne it. You would have been compelled to faint."

"Oh, I faint quite easily," she said, arching one eyebrow instead of two, "I came near falling from my horse as I went to mount last evening, and became unconscious for a little while."

"And was no one there to catch you?" I asked, with earnest heroism in my tone.

"Oh, of course, I took care to be provided with that safeguard. Do you think you could catch me if we were riding and I should fall?"

"I would catch you if you fell from the skies," I replied, warmly, involuntarily feeling my arm, as if it belonged to Hercules, and looking at her just in time to catch a glance of significance passing between herself and DeVare. Feeling that perhaps I was just a little ridiculous, I endeavored to leave the subject gradually by asking if she was fond of riding horseback, and begging the honor of an engagement for the next evening. She thanked me, and said that as she had introduced the subject I might have construed it into a hint, and she must therefore decline the offer. As I seemed so cut down, however, she agreed to make an indefinite engagement, the time to be fixed any time after that evening.

She then drew me out about our halls and libraries, till I had told of every alcove, and how well they were arranged for courting, and that all the students carried their sweethearts there, and ended by asking her to go with me there some evening after lecture. Another lazy smile, and she softly reminded me that she had introduced that topic also, and must therefore decline again, "at least," she said, looking at me sideways under her long lashes, "till you claim me as your sweetheart, as you state that it is the resort of lovers only."

I flushed and hushed for a moment, when DeVare rose from his seat with Miss Minnie, and said it was time for us to go.

Miss Carrover gave me her hand at parting, and insisted on my calling again with so much sweet earnestness that I made myself ridiculous again in my promise to do so.

We had scarcely passed outside the gate when I commenced:

"DeVare, is she not perfectly splendid! I'll vow I'm crazy about her."

"That was shameful conduct in those scoundrels to-night," DeVare said, without noticing my remark, "and had it not been for Miss Minnie and Lillian I would have punished them on the spot."

"Do you call her Lillian, Ramie?" I asked with surprise.

"If any of them want satisfaction for anything I said to-night," he continued, without heeding me, "I will have to request you, Jack, to act as my friend."

"You may depend on me, Ramie; but if there is to be any difficulty, I must be the principal, as it was all begun on my account."

"Oh, nonsense," he said. "I gave the insult to them, and of course I only can satisfy them. I do not expect anything, however, from that crowd, as they are too cowardly to resent an insult."

We parted at his room, and when I reached mine I made Ned put up his books for the night, and listen to my account of Miss Carrover.

When I had at last wearied him out, and we went to bed, I could not go to sleep for the dancing train of fancies that were rushing through my mind. I lay there till far in the night, recalling every incident of my visit, trying to make its memory as vivid as possible, thinking of every word she had said, and regretting the many foolish things I had said, which might lessen me in her estimation—(but oh! I hoped not!)—wondering how she who had seen so much of society, who had seen everything worth seeing in Europe and America, and knew almost everybody worth knowing, could be so interested in my talk—a youth just approaching manhood, unused to the ways of the world and unskilled in the use of the tongue. Then I would, by an ingenious process, known only to those who are vain, endeavor to convince myself that she did like me, and would eventually love me. I would imagine her telling Miss Minnie that I was a handsome fellow, and so entertaining; then wishing for me to call again, then giving me a preference in attention when I did call, then writing sweet notes of thanks for the many love tokens and gifts I would send her, then a moonlight stroll, a courtship, a kiss, and eternal happiness!

I would fall asleep only to rebuild and embellish in my dreams the magnificent air castles of my waking hours.

CHAPTER XXII

The morning after our visit I was in DeVare's room, waiting for him to come in from lecture, when some one knocked, and, in answer to my invitation, Ellerton, a Sophomore, who had been kind to me at first, entered, and asked for DeVare. Finding that I expected him in soon, he took a seat, and commenced some trivial talk about college matters. He had had nothing to do with me since I joined DeVare's club, and a salutation when we passed had been the extent of our intercourse since early in the session.

He spoke with regret of the last night's affair, and said DeVare ought not to have been so quick to resent the fellows' fun. This, of course, nettled me, and I was about to make an angry reply, when DeVare himself came in. He bowed to Ellerton, who rose and handed him a note. DeVare's brow contracted as he read it, and as soon as he finished he tossed it to me, and sitting down to his writing table, commenced his reply. The note he had received was from Brazon, demanding a retraction of the language used last evening, and an apology in the presence of both ladies, or the usual satisfaction. Ere I had finished reading DeVare folded and addressed his answer, and Ellerton, receiving it, bowed himself out.

DeVare looked at me and smiled as I asked him what he intended to do.

"My self-respect forbids that I should entertain a thought of yielding to the first demand; custom and public opinion compel me to grant the second. I wrote, therefore, that I had no remark to regret, and no retraction to make; and that I would accord him any satisfaction he might desire I took the liberty of referring him to you, as my friend."

"You were perfectly right in that; but, DeVare, I must take your place, and be the principal in this affair, as it was all undertaken on my account."

"That could not be, Jack, even if I were willing, which I certainly am not. Do not trouble yourself about it, for I do not feel one particle of concern or uneasiness in reference to it. You had best now go to Ellerton's room, and confer with him in regard to the arrangements. One thing I will mention: if there has to be a meeting get it put off till the end of the session, as the laws of the University require instant expulsion for any one in anywise connected with a duel."

I had scarcely risen from my seat when Ellerton again tapped at the door, to request me to walk with him over to his room.

I rose and followed him, feeling, I must confess, somewhat important as second in a duel which would create quite a stir, and yet feeling sadly conscious that it was a strange manifestation of friendship to be arranging preliminaries for my friend's possible and probable death.

When we reached Ellerton's room he motioned me to take a seat, and said:

"Brazon has read DeVare's note, and as he refuses to apologize, I wish to know when he will meet him, and with what weapons?"

"O! Ellerton!" I said, thoroughly unmanned, "cannot this wretched affair be settled without recourse to arms? I was the unintentional cause of it all, and, as DeVare will not hear of my taking his place on the field, I will submit to any humiliation to save him."

"I don't think your humiliation would do much good," he remarked, coolly, sticking his knife through a match lying on the table, and splitting the phosphorus into a blaze. "DeVare is the man who insulted him, and Brazon will alone be satisfied with his blood."

"I'll have his if he gets it," I said, savagely, recalled to myself by his words.

"Well, well, do not threaten," he said, throwing the match on the floor and rubbing it out with his boot; "let's proceed to business."

He got paper and pens, and we agreed on the following arrangements:

Time of meeting, the 3d of December; place, just in the South Carolina line; weapons, Derringer pistols; distance, ten paces.

"Is that all, now," I said, rising to leave.

"I believe so," he said, running his finger down the paper. "It's pretty far off now, and we'll have to keep our principals up to the point. I'm afraid they'll cool off and make friends yet."

"You need have no fears in regard to mine," I said, haughtily, "he'll make no overtures, and will certainly be ready when the time comes."

I reported all to DeVare, who expressed himself satisfied with the arrangements, and apparently dismissed the subject from his mind for any allusion he made to it during the days and weeks following.

The same evening I walked out, and received a very gracious bow from Miss Carrover, which set my heart in a flutter, though I was considerably troubled at seeing Ellerton in the porch with her.

That night I wrote to father, with many excuses and reasons for the request, to send me my horse and Reuben; and feeling perfectly assured they would come, made up my mind what to do when they did.

After a day or two I called again on Miss Carrover, and was fortunate this time in finding her alone. I enjoyed a very delightful *tete-a-tete* with her, and, among other things, told her that I had sent for my horse, and that when he came I would claim the ride she had so cruelly refused me the evening I had first called. She readily assented, and expressed the wish to ride him herself. Then she consented to sing for me; and, having been assured that her favorite would be mine, selected Meyerbeer's "Robert le Diable." Though her voice was very fine, yet it had been trained in such affectation of the opera that the song lost all of its melody and pathos in her rendition. She got up so high in her screams for *grace* that it was only possible to descend by a ladder, which, like Brother Weekly, she constructed of "er," and came hopping down with such an impenitent *gra-er-a-er-a-er-ce pour moi* that no one could have blamed Robert for his inexorable "*Non, non, non.*" At the conclusion of the piece I was, of course, profuse in my thanks and praise; but, fearing another such infliction, I begged for some instrumental music, and was tested, as to patience, by ten or twelve pages of banging and scaling.

Yet my visit was very delightful, and I departed more enraptured than ever, if such a thing was possible.

When I recounted my visit to Ned, he only laughed, and advised me seriously to attend more closely to my books.

"You know how much your father expects of you," he said; "and you may be sure this Miss Carrover does not care a fig for you."

"I know she does," I responded, warmly. "Even on this, my second visit, she has shown me plainly that she likes me well. I'll bet we are engaged before three months. Won't that be glorious, Ned? Surely, man, you have no eyes, or you would be enslaved yourself by her beauty."

"My vision is very good," said Ned, "but I don't see any thing enslaving about her. She is pretty, without doubt, and is probably entertaining; but there are others equally as good looking, and more capable of rendering you happy. Besides, do you suppose that a lady who has been the object of a great city's adulation can be pleased with any one in this little village of students—half of whom she regards as mere boys?"

"Umph, we are as good as any Adonis of Broadway. And then, Ned, a lady who felt at all bored by our presence would evince it in some way. A look, a careless word or a sneer would betray her feelings. No, Ned, you are surprised at my success, and only predict evil because you hate to confess the contrary is true."

"Well," said Ned, turning over the leaves of his lexicon in search of a flea of a word, "go on; but you will find she is only amusing herself with you during her rustication."

"But, Ned, I know she likes me; and won't it be splendid to call the beauty of Gotham mine?"

"Go your way, old fellow," said Ned, catching the flea and pinning it with his pencil on the margin of his text-book; "but, mark my words, in three months from to-day your adored will have discarded you, and you will then be regretting the moments you have wasted on her."

"That reminds me," I said, taking down my book, "I must cram Greek for to-morrow."

After an hour's study we retired—Ned well prepared, I just half.

CHAPTER XXIII

Several days have passed, and I am still in dreamland with Miss Carrover. I manage to attend recitations, but that is all. The tutor's instructions fall on an inattentive ear, and his questions receive random answers. My books are all neglected, and even when I try to study, my mind is so preoccupied that it proves a perfect Danæan sieve, and after an hour's vacant rambling over a page I close the book, with a more confused idea of its contents than I had before I opened it.

I visit Miss Carrover every other evening, at least, and in the interim am thinking of a word she spoke, a smile she gave; or am forming rainbow conjectures as to how she will treat me when I next call.

A week after the events narrated in the last chapter, I received a letter from my father, saying that he had read my letter with some surprise, but that, while he feared my horse would prove an hindrance to study, he did not like to refuse my first request, and had accordingly started Reuben off with him the morning before; that he hoped I would not let it deter me from applying myself diligently to my books, but that my report at the close of the session might be, as it always had been in my other schools, perfect.

I examined the date of the letter and found that it had been delayed a day, so that Reuben and Phlegon, starting the day before, ought to reach the University that day. I made a minute calculation, and found that they would arrive by one o'clock, and so, with a sigh of repentance over my dereliction of duty, and a firm resolve to do better, I determined, as that was Friday, to snap lecture, and watch for Reuben, waiting for Monday to turn over my new leaf.

Accordingly, when the bell for lecture rung, instead of going with Ned to the section room, I strolled through the campus and gave myself up to sweet thoughts of Lillian. It was one of my autumn days. The sun was shining with a still, mellow light through a golden haze, which seemed to have fallen on all Nature, so yellow were the leaves on the trees and the stubble in the fields. The air was still and dreamy, and the campus, usually so full of noise and life, empty and deserted. I tried to think of Lillian as the only one in the world besides myself; of the universe as being made for us two, and of how sweetly we would live for each other. But somehow my soul would not fall into the delicious reverie her name usually inspired. For the first time since I had met her I could not think constantly of her, but my mind was ever and anon recurring to father's letter and his admonitions. There was an aching at my heart, a restless unhappiness I could not understand. I wandered about for half an hour, then sought out the negro who rang the bell, obtained the belfry keys from him, and went up in the cupola of the South Building. Taking my seat on the window ledge, I gazed on the beautiful scene around. A large extent of country spread out before me, gently undulating, and specked here and there with lonely white houses or groups of negro quarters. The haze of the zenith softened down to a deep shaded violet as it met the horizon, and long lines of smoke stood stiffly around the verge, like gray sentinels guarding the Great Beyond. A little way off a herd of cows were grazing, and the hoarse monotones of their copper bells were just audible enough to be drowsy; while along the red line of the road that wound out of sight by the cemetery, a white top wagon, with sluggish horses, was slowly crawling on to Raleigh.

My mind now easily fell into reverie, but Miss Carrover was not its burden. Conscience, that had so long been tapping at the door of a heart too full of love to let it in, now gained a hearing, and told of wrong after wrong, of duties neglected, of promises of diligence forgotten, of honors so easily in reach unstriven for, of a doting father (of whose kind indulgence I was about to receive such a striking proof) so culpably deceived, of golden opportunities wasted which might never be retrieved—all for a love which was, perhaps, in vain—till remorse applied its tortures to my soul and I was miserable. Then came the struggle. Could I give Lillian up? Could I drive out all those sweet thoughts of her that had been such pleasant companions for me while away from her? Could I bear to think of her sighing for me, while I cruelly kept away? Above all, could I bear to think of her smiling on others and forgetting me, only because I had forgotten her? No, I could not do that, but I would go to see her less frequently; I would study harder; and redeem the lost time; I would gain the first honors; and yet love Lillian. Like Alan of Buchan, I would win both banners, and father would smile on my honors and approve my choice.

Patting down my conscience with these good resolutions, I chanced to look out on the scene again, and saw, coming down the road from Raleigh, a horse and rider. The horse was blanketed, but I knew by the lordly bearing and arching neck that it was Phlegon, and I clambered down from the belfry, and ran down to the hotel to meet him. The bell rang for the close of lectures at the same time, and the students were thronging from the various lecture rooms, and many shouted at me as I hurried through the campus. I reached the hotel just as Reuben rode up. I had hardly gotten through making inquiries about them all at home when the students, in large numbers, came down to the hotel, and commenced making comments on myself and my horse. Some of my friends, however, coming to me and desiring to see him, I made Reuben take off his blankets and move him up and down the street, to show his action. As Reuben stripped the cloth from his glossy hide, and the splendid form stood revealed in its matchless grace, a murmur of approbation ran through the crowd. And Phlegon was in every respect worthy. An English thoroughbred, he possessed the marks of an aristocratic ancestry, lords of the turf for many generations. The sharp pointed ears, the mild dark eye, and the tapering mouse colored muzzle, with its red open nostrils, were a coat of arms as perfect as argent fields and unicorns rampant.

His color was a beautiful claret, and his coat as glossy as if just washed in the ruby wine. His limbs tapered delicately, but the muscles were round and full of strength. He had evidently been the pet at home since I had left, and it was with no little pride that I ordered Reuben to take him round to the stables I had engaged for him. I went back to my room, feeling a good deal flattered by hearing some one say, as Reuben rode off:

"That's a crack Fresh, to keep a horse the first session."

That evening, of course, I rode out, and, riding out, of course passed the house where Miss Carrover was staying. She was on the porch with DeVare as I swept by. I bowed and said, "To-morrow evening!" and she kissed her hand at me and said, "Without fail!" I was happy again, and my good resolutions about such *very* hard study began to melt.

The next evening found me in the parlor, while Reuben stood at the gate holding Phlegon and the horse from the livery stable Miss Carrover usually rode.

As she swept into the room, holding up the long folds of her riding habit with one gauntleted hand, while the other threatened me with her pearl and gold riding whip, I thought I had never seen anything half so lovely, and I playfully bent on one knee as she said:

"You wicked boy, why did you come so late. I have been waiting ever so long for you?"

I apologised with all meekness, threw the blame on Reuben, and escorted her out to the block. As soon as she saw my horse she burst into an ecstacy of admiration, and vowed that I must have the saddles changed; that she could not allow her escort to ride a prettier horse than she was on. As I believed him perfectly safe, I ordered Reuben to change the saddles, then assisted her to mount, took her gaitered little foot in my hand to adjust it in the stirrup, and then, springing into my saddle, we galloped away into

She doubtless loves me, thought I, but of course she is not going to reveal it till I convince her of my sincerity. She has probably been annoyed with empty protestations of love from so many that she believes all men faithless, and my sudden and inappropriate declaration this afternoon was certainly not calculated to inspire any belief in its truth. She is a lady of too much tact and experience to discover the real state of her feelings till I have proved myself in earnest, and that I mean to do before another sun shall set. My horse, which she knows I prize so highly, will at least prove that I am not trifling.

I spent that night till bed time writing notes presenting her with Phlegon, and then tearing them up, till I almost despaired of getting one to suit me. Towards twelve o'clock, however, I completed one on the fanciest paper procurable, and, delicately perfuming it, laid it by till Monday morning, as the next day was the Sabbath.

Monday morning was the time I had appointed for my new leaf, but the excitement of sending my horse to Miss Carrover made me determine to put off the reform I had contemplated to next day.

After breakfast I told Reuben to take Phlegon, and go up to Mr. Pommel's store and get the saddle I bought there Saturday.

"What chu want wi' another saddul, Marse John? Dat one ole marse gin you rides better'n any saddul I ever sot on."

"Go and do as I told you, and don't ask so many questions. It is a side saddle I've bought, and I am going to give Phlegon away."

"Gwine to give 'way Phregon! What you 'spect to do wid me, Marse John?"

"You are to attend to him still, and saddle him whenever the lady wants to use him."

"Um-umph, dat's gone by me!" he muttered, as he walked off to obey my orders.

After he had gone with my note the anxious suspense of waiting for the answer was immense. I went up in my room and tried to study, but it was in vain. At the end of half an hour I heard the clatter of hoofs under the windows, and found Reuben returned on my horse. His teeth were gleaming to the first molars as he gave me Miss Carrover's note. I tore it open hastily, and read:

"Mr. Smith:

"Your unselfish generosity in offering such a superb contribution to my pleasure forbids that I should return

CHAPTER XXIV

I had secured the key from the librarian, and we did not, therefore, fear interruption, as the library of the Society was only open to the public on Saturdays.

As we walked from alcove to alcove selecting books, reading an extract from one, examining the engravings in another, and I realized that we were all alone in the great silent hall, I felt the resistless current of my love more strongly than ever, and determined to reveal it if I could, before we left the library. But the very thought of sitting by her side and telling her to her face that I loved her made a hot flutter rise in my heart that imparted its tremor to my limbs, and I began to think it were best to put off the disclosure a few days yet.

At length we took our seat on one of the sofas, and bent together over a beautifully illustrated copy of that passionate Persian poem—the Gitagovinda.

We opened to a picture of Rhada half concealed in the papyri, gazing on the inconstant Heri as he sports with the laughing shepherdesses. The sad, wounded look spread over the chiselled features told of the jealousy within her heart, and shaded the radiance of Heaven with the blight of Earth's sorrow.

"Isn't that face exquisite?" she said, after gazing for some time at it without speaking; "and the hand half raised, holding the broken stem of lotus, how perfect in outline. The whole picture is the loveliest thing I ever saw."

"You haven't had the advantage of a mirror recently, then," I said, tamely.

"That is fulsome and exceedingly stale," she said, with a smile that softened but did not quite destroy the sarcasm of her tone.

"Indeed, Miss Carrover, you are lovely enough to make Heraclitus cease weeping; but I would not seek your favor with adulation. Your experience as a flirt has doubtless taught you too well how to estimate the compliments of—er (I longed for my horse and spur again, but not having them with me I was forced to its utterance)—lovers."

"Do you call me a flirt," she said, closing the book, and setting it up edgewise on her lap, so that she might lock her beautiful fingers over it, "after all the consideration and regard I have shown you? Has anything in my conduct toward *you* indicated that I was flirting with you?"

"No; I confess with deep gratitude that, so far as I am concerned, you do not yet deserve the name. But I do fear your ridicule and sarcasm, or my bursting heart would tell its love."

"Poor little heart! do not burst," she said, patting me with one hand gently over my heart.

Of course I caught the hand and imprinted a very fervent kiss on it; a liberty which she resented by calling "Sir-r-r," with a great many r's, and vowing she would not speak to me again while we were in the library. I gazed at her a moment, and then broke out passionately:

"Miss Lillian—may I call you that?—let's cease trifling. I love you; but before you laugh me to scorn let me tell you how I love you. I have never loved before, can never love again, as I love you now. My life, my soul is wrapped up in you; my whole being is in yours; and existence without your love to possess or to hope for is utterly worthless. No other thought, no other object has been mine since I saw you; and I solemnly vow to you now, I care for, hope for nothing else on earth but your smile and favor. I cannot, dare not believe that you love me now; but give me one ray of hope, one straw to cling to; promise that you will learn to love me in years to come; that after long, patient devotion on my part, and satiety of conquest on yours, you will give me your heart. Dearest Lillian, promise me."

The sexton of the library had forgotten his broom, and it chanced to be leaning against the sofa arm near her. She quietly handed it to me, and said, with an affected sigh:

"Alas! I have no hope to offer, but there is a broom full of straws for you to cling to."

I dropped my head into my hands, and moaned:

"Oh heaven! the agony."

"Really, Mr. Smith, you act your part well. I can only regret that the programme of courtship you have evidently studied is a hackneyed one. Indiscriminate flattery, life and death pledges of devotion and vows of eternal fealty! The addition of a little poetry, about the fountain of your heart being sealed, to keep its waters, etc., would have made it perfect."

"Miss Carrover," I said, raising my head from my hands, and looking at her with a countenance so full of despair I saw she knew at last that I was in earnest, "it is enough. Before we drop the subject, though, forever, hear me. As I hope to be judged in eternity, every word I spoke just now was earnest truth. As you value the happiness of a fellow being, do me the justice, at least, to believe this my solemn assertion."

"Mr. Smith," she said quickly, her face losing the expression of incredulous derision it had worn, and assuming a seriousness I had never before seen on it, "were you really in earnest?"

"Before my Maker, I was."

"Can you pardon my unkindness, then," and she offered her soft little hand. I took it, but did not release it immediately, but sat holding it in mine, and gazing down at the floor. Though so near her, I felt that we were separated by an immense chasm, whose black depths were unfathomable; but now her last words threw a tiny thread of gold across it, and on this slender bridge Hope, like another Blondin, prepared to tread.

"I have been called a flirt," she continued, to my joyful surprise letting her hand remain in mine, "and perhaps the title is deserved; for I confess that I have constantly sought the conquest of hearts, and I enjoy nothing so much as a long story of love poured out for my mockery—not that I love to cause pain in others, but I have ever found men's vows insincere, deserving nothing better than scorn. Whenever I have had reason to believe one sincere I have always made the dismissal, if I rejected him, as kind as possible. With you, my dear friend—will you allow me to deal candidly?—I was much pleased, and enjoyed your pleasant vivacity and humor exceedingly; so that I will confess I looked forward to your visits more pleasantly than to almost any one else's. Thus, without intending it, I have encouraged a love which from the first I knew I could not return, but which I did not suppose was serious. If I esteemed you less I might bid you hope that I might retain you as a suitor; but the very earnestness of your love forbids that I should deceive you. I cannot love you, save as a friend. That is very trite, isn't it? Still, it expresses my feelings, and I trust that you will believe *me* when I assure you that I do and ever shall entertain the highest regard for you."

"Do not say you can not love me, Miss Carrover. Surely a love so devoted as mine will yet win some return."

She did not reply; but slipping the diamond ring on her third finger down to the tip, and holding it there with her thumb, she held it to me. I looked down on the inside of the gold band and saw, marked in ruby points, as if written in blood, the names Raymond and Lillian."

"Raymond!" I exclaimed, "who—what is the surname?"

"DeVare!" she whispered softly.

The golden thread snapped in twain, and Hope fell forever into the abyss!

I did not reply, for I knew it would have been folly to attempt to supplant Raymond DeVare, and I would not if I could have done so at a breath.

As neither of us had any further use for the library we closed it and walked home. Nothing special was said; only when I bade her good-bye she said, with the old irresistible look: "You will still visit me?"

I bowed low, and said, "If you wish me to."

On my way home I made up my mind to one thing, that, however much I might feel depressed, I would not let Ned find it out. He had provoked me enough with his predictions; he should not now have the triumph of saying, "I told you so."

After tea I took a long stroll with DeVare, and, as the conversation led to it, I told him all. He smiled when I concluded, and said he had been expecting as much. He then, in return for my confidence, told me that they had been engaged since early in the summer. That he and Carrover had gone to Newport, and he had met her there and loved her; that they were betrothed before he left, and that they were to be married the coming June, immediately after his graduation.

"That is," he continued, "if the meeting we have arranged for in December does not prevent it."

"Does she know of it?" I asked.

"No; and I would not have her to for worlds."

"But, Ramie, there will never be a meeting," I said, cheerily. "Brazon is too cowardly to fight; and if he were not, time would make the affair too trivial to be remembered, especially as it is safest to forget it."

"Brazon would never have begun," he said, "had it not been for the advice of others. Of course their purpose is to continue the affair, as they suffer no uneasiness on account of it."

"Well, Ramie, let us look on the bright side of things. I do not believe that the affair will come off at all, and if it does it will be without danger to yourself."

DeVare then gave me his personal history, stating that he was an only child; that his father had been dead a great many years; that his mother was perfectly devoted to him, and that this was the first session she had passed without spending most of the time at Chapel Hill or Raleigh, where he could run down to see her often.

"She will not leave New Orleans till the close of November," he continued, "when we will together go to Richmond to spend my vacation. The thought of the terrible blow to her, if I should fall, is the only thing that makes me shrink somewhat from the meeting."

CHAPTER XXV

The thirtieth November came at last, and found DeVare, Ned and myself on the train for Wilmington.

The fall session had closed that afternoon, and we had gone up to Durham's to take the night train. DeVare was going home with me, and would remain till the 3d December, when we were to go over to South Carolina, that Brazon might prove himself a gentleman by trying to take DeVare's life.

He and Ellerton were on the same train, in company with Frank, but there was no intercourse between any of us.

We reached Wilmington late the next evening, and were heartily welcomed by every one. It was delightful to be in my dear home again, every one so glad to see me, and all interested in the merest little detail of my experience. Carlotta was far more beautiful than when I had left her, and I thought, if years improve her as months have done, she will be the most superbly beautiful woman the world has ever seen. DeVare was perfectly enraptured with her, and vowed that were his affections free he would lay them at her feet. In fact, everything was made so pleasant to both of us that he declared my home the happiest he had ever known. My spirits were very much depressed. Do what I would I could not shake off a dull, heavy foreboding that seemed to shroud my heart in perpetual gloom. Even when I would forget it for a while, there was the same unrest, the same consciousness of something unpleasant, ever resting on my mind. Whatever were the consequences of the dreaded affair to the others, to myself they could be nothing else but disagreeable. If there were no bloodshed, I would incur father's displeasure to the last degree. I would be liable to indictment in law, and would, perhaps, be expelled from the University; while if DeVare was killed, — — but I could not allow myself to think of such a horror for the slightest moment.

Every day I prayed, with all the faith I could command, that it might not occur, and, if it did, that no blood might be spilled. I would have informed the authorities had I not promised DeVare to keep it secret. All this dread of it arose from the fact that I was only the second. Had I been one of the principals in it the romance of excitement would have kept up my spirits, and the necessity for heroic demeanor would have nerved me into nonchalance. DeVare seemed perfectly cheerful, and scarcely ever gave the subject a thought, but my loss of spirits was so perceptible that father rallied me in regard to it, and mother became really solicitous.

The night of the 2d December came round, and DeVare and I went to our rooms to make preparations for our trip next morning. I had told them down stairs that DeVare had a little matter of business in South Carolina, and that I had agreed to accompany him thither. We had very few preparations to make, as we expected to return on the evening train. As I said this to DeVare, when he suggested that we had best carry a valise, I remember the peculiar smile with which he replied:

"Perhaps *we* may not return at all, at least together. One of us may be in the baggage car."

"Oh, Ramie, for the love of Heaven do not speak in that way. If you have any love for me let me take your place to-morrow. I had rather die a thousand deaths than feel the dreadful gloom I do to-night," and I bowed my face upon the table, while my frame shook with emotion.

"Why, Jack," said Ramie fondly, laying his hand on my arm, "you unnerve me. What have you to fear?"

"More than you, Ramie! I had a hundred fold rather face death than the remorse I must feel if anything happens to you."

"Your youth and inexperience shrink from the responsibility of the position; but look on the bright side and hope for the best. Now come, sit here by the fire with me, while I give you some directions about what I want done in case I— —. You understand."

"Don't mention that horrid possibility, Ramie. I cannot bear it."

"Yes; but it must be mentioned," he said, crimping a strip of paper between his thumb and forefinger, while he gazed pensively at the coals flickering their red horoscope deep in the grate. "If I fall," he at length said, "have my body brought back to town and carried to the hotel; I do not wish to shock the feelings of your kind family by being brought here."

"It shall go nowhere else," I replied, impetuously, forgetting that the neuter "*it*" might grate harshly on his ear.

"Then have a metallic case," he went on, without noticing my interruption, "and have it expressed to New Orleans, telegraphing Mr. Dixon, our agent, to meet it and make necessary arrangements for interment. I expected my mother here soon, but I wrote her a few days since to remain in New Orleans till she heard from me again. I made my will yesterday, and had it signed and sealed, but there are a few articles of personal property I wish you to dispose of for me. My ring, with Lillian's and my own likeness in it, together with the box of trinkets and souvenirs you will find in my trunk, please give to her; my watch and chain send to my mother, and this I wish you to keep," and he placed in my hand a beautiful emerald cross, which he wore as a scarf pin.

He gazed again for some time in the fire, and then looked up and continued:

"And, John, write to mother and explain all the circumstances and reasons of the affair—omitting, of course, the slight connection you had with its beginning; and tell her that I die in the faith and communion of the Church, and in the hope of Heaven. I am speaking thus in case the worst happens. I trust, though, there may be no occasion for your carrying out these instructions. Now complete your arrangements and let's go to sleep; I want to feel well in the morning."

He retired to his room, which adjoined mine; and having occasion to go in there a few moments afterwards, I found that he was sleeping as peacefully as if on his mother's bosom. I could not sleep, but tossed from side to side in a fever of restless apprehension.

About day I fell into a doze, from which I was awakened by father's tapping at our door and telling us it was nearly train time. I found DeVare already up and dressed, and I rose, and hurriedly, shiveringly, slipped on my clothes and went down with him to the dining room, where mother had prepared an early breakfast for us.

"What time will you return?" asked father, as we got into the carriage.

"Don't look for us until you see us," I said, slamming the carriage door, and concealing beneath my shawl my case of Derringers, which Ellerton had agreed to use.

A thought of coming back alone flitted like a raven of despair across my mind, but I shook it off and assumed cheerfulness.

As we entered the boat I noticed Ellerton and Brazon on the forward deck, smoking with affected *sang froid*. We sat down near the wheel house, and watched the paddles as they churned the bluish-green water into white foam, and rocked the little skiffs passing near, with refluent waves. Across the river a short dash on the cars took us over the line and into the little town of C— —.

Here we hired hacks and drove out to the place Ellerton and I had agreed on—a picturesque spot, and one which Frank and I had visited when we were boys. It was a beautiful grass plat, of half an acre, lying between two hills, and bordered with a little gurgling branch.

We had hardly gotten out and dismissed the driver for half an hour, when the other carriage drove up, and Brazon and Ellerton got out, and with them a surgeon from the town.

We bowed to each other, and Ellerton and I stepped forward to measure the ground. We divided the sun and shade as equally as possible between them, Ellerton examined and loaded the pistols, and we arranged to place our men. Brazon was smoking with apparent indifference, but that it was assumed could be seen from the nervous, trembling way he would take his cigar from his mouth, and from the frequent yawns he made. DeVare was leaning against a tree in an abstracted manner, and started when I touched his arm.

"All is ready, Ramie," I said, conducting him to the spot assigned him. "Here, take this pistol, be cool and aim well."

He only looked at me and smiled, but said nothing. I told Ellerton he must give the word to fire, as I dared not, and I withdrew a short distance, and stood with uncovered head, breathing a prayer which I felt was a mockery.

Ellerton raised his handkerchief while I quivered with suspense; his voice rang out loud and clear:

"Ready! aim! fire!—one, two, three!"

At the word "one" Brazon fired, his ball cutting the foliage a yard over DeVare's head, while the echoes rolled in solemn groans through the woods around.

After the word "three" Ramie raised his pistol and fired into the air, the smoke curling gracefully up towards Heaven, as if from the altar of a peace offering.

We each ran to our principals.

"Ramie! Ramie!" I exclaimed, "this will never do; why on earth did you not fire at him? I am afraid now he will want another shot, as he sees your harmless intentions. A shot pretty close would have frightened him off."

"Perhaps you are right," he said quietly; "but then I might have killed him, and that is not my object."

Ellerton now approached, and, bowing, said:

"My principal claims another shot, as Mr. DeVare promised him satisfaction."

"He can get it," said DeVare, before I could interpose.

"He also begs," said Ellerton, addressing DeVare, "that you will do him the honor to fire at him, as he dislikes to aim at one who preserves your peaceful attitude."

"I shall do as I think best," replied DeVare, with so much dignity that Ellerton withdrew in some confusion.

Again were the pistols loaded and placed in their hands, and again rang out those deadly words, "Fire!—one, two, three!"

Brazon, who had become very nervous and excited, fired while the word "one" was yet on Ellerton's lips. DeVare gave a slight start, raised his pistol and aimed upward, then lowered his hand without firing, deliberately uncocked his weapon and dropped it beside him, then, closing his eyes with a sudden tightness, fell in a doubled-up heap to the ground. The heavy manner in which he fell, without regard to easing himself down, told me all.

I ran to him, and raised his head upon my arm; his eyes were still closed, and his face was pale as marble. He was drawing his breath in short gasps, at long intervals, while the blood was oozing from his lips, and trickling in little red streams down his chin and throat. The ball had entered below the right armpit, and ranged straight across toward the heart, and I supposed that internal hemorrhage caused the flow of blood from the mouth.

"Ramie! Ramie!" I called frantically, "are you hurt much? Speak to me, Ramie."

His eyes opened feebly on mine, and with considerable effort he whispered:

"I am almost gone, Jack."

The surgeon now approached with his case of instruments, and tearing open DeVare's coat, vest and shirt, examined the wound. A round spot, closed up with blood and torn flesh, showed where the death messenger had entered, and rose and fell with every labored breath. He contracted his brow as if in pain as the surgeon ran his probing wire in, but otherwise remained quiet and passive. The surgeon, as he drew his wire out and wiped it, put his mouth close to my ear and whispered:

"He cannot possibly live more than ten minutes. If he wishes to speak, tell him to cough up the blood from his throat and take a swallow of this," handing me a small vial that contained some powerful stimulant, "the ball has severed one of the large arteries directly at the heart, and he must soon bleed to death."

I put my mouth close to DeVare's ear and said:

"Ramie, do you wish to speak?"

He opened his eyes languidly, and with a motion of his brow signified yes. I wiped his lips and put the vial to his mouth. He swallowed a little of the liquid, which seemed to revive him for a moment. He tightened his clasp on my hand and said feebly:

"It is as I expected, John. Tell mother——" but the flow of blood choked his utterance again. I again put the vial to his lips, but he turned his head away from it, and in a whisper said:

"No, 'tis useless. Oh, my lonely mother, forgive me! Dear Christ have mercy——" A shuddering clasp of the white fingers locked in mine, a paler hue on the pallid face, and only Raymond DeVare's *body* lay in my arms. The great weight of impending evil I had so much dreaded had crushed down upon me, and I was almost senseless beneath the blow. I could not realize the fact, but sat in stupid wonderment, gazing at the lifeless features. Ramie, my fond, true friend, dead! So full of life and activity but a moment ago; now dead! Dead for my sake; dead because I was insulted; dead for a hasty word; dead on the warrant of cowardly society, that would now shrink from the poor fool who killed him at its behest. Dead! *dead!* DEAD!

I leaned my cheek down on the forehead, already growing cold, and murmured, weeping like a woman:

"No, no, Ramie, you are not dead? Speak to me, Ramie, one word, open your eyes; one more look, Ramie!

The surgeon touched my arm and said:

"The carriages have returned, as you ordered; we had better get the body in and drive back to C——, where you can telegraph to Wilmington for a case, and carry him home to-morrow."

I rose from the ground, laying Ramie's head gently on my handkerchief, and calling the coachman we lifted him up and laid him as well as we could across the seats of the carriage.

Ellerton and Brazon, who had been standing some distance off, smoking and talking carelessly, got into the other carriage, and, bowing as they passed us, drove rapidly on to the station. The doctor kindly asked, as we drove slowly on, what I intended to do.

"I don't know," I replied, vacantly.

"If you will allow me to suggest a plan, I would say go to our little hotel here, get a room for to-night, and telegraph immediately for a metallic case, which will, perhaps, come out on the evening train. The undertaker will seal it up for you, and you can carry it in to-morrow."

I thanked him for his kind advice, but told him that as I knew the conductors on the road I could take the body into the mail car with me till we got to Wilmington. I lowered the carriage curtains, and ordered the driver to go as close as possible to the track at the station and wait for the train. It was a very short time before the train came in, and I immediately sought out the conductor, who had known me since I was a boy, my father being one of the directors of the road. I told him my friend DeVare had been killed in a duel, and asked permission to carry the body in the mail car. He readily accorded it, and had the carriage driven close up to the door. But with all our precaution, quite a crowd gathered around as we lifted poor Ramie from the carriage and laid him on some cushions in the car. Some one had heard me call his name to the conductor, and it passed from mouth to mouth that "a young man named DeVare was killed this morning near here in a duel, and they are carrying him home."

The passengers in the coaches got hold of it, and I was very much annoyed by the impertinent yet natural curiosity with which one after another came to the door and looked at myself and the corpse. At last the whistle sounded, the train got under way, and I was free from interruptions. I leaned my face against a pile of mail bags, and gave way to miserable reflection. The present was too horrible to dwell on, and the future nothing but remorse and gloom. Remorse that I had not prevented the fatal affair at all hazards. Remorse that I had not conquered pride and satisfied Brazon with my own apologies and explanation; gloom that my prospects were blighted, father deceived, and angered into dislike of me, mother surprised and grieved beyond expression, and Carlotta horrified into repelling me; my career at the University, which I had resolved, after Lillian had discarded me, to make brilliant, now cut short in disgrace, and my hitherto exuberant spirits damped by an ever vivid remembrance of the terrible tragedy, in which I had taken so large a part. Then I thought of the shock I would give them at home as I drove up to the door with DeVare's dead body, and as I fancied the faces of horror and words of reproach, I shrank from the ordeal. My bitter reflections were interrupted by a hand laid on my shoulder. I looked up and found the conductor standing by me.

"There is a lady in the rear coach wishes to speak with you," he said, counting over some tickets he took from his pocket.

"Who is it?" I asked, looking at him vacantly.

"Don't know her. Perhaps she's some kin to you. She's a fine looking old lady, a little gray, sitting two seats from the back of the coach."

I begged that my friend might be unmolested, and made my way through the coaches to the last one. A lady was sitting two seats from the back, and the instant my eyes fell upon her I had to grasp the arm of a seat for support. The same noble features that were now lying so rigid in the car ahead; the same dark eye that I had so recently closed with a sorrowing hand! I knew in a moment it was his mother. I strengthened myself as well as I was able, and approaching her, bowed and said:

"Did you wish to see me, madam?"

She looked at me earnestly, as she replied:

"Pardon me, sir, but are you the gentleman whose friend has just been killed?"

"I am, madam."

"I heard a gentleman, a few seats from me, say the unfortunate man's name was DeVare. As that is my own name, and I have a dear boy who has been at college in North Carolina, I felt a restless anxiety to know more, and ventured to intrude on your grief."

I made no reply, and she continued:

"It was a silly fear in me, I'm sure. It could not have been Raymond, for he would have written to me."

I still said nothing, for the simple reason I did not know what to say, and, after a pause, she asked:

"What was your friend's given name, sir?"

Driven to a corner by her question, I made a stammering attempt to evade.

"It could not have been your son, madam," I said, with evident confusion; "my friend's name was Lionel."

Ramie's full name was Lionel Raymond, but he always signed his name simply as Raymond.

Her piercing gaze read my flimsy deception in a moment, and a quick pallor ran over her face, as if her heart had ceased beating for a while.

"My son's name was also Lionel. Surely, sir, you would not trifle with my feelings? I must go into the front car and satisfy myself," she said, rising from her seat.

"Madam," I said, putting out my hand to detain her, "I implore you to be seated. The train will reach Wilmington in a few moments, and you can then see for yourself. Heaven forbid that it should be your son!"

At this moment the conductor approached, gathering up the tickets for the last station. She called him to her and said, with an air of command it was impossible to resist:

"I wish to go to the front car and look at the corpse there. You will go with me, sir?"

"I should advise you, ma'am, to sit still," said the conductor, snipping a hole in the last ticket he had taken; "it's not a pleasant sight for a lady, and we'll soon get to Wilmington any how."

"I only wished your aid in crossing the platforms, but I will go alone," she said firmly, passing us both and walking rapidly up the aisle.

I followed mechanically, feeling that nothing could add to the intensity of my wretchedness. I assisted her from car to car, till, passing through heaps of mail bags, we reached the end of the coach where lay the still form of Ramie, wrapped in my travelling shawl. She kneeled by its side, and, turning back the shawl, gazed for a moment on the pallid face, and then, with a shriek that often now rings in my ears, fell forward insensible on the breast of her dead child. The mail agent came forward, and we tried all the usual restoratives without the slightest effect. No sign of returning animation responded to our efforts, and, making the best couch we could, we were about to lay her by Ramie's side when the whistle sounded for Wilmington, and the train drew up close to the boat that was to take us over the river. The conductor and the captain of the boat aided me so kindly that the body of Ramie and his unconscious mother were conveyed on board without attracting very much attention. A carriage on the other side took us to the hotel, where I had concluded it was best to go since Mrs. DeVare had become unconscious. I ordered rooms, despatched one messenger for a physician and another for father; then, without waiting for them to come, I left the hotel and walked rapidly homeward, for I began to experience very singular sensations in mind and body—a tingling numbness, that deadened my extremities; and alternations of sudden forgetfulness of all that had occurred, and vivid remembrance of it. I reached our door, and pushing it open, found Carlotta in the hall. She started at my haggard face, and exclaimed:

"Oh! John, what is the matter? where is Mr. DeVare? what has happened?"

"He is dead!" I said, with a vacant stare; then, turning, rushed up stairs, heedless of her calls for mother. I managed to reach my bed, when I fell across it into a great black chasm of oblivion.

CHAPTER XXVI

How strange those long days of insensibility now seem! How mysterious that vague consciousness of unconsciousness, when the mind closes all communication with the outer world, and lives in a state of semi-existence within itself! All sight was gone, yet a dull gray blank pressed down upon my eyeballs—gray and dull, though invisible; all hearing was gone, yet a singing sound lingered in my ears, as if a cap had been exploded near them; feeling there was none, yet an undefined pain and sickness pervaded my system, like a dream of deadly nausea. A gap in existence, a chasm in thought and sense, known through the veil of an uncertain consciousness! After a long while, as it seemed to me, vague, uncertain shadows began to flit across this dull blank before my vision. Gradually, after many flittings, they began to assume varying shapes; and, as the form and features of a negative slowly come into distinctness as the photographer washes the plate, so these shapes began to show distinctly as familiar forms and faces. But oh! how changed their expression! Those whom I had thought loved me most now wore the blackest scowl for me, and, pointing at me, called me Murderer! Father, mother and Carlotta stood around me constantly, regarding me with a fiendish malignity and hatred. But among all the faces that passed before me there was one that never changed its position or expression—always directly before me, almost touching mine; a face with a stony glare from its fixed eyes; a face with a snarl of hate on its white lips, from which bubbled a froth of blood; a face I could never escape, go where I would. I sprang over frightful precipices, I traversed burning deserts, I climbed rugged wilds, but everywhere, turning as I turned, *that* face was ever before me, freezing my blood with its hideous scowl. After awhile these visions became less distinct, and soon another blank succeeded, during which I one day unclosed my eyes and found everything familiar around me.

The room was darkened and silent. The occasional clicking of the coals in the grate, as they powdered their red cheeks with white ashes, and the foot-fall of a passer on the pavement below, were all the sounds I could hear. I tried to raise myself on my elbow to make out what it all meant, but I had scarcely made the effort when some one rose from a chair at the side of the bed, and Carlotta's beautiful face bent over me, with an expression of anxious inquiry, as if she thought I was still delirious.

"Where—where have I been? How came I in bed?" I said, in a weak, drawling voice.

"Oh, you are yourself again!" she exclaimed, with a cry of delight; "let me run and tell Mrs. Smith."

"No; stop! Tell me what I am doing in this dark room. What is the matter with me?"

"You have been very sick," she said, removing a wet cloth from my forehead, and wiping the dampness away; "you have been delirious for more than two weeks. But the doctor says you must lie still and not talk."

"But I *will* talk," I said, peevishly; "I *will* know how I came here. Where are Ned and Ramie?"

A half distinct memory of the duel and its consequences flitted across my mind, but it was all so confused that it seemed some horrid dream, and in helpless uncertainty I turned my cheek over on my palm and gazed at Carlotta, imploringly.

She stroked my forehead with her soft hand, and begged me to remain quiet, promising to tell me all I wanted to know as soon as I became a little stronger. Her touch and sweet voice were so soothing that I fell into a gentle doze, from which I soon awoke much clearer in my mind than before. And now a blighting remembrance of Ramie's death came over me, with such force as to nearly unsettle my reason again.

Mother soon came in, and, by skilfully diverting my thoughts from the painful subject, managed to remove some of the shadows that clustered around me.

Days lengthened into weeks before I was able to sit up, and how dreary would have been those convalescent hours had it not been for Carlotta! She seemed to have no interest outside of my room. Her attention was never officious or too constant, and it was rendered with so much tact it seemed as if I was conferring a favor by accepting it. I was so sure it was a pleasure to her that I never refused letting her do whatever she would for me. She would sit by my bedside for hours reading or talking to me, seeking to divert me by all means possible from gloomy thoughts or sad reflections. So bright was the sunshine of her presence that I was unhappy unless she were near me; and however dreary I might be feeling, as soon as she entered, my face and heart would sensibly brighten.

While she would never allow me to draw her into conversation about Ramie and his mother, yet I gradually learned the sad truth. After Madame DeVare was carried to the hotel every effort was made by the physicians to revive her, but in vain. The cataleptic stroke, induced by the shock she received, in spite of all their labor, proved fatal, and she and Ramie were buried together in the cemetery the same day.

Then Carlotta would listen with such a pleasant, talk-eliciting interest to my stories of college life that I could talk with untiring volubility. In return she would tell me of all that had occurred at home since I had been away, with so much originality of expression and artlessness of narration that I would lie and gaze for an hour at a time on her faultless face. Occasionally she would lift her eyes from her needlework, and whenever they met mine I always looked away with a strange and unaccountable confusion.

One day, in our talk, she asked me if Frank and I were still good friends. I told her no, and inquired why she asked.

"Because Lulie has changed so in her conduct towards me. She has been very reserved and formal with me since you left, and rarely visits me."

"Has Frank been paying her much attention this vacation?" I asked, taking a sip of the cordial that stood by my bed.

"I have not had many opportunities for observing," she replied, driving her stiletto through a floss flower on her embroidery; "but I have seen them together many times, and gossip says they are very much devoted. Perhaps it is at his request she has withdrawn her intimacy from me."

"No doubt of it," I replied; "she is perfectly infatuated, and he cares nothing whatever for her, except as a conquest to boast of. I heard him read one of her letters to a crowd in his room one night, and tell of liberties he had taken."

Her dark eyes opened with a flash of indignant astonishment as she exclaimed, energetically:

"And she trusts to such perfidy! I'll warn her, if she spurns me, for we have been fond friends. But no," she added, after a pause; "that would implicate you, and perhaps lead to another affray."

"I don't care," I said, punching in the end of the pillow, as if it were Frank's head; "tell her by all means. I would go to her myself, but she would think it was an invention of my own to supersede Frank in her favor."

"I hear Mrs. Smith coming up stairs," said Carlotta, folding up her work; "and as it is late in the afternoon I'll run over to Dr. Mayland's and have a good long talk with Lulie, and get back in time to bring up your tea."

"Bless your dear heart, how I love you!" I murmured, as I watched her tucking back the curtains and setting everything to rights ere she tripped from the room. I could not help instituting a comparison between her and

Miss Carrover, and I could find only one point in the latter's favor: that she was a grown lady, who had seen much of society, while Carlotta was, to my college dignity, only a child—too often present for the romantic sigh, and too constantly near for the heart-throb when I met her.

And, in thinking of Lillian, the faint shadow of a demon thought began to flit across my mind. The baseness of its ingratitude made me shudder as I shrank from it; yet it gradually grew, ever lurking deep down in my heart, as it whispered, through the reveries of the day and the dreams of the night, "Lillian can love you now; Ramie is dead."

Deeply ungrateful as it was to the memory of my noble friend, I could not help looking forward with pleasure to my meeting with her: when I could take her hand, and, looking into her fond eyes, hear her say, "Nothing binds me now; I am yours forever."

I would then endeavor to plaster over conscience by imagining how fondly we would cherish together the memory of DeVare; how we would pour our mingled tears upon his grave, and feel that his spirit was smiling upon our union. And I would endeavor to convince myself that I would be acting in exact conformity to the wishes of Ramie, could he express them; and I would say a dozen times in a day, "I am sure Ramie had rather she would love me than another."

A day or two elapsed and I was able to walk about the house before Carlotta had an opportunity of telling me the result of her visit to Lulie.

She said that as soon as she mentioned the subject Lulie had gotten into quite a passion about it, and said she had parents to advise her, and that she was under obligations to no one else for advice; that she would do as she pleased and take the consequences.

"May heaven help her," I said fervently, as we changed the subject.

CHAPTER XXVII

Ned and I are again at Chapel Hill, in our old room. We found our books and furniture dusty, but undisturbed, and a day's preparation sufficed to get us in harness again.

It was with great difficulty father had secured my re-admission. His first application was peremptorily refused, but by many letters and pledges to the trustees and faculty, and in consideration of my youth and inexperience, I was at last allowed to go on with my class.

For all this I had made extra resolves of diligence, and had promised father that nothing should divert me from intense application to my books.

Of Miss Carrover I thought but little. I had heard from Charleston, whither she had gone soon after the duel, that she was the gayest belle of its society. This disregard of what was due the memory of her betrothed, coupled with the gradually acquired conviction that my suit was hopeless, and a conscientious desire to do well in my studies, had somewhat impaired the romantic fervor of my admiration for her, and I heard with remarkable composure the statement that she would spend a week or two in Chapel Hill on her way to New York. I resolved at first not to see her at all; but, feeling that this was too great a confession of weakness, even to myself, and having, besides, in my possession the valuables DeVare had requested me to deliver to her, I determined to call just once, that I might mark her deportment before making up my final judgment on her character. Of one thing I was fully resolved, that whether she was gay or sad, whether kind and cordial or cold and distant towards me, no word or glance of mine should betray the faintest trace of the old love, or depart from the consistent seriousness of real bereavement.

When I entered the parlor at Professor Z——'s I found her surrounded by a throng of admirers. As she came forward to meet me, the same superbly beautiful woman I had once adored, her usual queenly air softened into one of kindest greeting, and gave me both hands in her warm welcome, my heart bounded wildly, and for a moment I had forgotten Ramie, resolves, and everything save the rapture of being near her again—of hearing her soft, rich voice, and gazing into her dreamy eyes. The presence of other gentlemen restrained me, or I believe I should have knelt at her feet.

Taking my seat in the circle, and dropping into a commonplace conversation, I gradually regained my senses and my self-control. And as I became composed, and marked the levity of her conduct—the jest, the sarcasm and the repartee—and then thought of the cold form in the cemetery at home, my admiration of her beauty was tinged with contempt for her frivolity.

Her visitors began to depart, and I was about to say good night without having accomplished my mission, when she handed me a slip of paper, on which she had scribbled the words "Don't leave."

Of course I waited, and we were soon in the parlor alone.

As the last one closed the door she moved on the sofa and said:

"Come, sit by me. Oh, how tiresome those fellows are! and I wanted to be alone with you so much. Now tell me all about yourself, for it has been a dreary, long time since I have seen you."

"I thought you were aware, Miss Carrover, that I was connected with a most unfortunate affair at the close of the session," I replied, nervously twisting my watch chain, for I hardly knew what reply to make, and felt embarrassed and awkward.

"Oh! do not speak of that," she exclaimed, burying her face in her handkerchief, and trembling with very inaudible sobs. "I was trying to avoid that subject. My heart has been almost broken in its agony. Only in the past few days have I been able to compose my thoughts and feelings. Oh, the terrible shock of the announcement!" Her voice was so muffled by the handkerchief over her face that her words were almost indistinguishable. Far better could they have been lost in the cambric folds than to have vibrated into eternal existence!

The only reply I could make was to give her the casket containing Ramie's ring and jewels, as he had directed.

She lifted her face, with eyes rather dry for such convulsive weeping, and taking the casket pressed it to her lips, as she said:

"And did he think of me! Oh, how can I ever love you enough for your kindness to him!"

I ventured to say, "Love his memory."

"I do, I do," she replied, looking into my eyes with hers clear and tearless. "Heaven alone knows how I cherish the memory of my noble Ramie!"

I did her the justice to believe her, but said nothing.

She continued, trying to open the back of the watch:

"But, my dear friend, for this mutual grief has made you seem nearer than ever before, there is one point on which I want your counsel. How must I act towards society? Must I open my heart to its hundred eyes, and, by a sudden seclusion and retirement, reveal my sacred sorrow to its gaze; or must I go through the hollow mockery of gaiety, and assume a cheerful face with an aching heart? Gentlemen call every evening, and I am at a loss to know what to do. If I refuse to receive visitors it will cause remark and inquiry, and my engagement with Mr. DeVare will be made public, with all the usual train of disagreeable comment. I sometimes think it were best to do violence to my own feelings, and appear in company as if nothing had happened, while I am here. I will soon be in New York, where I can adapt my conduct to my sad bereavement. Do you not think so?"

"Really, Miss Carrover," I replied, coldly, for the veil of her pretended sorrow was too thin, "I do not feel competent to advise you. You know best how the death of DeVare affects you; and, if you will pardon me for saying it, your smiles and favors to the frivolous throng to-night would indicate that your course of action is already determined."

"Oh, Mr. Smith, you blame me, I know you do, and perhaps I deserve it; but you cannot appreciate my feelings. I did love Ramie devotedly, for he was the noblest and best of earth; but no one knew we were betrothed, and to retire from society now would be only to reveal what he wished kept secret. Besides, I will be candid enough to confess that I find the best cure for a sad heart in a round of pleasure, and, knowing that seclusion and manifested grief were not expected of me, I have sought to drown my sorrow in a whirl of frivolity."

She paused, and looked at me for some reply, but, as I could make none but what would have offended her, I said nothing.

"I know serious people will blame me for this trifling," she continued, "but gaiety and pleasure are as much my element as the air I breathe. Those who know me will not cease to love me. And you, who once professed such devotion, now hate me, because I do not wear a widow's weeds! Please do not desert me when we ought to become better friends; love me still," and she laid her soft, beautiful hand on mine.

Who could have resisted? A moment before I was despising her heartlessness, now, at the electric touch of her hand, I was changed; the old flame burst forth again with resistless fervor, and I could take her, heartless as she was, to be forever mine, only so that she loved me. I almost crushed her hand in mine as I pressed my lips upon it again and again.

"Love you, Lillian! Heaven only knows how madly, how wildly I do love you. Only say just once that you love me, or bid me hope. I have never ceased to love you, Lillian, but your faith was plighted to another, and I crushed my heart into silence. But he who stood between us is dead, and, as God shall judge me, I have sorrowed sincerely over his grave; but nothing now binds you; you are free to love me if you will. Darling, darling Lillian, come to my heart and be its queen."

I put forth my arms to draw her to my side, but she drew back and said:

"No, sir, the change is too sudden. A moment ago there was a look of contempt on your face—nay, do not deny it—and now you would have me believe these wild protestations of your phœnix-like love."

There was a gleam of triumph in her eyes that told me she did believe me, and gloried in her wondrous power, but I was careless of everything save to be lord of her hand and heart.

"Lillian," I said, gazing into her face with such intense earnestness that even her eyes fell beneath my gaze, "you once believed me; will you doubt me now when I swear to you that I love you as no other man ever dared love you before—that I am willing to give up everything for your sake, even the memory of Ramie? If that stands between our love, I will forget that he ever lived and forget that he ever died."

I felt a shudder run from her frame into her hand as the harsh words fell from my lips, but 'twas only a shudder.

"You are sure you mean what you say?" she said, with a half credulous smile that irritated me, and a slight pressure of her fingers that soothed and made me hopeful. I waited for her to continue, and we both sat for a few moments gazing into the glowing coals on the hearth before us. Suddenly, deep in the fire, where the heat was whitest, a dull red spot appeared, that seemed to rise and fall as if there was breath beneath it. In an instant I was again kneeling on the damp ground, with a white face resting on my arm, and pale lips bubbling blood as they bade me farewell. It was as vivid as vision itself; and after the eyes were closed by the surgeon's hand, I could still see the pale lips murmuring, "False! False!"

My hands and forehead grew cold as ice, and my heart, in its remorse, beat audibly, "False loving false! False loving false!" My resolve was taken from that moment; I would not be shaken from it by scorn or tears. I dropped her hand and, rising, said:

"Miss Carrover, I did mean all that I said; you know that I have loved you; but forget it. Even if you could love me, which I dare not hope, it must not be—Ramie's spirit forbids it. Will you pardon what I have said tonight?"

She rose and stood before me, the personification of anger and scorn, her dreamy eyes now flashing, and her beautiful face flushed with her feeling.

"Do you fear that I am going to accept your paltry love, that you hasten to retract it? Not content with insulting me with your cant about what was due the dead, you have attempted a contemptible flirtation. To say that I saw through your pitiful design, would indicate that I paid some attention to your rhodomontade, which I did not; but 'tis useless to waste further words upon you; I can never sufficiently express my contempt; there! go, sir!" and with a gesture that would have graced Siddons she pointed her jewelled hand to the door.

With a profound bow, I said:

"Thanks, Miss Carrover, for the lesson of to-night. But before I take my leave permit me to remind you that you asked my adv— —" but she had swept magnificently from the room.

The next evening, while strolling with Ned on the suburbs of the village, I met Miss Carrover riding in a buggy with Ellerton, who had not yet applied for re-admission to the University, but was staying with a friend. She looked confused as she passed us, and averted her head, while I turned and stared at them till they were out of sight.

"Oh, Ramie, Ramie," I murmured, as we turned homeward, "better to wed death than the false creature of thy betrothal; better the worm at thy lips than her kiss; better the sod on thy cheek than her Delilah-like caresses."

CHAPTER XXVIII

About the first of April I received a letter from father, saying that they had at last concluded to put in execution a plan that had been spoken of before I left home—namely, going to Europe while I was finishing my studies. They would go first to Cuba, where they would spend some time at Carlotta's home, and where father could attend to the management of her large estates. They would then sail directly for Liverpool, and spend two or three years in England and on the continent. I was to graduate at Chapel Hill, then go to Berlin or Heidelberg.

I felt almost irresistibly impelled to write and ask permission to accompany them, but reflecting on it, determined to remain at Chapel Hill and study with renewed diligence.

A second letter, some weeks later, informed me that all necessary arrangements had been completed, and that father, mother and Carlotta would be in Raleigh on a specified night, on their way to New York, to take steamer for Havana, and requesting me to meet them, to say good-bye.

At the appointed time I met them, and while they were cheerful I could not help feeling sad at the thought of being left here alone; but I bore up bravely under the disappointment, and promised father that he should hear a good report of me.

After tea he and mother walked up town to see an old friend, and Carlotta and I were left together. While she was affable and pleasant as possible, I could not shake off a silent moodiness, and she, to divert me, and to relieve our rather dull conversation, brought me a casket of jewels that belonged to her mother. They had been sent to her by the agent of Mr. Rurleston's estate in Cuba, and had reached her since I left home. There were antique rings and bracelets of most exquisite workmanship, there were diamonds that would have made Mahmoud of Ghisni envious, and pearls that would have equalled the Zanana. I was very much struck by the design of a pair of bracelets. They were made in Etruscan gold and were a pair of serpents with ruby eyes and emerald spots. They were made long, flexible and spiral, so that when clasped upon the arm they seemed to be gliding up the flesh. There was some long family history connected with them, which Carlotta related, but I have forgotten its tenor. But the most interesting article in the casket was a beautifully enamelled locket, containing a picture of her mother. When she opened it and I looked upon the face, I was perfectly entranced. Its beauty was of that radiant perfection that seems only to have existed in the conceptions of Vandyke or Correggio. It was perfect in every exquisite feature, yet its wondrous fascination lay in their combination. The lustrous, pensive eyes, the delicately curved mouth, the soft, olive complexion, the oval outline of her face, were all beautifully relieved by the rich mass of raven hair that fell in splendid profusion over the bare, smooth neck.

Lillian's beauty depended greatly on her skilful adornment, and her brilliant appearance was ever in debt to her toilet, but this face needed no cosmetic, its beauty was nature's gift, and art could only enhance it.

It was my ideal, and my heart only withheld its homage because 'twas but a portrait.

Looking up from it to address Carlotta, I was startled to find in her face an exact counterpart of the picture, only her features were childish and immature. Her beauty was the bud, this the perfect bloom.

"Will she be like this when she is grown? Heavens! how I would adore her!" I thought, as I gazed from one to the other and marked the points of resemblance.

I had ever regarded Carlotta as a pretty child, whom everybody admired, but I had not thought of her as growing up into the perfect, lovely woman; but now a strange indescribable unrest awoke in my heart, and I felt that I should be far more unhappy when she was gone than I had thought.

While I had never, and could not then think of loving her, save as a friend and brother, yet the reflection that she was going away to forget me and perhaps to love another, was galling in the extreme to my feelings, both of pride and disappointment.

"Carlotta," I said, handing the picture back to her with a compliment, and looking at her with a newly awakened interest, "I fear that amid all the splendor and novelty of the scenes through which you will soon pass, you will forget almost that I ever lived."

"No, indeed," she replied, looking at me frankly, "there is no danger of that; gratitude, if nothing else, will keep your memory ever fresh with me."

"But you will be a grown lady ere you return, and will, I know, have many admirers. You will love some one of them, and I will be only a cipher in your past."

"No, no, you have been too noble and good to me. Do you think me so base? Here!" and taking a pair of scissors from her box, she cut off a long curling ringlet of hair and put it in my hand, "keep that as my pledge that I will remember you every day while I am gone, and no matter when we meet again I promise to redeem it, as the same little Carlotta you have been so kind to."

"Thank you, Carlotta, I will treasure it carefully," I said, folding it up with a strange thrill of pleasure for only a child's simple gift.

Father and mother came back now, and after a few words of parting and some tears, I bade them good-bye and hastened down to the office, as I was to return to Durham's on the night train.

Oh, what a pleasure to me was that single lock of hair!

For days and months after they were gone a glance at it would recall her dear face in all its beautiful earnestness, as she so unhesitatingly pledged her remembrance. And now that she was gone—for years, perhaps forever—I found—yes, I will confess it—child as she was, *I loved her.*

CHAPTER XXIX

The session and a vacation in the mountains passed, I commenced my studies as a Sophomore, and under this new dignity fresh trials of my moral courage every day arose. I was constantly being solicited to join some scheme of devilment, and though my conscience always bade me refuse, the voice of the multitude often prevailed, and I was thus drawn into many an affair of which I was afterward heartily ashamed.

Our class seemed determined to surpass all of its predecessors in annoyances to the Faculty, the derangement and often destruction of college property and the "devilling" of Fresh. One of the Faculty, whose views of discipline were rigid, and who could not brook the slightest disturbance in his room, was our special mark. Going into recitation we would load our pockets with gravel and acorns, and by dextrously throwing them over our neighbor's shoulder we would keep a perfect hail of them upon the floor, rendering recitation impossible. Sometimes a rat would be carried in and turned loose in the room, and every one would mount his seat in an apparent extremity of terror. Bugs, reptiles and even poisonous snakes were put on the floor, to run under the students' legs and cause a sufficient disturbance to suspend the lecture.

An attempt to "blow up" the professor was even made by placing a small quantity of powder under his rostrum; which, indeed, came near being a much more serious matter than was intended.

One morning, as Ned and I came out from breakfast, we were requested to go up to one of our classmate's rooms, where we found nearly the whole class assembled. The object of the meeting was, so we were informed, to consider the proposition to "dress" for L— —, the professor. To "dress" for a professor was to attend lecture in the most ridiculous and grotesque costume attainable, and had ever been regarded by the Faculty as the highest contempt for their authority, and an offence meriting extreme punishment.

The proposition was warmly seconded and approved, there being only one dissenting voice, that of Ned.

When the roll was called for the votes, he rose and said that, while he regretted to oppose himself to the class, yet the course proposed tended to defeat the object of their attendance upon the Institution, and was, therefore, wrong; that it was undignified and discourteous, and that he could not join them.

Amid cries of "Bootlick! order! Cheyleigh, you're right! silence!" Ned took his hat and walked quietly from the room.

When my name was called, poor, weak I, could only respond, "I am in for anything the class agrees on," while my heart was throbbing to follow Ned's example.

When we assembled, at eleven o'clock, could Falstaff have seen us he would have thought his troop perfect dandies. Great, tall fellows, six feet high, appeared in coats whose sleeves scarce reached their elbow, and pants that were far above their knees. Little fellows had on clothes that smothered them, and which were stuffed out with pillows till Daniel Lambert would have been a skeleton beside them. Others wore pasteboard collars, whose points extended far above their heads, while a whole window curtain of flaming chintz served them for a cravat. Some had their clothing on wrong side out, and one man had reversed his entire suit, putting everything on hind part before. A few had gone to the trouble of getting up costumes from the stores, and appeared as demons and devils with most hideous faces, and horns, hoofs and tails. The most amusing character of all was a rare genius from the mountains, whom everybody knew as Joe. A man of brilliant ability and rare attainments, he was a great favorite with the Faculty, and yet, from his innate love of fun, he was ever getting into some difficulty. He was attired, on this occasion, in an immense swallow tailed coat of brown homespun, and tremendous copperas striped pants. He had gotten a pair of shoe-store signs down town and wore them for boots, the legs coming up nearly to his waist and the feet about a yard long. He wore a tremendous pair of green goggles, and carried around his neck a rusty old log chain, from which was suspended a large circular clock to serve as his watch. A turn down collar of white cloth extending to his shoulders like a cape, and a whole sheet crammed in his pocket as a handkerchief, completed his outfit. He was unanimously chosen our leader and we marched to the section room. The professor looked serious and was ominously silent till we were all seated. He called the roll with unusual gravity, and then, that the desired defeat of the recitation might not be accomplished, commenced to examine the class; but the attempt was futile. One would reply that he would answer the question as soon as he could get his voice up out of his collar; another, that his pants were almost long enough and were stretching, and that as soon as they got past his knees he would take pleasure in telling all he knew. Joe, upon being called on, took out his clock with a great rattle of his chain, then drawing out his immense sheet, proceeded to wipe his goggles with it, and then blow his nose as if it was a trumpet. The ridiculousness of this proceeding called forth such a laugh from the class that the professor dismissed us in disgust, first summoning all of us to appear before the Faculty when the bell rang.

Immediately on our dismissal we held an informal meeting in the campus and agreed to appear before the Faculty in our costumes. There was a wide stare of indignation and surprise on their faces as we filed into the room and took our seats. The professor preferred his charges, and the president, having called on each member of the board for an expression of opinion, asked us if we had anything to say in justification of our offence. No one spoke for several moments, and they were about to proceed with the case when Joe slowly rose to his feet and said in solemn tones:

"Mr. President and gentlemen of the Faculty—I have somewhat to say in behalf of these my friends. Will you be kind enough to state what length of time you will allow me for their defence?"

He paused and waited a reply, looking as solemn through his great frog-eyed spectacles as if he was in the High Court of Chancery.

"Speak on, Mr. — —," the chairman replied, "we cannot entertain your nonsensical proposals for time, but we are willing to allow you to make any statement you wish, and to give any excuses you can for your conduct."

"My friends," said Joe, turning to us, "do you hear that? Bear me witness, and see that they accord the full measure of their promise."

So saying, he drew from under his coat the old clock, and taking the chain from his neck, he let it clatter with great noise on the floor, and laid the clock before him on a bench, after the manner of public speakers. He then carefully noted the time, cleared his throat, adjusted his specs and began:

"Oh, most worthy Paishdadians, the early dispensers of justice, in whom are centred the majesty of the Pharaohs, the wisdom of the Magi, and the dignity of the Conscript Fathers, both Roman and Sabine! I would not detain you with useless words, but simply tell why we have appeared to-day in costumes which you, in the plenitude of your wisdom, have deemed offensive:

"We are unfortunate young men, severed from the endearments of home and cut off from the paternal exchequer; no sewing sisters' love, no darning mothers' care! Can you wonder that our wardrobes have suffered such considerable depletion that we must make some changes or renew? As to renew was impossible, with remittances rarer than angels' visits, we wisely chose to change.

"The apparent absurdity of these changes is at once explained by their utility as well as their necessity. Permit me to enumerate a few, and point out their peculiar advantages. I have been, as you all know, of very studious habits; consequently the abrasion of my *sedes pantaloonorum* has been constant. As concealment was no longer possible I exchanged with a smaller friend, whose shortness of leg will enable him to draw the trite orifices up beyond the reach of vision, while the brevity of his unmentionables enables me to preserve my respectability by the display of a new pair of socks, which I borrowed.

"My fat friend here found that his garments were wearing out more on the inside than the out, and, consequently, exchanges with this starved anatomy, that the outside may catch up. He then squeezes into the lean man's suit, to reduce his pinguisity. My reversed friend here," pointing to the man who had his clothes with the front turned behind, "has been suffering with a chronic crick till his head has twisted entirely around. With an energy worthy of Ithacus he has resolved to retrograde through life, rather than submit to the tyranny of his neck and change his clothes; hence his remarkable attitude and crawfish gait.

"The other gentlemen present have reasons equally good for the fashions they have adopted, and which this out-of-the-way place may deem a little *outré*.

"This much, gentlemen, to show that my comrades, as well as myself, had cause for our conduct. But I see by the cold regard of your stern faces that you do not believe me. If it were not for the consumption of your valuable time I could introduce witnesses to prove what I have stated, but 'tis useless."

"Stop, sir!" exclaimed the president, "we have endured this farce long enough. Gentlemen," addressing the Faculty, "what are your opinions of the offence and its punishment?"

"Sir!" said Joe, with a green, piercing glance, "you have promised that you would allow me to make my defence, and I claim the privilege."

"Well, go on, sir, we cannot wait much longer."

"I shall take my leisure," said Joe, stooping down to look at the face of his clock. "Well, I pass on to my secondly, then. My firstly was a statement of facts; my secondly shall be argument, and my thirdly, appeal. I do then emphatically deny to you the right of jurisdiction in our case. You cannot take cognizance, even, of our proceedings unless you make the University of North Carolina a tailor's shop and prescribe the fashions for its students. What right have the Faculty of a purely literary Institution to say what shall be the cut of my coat, merely because I am a matriculate? By what authority do you object to my clothing, so long as it is decent? and I am sure none of my friends here can be accused of indecency of apparel.

"If, however, you insist upon your right, by what standard do you condemn our appearance? Do you know what the latest fashions are? Have any of you seen a Paris paper this year, and are you certain that your information on these points is later than mine. If so, I cheerfully waive the right to determine for myself, and submit to your direction. But why multiply remarks; if you can find us guilty of any infringement of the laws of the University, behold we are in your hands, to be dealt with after our sins, but we do protest against being condemned by some perverted construction of a remote rule.

"And now we know, although you have no right, yet you will try us and condemn us. We throw ourselves upon your mercy. Oh! be tender with us. We are young and unsophisticated; we are away from father and mother, and some of us, alas! are orphans; will you deal harshly with us simply for changing our fashion? Oh! ye who have sons, plead with those who have not, and obtain for us clemency. Do not, with puritanic bigotry, strain at a gnat of a garment and swallow a camel of cruelty. Oh have mercy! Have mercy! We have suffered the pangs of remorse, our bowels have yearned over our transgression and groaned for dinner, and we are ready now to get down upon our all fours and gallop out the door if you will only speak the word. Speak it—bohoo-oo! Spe-oo-ea-oo-kit!"

He pulled his great sheet handkerchief out, and spreading it on the bench before him, buried his face in it and sobbed aloud.

The Faculty did not smile, and we were too badly scared to laugh; and so Joe raised his head soon and wiped his eyes, took up his clock and chain and put it on again, then leaned back as solemn and sad as Heraclitus.

The President then rose, and without the slightest appreciation of Joe's effort, said:

"Your conduct, gentlemen, has been considered by the Faculty in an impartial and unprejudiced manner, and their unanimous vote is that you be dismissed for an indefinite period.

"The farcical character of your defence, delivered through your representative, and its absurd and contemptible conclusion, place it too far beneath our notice for any reply; but I wish to say a word or two to those who have engaged in this affair thoughtlessly. There is a very mistaken idea among students generally that it is manly and courageous to resist constituted authority, and that such a course will gain for them a reputation for independence and spirit. They forget that in this resistance, and in the obstruction of recitation, they injure only themselves, and defeat the very end for which they have come to college. Resistance to tyranny is sometimes worthy of admiration, but here there can be no tyranny, for the same rights and protection are guaranteed the students as the tutor, and an appeal to the right source would prove a far more speedy and effective remedy than the course pursued.

"Many of you joined in this shameful affair for the want of moral courage, and scarcely one of you really desired to enter into it. To those who originated the plot I would say, remember that those you persuade to join you suffer equally with yourselves, and your magnanimity will surely deter you from getting others into trouble; and I would beg those who were led into this, in future to consider the certain result of their conduct; disgrace and mortification, without a single point being gained. And I ask you all, does the paltry pleasure of raising a laugh, repay even the trouble of dressing, much less the shame each one feels or ought to feel? I hope that you will look at this question of deportment in its true light and act thereon. You have heard the sentence, gentlemen, and can retire."

We sauntered from the room, and, once outside, commenced a Babel of confused talk, which was broken up by our departing to our rooms to put on some decent apparel. I sat down and commenced to indite a letter to father, but found it impossible to write in the excited state of my mind. As we had to leave the Hill in a few hours after our dismissal, I began to pack my trunk. Soon after dinner, however, I learned that the members of the class who had not joined us, had gotten up a petition for our reinstatement. The Faculty required a pledge of future good behavior from each of us concerned before they would entertain the petition at all; and I found to my surprise that those who had been most anxious to get up the "dress," and who had been most violent in their outcry against those who refused to join them, were now the most solicitous of all that the petition should be signed, and were among the first to put their names to the pledge. There was one exception, Joe refused to sign anything or in any way recognize the right of the Faculty to condemn us. He declared he would stand by the principles set forth in his speech, and nothing could move him from it. In spite of his frolics he was a great favorite with the Faculty, and several of them went to him privately and endeavored to persuade him to sign the pledge. He thanked them, but firmly declined, and next morning took his departure. We all gave him three cheers as he drove off to Durham's, which he returned by waving his handkerchief till he was out of sight.

True old Joe! The last tidings I had of him were that, as Colonel in the Confederate army, he had refused parole at Appomattox and gone to the Dry Tortugas.

CHAPTER XXX

The Spring session opened with pleasant prospects for us all. I was conveniently situated for study, and resolved to make the most of my opportunity. The great college office in those days was Marshal for the commencement exercises. Even early in the session those interested commenced to electioneer for their respective favorites. Frank was one of the candidates, and in the race for popularity his demagogical spirit was wonderfully successful. He had never had much to do with me since the death of DeVare, but he now seemed determined to renew our old intimacy.

As he fully possessed the art of making himself agreeable, and hiding his cloven foot, I enjoyed some very pleasant hours with him.

He was even confidential with me; said that he was engaged to Lulie, and that she loved him very devotedly, but that he had not quite made up his mind yet.

"And when do you expect to marry her?" I asked one day, when we had been talking about her.

"Marry, did you say? Ha! ha! that is a good one. Marry, the devil! Why, you do not suppose that I am in earnest with her, do you?"

"You ought to be, if she loves you, as you say she does, and as I believe," I replied, with indignation in my tone.

"Well, perhaps I am," he said with a careless laugh; "without boasting, she is certainly infatuated with me, and I—I love to be with her, hold her hand and clasp her waist, and all that sort of thing, but whether you call that love or not I do not know."

"Why, you do not mean to say you have gone as far as that?" I asked, in surprise, for I had not supposed that Lulie, with all her infatuation, would permit such liberties.

"Umph! I should think I had; and I count myself deucedly fortunate; for it isn't every day a fellow kisses such lips as hers."

"Frank, you shock me."

"Do I? Oh, Lulie is very prudent, with every one else; but you see with her betrothed she feels a little freer. By the way, John, how did you make it with Miss Carrover?"

"I had a pretty fair game," I replied, cautiously, for I did not wish to be communicative. "Did you try your hand there?"

"Only a little," he replied; "a stolen kiss or two and a half squeeze was all I got from her. Ellerton had it out with her though."

"You surprise me," I said. "I thought she was very chary of her favors."

"Chary, the devil! I could tell you of a dozen men in college who were engaged to her. She lived on flirtation. 'Twas reported that you were swamped terribly. They say you were the only one in earnest."

"Those who say so know nothing about it," I replied warmly, for I was nettled at his words.

"Well, well, no offence I hope; but, changing the subject, you will come to my supper, Friday evening, will you not? I'll take no refusal. There will be a select company, and we cannot do without you."

He was so urgent in his invitation that I finally consented to attend.

As I started to the supper room Friday night, Ned said, in his kind way:

"Do not drink much, to-night, John. It is hard to count one's glasses in the midst of so much hilarity."

"Never fear for me," I said, gaily, as I ran down the stairs. Frank had secured rooms down town, and on reaching them I found the company all assembled. There were Markham and Bolton, two Seniors, to contribute dignity; Trickley, a Soph., who was brimful of song; Ellerton, who was considered a wit; two or three others whose names I have forgotten, and last a little Fresh named Peepsy, who was so exceedingly verdant that Frank had brought him down as a butt for us. I shook hands round and bowed stiffly to Ellerton, whom I had not spoken to since the duel.

The time before supper was laid was, as is always the case, dull, the Seniors discussing Mill and Say, Vattel and Montesquieu, as if the fate of the nation depended on their opinion, while the rest of us addressed each other in short sentences after long intervals of silence. At length a servant announced that supper was on the table. We passed through a folding door, and gathered around a table that was really groaning beneath its massive load of delicacies. Frank had ordered the supper from Richmond, and Pazzini had excelled himself. After the usual chair scrapings, waiter trippings, plate turnings and comic graces, some of which were shockingly irreverent, we got to work. With some flow of conversation and a laugh at Peepsy, who called Swiss Meringue a syllabub sandwich, we came to the removal of the cloth.

I had determined, on my way thither, not to touch wine unless courtesy compelled it, but now, as I caught the contagion of hilarity, and found that what I said was applauded and listened to—dangerous flattery—a reckless spirit of conviviality seized me, and I threw restraint to the winds, resolving to have a "good time" for once. Conscience had withdrawn into a corner of my heart, and revelry held its carnival.

The green seals were broken and the amber fluid bubbled in our glasses.

I drank one as we toasted Frank, another after his reply, and the third at a compliment to myself.

As the glasses were large, and I was unused to more than half a glass at a time, I felt what I had imbibed glowing over my system. A warm flush came into my face, and the mercury of excitement went up several degrees.

After we had exhausted all the cut and dried toasts, and all the studied things had been said, we were thrown back upon our own originality. Markham then proposed that we sing the old song of *Vive la Compagnie*, toasting each other in turn, while the man who was toasted must reply by a distich of the song.

Ellerton immediately rose with a brimming glass in his hand and said:

"A good idea, Markham, and to commence I propose, gentlemen, Mr. Smith, the block on which Miss Carrover sharpened the blade of her coquetry."

I felt the blood surge to my temples and a harsh retort rise to my lips, but I controlled myself, as the chorus paused for my reply, and sang:

"The block will be happy to sharpen a bit
What so much needs edge, as the gentleman's wit."

Amid cries of Good! good! we drank again, with a noisy "Vive la, vive la, vive l'amour!"

Others were then proposed, and with each toast my glass was filled. And now the first effects of the wine began to be felt. I became conscious of a slight unsteadiness of vision, and found that when I attempted to look at any object my eyes went past it like the pendulum of a clock, then went back again, so that I had to move them several times before I could concentrate on what I wished to see. Even then my sight was not very clear, for the lamps had misty rings around them, and when I reached out my hand for my glass I had to make an effort or two before I could touch it. The table, too, seemed to have a wave or elevation in the middle, and the wall on the opposite side of the room was not exactly perpendicular. My consciousness, too, was an unreal consciousness, as if I were dreaming of all these surroundings, and this uncertainty of vision somewhat confused me in ideas and actions. Remembering how much wine I had taken, a sudden fear came over me that I might be a little intoxicated, and with the thought an intense desire to conceal it. The best way to conceal it, I said to myself, is to talk on and convince them that nothing is the matter with me. Markham was sitting next to me and I resolved to speak to him of Lillian, for I was afraid that Ellerton's remark had produced the impression on his mind that I had been jilted.

"I say, Mis'er Mar'c'um," I said, leaning much more heavily on his shoulder than I intended, "you did'n think I loved Lill'yun the most, did y'r? Ellert'n was only jok'n. B'cause I got's much's she did in that game. Umph? Don't you think so. Umph? Say, don't you think so? Umph?"

"Who the devil is Lillian?" he said, turning a red face and bloodshot eyes upon me. "Hold up. Trickley is going to sing."

"All right," I said, pushing myself up from him; "just's you say; I'll tell you 'bout it again."

I saw Trickley indistinctly on the other side of the table and heard him sing something about

"The world is all an ocean and the people are the fish,
The devil is the fisherman and baits us as we wish;
When he wants to catch a boy he baits with sugar plums,
When he wants to catch a man he baits with golden sums,"

and closing my eyes to relieve them of the misty light I dozed in a half sleep with my head upon my breast till I was awakened by the applause at the conclusion of Trickley's song.

"H'rah!" I shouted, a little louder than any one else, smashing my glass as I brought it down upon the table.

"Com mere, Jim," I said, beckoning to the waiter who stood near me, "brush off these glass, and hold me up and sweep under me. D'you hear?"

Negro-like he was full of laughter at my condition, and snickered outright as he swept off the fragments of glass.

"Who're you laughing at, you scoundrel? Umph?" I said, boiling over with rage, and seizing a goblet which Markham barely caught in time to save.

"I declare, sir, I wasn't laughing at all, sir," said Jim, frightened at my anger.

"You're a lie, aint you? I say, aint you a lie? Markham, lend me your pist'l."

Markham was just drunk enough to do it, and handed a Sharpe's four-shooter, but the negro had fled from the room, while Frank and Ellerton took the pistol away from me. Seeing how much intoxicated I was, they told me the poor negro had no idea of laughing at me, and that I had hurt his feelings very much, and ought to beg his pardon.

"Bring him in and I'll do it;" as I spoke he came in again with some cigars, and I called him to me. He had not lost all of his recent fright, however, and hesitated about coming any nearer.

"Why don't you com mere, Jim. I'll throw a chair at you 'f you don't come," I said, making an effort to rise. At length he drew near enough for me to touch him, when I threw one arm around his neck and said, with half sobs:

"I beg your pard'n, Jim; I won't hurt you. Are you 'fraid of me? Umph? I love you, Jim, b'cause you're all right, aint you?"

The others pulled me from him, and told him to get on the other side of the table.

"No; I want Jim to com mere. I know what I want; you all don't know what I want."

"No, no, Smith, let Jim alone. Here, take a cigar," said one or two, offering a case.

"No; I want Jim. Jim's all right," I said, looking sleepily defiant.

"Wait till after supper," said Ellerton, "then you can see him. It's your time to give us a song now."

"Th—hat's all right, Ellerton; you'll help me sing, won't you? Now, I'm going to sing:

"Then fill up your glasses—and your tumbler 'sand your
goblets, And drink to the health of it—all up and ask—for
more" — —

"Oh, we've had enough of that, Smith. Sing us something, or we will have to try Peepsy, here," said Trickley, who had been trying to make Peepsy say something all the evening.

"Vive la! vive la compagnic!" I sang, winding up with a hiccup.

"Smith, that's stale, and boring as the devil," said Ellerton; "hush! and let us hear the Fresh sing."

I was too stupid to make any reply, but made out to hear poor little Peepsy protest that he knew but one song in the world, and that was a hymn. But they would all take no refusal, and swore that unless he sang it they would tie him and leave him in the street all night, a threat he implicitly believed. I was almost in a second doze when I heard his little, quivering voice, as he sang:

"I love to steal a while away," etc.

A song learned at his mother's knee rendered in a drunken carousal! Poor little fellow, he was not in fault!

Ellerton now proposed that we light our cigars and go up to the campus to have some fun.

The Seniors said it was too undignified for them, and took their leave, and little Peepsy begged so hard we let him off.

When I rose from my chair the floor seemed to rise in waves before me, and, attempting to collect my senses and steady my feet, I fell, and, striking my head against the table leaf, lay unconscious till they carried me out. The fresh air revived me somewhat, and we staggered on with a noise and tumult that called several others from their beds to join our plans, which were to bar the doors, tar the benches and put a cow in the belfry, if possible.

Drunk as I was, I recognized in the accessions to our crowd the lowest men in college—fellows that I never spoke to, and who were evidently surprised at my plight. But it was no time for proud reserve, and so I led the way, shouting every few steps:

"Come on, boys; we're all right, ain't we?"

We procured some tar and smeared on all the benches in the accessible rooms, barred the doors and then went up to the belfry, which we burst in to get to the bell. While a part staid to ring it others went down to look for a cow to bring up. I sank down on the steps in a stupid sleep, with the thought piercing my drunken brain like a sword, "I am disgraced for ever. My parents will be mortified and my friends desert me."

I was awakened by a terrific noise near me, and some one's stumbling over me. 'Twas some time before I could see what was the matter, but at length, by a dingy lantern, I saw students above me with ropes in their hands. The ropes were tied to the horns of a cow that was standing with glaring eyes and frightful bellowing a few steps below me. I was too much frightened to move, and with great relief heard Frank reply to some one who suggested to run over the fool:

"No, no; that's Smith. He's all right. Help him up, Donnery."

The person addressed caught me by the arm and gave me a rough jerk that landed me on the top step, from which I managed to crawl off to one side out of the way.

"Now for it I" exclaimed several voices below; "pull, Donnery, you and Haggam pull."

They seemed to strain and tug at something without effect, and Haggam said, with a long breath:

"What makes her so devilish hard to move? She came up the lower flights very well."

"She got scared of that drunken fool on the steps," I heard the coarse voice of Donnery reply, and, intoxicated as I was, I breathed a solemn vow to Heaven that I would never merit that term again.

Drawing the ropes tight again, Donnery shouted to Frank:

"Twist her tail, Paning, — — her! that will move her."

"I have," said Frank, "and she won't budge."

"Let me get hold," said a great rough fellow standing by him, and, taking the vaccine caudal in his two hands, he gave it such a wrench that, with a horrid roar, the poor creature clattered up the steps, her hoofs sounding on the wood as if the building were falling. Once on the floor, they drove her on to a lecture room, and nailing up the door, left her there. Having finished this job they dispersed, Frank calling out good night! to me as he passed. I heard some one tell him he had better see to me, and heard him reply carelessly:

"Never mind, he rooms on this floor, Cheyleigh'll find him," and my vow gained all the more strength from his neglect.

I had just sense enough left to try to find my room, and was trying to totter to my feet, when some one took hold of my arm and said:

"Mr. Smith, let me help you. Are you hurt much?"

It was little Peepsy, who roomed on the same floor, and whom I had laughed at so, at Frank's supper. He kindly endeavored to assist me to walk, but I was too drunk to make any progress, even with his assistance, so I sat down on the floor while he went to call Ned. A dizzy sickness came over me, and I essayed to lean on one arm to steady myself, but my elbow doubled under me and I fell over heavily on one side, bruising my forehead against the hard plank. The only consciousness left was a sense of shame, and I murmured, "What would father and mother say if they could see me now."

A light appeared at the farther end of the corridor, and I saw Ned approaching. A last tinge of pride made me desirous to seem less intoxicated to him, and, as he came up, I called out, trying to raise my head:

"Hel-lo-old fellor, I'm all right; I want t'go t'me room, Ned. Where's se key?"

Ned did not make any reply, but with Peepsy's aid got me to our room and assisted me to bed.

I had scarcely tumbled lifelessly upon it before I was asleep.

When I awoke all was still in the room, the sun was shining very brightly out doors, and looking at the clock on the mantel, I saw that it was nearly twelve. Oh! the torture of that awakening!

My whole body seemed to be scorching in horrid flames, and my tongue and throat cracked with the heat, while a raging thirst consumed me. Yet I was so weak and feeble that had water been near me I could not have stretched forth my hand to touch it.

But physical suffering was nothing to my mental torture. My instability of character, my broken resolves, my ridiculous and disgraceful conduct, my wreck of all pretensions to moral character, the surprise and pain of my friends, the sneers of my enemies, and my own consciousness of degradation, all crowded upon me till I felt that my disgrace was irretrievable.

With a sigh of relief I heard the bell ring, and put a stop to the train of my remorseful reflections.

Ned came in, with a kind smile on his face, and, at my whispered request, gave me a goblet of cool, fresh water. How intensely delicious it was! Better far than the amber Chian or red Falernian, mellowed by years in the vaults of Mecænas, the pure, harmless beverage God hath brewed for His creatures!

CHAPTER XXXI

Apologizing for the prolixity of my last chapter on drunkenness only by the hope that a recital of my own ridiculous behavior may induce some slave of Bacchus, who may recognize any part of the account as familiar, to renounce his allegiance and be free, I invite my readers to take another skip with me.

A year has passed and it is Commencement week. I am a Junior, while Frank is to graduate.

Since his defeat, last year, for Marshal, he has gone rapidly down, till he has lost all moral and social position in college. He is drunk nearly all the time, and has gathered around himself a crowd of low associates, that place him almost beyond the pale of recognition. We have had very little intercourse since his defeat, though I have recently desired to notice him more out of pity than anything else, because so many others cut him. His brilliant mind, in spite of his dissipation, still achieves something in his studies, and it is thought he will get one of the honors in his class.

The Saturday before Commencement he surprised me very much by coming to our room with an open letter in his hand, and saying:

"John, I have just received a letter from Lulie. She and one or two of the Wilmington girls are coming up to our Commencement, and, as I will be busy in speech making and graduating, I must beg you to help me out in attending to them."

"It will give me great pleasure to do so," I replied. "What day will they get here?"

"On Monday," he said, looking at the letter. "I believe you have not been to Wilmington since your father left, but you used to know all these ladies. You must introduce some fellows to them, so they will have a pleasant time."

"Of course I will; but take a seat, Frank, you have not been in my room before in a long time."

"No, thank you, I have an engagement at twelve."

He left the room, and I sat for some time in unpleasant reflection. If Lulie came to Chapel Hill, and received attention from Frank and his set, she would be put down as second class, and my circle of friends would hardly wait on her, even at my request. Knowing her high social position at home, I knew that Dr. Mayland, as well as herself, would be deeply mortified when they knew the character of her associates, if she visited Chapel Hill under Frank's auspices; on the other hand, if I went to her and warned her when she came she would regard my information as a fiction of my prejudice against Frank, and despise me for it. Yet I felt sure he did not love and respect her, for only a day or two before he had said, when I asked if he were going to be married after Commencement, that he was going to see something of life first, that Lulie would keep for a year or two yet without spoiling, and that, even if she did prove false and love another, he had about tired of her.

After thinking over the matter I determined to wait and see whom Frank introduced to her, as his own pride might induce him to select companions suitable to her refinement and culture.

Going to the post-office that afternoon I received a letter from father, dated at London, saying that they would start the next day but one for the United States. They would land at Halifax, and come through Canada to Niagara, where they would wait for me to join them as soon as my college exercises were over. He spoke of the wondrous beauty of Carlotta, now that she was a woman, and said that fortunes and honors in profusion had been laid at her feet, but that she had refused all, and he did not think her heart had yet been touched. Her cousin, Herrara Lola, a young Cuban of rank and fortune, had joined them at Madrid, and had been travelling with them ever since. He was coming South with them to spend the summer and autumn, returning to Havana in the winter.

"And your mother and I fear," continued he, "that when he leaves he will take away with him our beautiful Carlotta."

I closed the letter with a great aching restlessness in my heart. Lose Carlotta! I had feared it ever since I had told her farewell, but my heart had not dared to acknowledge even to itself the possibility of such a loss. As I had received letter after letter telling of her ever increasing charms of person and character, I had longed with a great desire to see her once again and tell her how I loved her far more than any other dared to love, a desire made all the stronger by its utter hopelessness. And I had taken out my little ringlet each day, and, kissing it tenderly, wondered if she kept her pledge and ever thought of me. As I had learned the past winter of her successful *debut* in society, and her numberless triumphs, I felt that my hopes were forever fallen. She would return now puffed up with pride and conscious of superiority, while I would only appear to her as a rustic younger brother, whom she would be ashamed to exhibit to the arrogant Herrara.

"I won't go to Niagara," I said, savagely, crumpling the letter in my hand; "they will all look down on me now, and even father and mother will think I lack polish, after their European tour, for travel invariably breeds conceit."

I took up my *Herald* to divert my thoughts, and running my eyes over its columns, saw the following among the marriage announcements:

> "Marshman—Carrover. At the residence of the bride's
> uncle, Mr. Isaac T. Carrover, No.——Fifth Avenue, by
> the Rev. Dr. Deeler, assisted by the Rev. Mr. Prynn, Hon.
> Palmer Marshman, M. C. for the—th Congressional
> District, to Miss Lillian Carrover. No cards."

Poor Marshman, thought I, the rose leaves are plucked, only thorns for thee!

CHAPTER XXXII

When Frank and I entered the parlor of the hotel, after sending up our cards to Lulie and the other ladies from Wilmington, we found the room full of company. Strange faces among the ladies, and familiar faces among the students, were grouped on every side. All were bowing, smiling and talking in the most eager and interested manner, as they filled their dancing cards with engagements for the ball, or brought forward friends to be introduced. We had only to wait a few moments, when we heard light footfalls and the rustle of dresses on the stairway, and the next instant Lulie and her two friends came into the room and greeted us cordially.

What a fairy vision of loveliness was Lulie! Her exquisite figure, as *petite* as Titania's, perfect in the bloom of womanhood, a vine-work of brown ringlets clustering around her shoulders, a sparkle in her bright eyes, and a roseate hue on her dimpled cheeks! The same beautiful being I had once adored, though more perfect now in her bewitching loveliness; the same cherry lips I had kissed before the nursery fire; the same roguish glance that had so often brought my heart into my mouth, as our eyes met across Miss Hester's school room, and the same silvery laugh that I had thought was the sweetest music in the world. A tinge of sadness came over me as I bowed over her hand and thought of what might have been.

We passed a half hour very pleasantly, talking about old times and scenes, and making engagements for the festive occasions before us; but oh! what a yearning desire I felt to shield her from all possible harm, as I marked her fond looks turned, so often and trustfully, towards Frank's bloated though still handsome features.

I was to escort her that night to the "Fresh" Declamation, and when we walked up the brilliantly lighted aisle of the chapel, which was thronged with the beauty of the State, I saw many a look of intense admiration directed towards the little fairy on my arm. Next morning a score of my friends came to ask the favor of an introduction, so that Lulie held quite a levee down at her hotel, though each one who called asked me in some surprise afterwards, how she came to be so intimate with "that fellow, Paning."

Frank carried her that night to the "Soph." speaking, and I could not but feel ashamed for her, as I marked the looks of surprise and coldness on the faces of my acquaintances, who, I felt sure, to a certain extent, classed her by her escort. After the speaking we had a little hop in the ball room, and I noticed she remained in the room only a short time, dancing one or two sets with Frank's friends, men whom Dr. Mayland would have ordered from his parlor. I felt it was my imperative duty to advise her of it all, but I was so sure that she would attribute all my counsel to prejudice against Frank, and despise me for it, that I hesitated and delayed.

Next morning, while I was lying across my bed, enjoying the perfumed breeze that floated up from the flowery campus, Harrow, a friend and classmate, came in and sat down by me.

"Say, Smith!" he said, shading a match with his hands to keep it from being blown out, and speaking on each side of his cigar, "is that little beauty who was with Paning last night a friend of yours?"

"Yes," I yawned; "why do you ask?"

"Because if she was anything to me I would either whip Paning or carry her away from here."

"Why? What do you mean?" I asked, rising up on one elbow.

"Well, well," he said, tossing the match out of the window, "it's none of my business, perhaps; so let it be."

"No, but you must tell me, Harrow; what have you seen or heard? The young lady and I at one time were great friends, and I still esteem her very highly, though she has not liked me much since that scoundrel Paning has taken possession of her heart. But I will do everything I can to serve her now. What do you know about them?" I rose up and sat by him on the edge of the bed.

"Paning does not respect her much, does he?" he asked, blowing smoke rings in the sunlight.

"No, that's just it. She believes him to be the purest and best under Heaven, and trusts him blindly, while he, a villain, is trifling with her, and keeps her love only because he is proud of it. If he respected her he would not obtrude his polluted presence on her. But tell me, Harrow, what you know about her," I continued; "if you wish, I will keep secret all you confide."

"The deuce, no," he said quickly; "I do not care for Paning. I would tell him about it myself, only I have no right to interfere."

"Speak on, Harrow; what is it?"

"Well, for one thing, the very fact that she receives attention from such fellows as Paning and Donnery has lowered her in the estimation of your acquaintances; and then, even during the short time she has been here, those low fellows have originated enough scandal about her to damn a dozen women at the social bar."

"No! Harrow, you cannot mean that; I have not heard one word against her."

"Of course not," he said, smoking vigorously; "nobody speaks of it before you."

"She's as pure as an angel," I said, indignantly.

"I believe she is," he replied, lolling back on the pillow; "but if she allows Paning to carry her into the company he does, she will not be thought so by others. Last night I had no lady with me, and, getting tired of dancing, I went up into the library, which you know was lit up for promenading couples. When it was pretty late, and everybody had gone down, I took down a book, and, reclining on a sofa in one of the alcoves, began to read. I had not read far before Donnery and another low fellow came into the library, each with a lady, or I had better say woman on his arm. They made some show of looking at the books and paintings, and while thus engaged Paning and Miss Mayland came in. She was leaning on his arm with an air of devotion and confidence I have never seen equalled, and they were speaking in soft, loving tones. Donnery met them, and, in his coarse way, introduced his companions. After some noisy conversation, full of slang and rude jest, they agreed that the hop was a bore, and Donnery said he would go down to Muggs' and get some wine if they would wait and drink it in the library. They all assented except Miss Mayland, and I distinctly heard her ask Paning to see her home; but he vowed she must not leave yet, and she remained, though I knew from her silence that she felt out of place and ill at ease. When Donnery returned they took the librarian's table and made a gay party around it. Though I could not see them, I knew that Miss Mayland was blushing at the songs and toasts that passed around; and I inferred, by Paning's calling out in a loud tone, 'No, not yet, Lulie,' that she was again begging him to leave."

"Harrow, did all this really occur as you have described it?" I asked, in indignant astonishment.

"It did, upon my honor," he replied. "Several ladies and gentlemen, on coming to the library door and seeing who were in there, turned back down stairs, and soon after I left myself."

"I'll tell her of it to-day," I said, throwing off my slippers and drawing on my boots. "Paning must be the veriest villain alive to take the woman he loves, or pretends to love, into such company."

"He certainly did so," said Harrow; "and, as I said before, I heard much comment this morning from those who saw Miss Mayland with such a set."

When he rose to go I thanked him for coming to me with the information, and begged that he would explain and apologize for her presence in the library with Donnery and company to those whose opinion I valued, and whom he might hear allude to it.

During the day I was engaged so that I could not procure an interview with Lulie, and, much to my regret and annoyance, I saw her walk in the Chapel in the afternoon on Donnery's arm, while his coarse face was lit up with an expression of triumph as he took his seat "among the high up ones," as he said in a loud whisper to one of his friends leaning in the window.

That night the ball was to come off; and, as I buttoned my kids, and gave the last adjusting pull to the waist of my "spike," I resolved that, as soon as I had paid the required courtesies to the lady I was going with, I would seek Lulie, and, whether it offended her or not, give her my last warning against Frank.

It was with difficulty I found her amid the throng that swayed and surged through the ball room. She was in rather a retired corner, receiving very little attention from any one. She had few engagements or none for the dance, and her usually bright face wore an expression of weariness and mental pain as I approached. She welcomed me gladly, and accepted my proposal to stroll in the campus with eagerness. The avenues were lit up, as there was no moon, and strolling down one of these, we turned aside to a rustic seat beneath a large oak. It was a quiet and secluded place; even the music in the ball room sounded soft and indistinct across the maze of shrubbery.

The opportunity was now mine, but I shrank from my duty. She would not appreciate my motives, I was sure, and would repel my counsel with scorn and indignation. Yet could I suffer Frank to betray her into imprudences that would tinge the purity of her character? Could I permit his villainous designs, palpable to all eyes but hers, to go unexposed? Could I see her threatened with evil she would not suspect till it was too late to avert it, and not warn her? No, however thankless my task might prove, for the sake of her dead mother I would tell her of her danger.

"Lulie!" I said, after some moments of silence and reflection on my part.

"What is it, Sir Solemnity?" she replied, looking into my face by the dim light of the distant lamps.

"I wish to speak to you on a very important and delicate subject, and I want you to promise me that you will believe my motives pure and disinterested in so doing. Do not fear that I am going to renew the fishing scene of our childhood; I know too well that my love is hopeless. Let memory sleep; 'tis of the present now I wish to speak; and I want you to take off your glove and put your hand in mine, and if in what I am going to say you believe there is one single word prompted by aught save the most sacred friendship, instantly withdraw it, and I will say no more."

She undid the lace-edged kid with a slight tremor in her fingers, and, dropping it heedlessly on the ground, laid her little hand confidingly in mine.

"There is my hand, John," she said, "but you really frighten me with your solemn preface."

"Well, then," I replied, with an effort at a smile, unheeded, perhaps, in the darkness, "to come directly to the point, do you love Frank?"

I felt a quiver in her fingers as she said:

"Dear John, do not be offended, but we must not talk on that subject. I know what you would say, but 'tis useless; I cannot believe you."

"But, Lulie, perhaps you do not know how important it is that we should speak on this subject. Will you answer another question, then? Do you believe that Frank loves you?"

She drew her head back with the merest touch of pride, and said, with a tinge of steel in her tone:

"Yes, I do believe he loves me, because he has proved it in a thousand ways; and I do not fear to answer your first question. I do love him with all my heart. There! that confession is unladylike, but I make it to you alone."

I bowed in acknowledgment and continued:

"Pardon me again, Lulie dear, for pursuing my catechism. You were in the library last night?"

"Yes!"

"Do you know the character of those to whom Frank introduced you, and with whom he forced you to spend an hour?"

She made no reply, but I could feel her hand growing cold as the blood left it for her burning cheeks.

"Do you know the social and moral position of those men he has permitted to wait on you since your stay here? Do you know how he speaks of you to others? Dearest little friend, though you hate me for it, I *must* warn you. Frank does not love, does not even respect you. He only retains your love as a trophy of his power. As God knows my heart, I have no motive but to save you. Will you heed me, Lulie?"

She drew her hand quickly from mine, and, covering her face, remained silent a long while; then putting it back in mine, she said, with a sad earnestness I can never forget:

"I do not doubt the sincerity of your motives, John; but your words are wasted. Frank has loved me too long and too fondly for me to desert him now at your bidding. 'Twas naughty of him, I know, to carry me into bad company, but he did it thoughtlessly, and I forgive him for it."

"But, Lulie" — — I interposed.

"No; let's not speak of it any further. You cannot know how strangely sad I feel. A great gloom has fallen on my heart, which, indeed, has been hanging over it since I came here; and oh—I do so want to lean on mother's breast and cry. Dear John, I shall ever love you dearly for your kind interest in me," and before I could prevent it she lifted my hand to her lips and kissed it; "but you are mistaken about Frank. *I* know that he loves me, and God knows that I love him, and will trust him even to death."

We rose from our seats, but instead of returning to the ball room, she asked me to see her to the hotel, where I bade her good night and came back up the campus. As I passed by the seat we occupied, something white in the darkness caught my eye, and on picking it up I found that it was her glove, which she had dropped while we were talking. On taking it to the light I found that some one, in passing, had trodden upon it, and ground it into the damp earth, soiling it hopelessly.

"Heaven grant it may not be a type of her life!" I said fervently, as I laid it in my bosom.

CHAPTER XXXIII

I concluded, after all, to go North. What if father, mother and Carlotta had travelled while I was studying in a quiet little village? I felt equal to them in learning, and resolved that I would be in manners and polish.

I spent a few days in New York, which was very dull, as everybody was off at the summer resorts. With a pretty heavy draught on father's bankers, I filled a trunk or two with the latest styles and started for Saratoga, where I would spend a few days before joining our family party at Niagara.

Having paid the hackman as much again as his legal fare, and having seen my trunks checked through, I took my seat on a stool at one side of the already crowded deck of the Hudson river boat, which was steaming and hissing at the wharf like a chained griffin, and gazed, with the interest of novelty, at the scene before me. The long forests of masts and yards, with here and there a graceful flag or long fluttering streamer; the busy, fussy tugs, running hither and thither like noisy gossips, coughing and sneezing with bad colds; the patient jades of ferry boats, with their anxious human cargo, hardly waiting for the dropping of the chains; the ocean steamer looming its dark hull in the offing, and curling its black festoons of smoke on the morning sky; the white sailed skiffs leaning gracefully from the wooing wind, and the small row boat which a bare-armed sailor is sculling right under our prow, his blue jacket lying on the seat behind him, and the motion of his body, as he rocks from side to side, slushing the water about in the bottom of the boat, and wetting one sleeve of the jacket on the seat; the anchored ships, here and there, looking like immense laundries, with their rigging and sides covered with the clothes of the crew, all made me forget for a moment my own existence, till I was aroused to a consciousness of it by a shrill voice piping in my ear, "*Herald! Times! Tribune!*"

Having bought a paper, I turned round on my stool and commenced to read. People continued to crowd in; a hoarse whistle from our boat, or some other, I could not tell which, a few taps on a very hoarse bell, and with a shiver, as if the water was cold, we glided from the wharf.

I had read, perhaps, half a column when the rustle of a dress against my crossed feet attracted my attention, and I peeped under the edge of my paper. It was a very handsome black silk, and, being caught up over my foot, showed a beautiful bootee beneath it—an interesting bootee of purple glove kid, with a dainty high heel, and a firm curving instep—a bootee tapping the deck carelessly, as if about to execute a pirouette on its flexible toe. Standing against the silk dress, close to the bootee, was a pair of boots—large, dignified boots—with broad heels and thick soles, and coming down over their flat insteps were black pant legs. Lifting the edge of my paper a little I came in sight of the skirt of a black cloth coat, and hanging down by the skirt of the coat was a large white hand holding a morocco travelling bag—the hand of a middle aged man, white on the fingers and near the thumbs, and shaded with dark hairs on the side toward the little finger, on which was an onyx seal ring with P. M. in monogram. I knew the bootee belonged to a pretty woman, and the boots and hand to an intelligent elderly man, and to confirm my surmisings I took down the paper with a rattle and looked up at them. The lady turned her head and looked down at me the same instant.

"Why, Mr. Smith! is it possible?" she exclaimed.

"Miss Carrover!" I said, rising and blushing.

"Mrs. Marshman, sir. Mr. Marshman! an old friend of mine, Mr. Smith, of North Carolina."

Mr. Marshman, a frowning man, with heavy gray brows and a grayer moustache, gave me his hand and a "glad to know you, sir."

"Let me make you acquainted with our party," said Mrs. Marshman, turning to two ladies and a gentleman, "Mr. Finnock! Mr. Smith, Miss Sappho Finnock! Miss Stelway!"

I made my obeisance, and, completing the usual commonplace remarks, "took in" the party.

Mrs. Marshman, as beautiful as ever, but a trifle more mature and less dashing; Mr. Marshman, as above described; Mr. Finnock, a pale young man, with very blue eyes and very red lids, and light mossy side whiskers; he was exquisite in style and supercilious in demeanor, and very much devoted to Miss Stelway, a dark skinned young lady, with a short upper lip and very large front teeth, who looked at everything on the river with an opera glass, and whose conversational powers seemed limited to the constant ejaculation of:

"See there, how pretty!"

She was rich, though Finnock's attentions *may* have been disinterested.

Miss Sappho Finnock was a little lady, not very young, with thin, sandy hair, which she plastered, classically, around her forehead, and wore in wiry little curls around the back of her neck. Her eyes were as blue as her brother's, and were "near" in their sight, so that she wore circular gold-rimmed glasses, that magnified her eyes ludicrously when seen through them. She wore fawn gauntlets, and her fingers, when she drew off her gloves, were thin and bluish towards the ends. Her waist was straight from her arms to her skirt, and her neck long and corded. She was constantly taking notes in a gilt-edged book, and peeping at me sideways under her glasses, as I sat by her, which I did most of the way up the river. She opened her eyes a little wider whenever she spoke, as if she was surprised at her own voice, and spoke with a sudden quickness and a little jerk out of her head, as if she wanted to throw the words at you. I soon found that as Mr. Marshman would not give up Lillian, nor Finnock Miss Stelway, Miss Sappho Finnock was to be my companion for the voyage. I was not displeased, for she was entertaining for her very sentimentality, and was not disposed to laugh at any ignorance of the world I might betray, or any social solecism I might commit.

In reply to Mrs. Marshman's inquiries, I informed her that I was going first to Saratoga to spend a few days, thence to Niagara, where I would meet our family, just returned from Europe. At the mention of Europe, Finnock and Miss Stelway regarded me with more interest, and Miss Finnock increased her smiles and side glances.

We all talked together for some time, when Mr. Marshman left us to go to his state room, Lillian took a novel from the morocco bag, and Finnock and Miss Stelway going to the railing to lean over the water, nothing was left for Miss Finnock and myself, but to walk to the prow of the boat and take a couple of vacant seats that were there.

"I always think of the Culprit Fay when I pass old Crow Nest" she said, arranging her skirt. "Are you not fond of poetry? I am, passionately."

"I enjoy poetry very much," I said, not knowing how tame the reply would sound till I had made it.

"I declare I almost cry when I think of that dear little Fay cleaving the waters to catch the crystal drop, while the great monsters swarm after him. What do you think is the most descriptive line in the poem, Mr. Smith."

"Confound Rodman Drake!" I muttered to myself, for I had not read his poem, having scarcely touched anything save my text-books since I had been at Chapel Hill. Fortunately, I remembered a lecture of our Professor of Rhetoric, on American poetry, in which he had quoted from the poem in question; I therefore replied, pausing as if to consider:

"Really, Miss Finnock, the whole poem is so full of vivid descriptions and striking thoughts that it is hard to make a selection; but I think perhaps the finest passage is that which describes the firefly steed flinging a glittering spark behind."

"Ah, yes," she replied, "I remember that. But I think the tiniest, sweetest idea is, 'their wee faces giggling above the brine.'" To express the *tinyness* of an idea, she squinted her eyes painfully, and squeezed her forefingers and thumb together, as if she were holding a flea.

"To tell the truth, Miss Finnock," I said, hoping to take her out of her depth and thereby change the subject, "I greatly prefer the old classic writers, or even the earlier English poets, to the maudlin sentimentalists of the present day."

"Oh, you prefer the classics, do you?" she exclaimed, brightening her dim looking eyes, "then I am glad we are congenial. Homer is too nervous in his style, but Pindar is so sweet; and Sappho—do you know I am named for her?—isn't her poetry rapturous? and dear Horace, how pointed and terse he is. Do you know I have studied harder than anything his Art of Poetry, for I sometimes try to write verses myself. Did you ever write poetry? It is really difficult. And you say, too, you like the old English poets? How glad I am! I have a copy of Chaucer in my trunk, and we can read over some of his Canterbury Tales together. Then there's Spencer; isn't his Fairy Queen perfectly charming? And Sydney's Arcadia, do you like that? Sometimes, when I am sad and gloomy, I even like to read the melancholy musings of poor John Ford. You've read Ford, have you not? and Marlowe?"

Great Heaven! thought I; take her out of her depth indeed! I have only taken her into it. My only hope to change the subject, and prevent an exposure of my ignorance, is to speak of her own verses, as I know she will not quit that theme as long as I appear interested. I said, therefore, as soon as she ceased speaking,

"You say that you write verses, Miss Finnock? I am sure they are lovely; and I would esteem it a very high honor and privilege to be permitted to read your composition."

"Oh, I could not think of it," she said, with an attempt at a blush; "besides, my portfolio is in my trunk, and therefore inaccessible."

I protested my readiness to go below and have her trunk opened, that I might satisfy my desire to read her beautiful thoughts, and I insisted so earnestly that she would give me her keys and permit me to search, that she said, while she thanked me for my obliging spirit, she would not trouble me any farther than to get her reticule from Mrs. Marshman, for, if she was not mistaken, she had in that some verses on the Hudson that she had composed the summer before.

Of course I was delighted to bring it to her; when she opened it and took out a yard and a quarter of printed poetry, which she commenced to read, first making me promise, a naughty boy, not to laugh at anything in it.

She read the entire yard and a quarter with heaving bosom and unusually dilated optics; but I cannot inflict upon my readers more than an inch or two.

The theme of the poem was the launching of the first steamboat, and in her eyes it seemed an epic fit for Virgil. The lines were these:

THE HUDSON.

"Oh thou mighty, sweeping, rushing river,
Through thy cloud-reflecting bosom grand,
With unfledged wheels the first steamboat proud-
Ly plows, while on its trembling bulwarks stand
The gay, triumphant and prophetic crowd."

"Oh, that is perfectly enchanting," I exclaimed, when she had completed the ninety-third and last verse, feeling assured that, when she thought so highly of the effort herself, no commendation could be fulsome.

"Pardon the abrupt praise, but Mrs. Browning could not have expressed the idea of the untried wheels more strikingly than you did, by the single word 'unfledged.'"

"You flatter me, indeed, sir," she said, looking immensely pleased; "but, to be candid with you, I thought myself that the expression was original and effective. Can you imagine how I got such an idea?"

"Not unless the fairies brought it to you," I said, gallantly.

"I was at Yonkers last summer, while composing this piece, and saw a young duck, with unfledged wings, learning to swim, and immediately I thought of the steamboat. Remarkable coincidence, was it not?"

"Very remarkable, and all the more striking from that very fact," I replied.

"But the most striking stanza in the poem," she continued, running her little thin fingers down the paper, and pinching it at a certain verse, "is the sixty-eighth. Do you remember it?"

"They are all stamped so indelibly on my mind, by their wondrous power and beauty, that I cannot distinguish them by mere numbers; but I can easily recognize it if you will read it again." This I said leaning forward with an increased air of attention and interest.

"There is no merit about the lines, except that they convey to the mind a vivid impression of the circumstances," she said, with a preparatory cough, and read:

"And should a comet from the starry sky
Fall with its fiery tail along thy bed,
Oh! what a yawning, cracking chasm dry
Would stretch from parched mouth to fountain head."

"Miss Finnock!" I said, rapturously, "you are as daring as Milton in your conceptions. Even Dante does not surpass the appalling picture you draw. I can almost see the long, rugged chasm down which the ships are rolling over and over, snapping off their masts, the fish floundering in the steaming pools, while the red serpent of desolation winds its way down the hissing bed."

I did not deem it necessary to correct her astronomy by a hint at the nebulosity of comets, or at the absurdity of the idea that a tail, ten millions of miles long and half as many broad, could be squeezed into the channel of the Hudson. I could only admit to myself that if the tail of a comet was red hot, and small enough to fit the river, her picture of the effect of its fall was graphic.

She thanked me with many blushes, and as I paused in my comments she folded up her poetry reluctantly, and returned it to her reticule. As the bag opened I saw a book in it, and my respect for her erudition, before which I positively trembled as she ran through the names I have mentioned, was considerably lessened as I recognized Spalding's English Literature, and felt that her learning was "crammed."

As I felt as confident in my smattering as hers; I talked more boldly, and we spent the morning in a conversation on literature that would have made Porson envious at our attainments.

When dinner was announced our party had a private table in the saloon, and I was embarrassed to find that Mr. Finnock and Miss Stelway were regarding my table deportment as if that was the Shibboleth on which they would cut or notice me. Miss Finnock, however, kept me more employed in attentions to the outer woman than to the inner man, so that I got on very well, except pouring her glass too full of wine and making too loud a sip when I tasted mine.

Mr. Marshman had invited an elderly gentleman to dine with him, and was so absorbed in a political discussion that he completely ignored my presence; indeed, he seemed to forget that there was any one present except himself and his patient listener.

Mrs. M. was much annoyed by his neglect of his guests, and wasted many nods and frowns on him. As he paid no attention to them she spoke to him:

"Mr. Marshman, pass the claret to Mr. Smith."

But she might as well have addressed the post of the saloon, for Marshman was at that moment closing his most forcible argument in favor of his assumption.

"Mr. *Marshman!*" exclaimed Lillian, a flush on her cheek and a flash in her eye, "do you know where you are? Mr. Smith's glass is empty."

"Oh!—yes—pardon me, my dear," turning with a confused smile to her, and anything but a smile to me as he ran my glass over with the crimson fluid.

For a while there was an awkward pause, during which I felt very much embarrassed, as having been the innocent cause of the disturbance.

Mrs. M. soon resumed her smile, and said:

"Mr. Marshman thinks he is on the floor of the House whenever he gets to talking, and forgets his surroundings."

"Well, my dear," he said, pouring out a glass of brandy, "excuse my absent-mindedness. Come, Mr. Debait, since they will not let us finish our discussion, we will have to join the young folks."

Mrs. Marshman gave him a sign to notice me, and he said, in a patronizing, Congressional way:

"What are the times in North Carolina, Mr. Smith? Whom will your people support in the next Presidential election?"

I was informing him that, as a student, I had not taken much interest in politics, when Mrs. M. cut in:

"Mr. Marshman, you ought to observe Mr. Smith very closely. He is the only one who ever really flirted with me."

"Is he?" returned Mr. Marshman, trying to keep his good humor, though evidently disliking me. "What did *I* do with your heart?"

"*You* flirt? Oh, life!" and Lillian laughed scornfully, as she looked around at us all. "I was afraid I was getting a little *passé*, and just took you when you proposed, which you did, you remember, with much agitation and tremulous fervor."

We all smiled, as was expected, except Mr. Marshman, who only drew his bushy brows a little nearer together.

Lillian went on (as what woman will not when she is succeeding in a tease?).

"You know, Pam, I put you off indefinitely; and, strange to tell, I received your first letter the very night Mr. Smith and I came so near loving. If he had talked differently then, perhaps the answer you received would have been different. You really owe him thanks."

But Mr. Marshman, instead of taking the jest, grew very red in the face, and, pushing his chair back, said, angrily:

"You can make the change now, madam, if you desire it," and left the saloon.

We looked at Mrs. Marshman, but she was not in the least disconcerted.

"Poor, dear Pam," she said, running a spoon under the peel of an orange, "he loves me so dearly that he is morbidly jealous. I'll have him pleasant by tea."

Miss Finnock occupied the remainder of the hour by making original remarks and comparisons, if similes without a shadow of similarity could be called original. She said the nut crackers were like adversity, because their crushing discovered the sound fruit; that Italian cream was like a coquette's cheek, both pink and cold; that the heart of the melon was the heart of humanity, and the black seed black thoughts; that the lemon floating in the finger bowls was like the selfishness that mingles with the purest waters of life; and much more to the same effect.

As Finnock preferred Miss Stelway to the wine, we left the table with the ladies, and going up on deck I excused myself for my siesta.

As I turned over to the cool side of my pillow, and slid back the shutter to get the river breeze, I murmured as I dozed off:

"If little Sappho won't get in earnest I'll make love to her, just for the fun of it."

Late in the afternoon we all met again on deck, and, to my surprise, Mr. Marshman was by Mrs. Marshman's side, full of smiles and urbanity. I could not help thinking of Themistocles' chain of government.

Miss Finnock was unusually sentimental, and her style of conversation was a continual flow of heroic verse, with all the necessary inversions and syncope. She said that the river flashed its wavelet eyes beneath the sunset's golden veil, that the mountains donned their purpled robes, their bald, bare summits, glory crowned: that the houses nestled 'long the shore like white ducks resting from their sport; the steamboats puffed like wearied beasts, the sail boats glided, graceful swans; and I have no doubt she would have gone on to personalities about her lonely heart and mine, had not her brother called her to Miss Stelway.

As they had to spend a day in Albany, we parted there with many promises to renew our acquaintance at the Springs. The next day found me with good rooms at the Union Hotel, Saratoga. As I did not know a single person there, I found it, of course, very dull, and spent the day sauntering around to look at the various objects of interest. That night there was a ball at the Union, but there was such a press in the ball room that I might as well have been in the Mammoth Cave without a light, for all I could see.

I retired early, leaving directions to the servant to call me soon in the morning.

CHAPTER XXXIV

The sun had not been up long when I reached the spring, and found the little boys already busy with their long-handled dippers. I gulped down a glass of the water, which is a bad mixture of soda and Epsom salts, and was strolling over the grounds, thinking how pleasant 'twould be to have even little Miss Finnock along with me, when the rattling of the circular railway caught my ear and I walked towards it. A gentleman and lady were riding in the car, who riveted my attention at once. The gentleman was strikingly handsome. A snow white Panama hat, whose flexible brim, bending up before the current of air, showed a high, white forehead, and black eyes so piercing in their glance that I involuntarily shrank back as they whirled past me. A very heavy moustache, parted in the middle, fell on each side of his lip like a stream of ink; a graceful, massive frame, yet a small hand turning the crank of the car and a small foot with high instep rested on the edge. This much I saw as they rattled by, and strange to say, so full of admiration was I for the man that it was not till they were coming around again that I noticed the lady, who was much the handsomer of the two. She was clad in a blue morning robe, whose ample folds floated gracefully out from the side of the car. One tiny gloved hand rested playfully on the flying crank, while the other held in her lap the broad straw hat she had taken off. Her eyes were as black as her companion's, but were soft and gentle in their expression; her hair, superbly massive in its loose folds, was as black as a raven's wing, and fell in wavy profusion far below her waist. These were the general outlines of her features, for I could not see her face distinctly, so swift was the speed of the car. But even that glimpse had thrilled me, and an indefinable something in the face seemed to speak familiarly to my heart, and awaken wild, vague visions of something forgotten—perhaps the memories of previous existence, as Plato calls them.

"Have I seen her in my dreams?" I murmured, "or is she the star of my destiny which intuition thus reveals, that her beauty should so thrill me?"

A romantic youth, fresh from college, on the lookout for adventures, with a very large fund of admiration, on which beauty could check at sight; is it a wonder I was in love a second after this bright vision of loveliness floated by?

I waited for them to come round again, but I saw the car stop on the other side, and hurried through the crowd only to see them enter a gold mounted phæton, drawn by a splendid pair of blood bays, the driver and footman in liveries almost too gorgeous for Republican America.

"May the Fates grant he may only be a brother! They look alike," I muttered, as I walked back to the hotel.

I sought for them in vain during the day around the hotel, though I thought once I saw the black moustache behind the green baize door of the billiard room, but, on entering, I could not find it.

That afternoon Mrs. Marshman and party came up from Albany, and took rooms also at the Union. How cordial was Miss Finnock in her manner towards me! and how long she let her hand remain in mine when I shook hands with her! Poor, little cold hand! I felt as if I was pressing a frog with five legs!

The ladies were too much fatigued to go to the dance that night, so Finnock and I walked across to Congress Hall after tea. I told him of the wonderful beauty I had seen in the morning, and asked if he could not contrive to get an introduction for us.

"Oh, yes," he said, carelessly, "presyume so; she's the same Monte wrote me about. Devilish pretty, rich, and so forth. Engaged to that fellow, Monte says. Pious old couple to take care of her. But yonder's Monte now."

He carried me up to a throng of foppish young men who were lounging on the steps of the hotel. They spoke, after Finnock's introduction, with a cool kind of condescension that irritated, and, to a certain extent, humiliated me. While in my heart I despised them for their foppish uselessness, yet I felt they somewhat looked down upon me as being from the country, and I desired their attention and consideration more than I did the esteem of the most prominent gentlemen of my acquaintance; such is pride!

"Why, Finnock, where the devil did you spring from?" said Monte, a tall, languid fellow, with dark red hair, roached up in curling puffs on each side of the central division; somewhat lighter whiskers flowing in long wisps from each ear to the corner of his mouth, while his short chin, shaved clean, imparted an angry bull dog expression that required all the languor of his weak eyes and single eye-glass to soften. "I thought you were going across the pond?"

"No, not yet," said Finnock, carelessly, "the old man swears that stocks are too low to think of Europe. I told him I didn't care, I would either take three M's for Europe next winter or two for the Springs and Newport."

"Say, Finn.," continued Monte, "have you heard about Sedley?"

"No, anything bad?"

"Rather! got a lift from Lola, took the blues, and went into the jungle."

"'D the tiger hurt him?"

"A little—fifteen hundred or so. He left next morning, and I expect has committed suicide."

"Who the deuce is Lola?" asked Finnock.

"She's the rage now—prettier than Venus and richer than Plutus himself. Don't you remember my writing you about her?"

"Ah, yes, I do remember," said Finnock, "but where is she from, Monte?"

"The devil knows," said that gentleman. "I found her here when I came and as all the first ladies were jealous and angry, and all the best fellows in love with her, I went in without questioning her previous history."

"Sed. was euchred badly," put in a bloated young man, with protruding bleared eyes and very red nose; "held a good hand, too, but played his cards badly and lost. They say he went a five hundred diamond ring, but she sent it back."

"That was hard on him; but, Monte!" said Finnock, "Smith and I want an introduction, cannot you present us?"

"Certainly," said Monte, getting up from his chair, and shaking one leg at a time, to make his pants smooth, "but it's useless, that black eyed fellow with her has it all his own way. She will waltz with no one else, pretends to be squeamish, but it is all because he will not let her. The devil take these old marching Lancers and trotting quadrilles; give me a soft hand and a trim waist, and my toe is at your service. Let's have something to drink!"

All assented, and I followed them into the bar-room. I did not wish to drink, but my moral courage shrank from refusing before a throng of exquisites, who were just admitting me to their fellowship. Accordingly, when the others had called for juleps, cold punches and "straights," I responded to Monte's inquiry, by stating very faintly that I would take a sherry cobbler, believing that was the weakest drink I could name. Monte repeated the orders to Snyder, the bar man, with the injunction to make them strong, and we all stood around trying to keep up a desultory conversation, but watching, with more interest, the preparation of the beverages, as men always do at a bar.

Snyder, a large fat man, in his shirt sleeves, with a large diamond pin on his large bosom, and a heavy moustache on his heavy lip, who had been looking off vacantly while we delivered our orders, now started as if he suddenly remembered them, and calling an assistant, took down the bottles, put in the white hailed ice and sugar, the sprigs of mint, the slices of lemon, and set the dewy glasses on the counter. With a bow and a health we drank, and then Finnock swore we should have another round. This time I had weakened enough in my resolution to try a julep, and feeling a tinge of the old excitement coming over me, I asked, as we turned to leave the bar, the privilege of treating.

"Have you some good champagne—green seal or Verzenay—the best now?" I asked the barkeeper, assuming something of the bully in my tone.

"Not champagne at the bar!" said Monte, "that is sacred to the table."

The barkeeper pointed us to a curtained apartment, and sent in the champagne and some biscuit.

We spent, perhaps, half an hour behind the curtain, and when we came forth I felt as if I was again at Frank's party. Though the others had, perhaps, imbibed more than I, yet it had not affected them so sensibly, and, muddled as was my brain, I saw they were enjoying my condition.

They proposed that we have a peep at the Tiger, and I agreed very readily, having a faint idea that we were going to a zoological exhibition.

The zoological garden proved to be a brilliantly lighted room, redolent of cigars and full of tables, around which were grouped eager, anxious faces. I had never gambled in my life, but felt compelled to show my contempt for money by staking a few dollars on a game or two. I soon lost something over a hundred, and was getting more and more reckless, to the extent of much larger stakes, when Monte proposed to leave, saying to one of his companions, in an undertone, which I, however, heard:

"That will do for to-night, not too much at a time."

Monte proposed to take us over to the ball room and introduce us to Lola, the sensation, but I objected that I was not in evening dress. Monte swore I was fit for Buckingham Palace, and dragged me along to the room. Our party was very noisy as we entered the ball room, and several gentlemen moved away from our group in apparent disgust. The brilliancy of the scene dazzled and confused me, and I stood staring stupidly about, holding to Monte's arm for support. The floor was full of dancers, who were circling in a spirited Mazourka.

"There she is, Smith!" exclaimed Monte, "isn't she superb?"

Just in front of us was the belle of the season—my unknown beauty of the circular railway, floating gracefully in the embrace of the black moustache.

Her hair was now caught up in a magnificent coil, and its black folds were adorned with a beautiful spray of pearls. Her eyes—and oh! how melting and tender was their look—splendid in their depth of expression, were turned up to the face of her partner, and her form, perfect in its outlines, reposed with easy confidence in his arms. Her arm, round, smooth and dazzling, was shown in fine relief against the black cloth of his coat, and her neck, white as snow, tapered exquisitely from her bare, dimpled shoulders to the shading of her hair.

How my heart throbbed with admiration as she passed me; and again that strange memory of a dream of her face came over me!

Again they came around, and her full face was turned toward me. Heavens, can it be? yes, there, on that lovely arm, just above the tinted kid, a serpent in Etruscan gold wound its coils up the flesh, and I knew it was Carlotta.

"Monte!" I said, grasping his arm tightly, "that's C'lotta; I know her, I raised her. Lem'me go and speak to her!"

"Wait, Smith, don't be a fool!" he said, impatiently shaking me off, and making his way across the room, as the music had now ceased.

I turned to the others of our party and kept repeating, "That's our C'lotta, I know her 's well 's I want to. She knows me soon 's she sees me."

An elderly gentleman, who had been much annoyed by our noise, and who had been looking very steadily at us for several minutes, now got up from his seat and approached. I looked at him now for the first time, and oh, shade of Hamlet! I recognized my father. The most fervent wish of my heart was that there might be a Samson underneath that floor with his hands already on the pillars.

He did not smile as I pressed his hand, but said, "Come, go with me up to our room, John."

His presence, and my chagrin and surprise did one good thing—it effectually sobered me.

As we walked out of the room he left me for a moment, and when he rejoined me a lady was on his arm—my mother. There was as much sorrow as joy in her kiss, and we proceeded in silence to their rooms. I took the proffered seat, and no one spoke for some time; then mother burst into tears and said:

"Oh, my child! my child! you have almost broken my heart. To think that I left you such a pure, noble boy, and return to meet you drunk, and in a disorderly crowd. Oh, John, how cruelly you have deceived us!"

I threw myself on my knees, as I used to do when a child, and buried my face in her lap.

"Mother," I said, humbly, "I have not deceived you; let me explain."

"My son," said she, "there can be no explanation. I saw you intoxicated myself; and even now you are under the influence of liquor."

Her last words somewhat nettled me, and I resumed my seat, saying as I did so:

"I am entirely sober, madam;" which, indeed, was the truth, for all the fumes and effects of the liquor I had taken departed instantly from me on the discovery of my parents. Father, who had been regarding me with much pity, now spoke:

"Do not be too hard on him, Mary; perhaps this is his first offence."

"It is, it is," I said, gratefully; then suddenly remembering, I said, candidly: "No, I will confess I was under the influence of wine once before this," and I told of Frank's party. With that exception this was my first time, and I promised that it should be the last.

They both seemed mollified, and seeing that I was really not under the influence of liquor, they gradually fell into conversation with me, and we forgot all unpleasantness in our mutual inquiries about each other's health, and a general hash of all that had occurred since we parted. The evening wore on, and I commenced to make preparation for my departure; I had just taken my hat when a rustling was heard in the corridor, a musical "Good night!" and Carlotta came in, holding up her satin trail with its shower of lace. She started back on seeing a stranger in the room, but the next instant, as I rose to meet her, she dropped her skirt, and, holding out both hands, exclaimed:

"John! dear brother!" and putting up her rosy lips she kissed me, then stood looking at me with earnest happiness in her glance, as if she was really glad to meet me. What a joyous feeling there was in my heart! An hour or two before I had coveted just the honor of an introduction, now I had pressed her hand and kissed her! There was a delightful surprise, too, about the kiss, that made it all the more thrilling. We had never been very intimate, though living in the same house, and while confiding many secrets to each other as children, as I have told, yet there was always a shadow of reserve between us, and it was only by observing, at a distance, the beautiful depth of her character, I had learned to love her. After a three years' residence in Europe I had expected to find her haughty, vain and supercilious, and had rather dreaded the meeting; but now I found that the flattery and adulation she had received, instead of turning her head, had only conferred the insight of experience, and made her own heart more earnest and true.

These thoughts of her ran rapidly through my mind as I gazed at the beautiful, brilliant woman that had bloomed from the lovely child, whose image I had cherished since we had parted.

We sat down with father and mother, and as we all had much to say, there were not many seconds that escaped unfreighted with a word. Carlotta seemed much more ready to listen to me, though, than to talk, and instead of telling what she had seen and done seemed intensely interested in my dull affairs.

Father asked her if she were not going back to the ball room.

"Oh, dear, no," she said, drawing off her gloves, "I had much rather stay here and talk with John; beside, I am tired. I had a long sail on the lake to-day, and drove out with Cousin Herrara this afternoon. Please unfasten my bracelet," and she extended her arm to me.

As I took her soft white arm in my hand can you wonder that I pretended to be awkward, that I might prolong the undoing of it?

"*Apropos* of the ball, John," she said, while I was fumbling at the bracelet, "Mr. Monte asked the privilege of introducing two friends, Mr. Finnock and Mr. Smith. Did he refer to you?"

I told her he did, and what a romantic fervor I felt after I had seen her at the railway, and she and father rallied me on losing it as soon as I found her out, and mother helped me to deny it, and we were all so pleasant together we forgot the lapse of time. Looking at my watch and finding it nearly day, I bade them good night, and went to my room.

Like a child with a new toy, I felt a continual surprise and delight that the brilliant belle of the Springs was *my* Carlotta. Mine? The thought of Cousin Herrara placed a very large mark of interrogation after that word. As all indications pointed to the fact that she was his, and would ere long leave our home, the question came to me, bitterly: Can I give her up?

CHAPTER XXXV

A late breakfast found Mr. and Mrs. Marshman and myself at the table, Finnock and the two young ladies having gone for an ante-gestacular walk.

After a smoke I hurried over to Congress Hall and found Carlotta and Herrara Lola in the parlor. She was looking perfectly lovely in a morning dress of India muslin, and with her hair flowing loose through a band of gold. For the first time now I felt the abashment I had dreaded, and realized the disadvantage at which I appeared, in person and manners, after my long residence among books and boys, as I met the glance of Herrara's dark eyes, and imagined I could detect a smile at my discomfiture beneath the jetty fringe on his lip.

"Cousin Herrara!" said Carlotta, "this is John, my brother; you almost know him, I have spoken to you so much of him."

I bowed low over his hand, which was soft, and small as a woman's, as he said, with just enough Spanish in his accent to soften the English:

"I am glad to meet you, Mr. Smith. Lola has made us acquainted ere this occasion."

His manners were those of a courteous iceberg, and I endeavored to adjust mine to a reciprocal degree of frigidity. I had just commenced a stereotyped reply when the same horses and carriage I had seen at the railway drove up, and he remarked to Carlotta:

"I ordered the carriage for our usual drive, but I presume you now prefer renewing old times and terms with your friend."

"Certainly, Cousin Herrara, I will stay with John, as I have not seen him for years, and am with you every day."

"I resign her then to you, Mr. Smith," he said, turning off, while I thanked him with an attempt at one of his bows. He approached a group of gentlemen outside the door and asked two of them to ride with him. The three got into the carriage, a few plunges of the noble animals and the spokes in the wheels became almost invisible as they whirled up the street.

"A superb equipage!" I said, as we took our seats near the window.

"Yes, Cousin Herrara purchased the turnout from a Cuban acquaintance here a few days since. He is going to send it to Havana."

"You are very fond of Cousin Herrara, are you not?" I asked, with something of petulance in my tone.

"Indeed I am," she said, frankly; "he is as kind and loving as he can be, and is always attentive without being obtrusive. I am indebted to him for almost all the pleasure I have seen since I left Wilmington. But, come, tell me all the news about the dear old place," she said, laying her cheek on the downy tips of her fan. "What of Lulie and your Chapel Hill love?"

"Lulie is still Frank's slave, and a remorseless cruel master he is," I said.

"Then you and she have never renewed your old feeling?"

"And never will," I said, solemnly. "The other lady to whom you refer, DeVare's fiancée, is here now as the Hon. Mrs. Marshman. Her old Congressman is, however, too jealous for her to receive attentions from gentlemen."

"Really, you seem to be unfortunate in your loves."

"Indeed I am. I even fear that——" I found that the sentence might prove too pointed for the occasion, and I would not complete it.

Without asking for the remainder, she changed the subject into inquiries about all her acquaintances, and put me through a regular examination. When she had concluded, I told her I would now put her on the witness stand.

"Do you love Herrara, Lola?" I first asked.

She looked at me steadily, as if to read my motives, and then, as the smile came back to her face, said, "That is too pointed and abrupt; try circumlocution and I will be more communicative."

She was so quiet and self-possessed in her evasion that I felt more than ever convinced that she loved her cousin, and said, with an attempt at ironical pleasantry:

"You are engaged to him, and can't deny it. Invite me to the wedding, please."

She laughed carelessly, as she looked out the window and replied:

"Your method of extorting information is so ingenious that I would dread its inquisition, were I not happily relieved by seeing yonder the object of your inquiries."

As she spoke Lola's phæton rolled to the door, and he and his companions got out. He came in, drew a chair to Carlotta's side, and taking her fan from her hand fanned his face vigorously, turning it from side to side to catch the wind, and lifting the dark, curling hair from his high, handsome forehead. As soon as he approached I again felt that shrinking in his presence, that consciousness of a consciousness in him of superiority, though my own pride would not acknowledge it. He was such an Apollo in face and form, so elegant and *recherche* in style, that I was sure Carlotta could not help regarding me as plain and unsophisticated; and, feeling desirous of escaping the consequent awkwardness of my situation, I was about to go to my hotel, when Carlotta spoke:

"Herra, you ought to have remained with us. I am sure you would have enjoyed our conversation more than you did your ride."

"If you conversed at all I would," he said, folding her fan and returning it. "The road was so dusty we could not open our mouths. But you are fortunate, Mr. Smith, if you can entertain Carlotta for half an hour. Ten minutes is her maximum time of interest in what I say."

"Now, Herra," said Carlotta, "You know I was with you a whole hour yesterday; but you would have been as much interested in Mr. Smith's conversation as I was, as it was about yourself."

I only heard his nonchalant "Ah! indeed!" when, with a hot flush on my cheek, and an angry resentment in my heart, I rose, and without a word of adieu left them, and walked across the street to the Union. I knew they could see me from the window, and I fancied them laughing at my discomfiture. I was just debating whether I would leave the Springs and continue my tour of travel alone, or stay there and make love to Miss Finnock, when I saw the little flat face and wide eyes of the lady in question peeping out the parlor door. As I approached she smiled a froggy little smile, and said:

"Have you seen my brother or Mr. Marshman? I have been expecting them some time."

"No, indeed," I replied, offering my arm; "shall we go in search of them, or wait here in the parlor?"

"We had best wait, perhaps," she said, glancing toward two chairs in a shaded corner.

We took our seats, and her ceaseless little tongue began:

"Oh! Mr. Smith, you should have been with us this morning."

"Why and where?" I said, affecting Laconicism.

"Mrs. Marshman and I walked out to the Indian encampment near here, and we saw there such an interesting old woman. She claims to be of the royal line of chiefs, and, in her broken way, talks very prettily of the encroachments of the whites upon the hunting grounds of her fathers."

"To one of your poetic temperament, Miss Finnock," I replied, "she must indeed be an object of interest. What a romantic sadness attaches itself to a contemplation of the destiny of these forest children! Poor, fading race! A few squalid beggars are all that are left of the legions of feather-decked warriors who once fought their battles here. Ever receding before the resistless march of civilization, the last tribe will soon chant their death-song on the shores of the Pacific, and sink with the setting sun in its waves."

It roused her, and I saw by the spread of her nostrils that her soul was on fire. My remarks were part of an old speech at school, which I happened to remember, but they served very well for a match to the powder of her romance. She gazed at me as if in raptures while I was speaking, and when I ended she clasped her hands, with tears, or water, in her eyes, and exclaimed:

"Yes, indeed, Mr. Smith, there is a romantic interest that clings to the memory of these Nature's lords. Their mysterious origin, their nobility of soul, their mute adoration of the Great Spirit, the wild poetry of their legends, all have combined to make me admire them with all the fervor of my nature. Oh! what indeed must be the agony of their bursting hearts, as they stand on some lone mountain, and read in the smoke of the steamer their certain doom. Ah! when we think of their wrongs, the tomahawk becomes the battle-axe of freedom, and the scalping-knife as sacred as the dagger of a Corday."

Fearing, if I encouraged her, she might pack up and go West, to become the Florence Nightingale of the Comanches, I begged pardon for changing the subject, and asked her if she had seen my sister.

"Your sister!" she exclaimed, in her surprise, "I thought you were travelling alone, and expected to meet your family at Niagara."

"So I did, but it seems they telegraphed of the change in their plans after I had left the University; and so I was very greatly surprised to find them here."

"She is not your sister, except by adoption, is she? I have heard Mrs. Marshman speak of you in connection with her. You are expected to love and marry her, are you not?"

"No, I cannot love on compulsion," I replied, looking very steadily at her; "the emotion must be spontaneous, and unaffected by circumstances."

"You express my sentiments perfectly," she said, looking at me with a glance that was meant to be searching.

"Have you ever loved, Miss Finnock?" I asked, artlessly. Her eyes fell to her lap, and her fingers twitched each other as nervously as if she were a mute and were spelling.

"I cannot say that I have," she replied, after a pause. "I may, as a child, have felt heart throbs and bashfulness as the little boy over the way came to trundle hoops with me, but I have never felt that fervid and deep emotion which accords with my idea of love."

"May I ask, then, Miss Finnock, if you have given nothing in return for the many hearts laid at your feet?"

"There have been no— —;" she commenced the truth but caught herself, and said:

"I have never had an offer of love I believed sincere, nor, indeed, one that I could reciprocate."

I knew that I ought not to say anything more, but Carlotta had offended me, and I was reckless.

"But did you believe a love sincere, would you return it?" I asked, deepening my tone of voice to the dramatic.

Her eyes came timidly up to mine, and then fell again as she said softly:

"That depends on whose the love was."

"Miss Finnock!" I said, drawing hearer, "If I— —."

"Hush! hush! here comes Lil," she said, raising her hands in warning. "Oh, how provoking!" she added, with a look that was intended to be sweet.

As I looked up, Mrs. Marshman entered the room, and little knowing how *de trop* she was, took a seat near us and commenced some ordinary topic of conversation. I felt relieved, and was therefore quite affable, but Miss Finnock seemed put out about something, and was scarcely civil in her replies to her. She soon excused herself, and leaving Mrs. M. and myself in the parlor, ran up stairs. She was gone about ten minutes, and returning, brought with her a bark-and-bead cigar case, which, after a moment's hesitation, she gave me, with the remark: "I purchased that from the old Indian, Mr. Smith, and I beg that you will accept and preserve it as a *souvenir* of this morning, and of our mutual admiration of the red man."

"Why, Saph!" said Mrs. Marshman, while I was bowing my acknowledgments, "you do not know Mr. Smith well enough to make him a present."

"Mr. Smith appreciates the gift, and will not misconstrue my motives. I dare say he will remember our conversation," she added, glancing archly at me.

I assured her that I would, and would eternally treasure the case, with pleasant memories of the fair donor, and of our delightful converse, and even ventured on the hackneyed rhapsody about death alone being competent to part the said case and myself. She bowed and blushed, and I toyed with the case in the momentary silence that ensued, and opening saw that there was a crumpled note deep down in it. Just as I was inserting two fingers to reach it a waiter approached, and presented his salver, on which lay two cards. I looked up in surprise as I read the names, "Herrara Lola" and "Lola Rurlestone," and asked where they were.

"In the lower parlor, sir," he said, bowing as I rose to follow him. I excused myself to the two ladies, and thoughtlessly left the cigar case on an ottoman where I had laid it when I took up the cards.

In the lower parlor I found Carlotta and her cousin waiting for me. Carlotta was standing near the piano, looking expectantly towards the door, while Herrara was leaning carelessly against the instrument, turning over the leaves of a music portfolio.

"John, what on earth did you mean by leaving us so abruptly," said Carlotta, making a feint of striking me with her glove. "I would have thought you offended if I could have imagined any cause."

"You ought to have known me better," was all I could think of for a reply.

"Well, it makes no difference now, but you must go back with us. Mrs. Smith sent us over after you. She says she has scarcely spoken to you since we found you."

"I am at your service," I said, and Herrara rose up from the piano languidly and said:

"Mr. Smith will escort you back, Lola; I'll go to the billiard room."

"May I tell him, Herra?" asked Carlotta, as he walked off; "it's such a short time."

"I don't care," he replied, as he lifted his hat gracefully and left the parlor.

"May I ask what it is you wish to tell?" I said, feeling an interest in all secrets between them.

"Everybody believes here that Cousin Herrara and I are engaged, and I assure you it is very inconvenient, for it deprives me of a quantity of attention which you know I would receive, and I believe from your conduct you have fallen into the same error."

"I have had sufficient reason for such a belief," I replied.

"Well, it's no such thing. He is engaged to a lady in Madrid. He returns to Cuba next month, and then sails to Spain for his beautiful bride."

"Then you are still in the market?" I said, with an unaccountable feeling of relief at my heart.

"Of course I am," she replied, as we ran across the street to Congress Hall.

We had hardly joined father and mother in the parlor before a servant appeared with cards for Carlotta, and soon Monte and two others entered.

As she received them across the room I was left to a quiet talk with my parents. We had not told each other a tithe of what we had to tell when I saw the gentlemen rise and accompany Carlotta to the piano. As she seated herself gracefully at the instrument, and gave the warbling keys the petting of a prelude, there was a hush round the room, and I listened eagerly for the first note. She sang a soft Italian air, as full of mellow, rich trillings as a nightingale's song, and her splendid voice, perfect in its culture, rose and fell with exquisite melody and wondrous expression through the difficult measures. Its floods of glorious music so filled the room that we could not have told where the notes came from but for the throbbing of her Parian throat. When the last sound had died away, like the sobbing of a silver bell, every one gave the rapt applause of silence, till Monte, with his affected drawl, asked for a half dozen screeching arias. When she had sung enough the gentlemen left, and I was hoping that I would have her to myself, when another waiter appeared with more cards, and I found I would only have to play spectator at her levee.

I intended to move over to their hotel, but found, on application at the office, that it was too much crowded, and kept my rooms at the Union. That evening at tea I found Mr. Marshman and lady present, but Miss Finnock had finished and gone to her room. Underneath my plate I found the cigar case and a note. I looked up in some confusion, and found Mrs. Marshman smiling at me, as if she thought our love was a foregone conclusion.

"Sappho is a dear little girl, isn't she?" she said, as I unfolded the note.

"Very," I replied laconically, finding, without surprise, that the note was a string of verses, as follows:

"Forgotten the gift, the giver, alas!
Cannot claim the least thought in the day.
With me all the moments and seconds that pass
Bear an image of thee on their way.

This morning, suspenseful, I hung on thy speech,
And Time, oh, too swiftly did fly;
The cup is dashed down before my lips reach
It, and bliss is cut off with 'If I——'

And oh! what a vista of happiness opes
At the touch of the Sesame 'if;'
What a sun-colored life, what a Canaan of hopes
Do I glimpse through the unclosing rift."

There was no signature, but a holly leaf was pinned at the bottom of the verses. The emblem of holly I knew to be "Forgotten;" but if I had picked the verses up in Bessarabia I would have known Miss Finnock wrote them. I folded them up carefully and put the cigar case in my pocket, and finished my tea in silence, Mrs. Marshman having risen from the table while I was reading. I was really annoyed at the turn things had taken. If Miss Finnock had been an experienced flirt I should have regarded the affair as capital fun, but I felt sure Miss F. was in earnest; for, though she was old enough, she had never had much experience, and I had not attained that very desirable point of social education when I could knowingly trifle with a young lady's feelings. I resolved once not to see her again, but remembered that I had an engagement to visit the encampment with her next morning.

"Well," I said, resignedly, as I lit my cigar on the lawn, "I will certainly not commit myself farther. No word or hint of love will I give to-morrow."

CHAPTER XXXVI

The waiter's reveille was very unwelcome next morning, but I rose and dressed and found Miss Finnock already in the parlor.

"Oh, the morning air is so bracing, is it not?" she said, as we left the hotel; "it buoys one up so; I feel so light-hearted and free early in the morning; I am as airy as a feather," and she almost skipped in her youthful exuberance of spirits.

"You had better weigh," I said, somewhat morosely, as we passed the old lame man and his scales.

I confess I was out of humor. Can you blame me? To be roused at such an hour, to parade over to see tiresome Indians, with a fidgety little woman, who was trying to captivate me, and whom I hated now. Would not her very flow of spirits be provoking?

"See yon dew-drops how they sparkle," she exclaimed, pointing with a finger on which shone a diamond ring over her glove. "Nature, unlike the ladies, wears her jewels at morn."

"Then the ladies are not natural," I said emptily.

"Oh! I confess we are quite artificial in many respects, though not artful—at least I am not."

"Really, Miss Finnock, do you confess to artificial aid in your beauty?"

"If I had any beauty it would be artificial, of course. You admire beauty, do you not—your lady love is so beautiful?"

"To whom do you refer as my lady love, Miss Finnock?"

"Why, the lady who called you away from me yesterday. Please tell me if you love her. Now, confide in me, won't you?" and she looked up at me with an affected squint in her broad little eyes.

"I would trust you, Miss Finnock, but there is nothing to confide."

"Then, of course, there is no love, as that is something of great importance."

"Do you think so?" I said, vacantly, as we entered the camp ground. We spent half an hour strolling about, and after I had given five dollars for an old bead basket, that was said to have some Indian legend connected with it, and presented it to the little enthusiast, we turned back to our hotel. I was unusually dull, for I felt that it would be inconsistent with previous attentions and her expectations to introduce commonplace topics, and I had determined not even to hint at love. She seemed to notice my reticence, and tried to rally me.

"You do not seem as cheerful as usual, Mr. Smith. Can I have offended you in any way?"

"Thank you, Miss Finnock, for the hint that I am not entertaining," I said, glad of anything to take up; "let us hasten our steps that you may be the sooner relieved of my presence."

"Oh, how cruelly you misinterpret my meaning. The pleasure of your company is as great—I mean that——" she feigned confusion, "I like to be with you, but there is such a change in your manner since yesterday."

"Is there?" I said, mechanically, and thoughtlessly continued: "I was hardly aware of it. I am sure my feelings have not changed."

"Have they not?" she exclaimed eagerly; "neither have mine."

'Twas too far gone to correct, and so I said nothing. After another pause she tried to look roguish and said, "Did you not chastise the waiter for his interruption yesterday?"

What could I say but that I feared she had already rewarded him for so opportune an entrance.

"I regretted it as much as you possibly could," she said, softly looking down at the beaten path.

It was abrupt, perhaps unkind, but I inquired if she would take a glass of water, as we were just then near the springs. She assented with a slightly reproachful look, and we approached the circular railing, which was surrounded by a throng of health-seeking drinkers, all eagerly waiting for the glasses from the long whirling dippers.

It was the same crowd that is always there. The stylish young lady, who puts her glass down after the third sip; the pale young man with the large Adam's apple, which goes up and down his throat like the piston of a pump, carrying down whole gills of water at every gulp; the tall school girl, with her hair plaited in ribbons, leaning over to the glass and holding her dress back with one hand from its drippings; the fat bad child, his mother holding a glass to his mouth, and resting her hand on his head as if it was the faucet she had to hold open for the water to run down; and the delicate, meek boy, who has been brought to the springs by his father, who is now standing by, watching with deep interest and a notch stick the glasses he takes. Poor little fellow! standing with a Hogarth's curve in his shoulders, both hands grasping the glass, he swigs away, while the veins and leaders in his neck swell and tighten, and the dark lines under his eyes grow deeper, and his eyelids redder, as they disappear behind the rising edge of the tumbler. He takes it down and blows out: "How many's that, pa?" and receiving the plaudit, "Five, my dear boy," is led away to the hotel, to spend the day in his room, instead of playing himself into health with other children.

When Miss Finnock and I had left the pagoda, and were walking up the hill towards the hotel, she made a pretence of pondering over something, and suddenly said:

"Mr. Smith, will you tell me something if I ask you?"

"Most assuredly, Miss Finnock, if it is in my power to do so."

"Well, I want to know—no, I can't ask you now, I'll wait till we part at the hotel."

When we ascended the steps I begged to know her question.

"Oh! I cannot tell, it sounds so silly," she said, twirling the Indian basket with assumed bashfulness.

"I must bid you good morning, then," I said, turning to leave.

"No, I will tell you; I don't mind; I only wanted to know the remainder of the sentence you left unfinished yesterday."

"I will tell you soon," I replied, bowing and leaving her, for I knew not what else to say. Now I am in for it, I said to myself, as I walked across the street to Congress Hall, to breakfast with our family. I will consult Carlotta upon it and take her advice.

As unpleasant as my walk had been in some respects, it had imparted an appetite that made porterhouse steaks and *omelettes souffle* disappear with a celerity alarming to the proprietors. As we rose from the table Carlotta told me that she and Lola were going over to the lake, and insisted that I should join them. As I now felt no delicacy about obtruding, since she had informed me of the relation she sustained to him, I consented. Lola and I had scarcely finished our cigars when his carriage was announced, and, going up to our parlors we found Carlotta waiting, the picture of perfect loveliness, beneath a broad sun hat. The road was already filled with vehicles, and the dust was floating in clouds about our faces; Lola leaned forward and spoke to the driver; "Go ahead, Michael," and with dizzy speed his splendid horses whirled us past every team, and we were breathing again the pure fresh air.

When we reached the lake house, and had refreshed with some ices, I went down and secured a boat for a sail. Lola said he preferred the bowling alley, and Carlotta and I took our places in the graceful little craft I had chosen. My experience on the Sound at home had made me a good sailor, and I dismissed the boatman.

Running up the sail and getting before the wind, so that there was no danger of a gybe, I lashed the rudder so as to direct our course across the lake, and took my seat by Carlotta under the awning. The scene and situation were enchanting. The purple hills held the crystal lake in their bosom, like an immense dew drop, while soft fleecy clouds floated off from their hazy tops like smoke from an altar. The glittering surface of the lake was crimped by the breeze into myriad ruffles, that rustled their little foam against our vessel's side. Other boats were sailing far off, and with their glistening canvas looked like white herons flying hither and thither with a slow, objectless flight. Behind us was the lake-house, its verandahs thronged with people, its carriage way crowded with constantly arriving and departing vehicles, and at the water's edge, a long walk-way extending out into the lake—all receding farther and farther from us. By my side was Carlotta, a bright glow on her cheeks, her beautiful eyes beaming with pleasure, and her magnificent hair caught up in an immense coil, that seemed oppressive in its weight as it was bewitching in its negligée. One glove was withdrawn and her sleeve pushed high up the swelling arm, while the dimpled hand dangled in the rippling waters, that reflected the smooth white fingers in crooked, dancing outlines. Out on the lake alone, and Heaven only knows how I loved her! yet I did not dare to disclose it. The very intimacy of our childhood, the relations we bore to each other in our family, the brilliancy of her career in society, and the constant adulation she received, all made me feel that she could regard my tame proposal of love with nothing less than ridicule. So, while my heart fluttered with its restrained emotion, I spoke carelessly and lightly, admiring the view with her, and quoting Wordsworth and Tupper with pedantic inaptitude. Leaving scenery we became more personal, and, after asking her secrecy, I told her of my affair with Miss Finnock and asked her advice.

"And you promised to finish the sentence soon?" she said, laughing, and flipping the water from her fingers' ends as she drew on her glove; "what was its intended conclusion?"

"I was about to ask her that, if I were to offer my hand and heart, would she accept?" feeling a little ashamed of the commonplace phrases.

"A subjunctive courtship, truly," she said, smiling, as she took off her hat and threw back her hair from her white forehead to catch the fresh breeze. "Well, you have, indeed, committed yourself. You have attached too much importance to the matter, by deferring it, to give it some trivial conclusion, such as, 'were I to raise the piano would you play?' or, if I call this evening, will you ride with me? You have promised, and her heart is beating high with expectation."

"It will beat a long time before it is satisfied, then," I said, somewhat morosely.

"Suppose you write her a note, and candidly inform her that your feelings have undergone a change," she suggested archly.

"That would wound her feelings," I said, "and I cannot do that."

"But are you sure the lady loves you? That is a matter of some importance."

"I have every reason to believe it."

"I see nothing that you can do but wait the issue of events. Wouldn't it be funny if you had to marry her, or be sued for a breach of promise?"

"Pardon me for not seeing the fun in either case," I replied, shuddering at the bare idea of marrying her; "but see, here comes another boat!"

The large boat at the lake house had been manned, and was rapidly catching up with us, under the pressure of sails, and oars to which a couple of stout Irishmen were bending. As they drew nearer we saw that the occupants were Mr. Marshman and party. Miss Finnock was sitting in the prow of the boat, armed with an opera glass, which she now lowered from the hills to our boat. I fancied her eyes grew wider apart as she saw who my companion was. Their boat came swiftly on, foaming at her prow, and bearing down upon us like a pirate on a prize.

They were near enough now to bow, and I raised myself from my reclining position to touch my hat. Mr. Finnock was steering, and I saw he knew nothing about it.

As I had tied my rudder I did not unloose it, as I thought of course they would pass by. Such was Finnock's intention, but attempting to bear to one side, he gave the rudder too strong a turn, and to correct that turned too much the other way, and their boat, at full speed, ran obliquely against us. Carlotta and Miss Finnock both had risen to their feet as they saw the impending collision, and were both precipitated into the water, between the boats, which separated as soon as they struck.

Carlotta had scarcely touched the water before I was by her side.

Did you ever see waves close over one you love? then you know the horror that stamped the whole scene upon my memory, indelible in its distinctness, and perfectly vivid in its minutest detail. Her frightened look, as the boats came together, her agonizing cry for help as she fell, the dull splash of the water, the eddies that curled above the place she sank, all are present still. I remember now how clear the water was, and how, as with one stroke of my hands, I reached the spot, I saw her dress floating scarce beneath the surface, and then her face, distorted in her convulsive struggles for life, slowly rising upward. To draw her head above the surface was the work of a second, and as soon as she had cleared the water from her eyes and mouth sufficiently to become conscious, I bade her take my hand, and with the other commenced to swim to the nearest boat. As soon as she realized the situation she regained her presence of mind, and clung to me tenderly, though not so as to impede my movements. The large boat was not more than a dozen feet from us, and the occupants, as is usual in such cases, were in a frenzy of salvation, throwing overboard for our assistance, everything that would float. One of their intended life-buoys—a heavy oar—struck me on the head, almost stunning me, but I shook the water from my eyes and struggled on. The next moment my feet became entangled in a web of garments, a bubbling shriek burst forth close at my ear, and my arms were pinioned by the frantic Miss Finnock, who rose near me.

"B-r-r-sh ok—ok—Oh! chtl-Mr. Smith k-k—tl save your-k—d-arling, tlsave me k-ok—Oh! tlsave-k-me. D-ts-earest tsave me;" and, sputtering and choking, she clung to my neck, dragging me down irresistibly. As soon as Carlotta saw my danger, she let go my hand, and said, in her trembling voice, "Save yourself, John!"

But all this occurred in half the time I have taken to write it, and the people in the boat had now recovered their senses. The two Irishmen were in the water, and Mr. Marshman and Finnock stood ready with ropes to aid them. Carlotta was first drawn on board, then Miss Finnock and myself. Mr. Marshman fortunately happened to have a flask of brandy along, so the ladies went to work on the ladies, the gentlemen on me, while the boat hands overhauled our little boat, took down the sail, and lashed it fast to the large one. At first I felt weak and dizzy, but after a while I was able to sit up, though I could not render much help to the others. Carlotta was very pale, and her loosened hair, rendered still more glossy by the water, hung in jetty masses around her marble features. She was conscious, though faint, and lay helplessly in Mrs. Marshman's lap, occasionally raising her soft eyes to mine with an expression so full of grateful meaning that it thrilled me into life and activity. Miss Finnock had fainted, of course, and lay like one dead in Miss Stelway's lap.

The pallor on her face did not tend to increase her beauty, and a large roll of wet hair was hanging to her own knot by a single hair-pin.

Finnock and Miss Stelway were chafing her hands, and trying to get some of the brandy between her lips. Mrs. Marshman suggested unfastening her clothing, but after Miss Stelway had stolen a hand under her bodice, she withdrew it hopelessly, as if there was rather too much to undo and cut.

Very soon Miss F. commenced gasping, like a fish on a sand bank, and opening and closing her eyes in the most approved stage-faint style. Miss Stelway kissed her forehead, and called her "dear Saph," with a fine resuscitating effect, for little Sappho began to utter broken sentences in faint but nervous sudden tones, jerking the words out, as if she could not control them.

"Oh where—where—is he?" she said, looking straight up into Miss Stelway's face. "She sunk—him—I know she—did. I saw—her cling-ing to him."

With Miss Stelway's assistance she sat up, and her eyes met mine. When, with an affected scream, she buried her face in Miss Stelway's bosom, and sobbed.

"There, darling," said Miss S., "compose yourself; we all are safe, and are nearly at the shore."

"Oh, Nellie," said Miss Finnock, between her sobs, "did—they—all—see my—feet?"

Those at the Lake House had seen the accident, and Herrara met us at the shore with his carriage. We drove rapidly back to the town, and were met by mother, with uplifted hands and a face full of horror. Afraid of forming a scene, I bade them good morning, and went over to my room to change my clothes. A strange happiness was at my heart, for Carlotta had pressed my hand, when we parted, with grateful fervor.

CHAPTER XXXVII

Our accident formed quite a subject of sensation in Saratoga, and, in a small way, I found myself the hero of the occasion, and scores of the "fellows" echoed Monte's sentiments, when he said:

"Smith, I vow I would like to have been in your place. 'Twas jolly, I know, saving that angelic Lola. The devil take your good luck! did she hold on tight?"

The afternoon following the day of the disaster I went over to Congress Hall, and sent up my card, and inquiries after Carlotta's health. The servant returned with a card from mother, saying Carlotta was almost well enough to go out, but that she was now sleeping under the influence of an opiate, and must remain quiet all the evening. They were in their parlor, and insisted that I should join them. I immediately went up stairs, and was met at the door by mother, with her bonnet on. She invited me in, in a whisper, and explained that she had just gotten ready to do some shopping that was necessary. She pointed to the centre table, on which were some new books, and begged me to amuse myself for a quarter of an hour, when she would be back, or Carlotta would awaken.

I accordingly took my seat, nothing loth to watch over such a beautiful charge, and picking up *Beulah*, which was the sensation just then, began to read. The room was very quiet, and the shaded light from the soft green curtains was very pleasant, but I could not become interested in the book, and, laying it down, I moved a chair noiselessly near Carlotta, and sat silently looking and loving. She was reclining on a folding lounge of pink damask, that reflected a faint tint on her face, which was white as marble. Her hair was parted simply over her forehead, and fell in voluminous waves over the pillow, while her lashes lay in deep black crescents on her cheeks. One soft hand rested under her face, while the other lay at her side, its tapering fingers half closed. No quivers of the lids, no slightest motion, told of life, save the rise and fall of the snowy frill at her throat. Oh, hopeless love! the saddest of all earth's sadness, the deepest of all earth's gloom!

She could not, did not love me, I knew from all the past and the present. To tell her of my love would only distress her and make home unhappy. Mine alone must be the struggle and the victory. I would kneel by her side, touch her cheek but once with my lips, and henceforth only be her brother.

I rose softly and knelt by the sofa, and my face bent over hers. That kiss was to be the seal of my silence, and I was, from that moment, to bury the love of my life in my own heart, and trust to Time to build its tomb. I steadied myself with one hand on the back of the sofa, leaned down, and whispering only that one word, "Darling!" kissed her cheek. As gentle as was my touch her eyes unclosed and she looked in my face. Overwhelmed with shame and confusion, I could not move or speak, but kneeled motionless with our faces almost touching, and my eyes fixed on hers. The next instant her soft arm was laid timidly around my neck, and, with a look that thrilled my very soul, she said, in a tone of wondrous tenderness, "John!" It was only one word, but it told me all; and the next instant, in a delirium of surprise and joy, I had clasped her in my arms, kissing her brow, and cheeks, and mouth, and murmuring, "Darling, do you love me?"

And when Reason had returned, what a Heaven on earth 'twas to sit by her side, to hold her hand in mine, to feel the glorious resurrection of hope and love from the grave to which I was about to consign them, to know that the very truth and sincerity of her nature assured the certainty and earnestness of her love for me! Then it was such a delightful surprise, so different from what I expected, that I feared it could not be true—that it was all a dream. "Carlotta," I said, looking at her fondly, "is this real, do you love me? Is it possible that, after all my fears, all my despair, you will be mine, my own darling—mine to love, cherish and honor, with a devotion man never knew before?" She looked up into my face with a depth of truth in her dark eyes that dispelled every doubt, as she said:

"I have always loved you, John."

"Always, Lottie? What hours of unhappiness 'twould have saved me had I known it; for, though I have loved you constantly during these long years of our separation, yet I have felt that my love was hopeless, and while I treasured that dear curl, the pledge of your remembrance, I somehow felt that you would remember me only as the friend, perhaps the brother of your childhood. As I received letters telling me of your growth into beautiful womanhood, and of the attention and devotion that were lavished upon you everywhere, I felt that the gulf between us was widening—that you would return proud and supercilious, inflated with your success, and contemptuous of my quiet student life. Almost fearing to meet you, I delayed along my trip, hoping that when I reached Niagara I would find our party gone; hence I stopped at the Springs, intending, after a week's stay, to run across to the Falls. You know the rest; how cordially you met me, and how the thraldom of my life was sealed. The love that had glowed so steadily during your absence burst into a resistless flame before your superb beauty and lovely character. Yet O, darling, the anguish of the thought that you would never love me—that another would soon claim the hand that held in its grasp my soul! I could have borne it better had I found you haughty and vain, for then resentment would have aided me; but I found that you were still the same sweet Carlotta that had told me farewell in Raleigh; that the brilliant belle of every occasion was as guileless and pure as when I found her on the beach; that she was unspoilt by the caresses of society. How I worshipped you none can ever know, and I longed to fall at your feet and tell you all, but I felt sure you would laugh at the idea of 'John's loving,' and this evening I was going to kiss your cheek, and bid farewell forever to my love, when you awoke—and thank Heaven for it! And now, darling, tell me again that you love me, for your voice, talking of love, is the sweetest music in the world to me."

She smiled such a tender, loving smile, and, nestling up close to me, said:

"I have loved you, John, ever since we met. When I clasped your hand first after the shipwreck there was a thrill in my heart that ever came back when you were near me. So fearful was I that you might detect this feeling, that I tried to be reserved and silent in your presence, and even avoided you as much as possible. Conscious of my own love, I felt, child as I was, that every one else knew it, and hence my extreme sensitiveness at any connection of our names together. You doubtless remember the scene with Mrs. Smith, when you were asleep in the hall, or pretending to be. That explained the nature of my feelings. I shrank from the position I seemed to occupy—that of awaiting your love, and of being trained to suit that love if you pleased to confer it. While I saw you so full of Lulie and Lillian I buried my feelings in my own heart, and strove strenuously to crush them out of existence; but there were times when you were tender and loving to me, and then they came resistlessly. Do you remember one night, years ago, when we were out on the stoop, and you took my hand and held it awhile? No words can ever tell how I have treasured up that little scene. When you told me farewell, the night of our departure for Europe, and I gave you the curl, it was an earnest pledge of what I faithfully performed."

"Darling, do not speak of Lulie and Lillian. One was only the passing object of boyish affection, and the other a heartless though brilliant woman, who flattered me by her notice into an admiration that was as vain as it was transient. Dearest Lottie, your heart believes me, I know, when I vow that the purest, fondest love of my nature is yours, that without it all life is void and blank. Darling, have you loved me always, have you never wavered in your love, as affections more worthy, but none more devoted than mine, have been laid at your feet?"

"Never, John. No faintest shadow of love for another has ever passed across my mind, and the only pleasure I took in the attention I may have received has been the thought that, if others see aught in me to love, perhaps, when we meet, *he* will."

"He being myself?" I asked, looking at her with a smile.

"He being yourself. There, I have made enough unladylike confessions for one afternoon; but 'tis all a proof of my trust and confidence in you."

"As God shall help me it is not misplaced," and I lifted her hand tenderly to my lips. "Never was man as proud of as beautiful and pure a love as I am of yours, and never was a love guarded and cherished as I will yours, and I will seek no higher happiness on earth than to keep that dear brow as bright and beautiful as now. Darling, look into my eyes and read the truth of love."

She looked, and would have read, perhaps, had not the door opened just then, and mother entered from her shopping excursion. As she saw us sitting lovingly together, Carlotta's hand in mine, she was so utterly astounded that she stood without moving, her hands full of bundles, which kept dropping on the floor.

To prevent further embarrassment, I rose from my seat, and taking mother's hand, led her to Carlotta.

"She is going to be my wife, mother," I said, and without waiting to hear her reply, left the room.

How bright and beautiful all nature seemed. The cloudless sky, the rich green foliage, and the fragrant roses scenting the evening air—all were in unison with my heart. The very birds in the lawn seemed to twitter congratulations. Nothing could have ruffled my temper; a bootblack might have thrown his brush in my face, and I would have picked it up for him with a smile. I felt that I could even be kind and courteous to Miss Finnock.

In this pleasant frame of mind I went in to tea, and found the two gentlemen and Mrs. Marshman at our table, Mrs. M., after inquiries about Carlotta, and some compliments to her beauty, thought of a note for me, from Miss Finnock; and, as she gave it to me, said that Sappho had been quite indisposed all day, and had suffered severely from her fright, and the shock of the cold water.

Excusing myself, I opened the little three cornered note, and read:

"Will the generous and unselfish preserver of my life do me
the favor to call this evening at our parlor, No.—, that I may

unburden my heart of its gratitude, and offer a hecatomb of thanks to his self-sacrificing spirit. Call at eight.

Waiting."

In much smaller writing, just beneath this, were some verses, as usual, across which she had drawn her pen, as if to erase them, taking care, however, to leave them sufficiently legible—

> "But for thy hand I might have slept
> Deep in the bosom of yon lake,
> And no one for me would have wept,
> And none have wished that I might wake."

That's the first sensible poetry you ever wrote, I muttered, as I read it. But there was more:

> "I would not shun the wild waves' wrath,
> Could we sink clasping hand in hand,
> To walk together pearly paths
> Of mermaids, down the coral strand."

You ought to have said "path," Saph; you've spoiled your rhyme; and "mermaids" and a "coral strand," out in this little lake, are very much strained, but so are the verses. I was, as I have stated, in a pleasant frame of mind, and thus jested to myself with the verses as I read them. The next verse, however, put the case a little more strongly:

> "I fain would seek a watery grave,
> To dwell with thee in grottoes bright,
> Or roam through halls where the sea-weeds wave,
> And love would make the darkness light."

To think of marrying her anywhere! much less down in a grotto, with sea-weeds and bad colds, and coral, etc. No, I could not "fain," as she did; but I glanced at my watch as I rose from the table, and found that it wanted a quarter of eight. Fifteen minutes with a Partaga, and I tapped at the door of her parlor. Miss Finnock after Carlotta! 'Twas like a dessert of nutgalls after Hymettean honey; but I felt that the necessary exercise of my ingenuity would be rather pleasant than otherwise, and looked forward to our interview, with anticipated pride in my skilful retrogression.

When I entered I found Miss Finnock reclining in an easy chair, and looking as little like her Lesbian nomenclatress as scant strings of hair, an unmade, stiff figure, and pale blue eyes, in a sallow face, could make her. She smiled a faint little welcome, and pointed me to a seat in front of her.

"Please lower the gas," she said, shading her eyes with her hand; "you must excuse me, Mr. Smith, for seeing you in such *deshabille*, but I felt sure you would appreciate this liberty, and feel more free and unrestrained than if I had prepared formally to see you."

"I do appreciate and thank you for your consideration," I said, feeling assured that if she had known how different was the effect of her *deshabille* from what she intended it should be, she would not have been so considerate.

"I sent for you, Mr. Smith," she continued, in a whispering kind of voice, "that I might express my gratitude for your heroic efforts to save me yesterday."

I would have suspected any one else of irony, but I knew she was in earnest.

"Really, Miss Finnock, you overestimate my conduct," I said; "I must be candid with you, and tell you that I was doing all I could to save myself, which was almost impossible with yourself and Miss Rurlestone on my arms."

She looked at me with a queer little smile, and said: "What a trying ordeal for you! If no boat had been near us, 'twould have been an effectual test of your love, indeed. Would you have found it difficult to have made a choice, if you had seen you could not save but one?"

"Not at all," I replied, hoping she would construe the preference as intended for herself, and let the subject rest.

She played with the tassel of her wrapper, and said softly, "Which would you have chosen?"

I pretended not to have heard, and asked if she had suffered any serious inconvenience from the accident?

"Not much," she said, with something of a sigh in her tone. "I have been feeble to-day, but hope to gain strength rapidly. I expect to take a stroll every morning before breakfast, and to ride with brother in the afternoons."

It was a very fine opening for engagements; but I had had enough of strolls, and so I said nothing. There was a pause of some length, during which I saw a scrap of paper lying on the table, and as my name was on it, I looked at it more closely. The light in the room was very dim, and Miss Finnock was all the while stealing quick glances at me; besides, I knew 'twas highly improper to read it, yet under all these difficulties I managed to make out its purport. It was a note from Miss Belle Monte, Miss Finnock's dearest friend and adviser, to her "precious Saph," telling her that I was only trifling with her, that her brother had certain information that I was engaged to Miss Rurlestone; that my attentions to Miss F. were all insincere; that the best thing to do was to secure an interview with me, and, on my first committal, discard me promptly and finally.

I now saw that I had been invited to her parlor that she might have the credit of dismissing me, and I resolved that say what she would, I would not, by any reply, give her an opportunity of so doing.

"When do you think of leaving?" she asked, at length, lifting her head wearily from her hand.

"We will leave to-morrow or next day for Newport, where we will spend some weeks before going home."

"Oh, that is too soon," she said; "you have not seen enough of the Springs."

"As I have not seen my parents in several years, and came on here to meet them, I must regulate my movements by theirs. Besides," I continued, "they were here some time before I came, and desire a change—at least, Miss Rurlestone does, I am sure—as she has captured every heart here, and perhaps pines for more." This I said a little maliciously.

"Miss Rurlestone can probably account for your filial devotion—at least gossip says so."

"Gossip knows very little about such matters," I replied, cautiously.

"But is gossip wrong in this instance?"

"Oh, I must not commit myself," I said, with a forced smile.

"You are so tantalizing," she said, throwing her tassel at me, "and that reminds me that you promised to complete that unfinished sentence soon."

"What unfinished sentence?" I asked, with pretended ignorance.

"You must be forgetful, indeed; do you not remember your promise when we parted yesterday morning?"

"Pardon me; I do remember now," and instantly the thought flashed on me that I would candidly inform her of my intended flirtation, confess my sin, ask her forgiveness, and thus prevent her acting on Miss Belle Monte's advice. "I recollect now distinctly the sentence to which you refer, and its intended termination. My remarks were made in the same light style in which we were conversing, and I had no idea you would attach sufficient importance to anything I said to think of it at all afterwards. I was about to ask, if *I* loved you—if I offered my heart—would you reject it? I——"

"That's what I suspected, sir," she cut in before I could finish, and with a deprecatory wave of her hand dismissing what I had said as painful, "and while the suspicion flattered it pained me."

"But, Miss Finnock," I said, hurriedly, "you certainly misun——"

"Flattered, indeed, I was," she went on, without allowing my interruption, "because one so noble and gifted as yourself had conferred on me the honor of his love, and pained that I must refuse it."

I was too much astonished to reply, while she went on:

"But, Mr. Smith, while a calm review of my own feelings forces me to discard you, or if that is too harsh a word, to ask you to be *only* my friend, I can assure you that our brief intercourse has been exceedingly pleasant to me. It will ever be an oasis in the desert of my past, and I trust that the rainbow of mutual regard and esteem will ever arch brightly o'er our pathways, however diverse they may be. And when Time's fingers have plastered over the scars I regret to inflict, and you have found another love, whose voice may be sweeter, and eye brighter, and heart dearer than mine, I hope you will not think of this evening with anger, but with the pleasure of forgiveness."

"With pleasure, certainly," I managed to edge in, as she drew her breath.

"And at your life's close," she went on, in her peculiar strain, "may your barque furl its sails in a peaceful harbor, and having bosomed" (Sapphic for breasted) "every wave, anchor safely there."

As she paused, I broke in——

"Miss Finnock, you have wofully misinterpreted my meaning. I was only jesting, as I thought you were; and my words had no more serious import than the verses in a *bon-bon*."

"I hardly expected that you would thus try to evade the subject, Mr. Smith. But I have too much consideration for your feelings to place your name on my list of rejected ones. The result of our interview shall be strictly *entre nous*."

"Your list must be immensely long, if you put every name down with as little reason as you have mine. I will leave you, Miss Finnock; for I can gain

nothing in a contest with a lady who makes half the addresses she rejects."
This I said without thought, being thrown off my guard by her treatment;
and the moment after I had closed the door I felt like going back to ask her
pardon. Pride, however, suggested that she had overstepped the bounds
of womanly delicacy in her conduct towards me, and that she must take
outside treatment.

CHAPTER XXXVIII

Perhaps there was never a betrothal made under more favorable auspices than Carlotta's and mine. Perfect love and confidence towards each other, and the most entire approval of all interested in our welfare! When we met, father pressed my hand most cordially in token of his sanction, and mother kissed me, saying, as she did so:

"My dear boy, it is a consummation I have devoutly prayed for. You have won a prize, indeed, John; cherish it fondly."

To which my reply was, of course, redundantly affirmative and sempiternally votive.

As we were preparing to leave for Newport the day following I did not see Miss Finnock again, and was very glad of it, as our interview could not have been pleasant; and, in fact, I thought the rest of the party treated me with sudden coldness and reserve when we met at the table.

The night preceding our departure there was a grand ball at the Union, and though I had the honor of escorting Carlotta, her card was so full of engagements that I could only stand off and admire her, as a throng of her devotees surrounded her.

As blind as love is said to be, it is, nevertheless, very much affected by what others think of its object; and, besides flattering our own taste, it very much enhances our devotion to feel that others love what we love. Leander would never have swum the Hellespont if no one else had cared for Hero.

With all the fond pride of ownership I watched the crowd that flocked to Carlotta's side, when a set closed, begging the honor of a dance, striving to catch a smile, and wearying her with ceaseless and multitudinous attention; and, as I marked the disappointment on the faces of a score, and the conscious triumph of him who led her out, I thought that if they thus sought the pleasure of a moment with her, how supremely blest was I to own her love, and hold her promise to be mine for life.

I was selfish enough to want her all to myself, and brooked but poorly the immense popularity that engaged her time and kept her from me.

At Newport it was the same thing. Her fame had preceded her, and many of her Saratoga beaux followed her thither. Her appearance in the ball room at the Ocean House was the signal for the desertion of other belles, and our drives on the beach were series of stares, of envy from the ladies and of admiration from the men. It was amusing to mark the difference of expression on the faces of the occupants of a buggy or landau as it rolled past us; the gentleman invariably gazing at her, with a smile, as we approached, and turning his head to look back as we passed; the lady looking straight ahead, with a half curl on her lip, as if she would say, "Umph! she is not so beautiful after all."

It was not till we left Newport, and were returning to dear old quiet Carolina, that I began to realize that Carlotta was indeed my own. Herrara parted with us in New York, taking the steamer for Havana, and promising to bring his bride to see us the next winter.

After spending some days in the metropolis we started home, and then I was happy to sit by Carlotta's side in the train, whose very rattle made our conversation private, and talk of our future! There is no period so fraught with pleasure to lovers as that when, the first extravagance of the proposal and acceptance over, they sober down into conversation about their plans and prospects; when they talk of the home they are going to have, and how it will be furnished; when they tell of how they will live, and what they will have for dinner; when they make little confidences of their foibles of disposition and temper, that they may know how never to hurt each other's feelings; when they each draw pictures of their everyday life, that is to be, and dwell like epicures at a feast on the details; she telling of the nice cosy breakfast, with just two cups and saucers; of the fine cigars she will light for him, as she kisses him goodbye till dinner; of the pretty key basket she will carry on her arm, all the "long, dreary morning," till he comes back; of the afternoon nap, while she fingers his hair; of the evening drive, of the slippers ready for him after tea, of the "hateful newspaper" taken out of his hands that he may talk with her! Bright little heart! is there no tear, no frown, no headache in your picture? He telling of his compliments to her rolls and coffee, of his invariable kiss at parting, of his constant thought of her during the hours of business, of his haste to return, of his often pretending to be sick that she may nurse him in her sweet way, of the many thoughtful gifts he will bring her, of his helping to keep house and stealing her sugar, of his leaning on the piano while she sings his favorite songs, of her head upon his shoulder and his arm around her waist, as they sit together under the moonlight in their little porch, with all the necessary vines and flowers. When they both are thinking, yet carefully avoid speaking, of another tender phase of the picture—when something, not a chair, is rocking in their chamber, and a rack at the fire is full of white cloths, when the gifts he brings now are gutta percha and coral, and, instead of the moon the lamp is kept burning all night.

When we got back to Wilmington I found a letter for me from Ben, inviting me up to his wedding.

It was a characteristic epistle, and went on to tell me that as he "had laid by his crap" and was "outer the grass" he had concluded to take unto himself as an helpmeet, Miss Viny Dodge, though he frankly stated that his "daddy" said he "hadn't no more business with a wife than er oyshter has for gluves."

As the letter was dated two weeks back I knew that Miss Viny was already Mrs. Bemby, so I sent my congratulations, and regrets that I could not have been present, and a bridal gift for Mrs. B.

Our own arrangements were, that I was to return to Chapel Hill, complete my senior year, and be married to Carlotta immediately after my graduation; and then we were to go to Germany, that I might complete my law course at Heidelberg.

When Ned and I met again in our old room at the University, we both had so much to tell that we devoted several nights to the rehearsal of our adventures. Ned had spent his vacation at the White Sulphur Springs, and was, of course, well charged with news of himself. As each of us was more anxious to talk than to listen, our conversation was a series of mutual interruptions, and this difficulty of communication, perhaps, aided us in our studies.

When we finally got to work in earnest we found our position as Seniors very pleasant in every way. Our studies, though deeper and more comprehensive, were not so tedious, and allowed us more time for general reading. Ned was striving hard for the Valedictory, while I looked forward with some hope to the same honor; our rivalry, however, was always pleasant. With my studies and readings, and, above all, with Carlotta's sweet letters, I found time did not drag so heavily as I had expected when I parted from her, and almost before I knew the summer was gone the winter vacation came on. I went home and spent the time in one bright dream of happiness. I was with Carlotta!

I returned to college again in January, full of ambitious visions. Five more months and, with a brow burdened with honors, I would stand upon the rostrum of the University, and while the crowded hall was breathless with my eloquence, I would meet the light of Carlotta's eyes, and in their raptured gaze find my best applause. Then would come our wedding, arranged with all the splendor wealth could command; then a term of honor at Heidelberg; and then, with Fame's temple before me, I would climb until I stood upon its very dome. But across these bright visions there drifted now the red cloud of war, and in its murky bosom muttered our impending ruin.

I found the University, as I had left Wilmington, all ablaze with excitement over the secession of South Carolina. The number of students was much smaller than usual, and many of those who came returned to their homes, as State after State left the Union. Our noble Commonwealth, with her resinous nature, stuck tenaciously to the Union, and when she tore herself loose at last, adhered as closely to the flag of the Confederacy.

Letters poured in upon me from home. Father and mother urged me to remain at college till the session closed, and get my diploma, as it would be but a short delay, but I was impatient; I wanted to be preparing for the fray, and Carlotta's letter decided me. It was full of the fire of her soul, and while it breathed the tenderest love for me, it was fervid with patriotism.

"I know that study will be impossible amid the excitement of the times," she said, in conclusion, "and you will accomplish nothing by remaining at the University till the close of the session. You know, dear John, that I love you more than all else on earth, but if I did not love my country, too, I would be unworthy of your love, and if you were unwilling to defend her, you would be unworthy of mine. But I know your noble heart, and trust its fervid zeal.

"Remember, dearest, my hand shall gird your armor on, and my prayers shall shield your head."

CHAPTER XXXIX

When I reached Wilmington I found everything in a stir. Everybody wore a cockade, a miniature flag, or a uniform. Officers, with waving plumes, rode furiously up and down the streets; the roll of drums, as companies marched in from the camps, was heard at all hours of the day; and with every whistle of the train arose the thrilling shout of legions, passing on to the front. Ladies pricked their tender fingers sewing the stout gray cloth, or thronged the balconies to wave their dainty handkerchiefs at their favorites in the ranks.

War was in its youth; the scowl of battle had not yet gathered on its brow, and the flowers with which Beauty strewed its pathway were not yet bedewed with the red drops of carnage, nor withered in the smoke and heat of conflict.

Father had already raised a company, up at the plantation in Wayne, and they were now out at the camp of instruction near town. When I joined, they complimented me by electing me second lieutenant, and I felt as proud of the little yellow bars on my collar as Lord Dreddlington did of his Garter.

What a pastime was soldiering then; sleeping in tents for the first time, cooking our own meals, going out with a new gun to play sentry, marching through the dress parade in the evening, before the long line of carriages, filled with our sweethearts from the town!

I had moved out to the camp, and though it was very near town, I had to get a pass whenever I wished to see Carlotta. The very novelty of this, however, rendered it pleasant, and I no doubt wearied the commandant by my frequent applications. Our marriage had been fixed for the 15th of June, but as our company expected to leave for Richmond by the 12th, we made the appointment nearer by ten days, and on the 5th of June, 1861—a fair, cloudless morning—we were married. It was a plain, unostentatious wedding—different, indeed, from what I had anticipated. Only a few friends with us, a slight collation in the parlor, a short excursion to Smithville, and it was all over. Yet Carlotta was dearer to me, in her simple Swiss muslin, than she would have been in satin and lace; and I felt, as she looked up radiantly into my face, that she was prouder of me, in my suit of gray, than if I had worn the finest cloth.

On our return from Smithville I found a short letter from Ben, who had enrolled his name with our company, but had not yet come down to join us:

"Dear john," he wrote, "when Curnal Smith was up here, I couldent leave on account of Viny, but it's come now, and a fine one it is, and Viny is doin' well; so I'll be down sum'ers about the last of the week. i hate orful to leave Viny and the baby, and it'll be mity lonesome at night, not to trot him on my nee, but I be dogged if ime goin' to see the yankeys get into north Carolina if my carciss will help to stop 'em. Less me and you git together when we fight, cause I want somebody ime cwainted with to see me 'mongst the balls, and it'll help me to keep game.

"if i don't git to Wilminton in time, i'll meet you at Goldsboro'. Till Death, yours,

Ben."

CHAPTER XL

Father, mother, Carlotta and I are standing in the dim light of dawn, under the old shed at the depot. We lack only Lulie to be the same party who stood there five years before, waiting for the train. How things have changed! The little dark eyed girl that was gazing out of the car window then is the beautiful woman who is weeping and clinging to my arm now. Instead of mirth and cheerfulness, all around us now is sadness and gloom. Great rough fellows are dropping their first tears, as they strain a sobbing wife or little child to their bosom for the twentieth time.

Delicate youths, wearing a brave face in spite of their quivering lips, are holding in their arms fond mothers, who are putting back the hair from their idol's forehead, perhaps for the last time; and even those who have no one to bid them farewell, and who are attempting to look careless and indifferent, often lift their cuffs to their averted eyes.

We have no piles of baggage now; a plain pine box, filled with the delicacies loving hands have made, and a roll of blankets, are all that we check for.

How Carlotta clings to me, sobbing on my neck!

"Oh John, my husband, how can I give you up? And to think that I bade you go! I did not know what it was to part from you. Oh, if you are hurt, it will kill me—I know it will kill me. My God, protect him, for thy Son's sake!"

I kissed her again and again, and told her to look on the bright side; I reminded her of our duty to our country, and spoke of war as a field of honor, not of danger. But the agony of our separation was too close at hand, and my own heart too near breaking to reason her into composure and fortitude, and I gave way to my own grief, and mingled my tears with hers.

A whistle now sounded far across the river, then, with the roar of the approaching train, rose the thrilling cheers of its gallant freight. And soon the ferry boat, dimly seen through the mists, her very bulwarks crowded with men in gray, strikes out into the stream, and in brazen cadences the glorious strains of Dixie float across the smoky waters. Nearer and nearer comes the cheering, louder and louder swells the music, and in the red light of the rising sun gleams the Stars and Bars. As they neared the wharf father said: "Come, John, we must get our seats before the crowd comes in. Mary! God bless you, good bye. Good bye, Carlotta, my daughter!" and he walked with a firm step up the platform into the car. A mother's kiss and tearful benison, a sobbing scream and a convulsive clasp of my darling's arms, and I took my place in the train. Bowing my head on my hands I scarce heard the murmur of voices, the ringing of bells, or the quick thrang of the kettle drum, as the regiment from the boat formed and marched to the coaches assigned them. As the long train jerked forward I thrust my head out of the window and caught sight of our carriage and its two weeping occupants. They saw me at the same instant, and, with their handkerchiefs, waved farewell What an acme of agony in that last view!

We had reached Goldsboro before I had recovered my spirits, and I was gazing thoughtfully out of the window as we ground our way slowly under the shed, when a rough hand was laid upon my shoulder, and looking up I recognized Ben. He was the same awkward looking specimen of humanity, clad in a suit of copperas striped homespun. Instead of the old flapped hat he now wore an oilskin cap, which he had purchased that morning, and which still had the price card stuck on the brim. His hair was still long and sandy, though a trifle darker than when we went fishing together; his upper lip, with the scar across it, was covered with a soft yellowish fuzz, that told of an incipient moustache, and his chin was covered with stiff wiry little curls, that looked like the vegetation of freckle seed. Rough and uncouth as was his appearance, I felt, as I grasped his hand, that it was as full of nerve as Virginius', and that the old brown suit would always be the first hid in the smoke of battle.

"I am glad, indeed, to have you with us, Ben," said father, as they shook hands, "John here is a gloomy companion. He has hardly spoken to me since we left Wilmington."

"Well, I tell you, curnell," said Ben, laying a bag full of biscuit on the seat in front of him, "it streaked my gizzard powerful to leave Viny and the baby, and when I went to kiss the little varmint farwell the tears run round my eyes like rain in a gourd bloom; but I couldn't make up my mind to sneak at home, and let somebody else git shot for my folks."

"You have expressed your patriotism very pointedly," said father, clearing his throat to deliver his favorite speech on States' rights. "Our fair and sunny land is threatened with invasion by the Vandals of the North, and it becomes every man's duty to resist them. We are clearly on the side of right. The original compact of the thirteen States was, most evidently, no surrender of sovereignty. Each State retained its own laws, and was only sufficiently amenable to the general Government to preserve unity.

The very investiture of each State with the right to change its laws, to execute criminals, and to regulate its own elections, proves its sovereign independence. Do you not think so?"

"I don' know much 'bout politicks," said Ben, looking somewhat flattered that father should have asked his opinion on so deep a subject, "but seems to me that States is folks, and folks is sholy got the right to undo what they done therselves."

As I had heard these old arguments, differently dished, in every conversation or debate since the first of January, I was much relieved by more troops getting on board at the next depot, and crowding father and Ben out of their talk.

We passed Weldon in the evening, through Petersburg in the night, and were in regular camp the next day. Then war began in earnest; our lines were formed in front of cannon instead of carriages; instead of a flower-wreathed target a man in blue stood in front of our guns, and our bayonets now were sometimes red when we unfixed them.

But do not fear, patient reader, that I am going to inflict a long series of war incidents upon you. You have heard and read all that I could tell a dozen times; and though no pen has yet arisen to blazon North Carolina's deeds, I will only point to the battle record of the South, and resting her fame on the glorious valor of her sons, pass on, with only one chapter of letters, to the close of our struggle, when the banner we had borne through four years of shot and shell was furled, and the land we had bled for—conquered!

CHAPTER XLI

My Precious Husband—The little angel God promised us has come, and I am so happy. If you were only here, to see the little cherub nestling by me, I would be *too full* of bliss for utterance. To think it is *yours* and *mine*, darling! I feel sometimes that I *must* send it to you that you may see how beautiful and sweet it is. Mother says it is like me, but I see in it nothing but your image. I think it notices me some already, though it is only a week old, but I know there never was such an intelligent baby; the very first name it lisps shall be "papa," and it shall say its little prayers each night for dear papa's safety. I often weep over it, darling, as I think of the danger and hardship you are exposed to, and Oh! I do pray so fervently that no harm may befall you. We are making a fearful sacrifice for our country. God grant her independence may be won!

There is an old friend of yours here now—Frank, or rather Col. Paning, as he calls himself. He relates wonderful stories of his achievements in South Carolina, and wears his three stars very proudly. He is all devotion to Lulie, and report says they are to be married soon. Poor, infatuated girl, how I pity her!

We are getting on very pleasantly in our domestic affairs; the servants are all faithful and efficient, and Mr. Bemby reports excellent crops up at the plantation.

I would write more but feel wearied even with this, and mother, who has propped me up in bed, threatens to take away my paper.

Our love and kisses to dear father. Johnnie sends his little love to papa.

As ever your fond
Carlotta.

My Dear Wife:

I write to-night, because I know you will be uneasy when you read the telegraphic accounts of to-day's fight. I am grateful to say that I am well, and cannot even boast a scratch, though I have been to-day where a thought of life seemed folly. The hardest conflict of the war has taken place here, and even as I write the very air seems burdened with the groans of the wounded and dying. The loss of life has been fearful indeed, as the reckless courage of our soldiers drove them into the jaws of death. Our great commander and our men did all that human strength could do, but the position of the enemy was impregnable, and all our efforts to dislodge them were futile. To-morrow we retire, though we are not whipped, and if Meade dare leave his mountain entrenchments we will put him to utter rout. Would to God our retreat were all I must write, but the old proverb about the plurality of misfortune is but too true. Last night Ned, my dearest friend, died, and to-day father was taken prisoner by the enemy; he was at the head of our company, in a charge which was repulsed with heavy loss, and when we fell back, in some disorder, he was left within the Yankee lines. We trust that he is not wounded or hurt in any way, as, when last seen, he was standing erect, waving his sword, and calling on his men to rally. He will, I hope, soon get a communication through the lines to some of you. Even if he is sent to Elmira, or Point Lookout, he has so many personal friends at the North that he may make his situation comfortable. Help mother to bear up bravely, for she will need help. Prison life, however, is not so bad if one can get funds to purchase comforts, and you know the gentleman who is now holding father's property for him in New York will attend to that as soon as he hears that he is in prison. But, oh, darling! how my heart bleeds to write of poor Ned's death. You remember he came on to Virginia soon after we did, but his company was placed in another regiment, so that he was in yesterday's fight while we were not engaged. Last night, about dark, he sent for me to come to him, in the field hospital. When I reached his side I found him in a stupor, from which he roused only enough to recognize me, and faintly call my name, when he again sunk into that ever deepening coma that seems like the very mantle of approaching death. He had been struck in the breast with a fragment of shell, and his lungs were completely torn to pieces. The surgeons, seeing his hopeless condition, had given him an opiate and left him to die, turning their attention to those who could be saved. He was breathing with great difficulty, and with long intervals between the gasps, as I sat down by him and took his hand in mine. His pulse was scarcely perceptible, and I felt that his life would not last through the night. You, Carlotta, who know how I loved him, know how deep was my grief as I saw him slowly dying, his poor torn breast pouring out its life-blood with every labored breath. I sat, watching him in silence, 'till midnight, when he opened his eyes and attempted to sit up, but was too weak; he then commenced talking, in a confused strain, of angel armies he had seen marching all night, in white battle lines, over the blue sky, and of how they had formed a hollow square around his cot; and how their commander had approached and laid bare his bosom, that they all might see his wound, and how they had sung a song of triumph and filed back up the blue vault, out of sight. He then seemed to become conscious of his condition, and pressing my hand feebly, said: "I can't last much longer, John, but I am ready to die, thank God! Tell mother I said so. And, John, let me be buried under the old pines at home." He closed his eyes and was silent for an hour or more; when he again opened them there was that strange vacancy in their look that is Death's signet, and the tone of his voice was husky and cold, as he murmured, "The white army—has come—a-gain. I must—go. For Heaven, forward!"

He made an effort to spring up as he uttered the last word, but his strength failed, and he fell across my lap, dead. The bravest spirit that ever led a charge was marching through the pearly gates!

I had him buried this morning before the battle, and marked the grave, so it may be easily found. You must go down to Mr. Cheyleigh's and tell them how he died.

I close now to visit Ben, who is suffering with a broken arm. Love to mother, and a kiss to my dear boy.

May God bless and preserve you all.

Yours devotedly,

John.

Our Country Home, Oct., 1864.

My Dear Boy:

Though it has been nearly three months since your sainted father's death, this is the first time I have felt strong enough to rouse myself from my tears and grief, that I may write to you. My heart is broken, and I have nothing now to live for. I can only pray God for patience to wait His summons. But, my dear child, only those who are bereaved know how hard it is to say "Thy will be done!"

Sometimes I feel, so full of deep despair, as I look to the dark, lonely life before me, that I cannot help murmuring; and did I not know, from all our past, that God does all in love and infinite wisdom, He would seem now my bitterest enemy. O Christ! pardon the feeble rebellion of my burdened soul!

Dear Carlotta is as kind and tender as she can be, and does all she can to comfort and cheer me, but there are times when I feel that I shall die, when I think of your poor father's languishing on his coarse prison bed, with no comforts near, and only his enemies to smooth his pillow and attend to his wants. I know how he longed for *me* at his bedside, and how his dying thoughts came back to his dear old home. O John! it almost kills me to think I shall never see him again, never hear his voice calling "Mary" any more.

I hope and pray now for the close of the war, that I may go with you to Elmira and bring home his dear remains to our quiet graveyard—where mine, I trust, will soon rest beside them.

But I must not fill my whole letter with sadness. Dear little Johnnie is running all about now, and lisps our names very sweetly. Carlotta is holding him on her knee near me as I write, and he says, "Tiss papa for me."

You see from the date of our letter that we are up at the plantation. We brought most of our valuables up with us, and left the house in charge of Miss Wiggs, our housekeeper, who has taken her brother, the cripple, to stay with her, and says she is not afraid of the Yankees. All our servants left us except Horace and Hannah, who are touchingly faithful in their devotion. The negroes up here are too far from Federal influence to be much demoralized, and Mr. Bemby is gathering a very fine crop. Since we left Wilmington we have heard some very sad news about Lulie Mayland. Frank Paning, you know, has been in Wilmington for more than a year, in some position that exempted him from service. He and Lulie have been very intimate, and every one expected that they would soon be married. Lulie made a cloister of her home, and would see no one but Frank, who almost lived under her roof. Of late, dark rumors began to be whispered about them, but no one believed their slanderous import. At last, however, her shame could be no longer concealed, and your once bright, guileless little playmate is ruined for ever. Frank has fled, no one knows whither, though many believe he has gone to the Federal lines, which is, I think, probable. It is but the result of Frank's long studied designs of evil and Lulie's too implicit trust and confidence.

The blow has almost killed Dr. Mayland, whose health is very feeble. Carlotta has written to the poor girl, begging her to come up here to us, as her ruin will be less marked in this retired neighborhood. Lulie's mother was my dearest friend, and I would love and protect her child for her sake.

Alas! all the news we hear now is sad and gloomy. Fort Fisher must soon fall and Wilmington be evacuated; and I fear that even our home here will not be safe from the invasion of the enemy. But we are in the hands of the Lord. May He deliver our struggling country!

Write to us often, my dear boy, for you can never know what a comfort are your letters to your mother's sorrowing heart. May God enfold you with His arms of mercy! is her earnest prayer.

Headquarters,
Army of Va.,
February 28, 1865.

My Dear Smith: Your application for transfer to the Army of South Carolina has just been returned to us from the Department at Richmond, approved, and I take pleasure in enclosing it to you, together with transportation for yourself, servant and horse. We regret to give you up, but hope that you and Bemby may render as signal service to General Johnston as you have to General Early.

I remain, very truly yours,

Amos Halstead,

Acting Ass't Adj't

Gen'l

Major John Smith,

of Gen. Early's staff.

As explanatory of this letter, I would state that, when our regiment first reached the Army of Virginia, it was placed in the old "Stonewall" brigade. Ben soon began to attract the attention not only of the officers, but of General Jackson himself, for his daring bravery in battle, but chiefly for his skill in conducting foraging and scouting expeditions. So successful was he in stealing through the enemy's lines and gaining reliable information in regard to their strength and position, that General Jackson honored him with a special appointment for his own service. Soon after this a friend of father's, in high position, secured for me a place on Jackson's staff, and Ben and I were thus thrown together in many a field of danger and hair-breadth escape. After Ned's death, at Gettysburg, and father's capture and subsequent death in prison, I became more than ever attached to Ben, and we were fortunate in not being separated till near the close of the war. When Jackson fell at Chancellorsville we were both transferred to Ewell's command, and at his death to Early's—Ben receiving a commission as chief of scouts, while I was appointed aide-de-camp with the rank of major. After that memorable valley campaign, and when we had joined General Lee in the trenches around Petersburg, Ben was sent to General Beauregard, in South Carolina, to act as scout and spy; and as I felt lonely without him, and General Early had little need for staff officers in the trenches, I applied for transfer, with the result indicated in the letter.

When I reached the army, Johnston had, at Beauregard's request, been placed in command, and, with his splendid skill, was fighting Sherman at every step, yet drawing his small force farther and farther back without demoralization, and without a wagon's loss.

CHAPTER XLII

Eighteen hundred and sixty-five! *Annus iræ!* Year of blood and tears, famine and oppression! God send that Time's womb may be barren ere such another offspring shall curse our land!

Could one behold, as in a panorama, the South of '60 and the South of '65, even a devil would weep over the ruin wrought in five years.

In the one picture he would see wide-spreading fields, with waving, luxuriant crops, worked by throngs of joyous light-hearted negroes, who sing, in a resounding chorus, as they guide their sleek teams up and down the fertile furrows; he would see long villages of negro quarters, each house with its garden and patch, its pig and chickens, and its happy children playing at the door, while within some old camp-meeting hymn is mingling with the drone of the wheel and the clack of the loom; he would see premises adorned with all the appliances of wealth, stables filled with blooded stock, pastures grazed by herds of purest breed, kennels filled with well trained dogs, gardens of roses, orchards of fruit, and groves of magnificent oaks, amid which towers the stately mansion, its windows aglow with hospitality, and its porches thronged with fair faces and noble forms.

In the other he would see the broad fields lying idle and waste, the ditches overflowed, the fences broken down; no chorus sounds, no life is seen save in a distant corner of the field, where a "fourth part tenant" plows a little steer around an arid patch of corn. He would see the quarters all deserted, the children gone, the wheel still, and the loom silent, the very doors holding their wooden lips ajar to speak "desolation!" He would see dotted over the country the squalid huts of the freedmen, their children sick, and no one to secure the doctor's pay, that he may attend; their mortgage on the crop, made to the nearest merchant, for their year's support, consumed in midsummer by their own extravagance, and the invariable bull, scarce able to plow an hour in the day for want of food. Oh, Boston! "Hub of the Universe!" "Cradle of Freedom!" You drove a sharp trade indeed with Africa's children when you gave them the ballot in exchange for life, and comfort, and home! He would see the mansion amid the oaks, if standing at all, standing silent and drear, the smoke only rising from one chimney, the shutters all closed, and a woman in black walking wearily up and down the gloomy hall, while down in the garden, under the willow, rests a marble slab, with the inscription: "Killed at the battle of Somewhere."

But, as I was saying, it was the spring of '65.

The great army of Sherman had wound its blasting way from Atlanta to the sea. In its trail lay ashes and ruin; lone, blackened chimneys, plundered cities, and weeping women. The ever ascending smoke told its course; not the white smoke of honorable battle, but thick black volumes from burning homes, that, like the ink of a recording angel, wrote their hellish deeds upon the scroll of the sky.

Day after day our wary General fell slowly back before thrice his numbers, checking them, wherever he could, with a fight, and retreating after the fight, ere they could crush him by heavier forces. Back, still back, retreating with undaunted hearts, but alas! too few; skirmishing at Fayetteville, battling at Averasboro', the 17th March found us not far from Goldsboro' and near my home; but between us and that dear spot was part of Sherman's army and the commands of Schofield and Terry, who had met, one from Newbern, the other from Wilmington, in Goldsboro'. I had not heard from Carlotta since leaving General Lee's army, and for her and mother's safety I dared not hope. Mr. Bemby was their only protection, and with the Yankee army in Goldsboro', I knew that one hour would suffice for the house to be rifled and themselves insulted. The agony of my suspense was terrible; to be so near home and yet not be able to see my wife and child. My fears and anxiety almost maddened me, and I seemed to hear continually their cries for help and protection.

Ben and I had been sitting in our tent, as the day drew to a close, talking of our loved ones and thinking of some plan by which we could get to them, when he rose and said:

"It's no use a talkin' 'bout it, John, I'm goin' through the lines; I'll be darned if I musn't see Viny and the young ones."

"I'll go with you, Ben," I said; "shall we start tonight?"

"No, siree! not ef you think much of yer head; a Yankee would kill a angel ef he caught him flying in the night."

"It will be impossible to pass them in the day," I said, impatient of delay.

"Lem'me take keer of that," he said, rising; "I'm goin' to see Gen. Johnston now and get two days' leave of absence, and we'll git to the old man's to-morrow night, or the devil may take my nose to plow ashes."

He passed out under the flap of the tent, but in a second rushed back, dragging in an old negro man.

"Look here, John," he exclaimed, "here's Horace, he can tell us somethin' 'bout our folks."

I sprang forward to the old man, who stood grinning in the door, and grasped his arm.

"Horace, for God's sake, tell me about Carlotta and mother! are they safe?"

"Well, Marse John," said Horace, with great deliberation, looking at me with love and pride, "Sho nough, dis is you, but you is changed a sight sence I seen you; you's puttier'n ever."

But I was in no mood for empty compliments, and led him in the tent almost rudely, as I pointed to a stool, and said:

"Sit down, Horace, and don't speak another word about any subject till you have told me something of home."

He shook his head slowly two or three times as he replied:

"U'm—m! dere's news enough, Marse John, and bad at that."

"Have the Yankees been at our house yet?" I asked.

"Yes, sir, I should say they has, but they won't come again—not to the house."

"Why?" I asked, leaning forward eagerly, "What will prevent them?"

"Dere 'aint no house for 'em to come to, it's done burnt clean to de groun'."

"Burnt down!" exclaimed Ben and I, in one breath.

"That it is; but I'm mighty forgetful, here's a letter from Miss C'lotta."

He took off his old torn hat, and lifting up the lining, took out the back of an envelope, soiled and crumpled, and handed it to me. I snatched it eagerly and read—

"Dear John:

I write on this little scrap hastily, to let you hear something from us. Uncle Horace, who has alone been faithful, promises to get it to you, if he can. The Yankees have taken every thing from us, and burned the house. Darling mother, in escaping, was struck on the head by a piece of falling timber, and is in a most critical condition. My precious boy and myself are safe. We are now at Mr. Bemby's, whose house escaped, though his supplies did not, and we have to depend on his and Uncle Horace's ingenuity for our daily support. I feel I shall almost go mad with our trouble. God help me to bear it, and forgive my wild wicked thoughts! I fear you will be insane with fury when I tell you that Frank Paning was with the soldiers, piloting them around, and was very insulting to me. I cannot write more.

Carlotta."

"May God help me to be revenged!" I shouted, crushing the letter in my hand, as I sprang to my feet.

Ben rushed to my side, and, clasping our hands, we held our revolvers above our heads, and registered a fearful oath of vengeance or death. Then my feelings quieted down enough for me to turn to Horace, who was looking at us with a frightened gaze.

"Horace, may Heaven bless you as you deserve. Here is the only reward I can make you now; take it all," I said, drawing a large roll of Confederate money from my belt.

"No, sir!" said the old man, proudly, "I don't want nothin' for taking keer of Mistis and Miss C'lotta; 'sides, that ain't no 'count 'mongst dem blue coat debbels in Goldsboro'."

"When did you leave home?" asked Ben, as I put back my currency, rather crestfallen at Horace's very sensible reason for refusing it.

"Yistiddy mornin'. I been in camp all to-day trying to find you and Marse John, but dere's so many solgers comin' and gwine I was in a pyo maze like."

"Horace, tell me all those scoundrels did," I said, reading over the letter again. "Don't leave out anything."

"Well, you see, Marse John," he said, taking off his hat and laying it on the ground, while he wiped his forehead with a very dingy red handkerchief, "we hears de Yankees is comin' up from Newb'n, and Mistis axes me to hide de silver things, an' I like a fool gets Reuben to help me, 'cause Reuben swears he love Mistis better'n all de Yankees in de world. That's how come de silver gone, in de fust place. Den we hears they is in Goldsboro', and next morning, by sun up, a whole squad comes gallopin' up to the house, and bust de crib door open, and gets out de corn. I was standin' by, and says: 'Dere ain't much corn dere, 'cause Wheeler's folks got some yistiddy;' and they say, 'What Wheeler's folks?' skeered like. I say: 'Some folks on horses that come from todes Fa'teville, and stopped all night down in dem woods yonder.' Den dey jumped on dere horses 'thout puttin' ary foot in de stirrup, an' lumbers down de road 'thout techin de corn.'"

"But tell me about the house, Horace," I exclaimed impatiently. "I don't care about the crib and Wheeler's men."

"I'm a gittin to it, Marse John. You see mistis was poorly, and was stayin' in bed, and every one de niggers lef', an' I had to cook, and tote water, an' do every thing 'bout de house; an' that day, 'bout dinner time, I see a dozen blue coats come dustin' down de road. An' 'fore I c'd git to de house dey done kicked de door open, and was all over de rooms; and de first man I see was Frank Paning, and he had on a blue newniform, too. He knowed me, and looked sorter mean, but put on like he never been dere b'fore. They was all rippin' and cussin' all over de house, and Miss C'lotta she come and stood in mistis' room door, and her eyes was like coals er fire; but they never noticed her, only Paning say 'gim me de keys, my beauty!'"

"The villain!" I muttered, grinding my nails into my flesh.

"At last one on 'em foun' de key basket, and den dey begun in earness. They took out all dere was to eat in de pantry, and drunk up and spilt all de wine; they eat some of the preserves, and bust the glass jars on de floor; they kicked open de ole clock, and split the pianner led wid one er de weights. Then dey swore they was gwine to have some silver an' gold, or burn up de house; and they went into mistis' room, where she was sick in de bed, and cussed her, and asked her where de silver was. Mistis, nor Miss C'lotta neither, never said a word, an' one great big fellow, with cross eyes, come up to de bed and say: 'Look here, ole gal! that won't do; you got to hustle out er them bed close; you's silver sick, I reckon.' And mistis sees Frank Paning then, and says: 'Mr. Paning, for de sake of de pass pertect me!' an' Paning says, 'I don't know you; git up!' and two on 'em ketches mistis by de arm and jerks her outen de bed on de floor, and mistis faints like, while Miss C'lotta holds her head in her arms and cries. De Yankees rips up de bed and scatters de feathers all over de room, and when they find nothin', one on 'em say, 'Less leave; and Paning steps up to Miss C'lotta and says: 'Ef I can't git silver I'll take a kiss,' and smacks her right on de cheek; and then Miss C'lotta was mad for true. She jumped up quicker'n lightning and jerks a little bit er blue pistol outen her pocket, an' 'fore Paning could git away bang! went de little pistol, and Paning clap'd his hand to his shoulder and says, 'Damnation! the fool has shot me,' an' he pulls out his sode and starts todes her, and Miss C'lotta was a standin' lookin' straight at him with de little pistol levelled; and a tall man, that hadn't said much, kotch Paning by de arm, and say, 'That's a woman; let her 'lone,' and den dey all leaves. Then Miss C'lotta told me to run and fetch some water, and when I fotch the piggin I seed that de house was on fire, and de room was a fillin' with smoke. Miss C'lotta tuk some shawls and ropped mistis up, and tole me to help tote her out, for de fire was all over de house. And then we starts out, mistis tryin' to walk, an' little Johnny a holden on to Miss C'lotta and cryin', and jus' as we gits to de front door a piece of scantlin' fell outen de top of de porch and hits mistis plump on de head, and she fell — — ."

"Hush, Horace, for the love of God, hush!" I groaned, as I staggered to my cot in the corner. "Do not tell me any more. Try to make your way back to Mr. Bemby's, and tell Carlotta we are going to make the attempt to get to her. Ben, give him something to eat, please, and make your arrangements for our trip."

I turned over on my face, and lay in a kind of stupor. The horrors of Horace's narration seemed to paralyze all faculties of mind and body, and while Ben was off perfecting his arrangements, I lay through most of the night without moving, my ears ringing with Carlotta's cries of anguish, and my eyes scorching with the light of my burning home.

About daybreak I awoke from a fitful slumber, full of horrid dreams, to find Ben standing near me with a large bundle on his arm, and a covered basket in his hand. "Great Heavens!" I exclaimed, springing to my feet, "this tame inaction will kill me. I must start now; if you will not go with me, Ben, I must go alone."

Ben put his bundles down with great deliberation, as he replied:

"John, you know I'd go to Satan's summer house with you if you wan't goin' to live there, but there *is* such a thing as bein' in too much hurry. Less get somethin' to eat first, for we ain't goin' to start till after sun up, and we can't stop to cook dinners. What we've got to do ain't like goin' to preachin' with your sweetheart, no how."

I saw that he knew best, and let him have his own way.

"I have been to Gen. Johnston," he said, drawing some papers from his pocket, "and got two days leave of absence; here's his pass through our pickets. Now get your writing tricks and fill up this one as I say."

He drew from among his papers a regular Federal pass, already printed, with only the date and name to fill up, and gave it to me, telling me to write it for Mrs. Sarah Jenkins and her son. It seemed to me a foolish waste of time, but I did as directed, and signed it as all adjutants do, with such a flourish and complicated A. A. G. that Champollion would have been puzzled to decipher it.

"And now," said Ben, taking the two passes, "string up your nerves while I get breakfast, and then we'll dress for the frolic."

I ate some of the hard tack and drank the cup of coffee which he kindly brought me, and told him I was ready.

"Hold on yit," he said, as he finished his cup, "the sun's jes' gittin' up. We must change our clothes—here, you put on these, as you ain't as tall as I am," and he untied his bundle, and took out an old faded calico dress, a white cap and a large fly bonnet.

"You see," he said, as he spread out the articles, "we are bound to rig up outlandish, for we can't help seeing some of the Yanks. Here's mine," and he produced an old home-spun suit and a wide-brim wool hat. I now saw the design of his disguises, and giving his hand a warm grasp for his sympathy and assistance, entered into his scheme and began to make ready.

"I can tell you," said Ben, talking while I was shaving off my beard, "I had a hard time gittin' these traps. I rode about ten mile last night, and had to steal the bonnet at that, though I stuck a five dollar Confed. on the fence where I grabbed it."

After half an hour's preparation I stood as complete an old woman, with specs and muffled chin, as ever sold eggs or peddled cakes. Ben was his old self again, and looked as essentially rustic as when he carried us fishing when we were boys.

"Now we are ready," said Ben, when we were fully disguised. "Less go; don't mind what our boys holler at you, it'll help fool the Yankees better."

Just outside the tent door were two sorry looking horses, with rope bridles, and a side saddle on one of them; beside them on the ground was a hamper basket, with a cloth tied over it, and another smaller basket full of eggs.

In reply to my regret that our horses looked so poor, Ben said that our own were too good, that the Yankees would dismount us, and that these would be no temptation.

I got up to my seat, and after some instructions from Ben as to how I must hold my basket and how to hide my feet, we started off.

We took a circuitous route around Goldsboro', and striking the Neuse, kept down the bank of the river 'till we were near our homes. So well was Ben acquainted with every path through the woods that we did not come in sight of a Yankee during the day, 'till, just before sunset, we came into the road leading to our house, at its junction with the County road; and here we found three or four soldiers apparently on picket duty. We rode carelessly up and, on being halted, presented our passes, which were examined by one of the men, with the bars of a corporal on his arm.

"All right, you can pass," he said, returning the papers to Ben, while I sat with my face averted and my shoulders bent as if I was very decrepit. We had hardly started from the group when one of them called out—

"Stop, old lady, let us see what you have in your basket." Knowing that the closeness of interview required by bargaining for eggs would lead to our detection, I could not repress a tremor of apprehension; but Ben instantly relieved my embarrassment by kicking my horse into a trot, and saying in a loud tone:

"Go 'long, mammy; don't you know the man with stars on shoulder, what give us the pass, tole us not to talk to folks that was standin' guard?"

None of the soldiers said anything more to us and we rode on without molestation. We had scarcely gone a mile when we came to the large gate of our grove. It was standing open and strange cattle were browsing under the oaks. We looked down the long avenue, and instead of the tall white house, with its broad porch and door, distant woods, and the red evening sky beyond, were all that caught the eye. We galloped hurriedly down the avenue, and dismounted at the yard palings, a few steps in front of the ruins. Where the house had been was now a heap of ashes, that rose in little clouds as the March winds blew over them. The tall, silent chimneys stood with their mouth-like fireplaces whispering to each other of ruin and desolation, across the smouldering pile. The old cedar near the house, under whose branches I had wept, as a boy, over Lulie's cruelty, was withered and blackened, and even the palings on which we leaned were charred to coal. A broad rock chimney showed where the kitchen had been; and the well house and dairy, which were still standing, were scorched and blackened with the heat. There was no sign of life on the premises; all was silent and still, the stables were open and the horses gone, the negro houses all deserted, and not even a dog lurked around the lot.

The very evening was full of dreariness! The sun had gone out behind a hard, red sky, against which the wind blew in fitful gusts; now with abortive blast, as if to rekindle the flame of day; now with a frightened moan, as if afraid of the approach of night. The tall trees along the river tossed and beat their long bare arms, as if they longed to break their chains of root and flee from these scenes of waste and woe. From the swaying top of one of them a solitary crow flew, with black flapping wings, cawing as he came, and perched upon the topmost bough of the old cedar, like a spirit of evil, his black feathers blown into a ruff around his neck, and his head bobbing with every note, in mockery of the desolation.

His voice broke the spell of our silence, and I turned to Ben. He was standing with one hand on the gate post, the nails whitened by pressure against the wood, and his grey eyes glowing as if there were lamps behind them.

"Gracious God! what a sight!" I said, as I leaned against the paling for support.

"Ah—h—h," said Ben, the breath hissing through his clenched teeth, "and it's lit up a devil's bonfire in here it'll take blood to put out," and he tapped his breast, where the protrusion of a revolver could be faintly seen.

"But think, Ben, of Paning's doing all this. A double-dyed villain! to burn the very house that has sheltered him, and insult a woman whose hospitality he has received! *He* here at my home, directing a too willing enemy where to pillage; *his* foul lips forcing their polluted touch on Carlotta's cheek! Great Heaven! the thought drives me mad; may Infinite Justice help me to meet him once more!"

As I ceased speaking a strange unearthly wail arose on the air, and a poor wounded cat, roused by our voices, sprang, or rather fell from a box in the dairy window to the ground, and strove to make its way to us with piteous mewing. It was perfectly blind, as we could tell from its actions, and its fur and flesh on one side were singed and burnt by the fire. It was gaunt from starvation, and cried aloud with a hollow voice in its vain efforts to find us. I went forward and took it up in my arms, and saw then that it was a pet of mother's, that had been perhaps forgotten in the haste of leaving, and with fond local affection, was starving rather than quit the place. As I gazed upon the poor famished creature, with its white sightless eyes and emaciated frame, and thought of mother's fondness and care for it, for the first time losing control of myself, I burst into tears.

Ben touched my shoulder and said:

"Less go, John; we can't do no good staying here, and are wasting a heap of precious time."

Knowing that Mr. Bemby's larder now had no room for cats, I made the poor creature a bed in the dairy, and placing something to eat and some water by it, we left it. Throwing our bridles over our arms we walked on to Mr. Bemby's, which was but a short distance through the trees. As we approached the house I saw my beautiful boy playing near the steps. He looked up in perfect amazement as I ran to him, and his lips quivered with frightened surprise as a seeming old woman caught him up and strained him to her heart. Bearing him in my arms I entered the house, and at the sound of my footsteps Carlotta came to the door, her beautiful face pale with anxiety and alarm; for every footfall on the doorway now meant robbery or insult. She started back in affright at my wild appearance and grotesque disguise, but the next instant, as I murmured "Carlotta!" her arms were around me and she was sobbing on my shoulder.

"Oh, thank God! we have met again. Oh, John, my husband, what we have suffered since I saw you last!" she exclaimed, with convulsive weeping.

"I know it all, darling; Horace has told me. But compose yourself, dearest, and let us go to mother, if she be still alive."

"She is still living, but I fear will not live long. She grows feebler every day. I will go in and prepare her for your coming."

She left me and went into another room, while I placed my little boy, who had been staring at his mother and myself with a look of amazement, again upon the floor, and tore off my bonnet and dress.

"No matter what happens," I said, as Ben came in with his wife from the kitchen, where he had gone to look for her, "I won't wear this ridiculous costume, here at least."

I had scarcely done greeting Ben's wife when his mother came in, not so plethoric as when I had last seen her, but with the same good natured face and kind heart.

I could only grasp her honest hands with tears in my eyes, and bless her for her kindness to my dear ones.

"You needn't go to talk 'bout kindness," said Mrs. Bemby, wiping her specs on the corner of her apron. "Your mother's done a sight more for me'n I ever kin do for her, an' I want to keep a doin' long as God will let her live, which I'm afeard it won't be mighty long, for she's poorlier to-day 'n I've seen her yet."

To divert her from such painful remarks I asked if the Yankees had molested them since they had burned the house.

"Not such a mighty sight. They've tuck my chickens and vegetables, tho' they wan't nothin' in the garden but turnips, but we've got some meat an' a little corn. The wuss trouble we has is a continuwell fear they is goin' to break in on us. Mr. Bemby he's gone to town to-day to git a guard."

"A guard!" I exclaimed, in much alarm; "then if we are discovered here you all are ruined. Ben and I can settle with half-a-dozen by ourselves, but I am truly alarmed for you."

"Never do you mind, John," said Ben, as he trotted a little white-headed scion on his knee; "she'll fix all that; the old man aint coming back till to-morrow no how, and we'll be off by light."

Off by light! how the words sounded like a knell on my ears; off, to leave a dying mother and an unprotected wife and child in the lines of a merciless foe; off to fight, perhaps die for a now hopeless cause, leaving all I loved to misery and want. Ah, Mercy! let thy white wing oftenest shield the poor deserter at the stake, and Justice will have less complaint!

Carlotta now appeared at the door of mother's chamber, and beckoned to me. Walking softly, with a bowed head and prayerful heart, I entered a small dark room, dimly lighted by a single candle and a flickering fire on the hearth. On an humble bed in the corner, with her crushed head bound with cloths and liniments, lay my mother, pale and thin, her sweet face illumined with bright surprise yet strange bewilderment.

"Be careful," whispered Carlotta, as I paused on the threshold, "her mind is not perfectly clear."

In another moment I was on my knees at the bedside, my face pressed upon her pillow, sobbing, "Mother! oh my mother!" She did not speak, but laid her thin tremulous hand on my head and let it rest there. I was convulsed with grief to think of losing her after I had been away from her so long, and that she was dying under such distressing circumstances, without a home, under a strange roof, and with a consciousness of helpless dependence.

As in moments of great danger a retrospect of our whole lives rises before us, so in this deep distress all my acts of disobedience and unkindness toward mother; every time that I had wounded her feelings; every harsh word I had uttered, all came with cruel distinctness into memory to torture me, and I longed, in my agony, to ask her forgiveness for every one, and to assure her again and again of my love. But Carlotta's warning, and the strange look on her face, made me afraid to speak, and I knelt with my face on the pillow, silently weeping, till she herself broke the silence of the chamber.

"Carlotta," she said, in a voice so changed that I raised up to look at her, "this is John, is it not? When did he come? Does he know that his father is dead?"

Carlotta made a sign to me not to speak, and drawing a chair up to the bedside, she took mother's hand in her's and said:

"Yes, mother, this is John. He knows all about father's death, and about the burning of the house; and he has come through the Federal lines, at great risk, to see you. Can you not arouse yourself to talk to him! He wishes to know if you feel better to-night?"

Mother now gazed at me with the old look of fondness as she said:

"Is this my dear boy? and have you come to see your mother? God bless you for it! I will make the effort to speak with you; but oh! I cannot remain conscious. *Now* all that has transpired is perfectly clear and distinct before me, and I recognize my dear child's face, and know why he has come; but presently a dull gray cloud, or something from afar off, will float up and envelope my mind, and all I know or remember becomes confused. Carlotta, darling, help me keep the cloud away."

"I will, mother," said Carlotta, dampening a cloth and laying it on her forehead; but even as the cool moisture touched her skin the vacant look came again to her face, and she asked, looking at me with earnest inquiry: "John, have you brought your father home; is the grave ready? Go have it made wider. I am coming to lie by his side."

Utterly helpless, we both sat watching and listening to her incoherent mutterings about father's lonely grave, and her desire to go to it, till, dozing off into her stupor again, she was silent. In a few minutes she opened her eyes, and was for another interval herself again.

"John, my precious child," she said, trying to put her arm around my neck and draw me down to her, "God alone knows how I desire to talk with you, for this will be the last converse we will ever hold on earth. I do not wish to grieve you unnecessarily, but I feel that I am dying."

"O mother, do not say so," I sobbed, as I kissed her pale, emaciated cheek; "God is too good to take you away from us."

"He knows best, my son. His will be done! But I have not strength to say much, and even now I feel the cloud coming. Will you make me two promises? I want you to bring your father's remains from Elmira, and bury them with me under the old cedar at home; 'twas there I promised to be his bride in the long ago. And, John, something tells me that you had another motive, besides seeing me, in coming hither. Do you not seek Frank Paning's life?"

My face flushed hotly as the thought that she might ask me to forgive Frank flashed upon me, and I felt that even her last request could not persuade me to forego my vengeance. But I answered quickly:

"No, mother, as Heaven is my witness, I only thought of you and Carlotta when I came here; but if Providence should throw the viper in my path, even you would have me crush him."

"No, John, the dear Saviour prayed for those who nailed him to the cross, and bids us forgive as we would be forgiven."

"But, mother," I argued—though Carlotta shook her head at me and whispered, "do as she requests"—"Frank is so vile. He has partaken of our hospitality, and I have been his friend a thousand times, yet he has burnt our home, insulted Carlotta and murdered you; how can I ever forgive him?"

"You are full of wrath and hatred now, my son, and I cannot hope to change your feeling yet awhile; but I can ask, as my last request, your promise that you will not seek Frank's life—that if you ever meet you will forgive him for my sake. Do you promise?"

I did not speak, for the hot blood that had written my oath of vengeance on my heart was still throbbing there, and I could not at a word forget my cruel wrongs. While I hesitated the cloud came over her, and her countenance again was vacant and meaningless, and she began to murmur broken sentences about the Cross, and Christ's love, and her child's hard heart.

Then there came the heartrending thought that she might not again become conscious, and might die with my obstinate refusal weighing on her poor broken heart.

"Oh, merciful God! what is my unholy resentment compared with the peace of my mother's death bed?" I exclaimed, with unfeigned penitence, as I implored Carlotta to rouse her once more to consciousness.

Falling on my knees I began the struggle, and conquered self, and then I felt that I could forgive Frank, not alone for the sake of my promise, but for the sake of Christ and His Cross. With a faith I had never known before I prayed for mother's restoration, pleading the promise, "If ye shall ask anything in my name I will do it," and arose from my knees with that "peace that passeth all understanding" resting on my soul.

After a long while, as it seemed to my suspense, she rallied again, and addressed some words to me that showed she was rational. I hastened then to give her my promise, and assured her that I really, from my heart, forgave Frank, and would not harm him if I could.

She thanked me in her feeble way, and then asked me to sit near her and talk with Carlotta, that she might hear the sound of my voice, though she felt too weak to talk herself. Then, after Carlotta had put little Johnnie to bed in his corner, she came and sat by me, and with tearful eyes and aching hearts we talked of our parting on the morrow, when we would bid each other farewell, with a probability of never meeting again; when we would be separated without a possibility of communication; when each must suffer well grounded anxiety and prolonged suspense, because the other was exposed to constant and serious danger; when I must leave without having done a single thing to alleviate their condition, or render them less dependent on the Bembys. But 'twas all for the Stars and Bars, and for them I would bear it thrice again.

In the ever flowing tide of our sympathy and love we took no note of time, and when we were startled by a tap at the door I was surprised to find that the window behind me was a gray square of light, and that objects were becoming plainly visible out in the yard. It was Ben who had knocked, and who said in a whisper, as I opened the door:

"Day's broke, John; you'd better put on your fixins', and let's git out. The old man and his guard might git here before we leave, and that would spile our tramp and ruinate the folks here."

With a sudden sinking at my heart, like we feel when we hear the footstep of the doctor who is to lance a bone felon for us, I turned into the chamber and began to make ready for my departure. My poor Carlotta, who had borne all so bravely, gave way at last, and clung to me weeping.

"Oh, John! I do try to bear up, but it seems that my heart will break now if you leave me. I know you could not protect me amid so many foes, but I would feel so much braver, so much more secure, if you could be with me—if I could get your advice and counsel, and have you help me nurse dear mother. John, what shall I do if she dies?"

"Would you have me stay, Carlotta?" I said, to prove her. "I am in the Yankee lines now, and cannot be punished for desertion."

"Desertion!" she exclaimed, with a blaze in her splendid eyes. "Fondly as I love you, John, I would rather have you fall dead at my feet than leave our cause now because it is feeble. No, no, darling, go back to your command, and if we are conquered I will be proud of my husband because he wore the gray while I suffered at home."

Blessing her for her encouragement to duty, I strained her again and again to my heart, asking God's protection for her, and bidding her good bye.

Mother was sleeping soundly for the first time in several days, and I would not wake her, but touched her forehead tenderly with my lips, and then bent over my darling child.

I carried my disguise on my arm, for it seemed such a mockery of all the sad circumstances at Mr. Bemby's that I would not put it on till we had gone some distance from the house. When we had again become the old woman and her son we mounted our horses, and with sad hearts set out on our return to Johnston's camp. We had been delayed by Mrs. B.'s breakfast and our prolonged farewells, so that we found now that the sun had been up some time, and Nature was sparkling in dewy beauty. My feelings were too much depressed for conversation, and Ben, with Nature-taught delicacy, refrained from either futile attempts to console or irrelevant efforts to divert, and our ride began in silence. As we neared our home, and I saw the chimneys and the ashes, the old hot feeling came to my heart, and I remembered my promise to mother with something like regret. The next moment I was startled by hearing the exclamation "Humph!" very much accented, from Ben, and seeing him dash at headlong speed down the pathway to the house, or rather where it had stood. I followed as fast as I could, and saw, as I neared the gate, the cause of his movements. A figure in blue uniform, mounted on a powerful horse, stood at the palings, and another, dismounted, was raking over the ashes and cinders with his sabre scabbard. At the sound of our gallop the man on horse-back turned and saw us, and, driving the spurs into his charger, he fled up the avenue with a speed that defied capture. Ben was some distance ahead of me, and as I saw him leap from his horse and dash into the yard, I wondered that he should thus forget his usual prudence and throw aside his assumed character when we most needed it. In another moment I was at the gate, and saw him grasp the man in blue, who, with trembling hands, was untying his horse, and drag him by the throat towards me. The prisoner, oh! promise of forgiveness! was *Frank Paning*.

His arm was in a sling, from Carlotta's shot, I thought; his cap had fallen off, and his dark curls were clustering as prettily as ever around his white forehead, while his restless eyes turned any where but towards Ben or myself. Ben looked up at me with the lamps in his gray eyes burning red lights, and his lips so pressed over his set teeth that the old scar stood out like a cord; and drawing a long navy revolver from his breast, he offered it to me saying:

"Here, John, this is your mouthful; I won't take it from you."

"No, Ben," I exclaimed, turning my head away; "don't, don't tempt me. I promised my mother, pledged my word, at her dying request, not to take his life. I cannot break my last promise to her."

"John, I feel sorry for you," said Ben, solemnly, as if the obligation to spare Frank was a great affliction, and demanded his sympathy, "but I did not promise, therefore— —" and his thumb slowly drew the hammer of his pistol back, till it stood like a serpent ready to strike.

"Gentlemen," said Frank, in a husky, nervous voice, while he raised his hand hesitatingly towards Ben's, as if he wished to move it from his collar, but was afraid his touch would be the signal for the serpent to fall on the yellow, gleaming cap, "you surely will not do me any violence. I am your prisoner, and will give up my arms if you will receive them, and will do anything you say or wish. If you will not spare me for humanity's sake, only think of the danger you are in. Our troops are all around you, and there is even now a strong body of cavalry just beyond the bend in the road. You are both in disguise, and, if caught, will be hung as spies. If you harm me you cannot possibly escape, but if you promise to spare my life, I will pilot you safely through our lines, and then go with you to Gen. Johnston. I can give him very important information about Sherman's movements, and will do so cheerfully."

"You will?" said Ben, with two short grunts for a laugh, at the same time taking his thumb from the crest of the hammer.

"Mr. Bemby, for God's sake don't shoot me!" cried Frank, in an extremity of terror, clasping his hands over Ben's, that like a vice still held his collar. "John, don't, don't let him shoot me! Speak to him, please, and ask him to spare me! He won't shoot if you tell him not. Remember, we were friends once, and save my life now for the sake of that time."

He tried to throw himself on his knees, but Ben held him erect, and he stood trembling in every limb, and holding out his hands to me in a cowardly fright, that excited no feeling but disgust. When he appealed to the past, I remembered that Carlotta had made the same appeal to him only to receive an insult, and I had almost stricken him down with my own hand, when mother's voice again whispered in my ear, "Forgive, as ye would be forgiven."

My arm was scarcely lowered when the sound of horses' feet was heard, and, looking up, we saw a half dozen Federal cavalry coming down the avenue at a fast trot.

Frank's face lighted up with an expression of fiendish malice and triumph as he saw them, and, pointing to them, he said, with a sudden change from an abject to an authoritative air:

"Take your hands off, sir! Surrender, or I will have you both shot. You dare not harm me now," he added, with a sneer.

"We don't?" said Ben, with a hiss in his voice and a redder light in his eyes. Then, giving Frank's throat a grip that made his face livid, he pointed with his revolver to the ashes, and said through is teeth: "Look there, villain! is that your work?"

"Yes, by Heaven! it is;" exclaimed Frank, with a gesture of defiance, for the troopers were almost on us.

"Then, infernal dog, take your pay!"

Before I could speak there was a levelled brown barrel, a deadly report, and a red oozing spot in Frank's white forehead. He stood motionless a second, and then fell limp and doubling up to the ground.

"Now less scatter 'em yonder, and break for old Joe's camp;" said Ben, as he sprang upon his horse.

The Yankees halted with astonishment as they saw an awkward country lad and an old woman charging upon them.

But we were on them before they had time for much wonder. Bang! bang! one reeled, another fell. Bang! bang! another empty saddle! and we were past them a hundred yards before they returned our fire. They did not dare pursue us, and we galloped a short distance up the road, then plunged into the woods, and, riding on to the river, we took up its banks, picking our way cautiously through bogs and marshes, and avoiding every sign of habitation and life. So careful were we in our progress that we saw no human being during the day, and at nightfall found ourselves not far from the place where Johnston had his camp when we left. But all day long we had heard the roar of battle, growing louder as we drew nearer, and we knew that there had been a heavy engagement somewhere, and that the positions of both armies had undergone some change. As we determined to ride now in the night, we stopped some time before sunset in a deep secluded dell, to rest our horses till after dark. Ben slipped into an adjoining field and obtained some fodder from a couple of stacks that were standing near the woods, and gave a plentiful supply to our hungry cattle.

"The Yankees will get it all soon, any way," said Ben, apologetically, as he untied the bundles and shook them out on the ground.

At sunset we could hear the bugle calls of different camps, and mapped out our course for the night accordingly. As soon as it was dark we mounted our horses, which were much refreshed by food and their short rest, and set out to thread the maze of pickets extending miles around. As my disguise was useless in the dark I tore it off, preferring to ride bare-headed to having both sight and hearing impaired by the long, projecting bonnet.

Having located the camps by the sounds of the bugles, we made a wide circuit, which considerably increased the distance we had to travel. After riding for hours in cautious silence, and being, as we thought, very near our lines, our horses began to show signs of giving out. After an hour's more urging them forward they began to breathe hard and stagger, so that it would have been cruel as well as impossible to ride them further.

"What shall we do?" I asked, barely dismounting in time to keep mine from falling beneath me. Ben's horse was much better than mine, and would have held out a mile or two further, but he got down immediately, and taking the bridle from his horse, said:

"We'll have to foot it, I reckon, and leave these Arabs here; somebody 'll find them, and a fine team they'll have, won't they? I was afeard they wouldn't hold out when we started, but we couldn't er got 'long on good stock. Take your bridle off, so the varmint can browse, and less move on. 'Taint far no how, and I want to stretch my legs a little."

Taking the bridles and saddles off we let the poor jaded creatures go free, and set out on foot through the darkness. We had not gone more than half a mile when Ben caught my arm and said, in a whisper: "Shh! Listen!"

Not a hundred paces ahead of us we heard the unmistakable tell-tale of the horse, and the frequent betrayal of the picket—that peculiar flutter of the animal's lip as the breath is forced through the nose—that is very frequent, and audible at a considerable distance in the night. Simultaneously whispering the single word, "Pickets!" we crept forward with Indian stealthiness, feeling for twigs before we stepped, and parting the bushes carefully before we passed through them.

"What do you intend to do when we find them?" I asked, in a low voice, of Ben, who generally assumed the responsibility of directing.

"See how many of 'em there is, and act according. If there ain't more than two we c'n rope 'em and git their horses, but we must do it w'thout our pistols."

"All right," I whispered; "I'm ready."

We went forward a few steps, and there, not twenty paces from us, at the edge of a wide open field, loomed the figures of two pickets, seated on their horses. We crept a few steps nearer till we could hear their conversation, and paused to listen. They were grumbling about the hardship of standing picket 'way off where nobody ever came, and half a mile from any of the others, and they swore, half laughing, that they had been freezing there a month, and would never be relieved. One rallied the other on being afraid of the dead men in the field before them, and then, with an oath, said he was ready for dead or living, and that he had balls enough for both.

Ben placed his mouth to my ear and breathed the words, not spoke them:

"It is all right, they're alone, and will be sho to surrender when we tell 'em. But be ready with your pistol if the worse comes to the worse; we may have to shoot a little to git the horses."

I shuddered at the thought; for while I had been in many battles, where the balls fell like hail, and never yet shrunk from duty, yet there was something so secret, and, I must confess, frightful in this contemplated hand-to-hand encounter, with an adversary cach, out in the lonely night, with no eye to mark our victory or death, that I fain would have avoided it. I ventured to whisper to Ben:

"As there is no special necessity for attacking them, had we not better go around them and hasten to our lines? An attempt to take them will probably lead to an alarm and our own capture. You know I am with you wherever there is need, but I had rather be prudent now, for Carlotta's sake."

"'Twon't do for soldiers to think of the home folks, John, if they're going to fight right; it makes 'em too soft in the heart. But them fellows 've got two good horses, and we can take 'em in so nice. My rule is to never let a Yankee off; and, if you'd ruther not, I'll try the game by myself."

"You must beg my pardon for that insult, Ben, or you and I will fight," I said, in the same low tone, but with a flush on my face at his insinuation.

"You know I didn't mean to insult you, John; but less quit wasting time and git to work; what we've got to do is to creep up close and spring on 'em. When I take hold of one bridle you grab the other, and I'll do the talkin'."

Bending down almost to the ground, with panther-like tread we stole upon the unconscious pickets, while my hand was trembling and my heart beating audibly with excitement. Ben was perfectly cool and deliberate, for he was but reënacting, rather tamely he seemed to think, one of his many scouting adventures. We were now at their horses' heels, and Ben, putting his mouth again to my ear, whispered, "Be certain to go when I do, and keep your revolver in your right hand. Are you ready? Now!" and we both sprang to the heads of the horses and seized the reins. "Surrender! or you are dead men. Steady, boys! do not fire till I give the word," exclaimed Ben, in a loud clear voice, as we levelled our pistols on them.

They made no show of resistance, but cried out to us not to shoot—that they yielded themselves up; and when Ben approached to take their arms gave them up readily.

We made them dismount, and found that they had two strong, well built horses, of which we took immediate possession. In answer to our inquiries they told us that there had been a severe engagement near Bentonsville, and that Johnston was moving up toward Raleigh. They pointed toward his lines, which they said were not more than half a mile distant. Ben examined the horses' heads, and finding a halter under each bridle, he took them off, and telling our prisoners that while he was obliged for their information, yet for their safety and our own he would have to tie them, he made them turn their backs to two small trees and lashed their hands around them. "The relief'll be along pretty soon," he said, "so you won't git tired; and if you want to scratch your back, or wipe your nose, you'll have to rub up and down, or twist your head. Good bye, and don't forget to thank the Lord that we didn't kill you, as we ought to do."

Mounting our captured horses we again set out in the darkness, picking our way still cautiously, and halting ever and anon to listen and take our bearings, for we did not place that implicit confidence in the statements of our prisoners, regarding the position of our lines, that a charitable belief in the integrity of human nature would have encouraged us to do. But we had judged them wrongfully, for we had just passed through the open field at the edge of which we had left them, and struck another skirt of woods, when, directly in front of us, crack! went a rifle, and the ball whistled in uncomfortable proximity to our ears. The next moment we heard the gallop of the horse's feet as the picket fell back to the reserve.

"Quick!" said Ben, spurring his horse forward; "we must catch up with him and tell him we are friends, or we will be shot."

But catching up was not so easy, for he heard our pursuit, and dashed through the brush and undergrowth as if he had a contract to clear up the land.

As our speed was a matter of equal necessity we kept close behind him, when suddenly his horse fell, and he rolled over in the darkness.

"I surrender," he called out, as we rode up.

"What command do you belong to?" I asked.

"Wheeler's cavalry,—th Regiment."

"Where's your camp?" said Ben.

"Just behind us; yonder are some of the fires."

"Well, go back to your post; we are friends," I said, as Ben caught his horse for him. "I am Major Smith, of Gen. Johnston's staff."

"Yes, sir," said the poor fellow, who was badly frightened, attempting to make a salute as he rose from the ground, where he had been lying during the colloquy.

We left him and pushed rapidly on to the fires which we saw glimmering through the trees.

Without detailing the halts of the sentinels and our explanations, suffice it to say we reached our quarters in safety, got an hour's sleep, and rose with the army to continue our ceaseless but gallant retreat.

CHAPTER XLIII

If my pen alone, dear reader, could direct the scenes which must be presented to your view in drawing near the close of my narrative, rest assured they should be pleasant. I would tell of a grand triumphant army, marshalled for the last time beneath the Stars and Bars to hear the plaudits and farewell of their chieftain; of victorious legions marching home crowned with laurels, their very footsteps softened by the flowers fair hands are scattering before them; of every homestead, blessed with peace and plenty, greeting its hero returned from the war. I would tell of an Independent Republic, with Robert E. Lee at its head, growing into power and greatness among the nations of the earth; while, with all sectional animosity and bitterness buried beneath the blood of their children, the United and the Confederate States join hands in the noble alliance of progress and enterprise—exchanging products and commodities, aiding each other onward, yet vieing in generous rivalry. Alas! the stern reality presents a darker picture—the picture of a people, borne down by want and woe, yielding up at last their long and gallant struggle, and sitting down amid the ashes of their country to mourn their children dead for nought; a picture of two armies—small, indeed, and wasted by famine and disease, yet still stepping proudly as they remember their long record of victories— stacking their faithful arms and furling their shell-torn flags with tears of helpless bitterness; a picture of Southern roadsides filled everywhere with men in tattered gray, plodding, with blistered feet, their weary way towards homes where gaunt starvation hath so wasted the cheeks of loved ones that they will scarcely flush at their coming, and where, laying down the burden of war, they must take up the burden of fruitless labor!

Ben and I secured transportation on the cars from Durham's to Raleigh, and set out from there to walk home.

Ah! never to be forgotten are those days after the surrender! How the Yankees jeered and cursed us for being rebels, as squad after squad galloped by us, tramping along our dusty roads! And the people, God bless them! how kind they were to us, even in their poverty! Stripped to almost utter destitution by the enemy, they were willing, like the widow of Sarepta, to share with us their only cake. As we passed each gate they would come out with a pitcher of water, a tray of corn bread and potatoes, and, if the "bummers" had not paid their visits of mercy, a small piece of meat. Calling us into the yard, under the trees, they would press us to eat, and lament that they had not better to give. And as we eagerly ate their frugal fare, which was more delicious then than were the quails of Lucullus, and rose to thank them and pursue our way, they would put what remained in our pockets, and, asking God's blessing on us, turn into the house to prepare their humble offering for the next hungry troop.

Thus were the gloomy feelings of our homeward journey relieved by constant kindness and attention from every house we passed, and it was not till we neared Ben's home, and had left the public road, that I had time to feel the terrible suspense and anxiety about Carlotta and mother that had been in my heart since I left them. I dared not hope that mother was alive; yet my heart did so much shrink from knowing she was dead, that, as I came in sight of Mr. Bemby's, my feet almost refused to go forward.

As we approached we saw no one but Horace, who was working in a little garden near the house, and we motioned to him to be quiet. We opened the door of the house softly, and heard the sound of voices out in the little back porch, and saw the edge of some one's dress who was sitting near the door. Then we heard a chair put down from its tilted position, and Ben's wife leaned forward and looked sideways into the passage. With a loud cry of joy she dropped a lap full of work on the floor, and ran to meet her husband. She was followed by Carlotta and Mrs. Bemby. Where was mother? Carlotta, as I pressed her to my bosom, interpreted the anxiety of my look, and said:

"God has spared mother, John. She is much improved, though still feeble. She is out in the porch. Come with me."

I followed her out to the porch, and there, propped by pillows in a chair, pale and thin, but still alive, was mother.

I knelt by her, and we both murmured our thanksgiving to God for his mercy.

Then, when Mrs. Bemby had brought out chairs for us all, and Horace had brought a bucket of fresh cool water, how bright and happy were we all as we told of our adventures and wondered at our mutual dangers and escapes. Verily, it was worth four years of hardship to experience the joy of that morning out in Mr. Bemby's porch.

"But tell me, Carlotta, what caused this blessed change in mother?" I said, after we had finished our salutations, drawing my little boy to me, and taking him on my knee.

"She was relieved, and commenced to grow better the very day you left. A short time after you and Mr. Ben were gone a company of Federal soldiers came up to the house, bearing with them a dead man and two wounded ones. Mrs. Bemby and I went out to them and found, I shudder to tell it, that the dead man was Frank Paning. They wanted some spades to bury him with, and some cloths to bind up the wounds of the others. They said that two spies, one of them disguised as an old woman, had killed Paning, and, meeting these, had fired on them. We knew it must have been you two. Oh, John! did you forget your promise to mother?"

I said nothing, for I did not wish to involve Ben, but he spoke up directly:

"No, Mrs. Smith, John didn't kill him; I done it myself. We found him a rakin' over the ashes he'd helped to make, and when he saw his friends a comin' he tried to make us surrender, and I let him have a ball in his forred. 'Taint worth while to be mealy-mouthed about it."

"Well," continued Carlotta, with a shudder at Ben's words, "Horace got the spades for them, and Mrs. Bemby told them to bring the men into the house, for they were both suffering very much. We did what we could to alleviate their sufferings, and when the surgeon who was with them had bandaged up their wounds, and sent them off to camp, he asked if he could reward us in any way for our kindness. I thought of mother; and though my pride revolted at the idea of asking a favor of an enemy, I begged that he would see her and give her some relief, if possible. He went in and examined her head, and saying that it was an easy matter, took out some instruments and went to work. He raised up the fractured skull, and, as mother expressed it, lifted a great weight from her brain; then mixing some medicine for her, and telling me how to bathe her head, took his leave."

"Did you not offer to remunerate him in some way?" I asked.

"Yes, I offered him my watch, as we had no money, but he refused it with polished courtesy, and said he would only take a kiss from my little boy, as there was something about his eyes, as well as mine, that reminded him of a lady he had loved years ago."

"Did you not learn his name?"

"Oh yes! He gave me his card, and I think I put it in this basket;" and she commenced to search in her work busily. "Ah! here it is!" and she gave me the card:

"C. B. Sedley, M. D., New York!"

"Why, Carlotta," I said, "did not a young man of that name pay his addresses to you at Saratoga?"

"Oh! certainly; I remember him. How stupid of me to forget. Poor Charley! I do not blame him for not recognising the lady of satin in this old homespun."

"I must go to Goldsboro' to-morrow," I said, thinking gratefully of his kindness, "and if he is still there offer some testimonial of our gratitude."

"It's useless," said Carlotta, "he has gone on to Raleigh with the army, and I cannot let you leave me so soon."

Mr. Bemby now came in from the field, and greeted us warmly in his uncouth way, while Mrs. B. excused herself to see about dinner. It was a plain meal, of one course, but Delmonico has never served one that was more enjoyed, or surrounded by happier hearts.

The next day I went over to Goldsboro', and, obtaining a hundred dollars, in "greenbacks," the first I had ever handled, prepared to start with our little family for Wilmington the following morning, for I could not consent to impose longer on the good nature of the Bembys, and crowd them out of comfort in their little house.

The next morning, having bade them an affectionate and grateful farewell, we lifted mother carefully into the vehicle I had hired to take us to town, and were soon in the cars, mother, Carlotta, Johnnie and I, rattling down to Wilmington. We found that Miss Wiggs had been unmolested in her possession of our house, and that it was therefore ready for our reception.

Many of our former slaves now applied for positions in our household, but, as they had deserted us when most needed, I refused every one, and engaged an entire new set. About this time, also, I received a balance sheet from father's bankers in New York, showing a large accumulated balance in our favor, and, drawing on this, we began to surround ourselves with ante-bellum comforts, and to make home feel like home.

Soon after we had gotten somewhat settled I began to make inquiries about Lulie, for I felt the deepest interest in her welfare, and had ever thought of her downfall with deepest sorrow. As I could hear nothing definite in regard to her, though it was generally believed she had gone off with a Federal officer of high rank, I determined to call on her old maiden aunt, with whom she had lived since her father's death, which occurred early in the winter. To my surprise the old lady would neither see me nor answer any of my inquiries, but called out to me, in a shrill cracked voice, as I stood at her door, her long bony feet just visible in heelless slippers and blue stockings, at the top of her stairway:

"You needn't come here asking me about the little silly fool, for I wouldn't tell you anything if I knew, which I don't. She's gone from my sight and hearing, and I hope to the Lord you nor any one else will ever hear of her again."

Of course I could do nothing but give up the search, though I ceased not to hope she might yet be found and saved.

And now, as the summer wore away, came to me the question of life; not *how* we were to live, for our income largely exceeded our expenditure, but *why*. The boyish dreams I had so long cherished, of distinction in the political arena, were now vanished forever; and the practice of law, for which I had studied, under the Provisional Government was little better than a system of pettifogging, that was as undignified as it was profitless.

There was absolutely nothing to do, and the very *ennui* of existence seemed a terrible evil. So, when Carlotta proposed that we break up here and go to her home in Cuba, I acceded to the proposal with great delight, and, mother consenting to go with us, I began immediately preparations for our departure in the Fall. I could not help feeling some touches of shame and regret in leaving our dear old State in this her darkest hour, and had it not been for the beautiful Cuban home that was awaiting us, I could not have gotten the consent of my mind to go. But I felt, as a private individual, of little benefit to the State at large, and that my first duty was to render those dearest to me happy, and this I thought would be accomplished by the change.

As executor of father's will, I found very little trouble in settling the estate, there being no debts to pay and few to collect. The real estate in New York I determined to leave in the hands of our agent, in whom we had the utmost confidence, and who had doubly endeared himself to us by his kindness to father while he was in prison. I sold our residence and grounds in Wilmington to a blockade runner who had amassed a large fortune during the war, and was anxious to invest in town property. Early in the fall I went up to the plantation to see Mr. Bemby, and make arrangements for its disposal. Taking the surveyor over from Goldsboro' I had four hundred acres cut off for Ben, and two hundred for Horace, making them a fee simple title to it; the remaining three thousand acres I turned over to Mr. Bemby, to use the balance of his lifetime without rent. These kind people were profuse and sincere in their regrets at our leaving, and Mr. Bemby protested that he and Ben could make enough on the farm for us all to live in the house and never go out doors where we could see a Yankee. They all followed me up to the road, and I felt, as I shook hands and drove off, that, go where I would, I could never find more faithful hearts than beat beneath their homespun clothes. Ben rode over to Goldsboro' with me, and when we had gone some distance from the house he drew from his pocket a twenty dollar gold piece and handed it to me, saying:

"I want you to give that to the one it belongs to, if you ever see her."

"Whose is it?" I asked in some surprise.

"Miss Luler Maylin's," he said, putting the coin in my hand.

"Lulie Mayland!" I exclaimed. "Where is she; where have you seen her; I have been trying to find her ever since I came home."

"I saw her week b'fore last, right on this road, jus' above our house."

"How came she there? Tell me about it for Heaven's sake, Ben."

"Well, you know Frank Paning is buried up there in the woods by the road, and last Wednesday was a week I thought I'd go up and sorter put a pen like 'round his grave, to keep the hogs from rootin' 'bout on it, 'cause I tell you the truth, John, I ain't never felt right 'bout killin' him yit. I shot a sight of Yankees during the war, but I done it on account of the Confeder'cy, and I didn't feel like it was charged 'ginst me in the big book up yonder; but I put that bullet in Frank Paning on my own hook, because I was mad with him, and it's looked mighty close kin to murder ever since."

"By no means, Ben," I interrupted; "he had ordered you to surrender, and his friends were close at hand."

"Well, any how," he continued, "I was piling up the rails 'round the grave, and kinder askin' its pardon to myself, when I heard a carriage 'comin' 'long the road. I got up and stepped back a little for 'em to pass, for I was sorter ashamed of what I was doin'. But the carriage stopped right at the grave, and a Yankee officer got out, and then handed down a lady dressed finer 'n the top spot in a peacock's tail. The minnit I see her face I knowed 'twas the same young lady that come up here wonst with Mrs. Smith and you all. 'Soon as she got on the ground she run to the grave, and fell down on her knees, and put her head on the edge of the rail pen, and cried a long time. When she got up the man fetched some white flowers outer the carriage and she put'em on the grave; then turned to the man and said:

"'Do you think you can find the place, Curnel?'

"'Without doubt, madam,' he said.

"'I want the granite base very broad and strong, as the column will be very heavy,' I heard her say.

"'It shall be as you desire, madam,' he replied.

"They was about to git back in the carriage when she saw me, and come towards me with both hands stretched out.

"'O, sir!' she said to me, with her cheeks all wet, 'did you think enough of his grave to take keer of it; let me reward you.' And b'fore I could speak she put that money in my hand. I run up to the carriage as she got in, and tole her I did not want her money, but they drove off without saying any more."

"Do you know where they went to, and did she call the officer's name?" I asked, intensely interested in what he had related.

"No; but I went to town next day, and saw 'em going off on the train, and the man had a han' trunk marked New York."

"Poor Lulie!" I murmured; "would to Heaven I could find her."

The train was standing at the depot as we drove up, and I had to hurry to get on. Ben followed me into the car, and, taking my hand, said:

"Good bye, John, for I can't call you Mr. Smith, like I orter. Remember one thing, no matter where you go or who you see you'll never find anybody to think any more of you than Ben. I didn't have much religion to start with, and the war spilled what I did have out; but if I ever do get to the good place I'd like to see you there, for it won't seem natchurel without you."

The train moved off and he was gone—a true, tried old heart.

There was one more duty, a sacred one, for me to perform before our departure. I must bring my father's remains from the enemy's land, and let them rest in the soil he had died for. I found no difficulty in identifying his grave at Elmira, owing to the clear and distinct manner in which it had been marked by Mr. P., the agent referred to; and taking up the rude prison coffin, I had it enclosed as it was, without being opened, in a large metallic case, and thus brought it home.

Mother had given up her desire to have him buried under the old cedar, as she knew his grave would be neglected when we had passed away, and the property had fallen into strangers' hands, as it inevitably must some time in the future. So we carried his remains to the cemetery, and in the hazy autumn evening, while the sinking sun was mellowed by the purple mists, we laid him beneath the still green turf, where the yellow leaves were falling, in "whispers to the living," one by one upon his grave.

And now, with that solemn certainty that alone belongs to Time and Death, the day appointed for departure approached. On the evening before we were to leave, feeling that I ought to pay a farewell visit to Ned's grave, I went down to the livery stables—our stalls were empty now—and hired a horse and buggy, and drove, with Carlotta, down to Mr. Cheyleigh's. The old gentleman came out to meet us with his wonted cordiality, and was as cheerful as of old, but Mrs. Cheyleigh had never gotten over Ned's death, and I could read in her wan, sad face, the tale of incurable sorrow. We talked all the while of Ned and his death; and as I told her how the men all loved him for his goodness, and the officers honored him for his bravery, I could see that, like a Spartan mother, even in her tears, she was proud of her gallant boy.

At length I arose and went out alone to his grave. It was in a grove of pines near the house, and the brown pine straw hushed my footfalls as I approached, and the wind was sighing through the boughs. The grave was enclosed by an iron railing, and over it rested a plain marble slab, on which were an inscription and some lines in gilded letters. Opening the wire-work gate, with uncovered head and softened step I went up to the slab, and, bending over it, read:

SACRED TO THE MEMORY

OF

EDWARD CHEYLEIGH,

Born April 8th, 1840,

Killed at the battle of Gettysburg, July 2d, 1863.

"Tell them to bury me under the pines at home."

I would not rest in the mouldering tomb
Of the grim churchyard, where the ivy twines,
But make my grave in the forest's gloom,
Where the breezes wave, like a soldier's plume,
Each dark green bough of the dear old pines,

Where the lights and shadows softly merge,
And the sun-flakes sift through the netted vines;
Where the sea winds, sad with the sob of the surge,
From the harp-leaves sweep a solemn dirge
For the dead beneath the sighing pines.

When the winter's icy fingers sow
The mound with jewels till it shines,
And cowled in hoods of glistening snow,
Like white-veiled Sisters bending low,
Bow, sorrowing, the silent pines.

While others fought for cities proud,
For fertile plains and wealth of mines,
I breathed the sulph'rous battle cloud,
I bared my breast, and took my shroud
For the land where wave the grand old pines.

Though comrades sigh and loved ones weep
For the form shot down in the battle lines,
In my grave of blood I gladly sleep,
If the life I gave will help to keep
The Vandal's foot from the Land of Pines.

The Vandal's foot hath pressed our sod,
His heel hath crushed our sacred shrines;
And, bowing 'neath the chastening rod,
We lift our hearts and hands to God,
And cry: "Oh! save our Land of Pines!"

CHAPTER XLIV

However pleasant may be the scenes to which we are going, we cannot repress a feeling of sadness as we leave those with which we have been long associated, and which have become, as it were, part of our life.

As the train bearing us from our home moved off from the shed, I went out to the rear platform, and stood looking at each familiar place and object as they passed, with a fond farewell upon my lips, and a desire to stamp all so indelibly upon my memory that in years to come I might remember exactly how everything appeared. As I stood with my face down the track I could not see an object till it passed, and then I gazed at it as it receded, till other objects flashing by claimed my attention. Now the bridge overhead, where I had so often stood to throw bits of coal and wood at the engines passing underneath, its arch and railing almost hidden in the curling volumes of smoke our engine has left behind; now the machine shops, where as a boy I had gathered the spiral iron shavings as great wonders of art, still clinking noisily above the rattle of the train, and blinking their red eyes from every forge; now engine yards, with old rusty boilers cast aside, and broken smoke stacks lying on the ground; here a pond where I have fished, its yellow surface darkened with cinders and wrinkled with the breath of our speed; there the river where I have bathed, hidden by the trees itself, but its course revealed by some naked mast and gliding sails; now we rattle through the coal and lumber yards, almost brushing against great piles of timber heaped along the track, and almost grazing dusty carts, with coal-begrimed drivers in red shirts, and heavy plodding horses with brass-studded harness, nodding their heads at every step, as if to say they were used to the cars and could not be prevailed upon to shy; now flash by streets that open, for a second, elm-bordered vistas 'way up into the city, and close them as they whirl past; now we overtake and pass some one who knows me, walking along a very narrow sidewalk, and who bows and says something I cannot understand, and which I can only reply to by a great many shakes of the head; now we rattle by a little house with a dingy porch, and a goat with two kids browsing in front, where a schoolmate of mine used to live and invite me, and mother would not let me go; and now we roar out through the suburbs, where greasy looking men are smoking short pipes in rickety doorways, and red-armed women, with tumbled-down hair, are ever carrying water in painted buckets to the crazy shanties, and never seeming to use it, and where flocks of dirty children run out to wave and scream at the train; on till the last tenement is passed, and in the hazy distance I can only recognize the steeples of the different churches. Even these at last fade into the sky, and still, in my reverie, I stand there watching the black rails gliding like two long serpents from under the train, and the cross-ties ever flitting like steps to an interminable ladder down the track.

As I had several matters of business to attend to in New York, I determined to take steamer from that point to Havana, instead of from Charleston, as we first thought of doing.

The evening after our arrival in the metropolis being bright and sunny, I ordered an open carriage, and Carlotta and I, with little Johnnie, drove out to the Park. Ordering our coachman to let the horses go slowly, we gave ourselves up to the enjoyment of the beautiful scene. Pausing at each object of interest—here a marble statue, there a bronze, getting out at the museum, that Johnnie might see the animals, stopping on the edge of the lake, that he might feed the swans—time passed swiftly, and the sun was nearly down as we found ourselves over the terrace, the dress parade ground for the equipages of the Park. The press of vehicles here forced us to stop for a moment, and at the same instant a most superb turnout caught our attention. A pair of jet black horses, whose champing mouths almost bit their foam-flecked breasts, covered with harness that dazzled the eye with its gleaming plate, a glittering gold-mounted chariot, and a coachman and lackey in green and gold liveries! There were only two occupants—a handsome, middle-aged man, and a lady of striking yet haggard beauty. Clustering brown curls fell around her shoulders, and her hazel eyes were very bright, but her wan cheek was rouged, and the smile she wore was plainly forced and meaningless. All this we saw in a moment, and then we looked in each other's faces, and exclaimed in one breath:

"Lulie Mayland!"

Ere we could extricate ourselves from the throng of carriages and follow, their chariot was out of sight, and we could only return to our hotel in wonder and surprise.

That night Carlotta and I went to the Academy of Music. Parepa was to open the season with *Maritana*, and the vast edifice was crowded. The curtain was down for the second act, and Carl Rosa, with his nervous baton was wafting up from the orchestra a soft, exquisite aria, when the door of a box across the circle was opened by an obsequious usher, and a gentleman in an agony of fashion bowed a tremendous satin trail, a superb white cloak, and a profusion of diamonds into the seat. Laying a harp of camelias and tube-roses in his crush hat, he assisted her in removing her cloak, and, as a cluster of brown curls fell over her bare white shoulders, we recognized again Lulie. He seemed to bend over her with pleasant words, for she frequently smiled; but oh! the look of weariness and despair that at times would flit across her face! The curtain rose and fell, Parepa sang her sweetest, and the dome reëchoed the thunders of applause, but we sat regardless of the stage, with our opera glasses fixed on the box where Lulie sat. The gentleman, too, who was with her was an object of interest to me, for I could not divest myself of the idea that I had seen him somewhere. The deep red hair, parted so exactly in the middle, the flowing side whiskers, and the foppish dress, all seemed familiar, but I could not recall them, till presently he lowered his lorgnon and stuck in his eyeglass, and then I recognized Mr. Monte. I immediately rose and left our box to go to them, but before I had gotten half around the aisle I saw them both rise from their seats and leave the house. I followed as fast as I could through the throng, and reached the pavement just in time to see them drive off in their carriage.

When we returned to the hotel I rang for a directory and found Monte's name and place of business, and lay down to sleep, resolved to seek out Lulie, and, with Carlotta's aid, reclaim her if possible.

CHAPTER XLV

Mr. Monte was partner in a large dry goods house on Broadway, and from what I knew of his habits I judged that I would most likely find him in the store about two o'clock. Accordingly, after lunch I took an omnibus and rode down to the place. It was a massive five story building, with great iron and glass doors, that turned slowly on their hinges, and, closing with a loud bang, shut out the noise and rattle of the great thoroughfare. I stood for a moment confused by the murmur of voices and the tramp of feet, as the hundreds of salesmen and merchants swarmed over every floor of the vast building. The next instant the door sentry approached, and asked whom I wished to see.

"Mr. Monte; is he in?" I replied, feeling for my card.

"Mr. Monte!" he said, looking somewhat surprised. "What market are you from?"

"North Carolina," I replied.

"Oh, then," said he, walking with me to the head of some stairs that led to a gas-lighted apartment below, "you want to see Mr. Bantam. Ban-*tum!* Ban-*tum!*" he called in his loudest tone, accenting the last syllable, and giving it the "u" sound. "Mr. Bantam is from your State; he is down stairs now with Col. — — from Raleigh, in flannels. Will be up in a moment. How's trade in your section?"

"I am not a merchant," I replied, wondering what Mr. Bantam could be doing with Col. — — in flannel, and if the Col. had forgotten his under garments when leaving home.

At this moment Mr. Bantam, an elderly man, slightly bald, appeared at the bottom of the stairway and called out: "Who is it, Johnson?"

"A gentleman from your State."

"All right; I'll be up in five minutes."

"Wait a few moments, sir," said Johnson, going back to his post at the door.

Leaning back against a case of prints, I looked around at this hive of human bees. From floor to floor, from wall to wall, were heaped and piled, like immense breastworks, goods and merchandise of almost every description; case after case of prints, rolls upon rolls of cloths and cassimeres, long brilliant rows of dress goods, boxes of glittering silks, long counters of notions, great heaps of shawls, rugs and blankets; laces, ribbons, and white goods; every department marked by placards with hands pointing to it, and over each another placard with terms of sale: "30 days," "Regular," or "Net."

Everywhere, at every case, around every heap of goods were the salesmen and merchants, bending over fabrics, examining their texture, standing off to get the full effect of the figure; the one class praising and overrating, the other undervaluing and quoting prices from other houses. Just here, at the case next to me, is a fancy young man, with brilliant studs and a flash cravat, a pencil across his mouth like a bit, and his shirt sleeves held up by gutta percha bands, diving head foremost into a box and bringing up a piece of goods, which he exhibits with a slap, as if it were a horse, and winks at a passing comrade, who pinches his arm and says: "How is it, Saunders?" while the merchant, an old fellow from the country, with a broad felt hat and long coat, who licks his short stump of a pencil whenever he sets down anything in his memorandum book, which has his name in gilt letters on the back, and was sent to him by some advertising house, is bending down to examine it. Over there is a red-faced man, in a Cardigan jacket, showing — —. But here is Mr. Bantam, who reads my card and exclaims:

"Smith! I am delighted to see you. When did you leave the old North State?"

"On Tuesday last," I replied, rather taken aback by his familiar cordiality.

"Where are you stopping?" he inquired, bending the corners of my card.

"At the Fifth Avenue Hotel."

"That is the reason I missed you last night," he said; "I did not go higher than the St. Nicholas. Well, I am very glad you've come in. Hope you'll make all your dry goods bill with us. It's much the best plan to concentrate on a house, and we'll be sure to do you good. What department will you look through this evening? I used to sell your father a great many goods."

I begged his pardon, but informed him that my father had never been a merchant, and that I was not merchandising, but had called in to see Mr. Monte, one of the firm.

"You must excuse me," he said, familiarly patting me on the back, "I thought you wanted to buy. You want to see Mr. Monte? I expect you'll have to go to his house, No.—West 34th street. He hardly ever comes here. Bless your soul, he wouldn't know what to do if he did come. His money is all the house wants. Give him a new dog cart and a pair of ponies and he's satisfied."

"Then he is not much of a business man," I said, for the want of something else to say, as I took down his address.

"Not in this line. He knows how to get in the green room at a theatre, and is a first rate judge of wine; but his connection with us is simply confined to putting in some money every year, and drawing on it like Old Harry the balance of the time."

"I am very much obliged," I said, putting up my pencil; "I will hurry up to his house, if you think I will find him there."

"He is probably there now, but he will drive out to the Park at four."

I was about to leave, when a tall, elderly man approached Mr. Bantam, and said, deferentially,

"Dinkle, of your State, wants Domestics on sixty days. Shall I sell him?"

"I'll go see him," said Bantam, turning off; "Good bye, Mr. Smith. Call in again if you have leisure."

The tall, elderly man was about to follow him, when a sudden recollection of his face flashed upon me, and I caught his arm.

"Excuse me, but isn't this Mr. Marshman?"

"It is, sir," he replied, turning around to me again.

"My name is Smith, sir," I said, offering him my hand; "we met at Saratoga."

"I remember. How have you been?" he answered coldly, taking my hand without cordiality, while a flush I could not understand came over his face.

"You are connected with this house?" I asked; thinking, of course, that he was a partner.

"Only as a salesman," he said bitterly, and then added, after a pause, "It is not worth while being ashamed of it. Lillian's infernal extravagance ruined me, and I was compelled to do something."

I could make no reply, and there was a pause of some seconds, when he continued, with increasing volubility, as all men do when speaking of their misfortunes:

"Lillian's old uncle, from whom we expected a great deal, died insolvent. I spent half of what I had in my last political contest, and was defeated by the——treachery of my friends. Still, after that we had enough to have lived comfortably, by economizing a little; but Lillian would have her brown stone and her carriage, her silks and her laces. and now she has to take the street cars if she rides at all, and that isn't often. I could stand it all better if she wouldn't cut up so, and mope about her poverty, as she calls it. She turns up her nose at the neighborhood because we've had to come down to Bleecker street. She spends half her time crying and looking over old finery, and talking of better days. She puts all sorts of foolish notions into our little girl's head, and makes her continually beg me for things I have not the money to buy. I would ask you to call and see us, but 'twould not be pleasant for you, and only make her worse. It is improper, I know, for me to talk thus to a comparative stranger, but I am full of bitterness when I think of Lillian's conduct, and as you used to know her I have been communicative. Pardon me. Yonder's Mr. Bantam. I must go back to my customers. Good day! But take this piece of advice: don't marry a belle," he added, over his shoulder, as he walked off.

As I stood on the sidewalk to hail an omnibus, my sympathy turned from him to poor Lillian, reduced to poverty, and her very sighs and tears ridiculed, to any one who might listen, by her unfeeling husband.

When I knocked at No.—West Thirty-fourth street a servant in livery appeared and took up my card. I waited a few moments in a very handsome parlor, when he returned and requested me to walk up stairs. Going up with him I was ushered into a sitting room furnished with cosy magnificence, that is, with a splendid Moquette carpet, on which you were not afraid to tread; velvet divans, on which you did not hesitate to recline; a rosewood table, on which an inkstand and pens were scattered; a marble mantel, with a half-smoked cigar tossed on it, an *etagere* with a smoking cap, a broken meerschaum, and a Sevres vase of Latakia, perched among articles of rarest *vertu*. With my first glance around the apartment Monte came in through a folding door from his dressing room, wiping his hands on a Russian towel, and giving me one to shake that was still damp.

"Smith! old fellow, I am devilish glad to see you. When did you arrive? We had a gay time at Saratoga that season, didn't we! Where the deuce have you kept yourself ever since? Sit down."

"I thought you were aware, Monte," I said, adopting his free and easy manner, and lolling carelessly down in an arm chair, "that we had had a little unpleasantness down our way. I've been in camp four years."

"Ah, yes," he said, slipping his arm through the coat his attendant held ready for him, "I had overlooked that. So they made a soldier of you, did they—powder, blood and all? I was captain of a company our fellows here got up, but when they went down South I resigned. If the— — States wanted to secede I had no idea of getting my brains blown out to prevent them."

"We were defending our country, you know, and, of course, had to fight," I remarked, smiling at his idea of patriotism.

"I suppose so," he said, sitting down near me and arranging his cuffs; then looking up at his servant, who stood waiting, "James, tell Thomas to put the bay colt to the wagon; I will drive to Harlem this afternoon. By the way, Smith," he continued, when the man had left the room, "what ever became of that devil of a beauty that flirted with us all, and with whom you left the Springs?"

An angry reply rose to my lips at hearing him speak so of Carlotta, but knowing that it would defeat the object of my visit, I restrained myself, and replied "that she had been living down South during the war, but that I understood she was soon to return to Cuba."

There was a short silence, and I was wondering how to get at any information in regard to Lulie, when he put up his eye-glass and looked at me again.

"You've changed a great deal, Smith. I should never have recognized you without your card."

It was just the turn I wanted, and I replied:

"I saw you last night at the opera and remembered your face immediately. But, Monte, *apropos* of beauty, who was the lady you were with? She drew my attention entirely from the stage."

"Ah!" he said, drawing his eye into the least perceptible wink, "She was worth a gaze, wasn't she? I wouldn't tell every one, but you are a transient visitor: that was La Belle Louise. Half of New York is crazy about her—that is, you know, the b'hoys."

"Not demi-monde?" I asked, looking knowing.

"It was daring in me, wasn't it?" he went on, without heeding my remark. "But she wanted to go and I promised to carry her. Oh! but I shall have to lie about it to the ladies. I can cheat scandal out of the morsel if some fellow who knew her don't blow on me to his mother, and she let it out to her set. Confound it, though, who cares?"

"Has she many admirers?" I asked.

"Many seek the honor of her acquaintance, but I believe I am the favored one. I'll vow it flattens that deucedly though to keep her in diamonds," he said, drawing from his pocket a mother of pearl portemonnaie.

"I'd like to get a peep at her myself; just a peep, Monte. Where does she reside?" I said, taking out a card.

"Oh, I don't mind telling you. But it's no use, she won't see you."

"La Belle Louise. Number what?" I asked, pretending to write.

"She is at Madame Dubourg's, 42d street, if you wish to know," he said, somewhat coldly, as if he thought me impertinent.

Quick as thought 'twas on my card, and then I said, smiling:

"Oh, well, I was only jesting; I will leave day after tomorrow. But tell me, Monte, something of my old acquaintance, Miss Finnock."

"Little Saph.!" he said, regaining his good humor. "She is up the Hudson living with her brother, who married that horrid Miss Stelway. You remember them?"

"Very well, but is Miss Finnock not married yet?"

"No, of course not; who would marry such a bundle of sentiment? She often boasts of you, though, as the young Carolinian she flirted with."

"I met Mr. Marshman very unexpectedly down at your store to-day," I said, not caring to correct little Miss Finnock's boast.

"Marshman? Yes, he's selling there for us on a small salary—the best we could give him though. The old fellow got beaten, took to his cups and went to the bad very fast. They say his wife has to work hard to support herself and child, while he drinks up what he gets at our house. My mother sends them supplies very often, though she has not visited them, you know, since they left the top."

"Have you a check book here?" I asked, with a sudden resolution.

"Yes," he replied, handing me one from his *escritoire.*

"Will you do me the favor to get that to Mrs. Marshman," I said, filling up the check for a good round sum and giving it to him. "Please draw the money and send it to her so that my name will not be known in the matter, and do not let Marshman touch any of it."

"James shall attend to it to-morrow. But stay and dine with me. We'll drive out to Harlem, and get back to dinner at six."

"Thanks, I must return to my hotel, as I have an engagement there. Dine with me to-morrow. I am at the Fifth Avenue."

"Would be happy. The Sillery's very fine there, but I dine our Club on my yacht to-morrow. Speaking of La Belle Louise," he continued, following me down to the door, "Madame Dubourg told me she gets letters from North Carolina, and that she is continually sending money to Italy to complete a monument to go over some poor devil of a deserter from the rebel army, who was killed down there. Did you ever hear of her before?"

"La Belle Louise? I never heard the name till you mentioned it," I said.

"I supposed it was a mistake. Good day."

"Lulie, I have found you at last," I murmured, as I sauntered down Fifth Avenue to the hotel. "God grant we may save you!"

CHAPTER XLVI

Madame Dubourg's was a grand brown stone building, with broad carved balustrades, and stone vases of cactus. I had chosen the hour of twelve for our visit, as the parlors would most likely then be free from visitors, and we could see Lulie in quiet. When we alighted from our carriage there was a large-armed Irish woman washing off the stone steps, and a man in a paper cap standing on a high step-ladder, to rub the plate glass windows. They were talking and laughing together, but ceased as we got out, and looked at us and each other with some surprise on their faces. The woman gathered up her cloth and water bucket and disappeared through the area with an audible snicker, while the man fell to rubbing the wide panes with renewed diligence. There was a pretty silver knocker on the figured glass door, and as I let it fall the door was thrown open by a footman, who had put on his gold laced coat so hurriedly the collar was turned under, and from whose moustache some fragments of cheese were still hanging. He favored us with a prolonged stare of wonder, then presented a somewhat tarnished gold salver for our cards. I laid one in it, on which was simply written, "An old friend," and said: "To see La Belle Louise."

"You can't see her," he replied, with something of insolence in his tone.

I restrained my first impulse of anger, and slipping a five dollar gold piece in his hand, said quietly,

"Take my card up to her, and say nothing about a lady's being with me."

"I will, sir," he said, with a low bow, his manner changing instantly at the touch of the gold.

He ushered us through a wide hall, with mosaic floor, into a spacious parlor, furnished in dark green velvet, and opening into another of light green satin damask, and this, in turn, leading to a large conservatory of rare plants and flowers. Though the furniture and all the appointments were so magnificent, yet every thing bore the defacement of reckless vice. The splendid Axminster carpets, though partially protected by linen tracks, were soiled and worn by muddy boots, the grand piano had its rosewood surface scratched and bruised, the music books were torn and scattered, buhl quartette tables around the room were covered with sloppings of wine, broken glasses, wet packs of cards and dice, the embroidered flowers on the ottomans were frayed into strings, and the gorgeous paintings on the walls were splotched and blistered, and their gilded frames tarnished. We had walked through both parlors to the conservatory and returned to the first, when we heard a light foot-fall on the stairway, and Lulie came down into the hall and stood for a moment looking through the side lights out into the street, with the same look of wan despair upon her face. The next instant she walked lightly into the room, twirling the tassel of her morning robe over her forefinger. She advanced half across the room before she saw us, and then her eyes opened as if in terror, a leaden pallor spread over her face, as if life had fled, and pressing her hand to her heart, with the tremulous wail, "O God!" she sank down upon the floor, her pallid cheek resting on the cushion of a *fauteuil* that had been overthrown, and her colorless lips uttering low moans, that were piteous, indeed, to hear.

In a moment Carlotta was down on the floor beside her, lifting the poor bowed head to her bosom, smoothing the brown hair from the fair brow that was once so pure, and dropping the tears of her Christ-like pity on the upturned face. The poor girl had no strength to stir, but only put up her white hands feebly and murmured:

"Do not touch me; oh! do not touch me. God knows I am unworthy to breathe the air you do. Leave me! Cast me off as all the world have done," and again she would make those gentle, piteous moans.

As soon as Carlotta could command her voice she bent down, and kissing her forehead tenderly, said:

"Lulie, darling, we have come to save you."

"To save me? Oh, no; it's too late—too late!"

"Do not say so, dearest Lulie," urged Carlotta; "our carriage is at the door. Do not wait a moment, but come with us and leave forever this pit of perdition."

"Would to God I could," she said, shaking her head slowly, and speaking in the same low tone; "there was a time I might have gone, but not now, not now."

"But, Lulie, we are going away from this country to Cuba, where no one has ever known you. No one is with us except mother, who is even now waiting to receive you. We will forever bury the past, and look forward only to a new life. Lulie, come with us, and be my darling sister in our happy home."

She raised herself from Carlotta, and, placing her hands over her face, sat rocking herself back and forth, her very frame convulsed with the agony of her struggle. When she lifted her face again her mind was made up.

"It cannot be, Lottie," she said, calling Carlotta's name for the first time. "Heaven only knows how I appreciate your goodness and thank you for it; but I cannot go with you; I cannot throw the shadow of my presence on your household. The world has no forgiveness for my sin, and no life of penitence or purity I might lead would ever wash away the stain. I do not doubt your kindness; as God is my witness I believe that you would love me, but, do what you would to forget and conceal it, in your hearts I could never be anything but poor fallen Lulie—and the consciousness that you all knew of my ruin would make your very presence a torture to me."

"But, Lulie," persisted Carlotta, "this sensitiveness would after a while pass off, and our very kindness would beguile you of your remorse. And even if you suffer, I should think any change would be better than this life of shameless iniquity, so utterly opposed to the refinement and delicacy I believe still linger in your breast."

"Oh, Lottie, do not chide me. You, whose heart is pure, who have never known the wild reckless abandonment of all that is virtuous, all that is good, cannot understand the terrible remorse that drives me into vice, whose constancy will prevent reflection—aye, reflection. An eternity of hell is compassed in one hour of my retrospect. I cannot be alone; solitude would drive me mad. One thought alone has brought relief—relief mingled with horror—the thought of death! Oft in the night has it come to my sleepless pillow and whispered to me 'Die!' and yet, when I poured the poison in the glass, my trembling hand has dropped it from my lips. But the crisis has come," she said, fiercely, striking her hands together and wringing them till her jewelled rings cut into the flesh. "I will not shrink again. I *will* die!" and clasping her hands across her head, she gazed at me with such intense anguish and despair in her hollow eyes, I shrank from her face.

"Lulie, Lulie, dearest, do not speak so," said Carlotta, again putting her arms around her and trying to soothe her. "You cannot surely contemplate self-destruction. Think, Lulie, what an awful thing it is to die. There, darling," she continued, as Lulie's head drooped on her shoulder, "you were speaking wildly just now, you did not mean what you said. Come, the carriage is waiting. You *must* go with us; we cannot leave you here."

But Lulie only shook her head firmly and remained silent.

After a rather long pause Carlotta spoke again, in a low impressive voice:

"Lulie, hear my last appeal. For the sake of the long ago, when we were innocent happy children, and our hearts were bound with ties of love which have never yet been broken; for the sake of those dear old days, I beseech, I implore you to leave these unworthy associations, and seek with us a better life. Aye, Lulie, for the sake of your dead mother, I beg you to come. If a heart can be sad in Heaven, hers is bleeding now to see you thus; her precious little Lulie in such a place as this! Oh! will you not make her happy again?"

The fountains of her heart were now broken up, and with long shuddering sobs she lay weeping on Carlotta's neck.

I had not spoken yet, but had left all to Carlotta's tact and skill. I now knelt down by Lulie and took her hand, while my broken voice and tearful eyes attested the sincerity of all I said:

"Dear little playmate, by the memory of our childhood's love, by the thousand scenes and incidents that endeared us to each other—our nursery games, Miss Hester's school, the little parties when you first ventured to take my arm—by your first rejection of my love as we grew older, but above all, by the confidence you placed in me under the old oak at Chapel Hill, I implore you to trust us now and to put your future into our hands."

"Oh, spare me! spare me!" she cried, sobbing afresh, "for humanity's sake spare me! If you would not kill me, do not tell me of my joyous, sinless childhood. It is gone forever from me. Oh, my wrecked and ruined character! Oh, my blighted, broken heart! Mother! *mother!* MOTHER! God grant you may be blind in Heaven, that you may not see your poor, polluted child on earth. Lottie, do not torture me more; 'tis useless to persuade me; I cannot go. Leave me to my fate. If you are willing, put both arms round my neck once more and kiss me farewell. John, my noble, true-hearted friend, Good-bye!"

Carlotta strained her again and again to her bosom, then, seeing she was not to be shaken from her purpose, we slowly and sorrowfully left the room. At the door Carlotta's feelings overcame her, and resolving to make one more trial, she went back, and embracing her again, said:

"Lulie, I cannot leave you so. By the Blood of dear Jesus, by the Cross of our Redeemer, I beseech you to go with us to our home."

Poor Lulie caught her hand and pressed her tear-wet cheek and lips upon it, then pushed her from her side, not rudely but sadly, with despair in her very touch.

And so we left her sitting on the floor, with her head buried in her folded arms upon an ottoman. We were so troubled to leave her as we found her, that we wrote a long note and sent it up to Madame Dubourg's that evening from the hotel. The waiter soon returned with our note unopened, but on it, scribbled with a pencil:

"Dear friends, forget me!

Lulie."

Next morning, as we stood on the deck of the steamer for Havana, inhaling the breeze and enjoying the scene, while the giant wheels were throbbing us out into the ocean, we little thought that in the great city behind us, up in a room with perfumed and silken hangings, an overburdened heart, slower and slower, was throbbing, throbbing, throbbing a soul out into eternity.

CHAPTER XLVII

Carlotta and I are standing in the balcony of our chamber, gazing in rapt admiration on the gorgeous beauty of a Cuban sunset. The home we have come to is indeed a lovely one; it is situated about fifteen miles from Havana. The house, built of white stone, is like some Gothic castle, with its towers, and arches, and extensive proportions, yet has all the airy lightness of Italian architecture, in tasteful decorations and elegant finish. It stands on a slight elevation overlooking the sea, and is surrounded with all the appointments refined taste could suggest or wealth procure. White shelled walks, bordered with smoothly trimmed evergreens, wind through gardens of exquisite flowers, or beneath wire-trellised graperies, whose luscious clusters rival those of Eschol. Beautiful drives lead around lawns of green velvet, where fountains play with sparkling jets, and marble statues gleam amid the shrubbery, or down through long fragrant groves of oranges and limes, that drop their yellow fruit beneath the passing wheels.

Every chamber in the house is fitted up with elegant comfort, the long suite of parlors furnished in varied magnificence, the halls filled with works of art, and the library with rarest literature. All the domestic details, usually so troublesome when we move to a strange place, are arranged with perfect system and regularity, and a large retinue of well trained servants, subservient in demeanor, anticipative,

yet not officious in their attention, await our commands and faithfully discharge their appointed duties.

All these arrangements were perfected before our arrival by our very efficient agents, Messrs. Rinaldo, who have had charge of the estate since Mr. Rurlestone's death, and nothing was left for me to do but to assume control of the establishment.

Herrara Lola, grown portly and plethoric since I last saw him, yet still exceedingly handsome, is living near, and he and his lovely Spanish wife are our frequent guests. Indeed they, and a few Southern families who have fled to Havana, are the only society we receive, as we desire yet a while quiet and retirement.

I have heard once from Ben Bemby since we reached here. All were well, and in good spirits. His father, himself and Horace, had all gone to work vigorously on their respective farms, preparing them for the next year's crop, though he apprehended great difficulty in securing effective labor. His letter, though characteristic, showed a spirit of earnest energy and hopefulness, and was burdened throughout with messages of love for us all from true and honest hearts.

But, as I was saying, Carlotta and I were in the balcony, looking at the sunset. Cloudless and alone the god of day was sinking to his rest. A few fleecy racks towards the South were blushing with his good-night kiss, and a purple bank with silver fringe lay beneath him, like the pillow of his couch. Drowsily he sunk his head upon it, and drawing the ocean, like a burnished coverlid, over his golden face, was asleep!

The spell of our silent admiration was broken by Miguel, my valet, who approached with the mail from Havana. Running hurriedly through the letters I came to one directed to Carlotta and myself, and dated from New York the very day we sailed. Calling her to my side, I tore off the envelope and read:

"My only Friends—

When this reaches you I shall be in the grave, where the scorn and contempt of the world cannot harm me. The awful abyss of eternity is before me, and into its depths I blindly plunge—whither I care not—any where, any where to leave earth, with its curses on the fallen, and to crush out Memory's page of past purity. There is but one ray of comfort in the dark Hereafter—the thought that in the realms of gloom to which I am going I will not meet the sad reproof of my mother's face.

Dying, I leave no reproaches for the dead, no warning for the living. I fell through my own weakness, and my eternal doom will be just; but oh! my poor heart breaks as I think of what I was and what I might have been.

To you, who tried to save me, my life's last pulse will be a throb of gratitude. I dare not pray for you, but He who suffered Magdalen to weep upon His feet will reward you.

Farewell, forever farewell!

Lulie."

As I opened the sheet to read the last lines a little flower fell out on the floor. Carlotta picked it up, and, bursting into tears, placed it in my hand.

It was a little *snow-drop, with its petals powdered with soot.*

Carlotta has gone in with the letter to mother, and I sit alone in the balcony, thinking of Lulie. And the red light dies out in the West, and the stars shine down from the sky, and the stars shine back from the sea, and I am still gazing far over the gray waters towards the land that I fought for—a land where orphans' tears meet widows' wails, and maidens wear the mournful pledge of battle-broken troth—a land where want and woe are rife, and the burdened people bow beneath the yoke of conquest; and yet, from all the wealth and luxury that surround me, my Southern heart turns with all the yearning of a child back to my Southern Home.